The Final Judgement

Daniel Easterman

The Final Judgement

WHEELER
PUBLISHING, INC.
ROCKLAND, MA

★ AN AMERICAN COMPANY ★

14893224

Copyright © 1996 by Daniel Easterman

Published in Large Print by arrangement with
HarperCollins Publishers, Inc.
in the United States and Canada.

Wheeler Large Print Book Series.

Set in 16 pt. Plantin.

Library of Congress Cataloging-in-Publication Data

Easterman, Daniel.
     The final judgement / Daniel Easterman.
          p. (large print) cm.(Wheeler large print book series)
     ISBN 1-56895-432-8 (softcover)
     1. Large type books. 2. Fascism—Fiction. 3. Holocaust
Survivors—Fiction. I. Title. II. Series
[PR6055.A82F5 1997]
833'.914—dc21
                                                                              97-9211
                                                                                 CIP

On 14 March 1994, the Radio 4 Today program reported a showing of Schindler's List in the United States, where the "young American audience" laughed as an SS officer shot a Jewish girl.

Donald Thomas,
"Watch Your Lip: Policing
the Talk of Literature,"
Pen International, XLV:1 (1995), p.6

The Final Judgement

Part 1
THE SHOPKEEPER

1

Arzachena, Sardinia
5 December

The first thing that told Aryeh Levin something was wrong was the silence. It was the middle of the night, surely there was nothing out of the ordinary? But the silence worried him the moment he woke. He had known similar silences in the old days with the army in Lebanon, silences that came just before a burst of shelling or the dull thump of an explosion. He knew there was something not right about this one, too.

To begin with, what had awakened him? Had there been a noise? He normally slept straight through, unless his son Yoel woke and called him, which was rare these days. Chaya, his wife, was fast asleep next to him. He sat up and looked down at her, at her soft profile, her bare shoulders. She always slept on her stomach, had done so since childhood, or so she said. Moonlight fell across her face. He reached out to remove a strand of hair from her eyes. They had been married eleven years, but still he could not get over the pleasure of being in bed with her each night.

What was wrong? What had awakened him? He strained his ears, but could hear nothing, and he knew that was wrong, that a sound was missing that should have been there. He should get out of bed, go downstairs and investigate. But what should he look for?

It was then he realized what it was. The alarm system had stopped working. Ordinarily, a small unit in the bedroom emitted an almost inaudible beep every minute. It provided a means of checking that the system was in working order. He looked round. The little red light on the control panel had gone out.

Two things happened quickly after that. Yoel cried out, a loud, frightened shout in Italian, then Hebrew: *"Papa, papa, aiuto! Abba, hatzilu! Hatzilu!"* Simultaneous with the cry—or a little before it, a little after, who could tell?—the door of the bedroom burst open.

The room flooded with light. Two hooded men were standing just inside the doorway holding sawed-off shotguns. Chaya woke abruptly, saw the men, and started screaming. The taller of the two intruders stepped quickly to the bedside and struck her hard across the cheek with the back of his hand, the force enough to send her reeling back against the headboard.

"Sta' zitta, puttana!" he yelled.

Aryeh made to grab him, but as he did so felt the cold, hard touch of a gun barrel pressed against his neck.

"Non fa' stupidàggine." The voice was guttural, the accent impossible for Aryeh to guess. Sardinian, almost certainly.

He felt himself go limp. Beside him, Chaya was weeping silently, her hand pressed against her cheek.

"What do you want? I don't keep money in

the house. But you can take anything else you like as long as you keep your filthy hands off my wife and son."

In answer, the man who had struck Chaya took a long, coiled rope from a canvas bag he had been carrying over one shoulder. That was when Aryeh understood what was happening.

"My son!" he shouted. "Where is he? What have you done with him?"

His captors did not answer. Instead, the man with the rope reached for Chaya and pulled her naked and yelling out of the bed. Aryeh again made to help her, and again the man next to him pressed the gun against his neck. He knew the intruder would use the weapon if he had to. He had known men like this before: a different nationality, a different religion—if any of them could be said to truly have any religion but violence—but the same strict adherence to the rules by which they lived.

"Yoel!" he shouted at the top of his voice. "Yoel, don't worry. I'll get you back.... I'll find you, I'll ..."

The blow took him on the back of the skull. Unconsciousness was immediate, black, and hungry. It devoured him in a single, greedy gulp.

When he came to, sunshine was streaming into the bedroom. His head felt as though it had been removed with a wrench, then replaced with a jackhammer. Every time he tried to open his eyes, the pain was intense. A gray wave of nausea rushed up from his stomach; gagged as he was, he knew he would choke to death if he threw up. With an effort, he fought the sickness down until he could breathe without making himself sick. He forced himself to keep his eyes tightly shut, desperate as he was to see what had happened in the room.

Slowly, the screaming ache inside his head slowed down to a dull throbbing. He was sitting naked in a chair. He tried to move, but could not: something was holding him fast. He forced his eyes open.

They had tied him to a chair using lengths of rope. Near him, her eyes wide-open with fear and her mouth gagged like his, Chaya sat bound in another chair. She was also naked. Aryeh swore that if they had laid a finger on her, he would hunt them to the ends of the earth for his revenge. And then he remembered Yoel, and knew that he would hunt them anyway.

There was nothing he could do now but sit and comfort Chaya with glances. She must have guessed. She had known the risks of living in this place. They had arrived on Sardinia's Costa Smeralda eight years earlier, not long after Yoel was born. Aryeh had wanted his son to grow up away from Israel, away from the constant violence and racism that were infecting the country and that had turned the Zionist dream of his parents into a nightmare.

There had only ever been one drawback to Sardinia—its reputation as a center for kidnap and extortion. But after Aryeh's tour as a conscript with the army in Lebanon, that had seemed little more than a children's game.

Until now. Now, Yoel was gone, abducted and taken into the mountains to be hidden, guarded by shepherds who knew how to keep their mouths shut, until the ransom was paid. Or.... Aryeh tried not to think about that. But as he sat in the chair, sickened by the smell of vomit, weeping, dizzy, he swore that whatever happened, he would have his revenge.

They were found shortly after 8:00 A.M. by Maria Deiana, the housekeeper. Some of the wealthier citizens of the Costa Smeralda kept large staffs—labor on the island was cheap, as it always had been. Poverty was still endemic. The little money that had ever come into Sardinia from the Cassa per il Mezzogiorno had been channeled into the pockets of just about everyone who had been meant to benefit. Huge factories got built in Cagliari or Porto Torres, but they produced more smoke than jobs. The rich, as always, could well afford the services of the poor.

But the Levins kept a simple household. Maria was their housekeeper, cook, and nanny combined, and Aryeh paid her well. A gardener came two or three days a week. Neither he nor Maria lived in. That was all. Aryeh drove himself to work in Porto Cervo every morning, leaving Yoel off at the Abbiadori school in Arzachena on the way.

He heard Maria coming through the house, shouting their names, her voice puzzled and a little anxious. The family was usually up and about at this hour, and Yoel had always greeted her with a rundown of the day ahead. The boy spoke Sardinian dialect fluently, and neither Aryeh nor Chaya could keep up with him. He and Maria were the closest of friends; she had six children of her own, and Yoel often went to their home to play. Some of Aryeh's colleagues disapproved of such close contact with "the

6

peasants," but he paid as little attention to them as he had to friends in Tel Aviv who had warned him against associating with Muslims or Christians.

The first thing Maria saw when she entered the bedroom was Aryeh sitting naked in his chair. Her immediate reaction was a scream, followed immediately by a flurry of fingers as she crossed herself again and again. She then lifted her apron until it covered her face. Keeping it firmly in place, she stumbled across to Aryeh and pulled the gag from his mouth. Shocked by the sight of him, she had not noticed Chaya, just out of her line of sight.

"La signora!" she said. *"Dov'è la signora?"*

"It's all right, Maria, Chaya's all right. She's on the other side of the room. Now, take that ridiculous apron off your face and get me untied."

But Maria was not prepared to risk the impropriety of fiddling with knots on a naked man's torso. Squinting round the edge of her apron, she spied Chaya and made her way across the room to her. A naked woman was not entirely proper either, but she presented considerably fewer perils to Maria's honor.

The housekeeper untied the gag, then busied herself with the ropes that held Chaya to the chair, muttering all the while to herself in Sardinian. Her hands were trembling, and tears ran unchecked down her face. She did not even ask after Yoel: the moment she had entered the bedroom she had guessed what had happened. The Anonima had come for the child, and in a day or two there would be a ransom demand. She had lived with such things all her life. There

7

were men in her own family who had been imprisoned as *rapitori*.

At first, Chaya could not speak, only gasp in air frantically like someone who has been drowning. Her panting, wheezing battle for air reminded Maria that her mistress suffered from asthma.

"*Dov'è il vostro inalatore?*" she asked.

Chaya could hardly get the words out.

"*Ne ... nel ... cassetto ... Nella ... toi ... toilette.*"

Lifting her apron again, Maria Deiana crept across to the dressing table and opened the drawer. The gray-blue inhaler was at the front. She brought it to Chaya and held her hand steady while Chaya pressed dose after dose of the Ventolin into her lungs. Gradually, the wheezing smoothed out and Chaya's breathing became easier. Maria untied the remaining knots and let the ropes fall to the floor. She reached out a hand and wiped the tears from Chaya's cheek, then fetched her robe from where it lay across the foot of the bed. Still shaking, Chaya pulled it on. She was numb, unable to think or act.

The next moment, apron in place, Maria dashed out of the bedroom, leaving Chaya to untie her husband. In other circumstances, they would have found her behavior comic, but they were far from laughter. Chaya dragged herself weakly out of the chair. After hours of sitting immobile, every muscle in her body felt strained beyond measure. Each step she took was an agony.

They did not speak. Chaya bent down and laid her head against her husband's shoulder, speechless, like stone, and for a very long time she did not move. Then, coming slowly to life, she began to untie the tight knots that held him. The knots might have been evidence for anyone who knew about such things. Whoever had tied them was or had been a seaman, but almost certainly not a Sardinian fisherman. With broken nails and shaking fingers, Chaya loosened them forever.

When Aryeh was free, she turned suddenly.

"Yoel," she said. "I have to go to him. He'll wonder what's happening. I have to get him ready for school."

With a soft gesture that felt harsh, he grabbed her arm and pulled her to him.

"Yoel's gone," he said. "They've taken him. He's been kidnapped."

She looked at him as if she did not believe him, as if she had never believed anything he had ever said to her.

And then she screamed, and went on screaming until he held her to him and stroked her hair and silenced her. When she was quiet, he was more disturbed. He felt it was a quietness that might never leave her, not even if her son was returned.

He took her into the bathroom, where he washed and dried her face before doing anything about himself. From the shower he watched her, not knowing what to do or say. Water did not help to wash any of the bitterness or grief away. He toweled himself dry. Chaya watched him without moving, sitting on the side of the bath.

"Do you want a shower?" he asked. "It'll make you feel better. It's going to be a hard day."

And how many hard days would follow before Yoel was safely back with them? He knew these things could take weeks, even months, before reaching a satisfactory conclusion. And sometimes the families could not pay. When that happened ... Well, the kidnappers were businessmen, not gamblers. A dead victim was as useful to them in the long run as a live one. The next family in line would pay up all the faster. Aryeh was sick at heart because he knew how much he was worth, and he did not think the kidnappers knew just how little that really was. They would ask for more than he could possibly pay. And his son would die.

They returned to the bedroom and changed into fresh clothes. Watching Chaya dress, he was frightened by how much she had altered in a matter of hours. Yesterday, she had been tall, upright, full of life; now she was bent, her breasts sagged, her hair hung limp, her shoulders were rounded, and even her skin seemed gray. He did not try to look at himself in the mirror.

There was a knock on the door. Maria Deiana appeared carrying a tray on which were a large pot of black coffee and three large glasses of *aquavite*, the local aromatic version of grappa.

"I've called Dr. Talanas," she said. "He's coming as quickly as possible. And Father Cavia. I hope you don't mind, I know you aren't Catholics. But he knows how to help in these matters. How to keep his mouth shut. He'll be a help, you'll see."

They said nothing. What did it matter who they saw? Aryeh downed his *aquavite* in a single gulp, and followed it with a cup of *caffè ristretto*. After a second cup, he got up and crossed the

10

room to the telephone. Best to get it over with. He picked up the receiver and dialed.

"*Cento tredici. Desidera?*"

"*La polizia, per favore.*"

"*Sì. Che numero ha?*"

At that moment, someone banged their hand down on the telephone, cutting off the call. It was Maria.

"*Scusi, signore, scusi.* It would be a great mistake to telephone the police. Surely you have not forgotten."

Of course. How could he have been so stupid? The police were the last people he wanted involved. In 1991 new *antisequestro* legislation had been passed by parliament in an attempt to control the epidemic of abductions throughout Italy. The chief provision of the law—and the one that had caused the most controversy—was that, on notification of a kidnapping, the state had the power to freeze the funds of the victim's family. The theory was that if would-be kidnappers knew that no one would be able to pay up, they would be forced to think of better ways of earning a dishonest living. In practice, desperate families found ways round the law, money changed hands when the police had their backs turned, and the abductions went on as before.

Aryeh replaced the receiver.

"I'm sorry," he murmured. "You're right. I wasn't thinking."

He sat down on the edge of the bed. It was then it came to him that he had nowhere to turn for help. He was a stranger here, without ties or contacts. He had no influence, no levers to pull, no godfather to call on. All he could do was sit and wait for the telephone to ring.

11

2

The call came shortly after midnight. They had passed a day like no other. It had been as though they had been cut off at once from the world and from themselves, severed from every emotion but that of misery. All day they stayed within reach of the telephone, and all day it stubbornly refused to ring. Aryeh had phoned in to his office, pleading illness. Maria had tendered Chaya's apologies for not turning up at a bridge party in Porto Cervo. The day had dragged past minutes at a time, dreadful with silences and a nagging feeling of absence.

The doctor gave Chaya pills. It was all he could do. This was not the first time he had been called out to such a case, and it would not be the last. He said nothing, pretended to believe their story about bad news from Israel, and left with vague reassurances. He would confide in his wife, of course, and she in her small circle of friends. They would tell their husbands, and their husbands would chat in the bar. In a matter of days, word of the Levin kidnapping would make its way round the Costa Smeralda.

Dr. Talanas was followed almost immediately by Father Cavia, the parish priest. A short, brooding man from Orgosolo, he was well-versed in the ways of the Barbagian brigands, much less in the needs and feelings of their victims. He attempted to reassure Yoel's parents with platitudes, and suggested they attend mass in his church the following Sunday. No matter that they were not believers, he insisted, the Church was universal and Jesus had room in his heart for everyone. They asked him if Jesus had room for their son. Of course, he said, Jesus had room for everyone, even the boy's kidnappers. Aryeh asked him to leave.

Maria Deiana watched the priest go with a mixture of relief and fear. She wanted him involved, less for any spiritual solace he could have given them than for his potential usefulness as a go-between.

Father Cavia reminded Aryeh of his grandfather, Zalman. The old man had been a Lithuanian rabbi, black-bearded, black-coated, steeped in tradition—a *mitnagid*, intellectual and unemotional. As a child, Aryeh had always been afraid of him; now his fear had changed to pity as he watched the old rabbi struggle to come to terms with a world he would never understand.

Aryeh's father had been born and brought up in Israel, had fought in the '67 war, and had opened a French restaurant in Tel Aviv soon afterward. The food was as kosher as Aryeh's French mother was Jewish, but that was beside the point as far as the old man was concerned. He had wanted his sons to study Torah and Talmud, and to follow the Shulhan Arukh as he had done. Instead, he had seen the world around him change beyond recognition, and not for the better.

Aryeh had followed his parents in their liberal faith and their belief in a secular, Zionist state, but his war had been in Lebanon, and his childhood lessons had been shattered by the role in which he found himself. After finishing his army service in 1984, he had gone into partnership with his father and two uncles, opening a luxury hotel in Herzliyya. He married Chaya the following year, and for a while everything went well. They were happy together, the hotel was flourishing, they talked about starting a family in a year or two.

But there were tensions between their families. Chaya's family were Sephardic Jews who had made *aliya* from Morocco in the late sixties, one of the last Jewish families to leave the country. They were right-wing, impatient with the crippled liberal state of the European Zionists, and they made no secret of their hatred for Arabs. Chaya's oldest brother had until recently belonged to Israel's elite antiterrorist unit, the Sayaret Matkal, and had been involved in numerous raids across the Lebanese border, both during and after the invasion. By the time he and Chaya had been married two years, it seemed that Aryeh and his brother-in-law could not meet without an acrimonious argument breaking out over one aspect or another of Israeli policy.

When the *intifada* broke out in 1988, Aryeh found his confidence slipping faster than ever. Rabbi Meir Kahane was preaching hate sermons everywhere and calling for the expulsion of all Arabs from the Holy Land. Aryeh's grandfather took to spending his days alone in his room, praying and studying Torah; he would never criticize Kahane openly, but he had seen hatred like this before, and he knew where it could lead. In 1989 Aryeh and Chaya's first child had been born. An anti-Arab demonstration had passed the hospital that same day. To Aryeh, it had seemed like a portent.

In the end, he could see no future in staying where he was. He took his wife and child to the other end of the Mediterranean, to Sardinia. It was not a random choice. A Palestinian friend, Abbas al-Khalil, had moved to the island several years earlier and already had a thriving business in Olbia.

Back in the sixties, the Aga Khan and several of his associates had bought up land cheaply on Sardinia's northeast coast. They had proceeded to turn the area—the Costa Smeralda or Emerald Coast—into one of the world's most luxurious holiday playgrounds.

Aryeh's friend knew of a hotel that had just gone on the market in Porto Cervo. Aryeh had managed to scrape together enough money to invest in the business, and a month later he had bought the house in nearby Arzachena.

"Abbiamo vostro figlio." A woman's voice, hard and emotionless. "We have your son. He is safe, and he will not be harmed if you follow our instructions. How soon you see him again depends on you. Consider this a simple business transaction. A little money in return for your son's life."

The voice was not Sardinian, Aryeh was sure of that, but he could not place the accent with greater exactitude. Southern rather than northern, he thought. Calabrian, perhaps.

"How much?" he asked.

"Nothing you can't afford. Four thousand million lire."

Aryeh felt the breath leave his chest as though he had been punched in the stomach. He almost dropped the receiver.

"That's impossible," he said. "I don't have anything like that."

The line went dead and he was left staring at the receiver. His hand shook as he replaced it. Four thousand million lire! As had been his habit from his first days in Sardinia, he converted the sum to dollars: five million. There was no way he could find a sum like that, nor anything close to it. He had a twenty percent share in the Hotel Giudichessa Eleonora, but he had signed agreements when he entered the partnership making it impossible for him to withdraw his investment without several months' notice. Unless he was incredibly lucky and managed to keep Yoel's abduction a secret, his partners would see to it that the law was enforced and his assets frozen. In any case, his twenty percent was still well below the figure demanded. Even if he sold everything he had, he would still be short by at least two thousand million lire.

He had always thought that the kidnap gangs did their homework before selecting a victim. They were, as they always said, businessmen trying to earn a living, and there was no point in their spending time and money on an enterprise that would never pay. A mistake had been made. They had confused him with someone else, taken his child instead of another man's. He knew that he had to convince them of that, otherwise he would never see his son again.

That night he hardly slept. Beside him, Chaya lay in a drugged sleep in which she tossed and turned feverishly. For hours he went through his finances in his head, picking through every thread, unraveling every knot, weighing risk against risk, certainty against uncertainty. Daylight found him in the study at his desk, sweating, exhausted, surrounded by calculations that had ceased to have any meaning.

They rang again at nine o'clock, while he and Chaya were having breakfast. The same voice, devoid of all feeling. Somehow it made it harder that it was a woman.

"Have you had enough time to think it over?"

"Listen." His voice was trembling. "You're making a mistake. I don't have that sort of money. I've never had anything like it. You must be confusing me with someone else."

"We don't make mistakes. We know what you are worth."

"That's impossible. You can speak to my accountant, my bank manager, anyone you like. They'll show you. Even if I sell everything, I still won't have enough. We have to negotiate."

The woman's voice lost its equanimity.

"You disgust me," she snapped. "Your son's life is at risk and all you can think of is a scheme to save your filthy money. You should be ashamed."

She hung up. He sat listening to the burring on the line, unable to move. Chaya came across and took the receiver from him. Gently she unfolded his left hand.

"You're bleeding," she said.

He had been clutching his hand so tightly around the receiver that the nails had dug into the palm and drawn blood. He pulled Chaya to him and held her like a shield against his thoughts. She made no effort to comfort him. Inside, she was dull and empty. Nothing mattered any longer. Maria watched them in silence, powerless to help. No one asked her about the pain she felt at the boy's loss. She was only the housekeeper.

They rang again that night. A man this time, a foreigner, his accent difficult to place. He spoke in grammatically correct, slightly stilted Italian with the voice of someone in his late fifties or older.

"Mr. Levin," the man began, his voice soft and reasonable yet unemotional, unhurried, and precise, "my name is Bianco. I have been asked to speak to you in order to resolve the dilemma in which you find yourself. I would like you to consider me as a friend. I want to help you, and to help your son."

There was a pause, a whistling as if of wind on the wire. Aryeh wondered where they were, how far they had taken Yoel. The usual place was the mountains, the Gennargentu region. They would never find the boy there among thousands of caves and underground hideouts. The man's voice returned.

"Let me tell you that Yoel is in considerable danger. I think it is best you know that. We will get nowhere if you are cushioned from the truth.

18

The people holding him are not noted for their tenderness. If they do not get what they want soon, they will hurt him. Make no mistake about that, they will hurt him badly. And if they decide that you either cannot or will not pay, they will kill him. This is not a game; it is a most serious thing for such a small boy to face such a fate. He is already terrified, believe me. I have seen him. Even if all goes well, I fear he may not recover easily from the mental stress."

Aryeh listened with mounting pain and anger, fighting to control his emotions, knowing he had to pay attention for Yoel's sake. The stranger's matter-of-fact manner was, if anything, more hateful than the woman's coldness, as if something more than business lay beneath the surface. And Aryeh knew that Yoel would not be the only one to come out of this scarred, that a life of wounds lay ahead for all of them, whatever the outcome.

"Mr. Levin," the voice continued, still sweet and fragrant with reason, "I say all this not to frighten you, but in order to help you understand just how delicate your position is, and how precarious the well-being of your son. You say you do not have the necessary funds to meet the demands of Yoel's kidnappers, and for my part I am inclined to believe you. Not all Jews are rich, whatever some people think.

"However, I have to tell you that the people holding Yoel do not believe you. They say they have done their research, that you have ample resources, and that you are just holding out on them. You are, I think, in very bad trouble, and your son's life may be the price you pay for not being rich enough."

The stranger paused again. His silence strangled Aryeh's heart. Where was all this leading? Was there further cruelty to follow?

"So," the man continued, "I have come up with a solution to your problems. I am willing to pay the sum demanded by the kidnappers in return for something else that I know you possess, something which is of no value whatever to them, but which means a very great deal to me."

Aryeh's head was spinning. Who was this man? What could he possibly want from Aryeh that was worth four thousand million lire? Aryeh's share in the hotel? A cut of his future earnings?

"You're not making sense," he said. "I have nothing worth that much."

"On the contrary, you will find that what I have to say will make perfect sense. Do you want me to continue?"

Aryeh was still trying to place the speaker's accent. Something told him it might provide a clue to whatever lay behind all this. His own unfamiliarity both with the variety of Italian dialects and the ways the language was spoken by other nationalities reduced him to guesswork. All the same, he did notice some degree of similarity between the man's accent and that of one of his colleagues, a native of Bolzano in the Alto Adige region of Italy's northeast, bordering Austria. And he remembered once being told that German was more widely spoken there than Italian.

"Go on," he said. "I'm listening."

"What I want is very simple. It consists of two things. The first is a guarantee of silence.

You will say nothing to anyone of our agreement. Not to the police, not the carabinieri. Above all, nothing to those of your friends who might seek to interfere with my plans. The second is just as straightforward: information. Perhaps you have already guessed. I want to know the present whereabouts of the *bottegaio*."

Aryeh felt as though a thick hand had torn half his stomach from him. They were playing games with him, torturing him for no good reason.

"*Bottegaio?*" he said. "The shopkeeper? I don't understand."

"On the contrary, you understand only too well. Think about it—your son's life for the shopkeeper. Or, put it another way, the shopkeeper for four thousand million lire and the life of your son."

Aryeh's hand was shaking. This was worse than a nightmare.

"Please, I really do not understand. Who is the shopkeeper?"

There was a dull click as the line went dead. Aryeh remained standing, the receiver dead in his hand, sticky with sweat and fear. He stood like that for what seemed an age, not knowing what to do, where to turn, like an actor in a film when the projector has jammed, frozen in mid-action, unable to complete even the simple act of replacing a telephone receiver.

Chaya appeared beside him without a sound. She took the receiver from him and set it back on the phone.

"What did they want?" she asked. She could sense his fear; it belonged to her as well, like a child they had conceived together.

21

He shook his head. "I don't know," he said. "I honestly don't know."

That night he had his first nightmare, a taste of things to come.

3

The next morning the postman brought a small package. It had been posted in Cagliari, but that meant nothing. They could have people all over the island.

The package contained two items: a tiny cardboard box and a photograph. It was a colored Polaroid print showing Yoel against a plain backdrop. The boy's face was strained and stiff, his eyes unfocused. Aryeh did not understand immediately what the box contained. From a small transparent envelope he drew out something like a sliver of dull glass or plastic, half a centimeter wide and a centimeter long. He held it up to the light and, as he did so, realized that it was a tiny fingernail, torn out at the root. He dropped it with a cry and sank into his chair, shaking.

By the time Chaya came into the living room he had hidden both the photograph and the nail. The kidnapping had exposed his wife's fragility, and he knew he had to protect her from the possibility that harm had come to Yoel. Several members of her family had died violently in the past few years. A brother and a cousin had been killed within a month of one another in Lebanon. An uncle and aunt had died in a bomb attack on a Shas party rally two years earlier. Her mother had wanted to come with them to Sardinia, only to die of a heart attack shortly before their departure. For Chaya, Yoel's death or wounding would be a final blow, one from which she would not recover.

That afternoon, Aryeh visited his lawyer in Olbia, Michele Mannuzzu. He told him everything. Mannuzzu listened in silence, nodding from time to time, not rushing him, asking no questions. He was a farmer's son who owed his prosperity to men like Aryeh Levin. Money had come to him like a dream; it would pass away like one. Levin was not his first client to fall foul of the *rapitori*. He would not be the last.

"You know my affairs, Michele. You know I don't have that sort of money. What can I do?"

"Go to the police. If you don't have enough to pay, it won't matter if your funds are frozen."

"But that will be like a death sentence for Yoel."

"Not if the police manage to find him. They'll send in a team from Criminalpol. Good men. There's a chance."

"I'd rather negotiate. That way I can be sure. Do you think I can bring them down?"

Mannuzzu nodded slowly. He had eaten a large plate of *malloreddus* for lunch, and they were taking their toll. Half his mind was on his stomach. He thought he might be developing an ulcer.

"It depends. Certainly, they'll bring their price down. They always do. But whether they'll come down to what you can afford is more difficult to say. To be honest, I don't think so."

"The man I spoke with last night, Bianco....

23

He said he could arrange something. If I gave him information, he'd pay off the kidnappers. It makes no sense to me."

Mannuzzu shook his head. "Nor me." He fingered his small mustache. A tiny crumb came away between his nails. "Tell me what he said exactly."

Aryeh explained as well as he could.

"You say this man asked you for the whereabouts of someone called the *bottegaio*?" Mannuzzu asked.

"I don't know. Just *il bottegaio*—that's what I think he said."

"And you don't know who this shopkeeper is?"

Aryeh shook his head. "A mistake," he said. "He's making a mistake. I know nothing about this."

"I see."

The little *notaio* stroked his cheeks. He looked thoughtful, as though the name meant something to him.

"Aryeh," he said, "I think you may be in serious trouble. I will do what I can to help, of course. If they'll accept me as your *intermediario* I'll meet with this man Bianco and try to make him see reason. You'll need copies of all your accounts, investments, mortgages—everything. I'll do my best to convince them it's all genuine.

"But I'll need more information about this shopkeeper. It occurs to me that this may all be a terrible mistake. If I can prove that, they will let your son go unharmed—I'm sure of that. There is a code in these matters."

As he was leaving, Aryeh turned to the law-

24

yer. "Michele, what does it mean, the finger-nail?"

Mannuzzu swallowed. His saliva tasted bit-ter. Outside, the weather had turned stormy.

"Nothing," he said. "It means nothing. It's just physical evidence that they have your son, that's all."

Mannuzzu took the call that evening. It was the man again, Bianco. Mannuzzu explained who he was, that he wanted to discuss his client's problems. Bianco listened to him and agreed to set up a meeting.

"We don't have much time," he said. "This has to be finished quickly. Otherwise the boy will suffer."

"It's better you don't harm him," Mannuzzu said. "You'll get what you want all the faster without violence."

Bianco put down the receiver.

Mannuzzu turned to Aryeh. "German," he said. "Our friend Bianco is German."

The following morning brought a fresh packet. It contained a child's finger, the little finger from the left hand, minus the nail.

Mannuzzu arrived half an hour later to find his client white-faced and shaking in the study. The finger was still on the desk, its end bloody, wrapped in cotton wool. The lawyer sent for Maria and asked her to take the tiny finger to his car.

"It may not be his," Mannuzzu said. "They often use a corpse, the body of some child killed in an accident. It frightens you, but it lessens their sentence if they're caught. Try not to worry."

"It's not your son they're holding. You don't have to go through all this."

"I understand. But you mustn't lose sight of the fact that these are reasonable people. They have rules, and they play by them. If you lose your head and try to break those rules, then Yoel really will suffer. You have to let yourself be guided by me. I'll raise the matter when I meet with them."

"When will that be?"

"Soon. Possibly this afternoon. If they're as anxious to get this over with as they sound, they'll have made arrangements for an early meeting."

Maria came back.

"The *signora*," she said. "She is upset. She thinks the boy is dead."

"You haven't … ?"

The little woman shook her head fiercely. "She knows nothing. I have shown her nothing. It would frighten her to know what animals these people are. They are not Sardinians, I swear to you. Such a thing would be impossible. I knew Grazianeddu, many years ago. He would never have done such a thing. He was a *bandito d'onore*, the King of the Supramonte. What he did, he did for his people, never for himself. He would never harm the innocent. But with these foreigners, there is no honor, no *codice*, no courage—only greed."

"Thank you, Maria. Tell my wife I'll be with her shortly. I'll ask Dr. Talanas to see her again."

When Maria had gone, Aryeh turned to Mannuzzu. "Do you think she knows something? She seemed so certain the kidnappers were not Sardinians."

26

Mannuzzu shook his head. "She remembers Grazianeddu—Graziano Mesina. You may not have heard of him. He was a legend in the sixties, a hero to people of her generation. They let him out of prison a few years back. *Oggi* ran a series on him, made a song and dance out of it. The honest bandit who stole from the rich to help the poor. In all truth, he was a killer and a kidnapper, but it's probably true that he would never have harmed a child. They say the *latitanti* from Calabria were the first to mutilate their victims. To cut off their ears. But children, that was much later."

Aryeh remembered the voice on the telephone, the woman's voice. Calabrian, perhaps? Mannuzzu would have a good idea.

At that moment, the phone rang. Mannuzzu let it ring twice, then picked up the receiver.

"Pronto."

He spoke for about two minutes. Putting the receiver back on the rest, he spoke to Aryeh.

"They want to meet me this evening."

"Where?"

The lawyer shook his head. "I can't tell you that. I'm their cut-off. If anyone else is involved, if I'm followed, if they feel in the least insecure, they will kill the boy. Do you understand?"

Aryeh nodded.

"Have all your papers ready for me by five o'clock. Don't keep anything back: We don't know what they've already seen."

"When will you know?"

"I'll contact you at midnight or as soon after as possible. Stay here. Look after your wife. And don't worry—we'll get your son back. I promise."

At the door, the lawyer hesitated. "You are sure you know nothing about this shopkeeper? Perhaps he's a Jew, someone you have met at the synagogue."

Aryeh shook his head. "I know no one like that. I swear to you. Do you think I would risk Yoel's life if I did know?"

Midnight came and went. There was no call from Mannuzzu. Aryeh sat alone in his study, shivering, unable to move from the phone. At three o'clock, Chaya came for him.

"Come to bed, Aryeh. He won't ring now. Get some sleep. He'll be here in the morning."

"I can't sleep."

"Try. You're no use to me like this. You have to keep your strength."

"I'm frightened, Chaya."

She took his hand. "Yes," she whispered. "Come to bed."

In the morning, Mannuzzu did not appear. Aryeh waited until nine o'clock, sickening. When the *notaio* still did not appear, he rang his office. The secretary said he had not turned up that morning. Aryeh looked up the lawyer's home number and rang there. His wife answered.

"Michele's missing. He went out last night at seven o'clock. A car came to pick him up. He said it was a client, on business. He hasn't been back since. I'm sure there's been an accident."

"Don't worry, he'll turn up. There's been no accident. He's quite safe."

"Do you know anything about it?"

"No, but I'm sure he'll be all right. He's a careful man. He'll be safe."

He hung up, relieved to escape her questioning. Moments later, his phone rang. The woman's voice this time.

"Levin? We told you not to fuck about with us. This isn't a game we're playing. Next time you tell us what we want to know or you never see your son again."

The line went dead. Aryeh felt simultaneously angry and crushed. What did they want with him? What had they done with Michele Mannuzzu?

There was the sound of a motorcycle outside, drawing close to the house, then away again at speed. Aryeh ran to the door just in time to catch sight of the rear of a heavy motorcycle disappearing, driven by a man in black leathers.

On the doorstep lay another parcel. Aryeh picked it up with trembling hands. God alone knew what it contained. He carried it straight to the study, closing and locking the door behind him.

There were no stamps, but the wrapping paper was the same as before. A photograph tumbled out, another Polaroid. It showed Michele Mannuzzu's head and shoulders against a background that looked like wood covered in flaking green paint. Michele's throat had been cut from side to side. His chest and shoulders were thickly coated with blood. Aryeh let the picture drop to the floor.

A long time afterward, not knowing whether he was asleep or awake, he opened the cardboard box that had come with the photograph.

Beneath a layer of cotton wool sticky with dried blood he found an ear. Not Mannuzzu's ear, but a child's ear. And not the ear of a dead child, stolen from a country morgue. The small, narrow lobe was unmistakably that of his son.

That afternoon, Aryeh Levin made a phone call from a bar in Porto Cervo. He had no choice, no other direction to turn.

"Centosettanta. Centralino internazionale. Desidera?"

"I want to make a person-to-person call, please."

"Yes. What name, please?"

"Abuhatseira. Yosef Abuhatseira. Let me spell that for you."

She wrote the name down slowly and read it back to him.

"Where is the call to be made to, please?"

"To Israel," he said. "The town is called Qiryat Arba, in Samaria."

"I'm sorry, I ..."

"You'll find it under 'Occupied Territories,'" he said.

When he put down the receiver, his hand was shaking. He left the bar and went out to the street. Above the roofs of the little town, the sky had turned the color of hibiscus, as though the petals of a vast flower were opening in the last sad moments before darkness. Aryeh sighed. His heart was still beating, and the conversation still rang in his ears.

Had it not been for Yoel, nothing could have induced him to make the call. Abuhatseira was Chaya's brother, the one with whom Aryeh had

had disagreements almost from the start. Aryeh was a peacenik, a supporter of the Peace Now movement, a dedicated believer in integration between Jews and Arabs. Yosef, on the other hand, was, like many Oriental Jews, a right-winger, an "Arabs-out, Israel-for-the-Jews" man. He had fought with a crack special services unit in Lebanon and elsewhere, and had recently gone to live in Qiryat Arba, a controversial settlement in the middle of the Occupied Territories.

Relations between the two men had never been easy. More than one family gathering had ended in shouting and the slamming of doors as one or the other stormed off. More often than Aryeh cared to remember, Chaya had come to bed red-eyed and upset, torn between her husband and the brother she loved. Yoel, too, had been confused by the animosity he had witnessed between his father and uncle. If one was kind, wise, and gentle, the other seemed to his boy's eyes nothing less than a hero, battle-scarred, taciturn, and brave—someone about whom to boast in school.

Aryeh walked to his car and slipped into the driver's seat. Whatever his feelings, whatever his principles, he knew he could not let them get in the way. Suddenly, he too wanted his brother-in-law to be the hero Yoel believed him to be.

The Alisarda flight from Rome landed at Olbia airport in a squall of fine rain. It was shortly after eleven in the morning, twenty-one hours after Aryeh Levin made his phone call, one and a half days after Michele Mannuzzu's throat was cut.

Aryeh watched the little plane descend, catching light once as it cleared the cloud cover, then touching down in a spray of muddy water. He felt weary, drained of hope. He had become nothing in a matter of days, a cipher, just a tired man waiting for a plane to land. And his wife was at home in bed, staring at the wall.

The search for Michele Mannuzzu continued. The carabinieri had been scouring the mountains for days now without success. Aryeh had burned the photograph of the dead man and said nothing to anyone, not even Mannuzzu's wife. He felt sorry for her, but there was nothing he could do: his son's life was at stake. He did not want the police to make a connection with him that would lead them to start an investigation of Yoel's kidnapping. That would lead to disaster, he was certain of it. He had chosen his own path now and would hold to it.

The plane taxied to a halt and steps were wheeled against the fuselage. Aryeh left the window and went to join the families waiting for friends and relatives downstairs. It would not be a long wait: the passengers did not have to go through passport control. For all its differences of language and customs, Sardinia was still officially Italy.

Two policemen had visited him the day before, men from the Questura in Olbia. There had been rumors that Aryeh's son had been kidnapped. Was he in a position to confirm

32

them? He had told them the rumors were lies, that Yoel had gone to Israel a few days earlier to visit relatives. During term time? It was a religious festival, he had replied, Hanukkah, the feast of lights. Yoel had gone to spend the festival in Haifa, where it would be celebrated more lavishly than here in Sardinia.

Aryeh had smiled, telling them how Yoel had loved Hanukkah, but inwardly he had been broken, a thing of fragments, knowing how much Yoel had indeed been looking forward to the festivities.

The policemen had left soon after, but he knew they had not believed him. And he feared they might soon return.

The man he was waiting for was the last to enter the arrivals lounge. Even if they had never met, Aryeh would have known at first glance which one he was. There was no mistaking that look. Had he been asked to define it, he could not have done so. Even at a distance, it singled Yosef out from his fellow passengers.

Yosef came through the doors and made straight for Aryeh. The other passengers were busy greeting their families or heading straight to the baggage carousel.

Without hesitation, they embraced, old quarrels set aside in a time of need. Holding his brother-in-law, Aryeh could smell on his skin the unmistakable perfume of Israel, an indefinable smell of sea and desert.

"*Shalom*, Aryeh."

"*Shalom*, Yosef. I'm glad you've come."

They stood back and looked at one another. It was four years or more since their last meeting, and then, as always, they had argued. Not very tall, not very handsome, not very well dressed, Yosef Abuhatseira did not conform to the bronzed ideal of Israeli manhood. But no one would pass him in the street without registering his presence. Above all, it was the eyes, with their inwardness, their olive blackness, their immensity, their awareness of everything. And the mouth, firmly set and tense, as though at any moment he might smile or burst out laughing, as though all the energy of his face was there, coiled in those lips.

Yes, thought Aryeh, I did the right thing in asking him to come. For the first time in days he believed his son might be saved.

Aryeh made to pick up his bag, but Yosef lifted it and slung it over his shoulder without a word.

"Don't you have a case?"

Yosef shook his head. "This is all the luggage I need. The rest will be taken care of later."

They headed for the exit. Aryeh kept glancing nervously to the right and left, expecting either the police or one of the kidnappers to be following him.

"It's all right," said Yosef. "We aren't being watched. You can relax."

"How can you be sure?"

Yosef shrugged. "Believe me, I know."

Near the door, they passed a trio of wanted posters that had been placed there by the Questura. Aryeh looked at one.

RICERCATO
BAUDO, PINO, fu Pasquale, nato ad
Orgosolo (Nuoro)
il 4.5.71 ivi residente. Colpito da
plurimi mandati di catture per

**sequestro di persona a scopo di
estorsione—omicidio aggravato—
tentato omicidio aggravato—evasione
aggravate da Carceri Giudiziarie ove
espiava residua pena di ANNI 42 di
reclusione
TAGLIA VENTI MILIONI
che il Ministero dell'Interno
corrispondera a chiunque ne
agevolera la
CATTURA**

Aryeh could not tear his eyes from the face on the poster. Small, hooded eyes, thick lips, untidy hair: the dull features of a Barbagian shepherd in his mid-twenties. It was hard to think of the man as a ruthless killer, the author of "aggravated homicide."

Yosef took his arm and drew him away from the poster. He shook his head slowly. "Not this man," he said gently. "He did not take Yoel."

"How do you know?"

Yosef looked back at the poster, then away again. "You know hotels," he said. "I know men like him."

As they turned out of the airport, Yosef turned to his brother-in-law. "How long have we got?" he asked.

Aryeh flinched at the question. He had spent almost half an hour the night before persuading Bianco to give him some leeway. To gain time, he had pretended to understand what the man had meant by *il bottegaio*, and had said he had no immediate access to the information Bianco wanted. A period of forty-eight hours

35

had finally been agreed upon, at the expiration of which Yoel would be shot. No further delays, no more playing for time.

"That gives me until early tomorrow evening," Yosef said. "It isn't long. I have to locate the kidnappers and assess their strength before I can even think of getting Yoel out."

"You could go in as my intermediary," sugested Aryeh.

Yosef shook his head. "Only as a last resort. I'd lose the element of surprise. And they'd arrange a meeting place some distance from wherever they're holding Yoel. It's too much of a risk." He paused. "You say they killed the man you sent, this lawyer."

Aryeh nodded. The image of Mannuzzu with his throat cut had not left him.

"Do you know why they killed him?"

"Bianco said Mannuzzu tried to be too clever. He wanted a cut for himself."

"Surely that's not unusual in these matters."

"Yes, but I think Mannuzzu suggested he knew what this is all about. Bianco said as much to me: If I told anyone else, Yoel would suffer."

They drove north past Olbia and on to the road toward Arzachena. Aryeh checked from time to time in his rearview mirror, anxious to see if they were being followed. As they passed the side road leading to Pantaleo, Yosef put up his hand between the mirror and Aryeh's eyes.

"You're wasting your time," he said. "If they're there, they won't let you see them."

"You think we're being followed?"

Yosef shrugged. "We have to assume so. If they ask about me, tell them the truth, or as much as they need to know: I am your brother-in-law, I'm here at my sister's request, I won't interfere."

He hesitated, then asked the question that was most on his mind. Chaya was his little sister; they had always been close. "How is Chaya?"

"Not so good," answered Aryeh. "This thing is killing her."

"Have you told her I'm coming?"

Aryeh nodded. "She's expecting you."

"Does she know why I've come?"

"I don't think so. I just said you wanted to be with us."

"Good. It's better she doesn't know the truth."

They passed through Albucciu, asleep in the noon sun. In moments they had left it behind. Minutes later, the high cliffs surrounding Arzachena appeared. The road was almost free of traffic. Aryeh watched his villa come into sight. He had never before felt so without direction when coming home.

Maria had made lunch. There was *pane carasau*—crisp, round sheets of bread very like the Arab loafs of home—roast lamb, tomatoes, and *calcagno* cheese. They cheerlessly drank a dry Tortolì wine. Yosef looked tired; he had been traveling almost since the phone call had reached him the night before. He seemed more thoughtful than Aryeh remembered him.

When the lunch things had been cleared away, Aryeh called Maria back to the dining room.

"How is Chaya?" he asked.

"She's a little better today, I think. Sometimes she cries. Sometimes she sits very still. She is waiting. At the moment, she is sleeping, but only with the help of pills. Not a good sleep."

"Have you told her anything?"

Maria shook her head. "Nothing, *signore*. She believes the ransom will soon be paid, that she will have her son back soon, that he is unharmed."

He saw her bite her lip hard. He had found her more than once, silently crying in the kitchen.

"When she wakes up, Maria, please tell her her brother is here, her brother Yosef. She will want to see him. It may cheer her up.

"Now, I want you to tell Yosef what you told me yesterday. Please don't be afraid. He has come to help us."

Maria looked at the newcomer. She had seen men like him before, many times. They were not the sort of men a woman would be advised to know well. They had a mark on them, these men. Those she had known had all died young and violently. If she had been young again, she would have done anything for him.

She spoke in Italian while Aryeh translated into Hebrew.

"My brother has a pasture in the Supramonte, at Oliena. I went there three days ago to speak to him. He is my older brother, my oldest living relative. I told him what had happened, what the boy means to me, to his mother. He listened and promised to find out what he could. He is much respected. People speak freely to such a man. He has their confidence. Two days after we spoke, he came to me and said that he had found the place where the boy is being held. It is very hard to find, near the Gennargentu, but my brother knows. He says,

38

signore, that he is willing to take you there, but there must be no *polizia,* no carabinieri, no *mobile.*"

"Will he take my brother-in-law?"

She looked at Yosef again, once, and nodded. "Yes," she said. "He will take him."

5

When Maria had gone, Yosef asked if he might use the telephone. He made several calls, all to local numbers, all conducted in Arabic. That was not altogether surprising, since many of the businesspeople and tourists who had come to the Costa Smeralda in the wake of the Aga Khan's enterprise were Arabs.

Yosef had learned to speak Moroccan Arabic at home as a matter of course, and later he had been trained in the Palestinian and Lebanese dialects. Though he never spoke openly of his work with the Sayaret Matkal, Aryeh had always suspected that much of it had involved the interrogation of Arab suspects. Hearing him now, using Arabic in the interests of saving his son, Aryeh felt confused. It complicated matters greatly to find himself so dependent on someone he had so long despised, and to know that it was precisely on Yosef's qualities as a hunter and killer that he most depended.

Half an hour after the last phone call, there was a ring at the door. A well-dressed man in a business suit carrying a large- and a medium-sized attaché case asked to see Yosef. He was Italian, with a pronounced Napolitan accent.

In the living room, Yosef closed the blinds and lit the main lights before asking their visitor to open the larger case. It contained an arsenal. The top section held a disassembled Heckler and Koch PSG1 sniper's rifle. Underneath were a Beretta MP12S submachine gun, sixteen inches long, with a telescopic bolt; a Browning Hi-Power autoloader pistol; and ammunition for all three guns.

The second case contained a variety of gadgets, ranging from a Simrad day- and night-vision binocular telescope to a hunting crossbow and bolts. Next to the bow was a strange-looking device like a tiny metal scepter with a canvas strap at one end. Yosef lifted this last item from the case and held it up, smiling.

"Your Sardinians are very resourceful, Aryeh," he said. "I didn't think anyone could lay his hands on one of these, but here it is."

"What is it?"

"It's a British special forces device from the Second World War. A Peskett close-combat weapon. See, the knob at this end can be used as a bludgeon." He pressed a button at the other end and a long spike popped out. "This is a very efficient dagger. And this—" he lifted a tiny metal ball at the bludgeon end, drawing out a long metal cord "—is a garrotte."

He replaced the weapon in the case and closed the lid.

Aryeh found himself troubled by the joy Yosef seemed to take from the weapons. He had watched him handling them, seen the pleasure it gave him to touch them, asked himself what joy he might find in using them. But this was the man who had come to save his son, so he said nothing.

Assured that Yosef was satisfied, the man who had brought the cases prepared to go. He handed a bunch of car keys to Aryeh and told him where the vehicle was parked. Yosef would find clothing and other items he had asked for in the trunk.

"And this," he said, handing him a slip of paper, "is the address where your brother-in-law will find his interpreter. She's a woman, an Israeli who has lived in Sardinia for several years. She speaks both Italian and Sardo fluently. Your brother-in-law can trust her completely. I selected her myself: there will be nothing to worry about. Tell your brother-in-law he must take the *latitanti* first: If anything goes wrong with their employers, they will have been instructed to kill the boy. See he understands that."

He said nothing more, not even to wish Aryeh good luck. For him, as for the kidnappers, this was merely business. He just happened to be on Aryeh's side on this occasion.

When he had gone, Aryeh explained what he had told him. Yosef listened, nodding. Aryeh drew a sketch map of Arzachena and marked on it the locations for the car and the interpreter. When he had studied it for a few minutes, Yosef burned the paper and threw the ashes into the fireplace.

"Now," he said, "I would like to sleep for a while. Is my room ready?"

Aryeh showed him to his bedroom.

"Don't worry," said Yosef, as he made to close the door. "Yoel will be all right. There's plenty

41

of time now for me to find him and deal with his kidnappers. They won't be expecting me. In matters of this kind, surprise is nine-tenths of the battle. We'll get him out: I promise."

"What about Bianco? He won't give up easily. This information's worth a great deal to him."

Yosef nodded. "I agree. But once Yoel's safe, we've got him at a disadvantage. Let's get Yoel out, then we can decide what to do about our German friend."

Aryeh stepped forward and embraced his brother-in-law awkwardly. Yosef responded to the gesture warmly, pressing Aryeh hard against his chest, as though in some fashion to reclaim him. Or was it that, in being this close for the first time, Yosef himself sought to be reclaimed?

"Thank you," said Aryeh, drawing away at last, his face flushed, his expression one of bewilderment. "I'm sorry that ... I'm sorry we had to wait for this to bring us together."

Yosef smiled a tired, impatient smile. "Don't worry, we'll argue again. You're still a dove, I'm still a hawk. It's our natures. You chose to abandon Israel. I have chosen to defend the land God gave to us. That will always be a cause for friction between you and me. But Yoel is my sister's child, and you are her husband. That is what matters at this moment. Go and get some sleep: I will need your help tonight."

Alone in his room, Yosef sat for a while on the bed, collecting his thoughts, letting his body relax. Before sleeping, he would perform the afternoon prayer. Standing, he shook the tiredness from his head. "O Lord," he began, "open Thou my lips, and my mouth shall show forth Thy praise...."

Downstairs, godless and childless, Aryeh kept guard over the innocent-looking cases, trying hard to think of nothing.

Yosef had just finished reciting the *shmoneh esreh* when the door opened. Looking round, he saw a woman standing in the doorway dressed in a long toweling robe, her hair disheveled. Her eyes were red and looked tired, as though she had not slept properly in days.

"Who are you?" she asked. She spoke Italian. He had to guess what she meant.

"It's Yosef," he said. "I've come to get Yoel back."

She looked at him silently for a while, pushing a lock of hair back from her eyes.

"You're not Yosef," she said. "Yosef's in Eretz Israel."

He went up close to her, his arms open, his eyes filling with tears. He had never seen her so hurt, so broken.

"It's me, Chaya," he said, "your brother Yosef. I left Tel Aviv last night. Just myself: The rest of the family don't know a thing. Don't worry, it will all be over soon."

She backed away and went on staring at him, as though what he said made no sense to her. Finally, she turned on her heel, and, without another word, left the room, closing the door behind her. He heard her returning to her own room with dragging footsteps. A dreadful tiredness washed over him, and a sense of his own inadequacy.

He left that night after dark, taking the weapons with him. No one saw him leave, he made certain of it.

His contacts had arranged for him to meet the interpreter in Nuoro, the provincial capital on the edge of the Barbagia region. He arrived there just before eleven o'clock, his sister's image still fresh in his mind like a dangerous insect buzzing in a deserted room. A carefully drawn map guided him straight to the address he sought, a private apartment chosen for its anonymity and relative seclusion. He rang the bell once and stepped back to wait.

The door opened within moments to reveal a small, dark-haired woman in her early thirties. She was dressed plainly yet with much care in a black sweater and trousers. Yosef noticed at once the intelligence and energy in her eyes, and picked up at once the slightly amused puckering of her lips. He had expected someone very different, someone bookish and withdrawn, difficult, perhaps, to work with should he have to negotiate directly with the kidnappers in the end. This woman, he sensed immediately, would be cool and level-headed in a crisis.

"You must be Yosef Abuhatseira," she said in Hebrew. "I'm Maryam. Maryam Shumayyil. Pleased to meet you."

She stretched out a hand, and he took it, but only for the briefest of handshakes. He felt betrayed. Shumayyil was an Arab name. Nobody had told him the woman would be an Arab.

She saw the look on his face, identified it immediately for what it was.

"You thought I'd be Jewish," she said.

He nodded dumbly. He tried to tell himself it wasn't important, that he was just employing her as an interpreter, not proposing marriage. But it was no good. Over the years, and especially since his move to Qiryat Arba, he had developed a distrust of Arabs. The interpreter might not play a central role in what was about to happen, but he had to be able to guarantee her loyalty.

"It's nothing personal," he said.

"It never is." She paused, looking hard at him. The trace of amusement had vanished from her mouth, as though a sliver of something sour had been placed on her tongue. He saw something in her eyes that unsettled him. "You'd better come in," she said.

The temporary accommodations his contacts had provided for her were spartan: a few sticks of cheap furniture, a television, a hot plate. She stood out against it all, poised, contained, and almost mocking. In this light, he noticed to his surprise that she was pretty. More than that, she had a dignity and self-assurance that turned the prettiness to something more solid.

"Abuhatseira," she said, sitting down in one of the room's two chairs while he took the other. "Moroccan?"

He nodded.

She switched to Arabic.

"Look," she said, "I've been told next to nothing about your situation, and, unless something goes wrong, I don't have to know. But I've lived in this place long enough to have a shrewd idea of what's up. The fact is, you don't have time to look for another interpreter, even if you could find one, which I doubt. So, unless you're prepared to take unnecessary risks, it looks like you're stuck with me."

"An interpreter isn't essential," he said. "I can get by on my own."

"Like hell you can. Even if you spoke fluent Italian, you'd be lost in the Barbagia."

He shrugged. All he wanted to do was make his apologies and leave.

"Where are you from?" she asked.

"Jerusalem."

"You live there now?"

He shook his head. "No. Qiryat Arba."

A slow smile spread across her lips. "I see. Well, that explains a great deal. Maybe you're right, maybe you don't need an interpreter after all."

She got to her feet without taking her eyes from him. Her look was hard to assess. It was not hostility, rather something midway between bitterness and resignation.

"You don't owe me anything," she said. She picked up an overnight bag from the floor. As she headed for the door, she turned.

"Tell your friends I'll send back the retainer I've already been paid. Good luck. I hope you find your nephew."

He thought of Yoel, frightened and praying for rescue, and he knew that if anything went wrong, he would never be able to forgive himself.

"I'm sorry," he said. He, too, had switched to Arabic, almost without thinking. "I don't speak a word of Italian, let alone ..." He hesitated.

"Sardu," she said. "You'll survive. The locals are very tolerant of outsiders." She opened the door. "The key's on the table. Lock up when you leave."

"They're going to kill him," Yosef said abruptly. "Unless I stop them. He's only ten years old."

He wondered if she had children of her own. For a long moment, she stood looking at him, as though sizing him up. He felt diminished by the look, thinking himself measured and found wanting, set against some moral calibration he could not understand.

"Very well," she said. "For the child." She let the bag slide from her shoulder to the floor. "I'll do it for the child. Tell them that when you go back to Qiryat Arba."

6

They left before first light, heading into the Supramonte on foot, like shadows. Matteo Deiana, Maria's brother, led Yosef through the darkness without hesitation: He had spent his life in these hills, walked down these pathways in all weathers, knew them as well as his wife's body. They did not speak. They had left Maryam behind in Oliena, where she would remain until Yosef brought the boy. The shepherd and Yosef had said all they needed to one another the previous night. Matteo would show the way to the cave in which the child was being held, then wait, keeping himself hidden, until it was time to lead Yosef back again.

They headed along the valley of the Locol, into the foothills above Orgosolo. It was growing light quickly now. The peaks of Monte Corrasi and Monte Ortu appeared in the sky above them like ghosts. Where there had been flocks of stars was now a field streaked with silver and pearl. Yosef watched the mountain country being born around him and remembered his own childhood in Morocco's Middle Atlas mountains. With a pang, he recalled the mornings he had spent watching his father's pastures, the smell of hill flowers opening, the sound of sheep and goats. If he ever found peace, he would return to a place like this and raise sheep and watch the sun rise in the morning.

They halted briefly while Yosef recited the morning prayer. He washed first in a cold mountain stream, then strapped tefillin to his right arm and slipped his prayer shawl over his head. The shepherd watched him without curiosity.

Matteo moved like a young man, climbing the steepening slopes with almost as much ease and grace as he had enjoyed at twenty. It was hard to guess his real age, but his sister Maria was well over fifty, and they were separated by three siblings. He wanted to get past Orgosolo and deep into the *macchia* before anyone saw them. Once there, he could keep the foreigner out of sight on the old footpaths, ancient tracks originally marked by the feet of wild boar and mouflons.

Matteo was not ashamed of what he was doing, but he knew he was breaking the code of the mountains by betraying his own people to a stranger. What had convinced him to do so was the knowledge that the people behind the kidnapping were not natives of Barbagia. Their treatment of the boy had been enough to convince him of that. Almost certainly, he thought, they would prove to be an opportunist grouping of anarchists from the mainland

and organized criminals from Cagliari. They were merely using the shepherds as hired hands to keep the boy in a secure location. Matteo could condone kidnapping or cattle stealing under the unwritten Codice Barbaricine, or the ancient rules of the Anonima, but these outsiders were ruthless and greedy, willing to cut off a child's ear and finger just to speed up a transaction. He had no pity for them or for anyone willing to work for them.

On either side, shadows solidified and became heavy outcrops of limestone. As the light grew, the color of the stone shifted from green to blue-gray to silver. On a slope to their right they saw a group of isolated *su pinnettu*, old cottages built of yew trunks, their tile roofs thick with moss.

They clambered on to an outcrop. At the top, Matteo showed his companion a hidden path straggling through a tangle of blackthorn, myrtle, and arbutus shrubs. This was the beginning of the *macchia*, the vast undergrowth that had hidden generations of bandits and fugitives from justice. Both men carried weapons concealed in rucksacks. Yosef was dressed in old clothes belonging to Matteo's son, Allesandro, and carried his hunting rifle.

They entered a patch of woodland, where tall holm oaks blotted out most of the light. Bright clumps of broom grew in the spaces between fallen trees. Every so often they would pass the charred remains of a tree that had been burned in a fire long ago, but which went on standing like a memorial to its vanished companions. The birds fell silent as they passed, then picked up courage and started to sing again. When they left the trees, they were high up and the sun was on their faces.

He knew he could not have come here on his own. Partly because no outsider could have found his way unassisted to the cave where the shepherds held the boy, but mainly because the mountains were so riddled with unsuspected grottoes and deep gullies into which a man might tumble without warning and not be found for months or years.

Matteo took his arm and pointed upward through a narrow pass.

"*E' un po' piu in là,*" he said. "*Piu in alto. Il nascondiglio.*"

Yosef understood well enough what the Sardinian meant. He nodded. They would have to go more carefully from here on.

Every time he woke, the pain was there, and the terrible pressure on his wound from the bandages they had wrapped round his head. He would start crying, partly from the pain, partly from the fear and loneliness that had surrounded him from the moment the men had come for him. Then they would give him tablets, and the pain would recede a little, and he would be left with the fear and the loneliness.

He remembered his father's voice, shouting to him as they bundled him downstairs: "*Yoel, don't worry. I'll get you back.... I'll find you.*" But it had been days and still his father had not come. He wanted his mother very much, cried for her at night, softly, so that they would not hear him and beat him. They could cut off his other ear, cut off all his fingers—he didn't care, as long as they took him back to her.

He knew what had happened, had known almost at once. Bandits had kidnapped him and were holding him for ransom. It was something they had talked about at school, in whispers, in places where the teachers would not hear them. Everybody knew about kidnappings, about the gangs who took little children and held them until their parents paid enough money to have them back, and who killed them if they weren't paid what they wanted. There had been a little girl in Porto Cervo last winter, and a few years ago a boy at his school, an Arab boy whose parents were close friends of the Aga Khan.

One of his friends at school, another Jewish boy, Yigal, had told Yoel that his father took great precautions for his safety. Yigal was picked up every day after school by a chauffeur driving a Mercedes, and when he went to the beach or walking in the hills, bodyguards went with him. But Yigal's parents were very rich, richer than Yoel's. They would have enough money to pay the kidnappers. Yoel was frightened that his own father had been unable to find the money his kidnappers wanted, that the men would kill him if they did not get it.

They kept him in the dark a lot of the time, at the back of the little cave. The cave stank of stale food and goats. Yoel thought it was used in the winter to keep animals, and as a shelter for the shepherds. There were four men with him, all Sardinians, all shepherds, and they treated him like an animal. But they had not been the ones who cut off his finger and then his ear. That had been the woman.

He had never seen any of their faces. They

wore masks all the time, at least whenever they came anywhere near him. The shepherds came and went through the day and spent the night in the cave. There were always at least two keeping watch. Sometimes the others came to see him, the woman and the two men who had driven him away from the house. The woman had told him that if his father did not pay soon, she would have to hurt him again. She had said she was coming back soon with a video camera, and that he would have to make a film asking his father to pay, telling him what they would do if he did not.

Yosef moved a branch aside and focused his telescope on the mouth of the cave. He had spent the night opposite the hideout, watching and sleeping through the long hours till dawn. Matteo had gone off on his own to hunt, leaving a little food and water. He had said he would return that evening.

The morning had been spent in making a thorough surveillance of the cave and the terrain around it. He had established that there were four guards and that each of them carried a hunting rifle with him at all times. One of them came out now, his weapon slung over his shoulder, and made his way to the spot that Yosef guessed was being used as the latrine. The boy had not been brought outside, but earlier he had seen one of the shepherds carrying a covered bucket. There had been no sign of a fire, either outside or inside. The shepherds would be eating cold food rather than draw attention to themselves.

He was unsure of his next move, but he knew

he would have to make it soon, whatever he decided. If he moved in now he could be reasonably sure of taking the shepherds by surprise and rescuing the boy. That was his chief mission. But that last image of his sister, her mind so disarrayed as to be unable to recognize him, had left him with a clawing need for revenge. He wanted to send out a warning to anyone else who had thoughts of kidnapping Jewish children. That meant taking the organizers as well—either here or, if he could track them down, at their base.

He needed to know how Bianco communicated with the men at the hideout. Either one of the shepherds hiked once a day to a nearby village in order to telephone or they had a two-way radio. Yosef would have put his money on the radio, except that he never gambled. The telephone option was clumsy, liable to attract attention, and useless in an emergency.

That meant that if he was to take the shepherds first, he must be sure to do it quickly. One word of warning on the radio and Bianco and anyone with him would disappear. He would have given anything to know when the daily check-in call was made. Probably first thing in the morning. If it had already gone through, he knew he might have to spend at least another night before there was any likelihood of the main group turning up.

He switched off the telescope and slipped the lens cover back on. He had made his mind up. It was time to take the boy out.

The way down to the latrine was slippery, and it brought him dangerously close to the mouth

of the cave. But he had chosen his route carefully, remaining hidden in thick undergrowth
most of the way. At times he went on all fours,
like a beast stalking its prey. His mind was on
two things only now: silence and concealment.
If he could accomplish everything without a
sound, so much the better.

He circled round until he was behind the
latrine and well out of sight. Ahead of him, he
could see his target, the shepherd who had
stepped outside. The man was taking his time,
sitting on a log and smoking a cigarette. He
had left his rifle on the ground.

Yosef removed the Peskett from a pouch he
wore round his neck and slowly drew out the
long garrotting wire. It had been well oiled and
was in perfect condition. He moved forward
without a sound. The man was only a few yards
ahead of him now. He was singing gently to
himself, a popular love song. Yosef put the song
out of his mind.

He crossed the last few yards like a shadow.
All was speed now. The boy's life, his own life,
the honor and happiness of his family—all re-
lied on speed. Pity would slow him down, hold
back his hand. It would destroy him, destroy
the child, destroy Chaya. He was close enough
to touch the man. And at that moment he knew
he had been sensed. The shepherd stopped singing and began to turn. Yosef lifted the garrott,
swung the noose over the man's head down to
his neck, and pulled in a swift, unhesitating
movement. The thin wire sliced through the
shepherd's neck, cutting through flesh and tissue
like a knife through cheese. The body jerked
and slumped. Yosef drew back at once, letting

the blood gush, waiting till the heart had pumped its last consignment to the dying brain. The body twitched and lay still. Blood ran everywhere, reddening the grass.

He took his victim by the arms and started to drag him back and out of sight. As he did so, he heard voices coming from the direction of the cave. He looked up and saw three figures approaching the entrance. A woman and two men. They were wearing camouflage jackets and black caps. The woman was carrying something that looked like a video camera. They all carried modern rifles over their shoulders.

The group behind the kidnapping had arrived. One of the men might be Bianco himself. It was only a matter of minutes before they realized that one of their men was missing.

7

He was one against six. The three remaining shepherds or bandits he could dismiss. They seemed neither well-trained nor well-armed, and he was sure he could take them out without difficulty. But the three new arrivals were an unknown quantity. They might be ordinary criminals with no understanding of combat. Or, if Matteo Deiana's speculation was correct and they were mainland anarchists or right-wing terrorists, there was just a chance they would know how to handle themselves. They had carried high-quality weapons, and if they knew how to use them they could hold out against one man without backup.

He moved to the face of the rock into which

the cave ran and climbed until he was above the entrance and a little to the right. Any minute now, someone would come to check on the missing man. Yosef settled himself against a jutting rock and took the crossbow from his back.

There was a shout from below.

"Antonio! Antonio! Dove diavolo sei? Sono arrivati i pezzi grossi."

The voice echoed among the rocks and faded. Yosef looked down. One of the guards had come out of the cave and was scouting about for a sign of his friend. He was dressed in a leather jacket and faded jeans and wore a flat cap. A good-looking man of about twenty-five. Probably not a shepherd, thought Yosef, but a local man who had spent some time in jail and was now on the run. The man headed for the latrine. Yosef watched him go, raising the bow. He wound back the cord to the sear and slipped a bolt soundlessly into the groove. The man was in his sights now, as helpless as a rabbit.

He saw the man stiffen. He had caught sight of the blood. In the next second or two he would guess what it meant. Then he would shout. Yosef let the bolt fly. It took the man in the neck, silently. The blow should have hurled him to the ground, but unexpectedly he kept his balance, tottering, clutching the air, and then, with weakening fingers, scrabbling at the thing lodged in his neck.

Yosef watched him without pity as he started to turn round and round in a small, aching circle, as though by turning he could twist out the quarrel that was killing him. His tiny mouth was opening and closing, but not a sound escaped. His mouth had filled with blood. He stumbled, almost falling. Yosef watched from his hiding place. The dying man took three steps forward, then fell to his knees. He had two hands at one end of the quarrel now and was trying to pull it out. His hands were red with blood.

A second man stepped from the cave and saw the first struggling. A bolt, aimed precisely, took him in the side of the head, in the ear. He too fell without a sound.

The first man was entering a state of panic. He could not free himself of the thing that had entered his neck, could not even get a proper grip on it. He slumped to the ground, kicking. Yosef was already moving. He scrambled up the rock face until he reached a steep gully he had spotted earlier through the telescope. The gully allowed him to climb down out of sight of the cave mouth.

At the foot of the rock face a clump of arbutus bushes gave him ample cover. He could see the two men further up, one perfectly still, the other jerking from time to time like a fish on land.

He moved across the goat track leading to the cave and got himself into the *macchia* facing it. Bending low, he dodged through the undergrowth until he was in position opposite the cave mouth. Inside, it was pitch dark. He could see nothing from where he crouched.

They would be suspicious now. Suspicious and a little anxious, perhaps even afraid. Three men had gone out and none had returned. The silence would worry them most. The police or the carabinieri—even a Digos squad—would have announced their presence, called on them to give themselves up, asked them to release the boy unharmed. But there had been nothing: not a cry, not a shot, nothing.

He raised his telescope and focused it on the cave mouth. A dim light showed inside, but he could see nothing more. He laid down the telescope and opened his rucksack. Matteo had told him that there was only one entrance to the cave. He hoped that was true. He could not afford to leave them inside: They might harm the boy or try to use him as a shield in order to make their escape. He would have to try to flush them out.

On the open ground below him, the struggles of the man pierced by the bolt were growing weaker. A small pool of blood had formed round his head.

Something was wrong. The horrible woman and the two men who always went about with her had come back. They were in the cave now, talking frantically about what to do. Yoel did not know what had happened, but they had been put on edge by something not long after their arrival. His heart was fluttering: Perhaps his father had brought the police at last to rescue him.

He could not see them properly. They always kept the cave in semidarkness. He thought it was so he could not see their faces if they took their masks off. They had not bothered to put them on yet and had not so much as glanced at him. He could feel their nervousness. They had been like this when they first took him, sweating, harsh-voiced, and on edge. Later, they had been cold. Either way, he knew they were willing to hurt him.

Suddenly, one of the men started coughing. Then the others joined in, mildly at first, then rapidly getting worse. He looked toward the mouth of the cave and saw a faint cloud drifting across the light. They were coughing loudly now, and retching. And then it hit him, too, a stinging in the eyes and throat, then a feeling of brambles in his chest, and he started coughing.

The woman was standing over him. She had a scarf over her mouth and was shouting at him, words he could not make out. She reached out and grabbed him by the arm, wrenching it.

"They're gassing us," she muttered. "I'm taking you out of here. If you try to make a run for it, I'll shoot you. Stay close beside me."

He waited until they were all out. Luck was with him: The light wind had been toward the cave mouth, driving the gas inside. He had used a French Zig-Zag grenade, which leaped unpredictably, making it difficult for those inside the cave to locate and catch it.

They came staggering from the cave, leaning against the rock face and gulping in fresh air. The woman came last, dragging the boy with her. She had had enough wit—or experience—to get a wet scarf round her mouth and nose, and she was more alert than her friends. The gun she pointed at the boy was steady. He heard her shout something without understanding a word. She looked round, trying to pinpoint her assailants. The boy, his head and one hand bandaged, was having difficulty holding himself up. She caught sight of the men on the ground, both still now, and shouted out again, holding the boy tight against her as a shield, the barrel of the gun at his head.

Yosef took careful aim with the rifle and shot one of the men in the camouflage jackets in the head. As the man fell, Yosef was already sweeping to his next target. The other new arrival unslung his own weapon and opened fire blindly in the direction from which the shot had come. Yosef felled him with a single shot between the eyes. The shepherd had started running for cover, stumbling toward the bushes skirting the rock face. A third shot hit him in the back of the head.

When he looked again, the woman had thrown the boy to the ground and was standing over him, her pistol in both hands, pointing it at his head and shouting loudly. He did not know what to do. It would be easy to shoot her, but a reflex could send a bullet into the boy's skull and undo everything.

He had to draw her gun up and away from Yoel. But if he revealed himself to her and she shot him, Yoel would suffer anyway. She could not know Yosef was the only gunman, but if she managed to drag the boy far enough she would begin to guess. And once the boy ceased to be necessary as a shield and became a burden to her, he knew she would have no compunction in shooting him.

He took the Browning from the rucksack and chambered a round. On his back, his jacket had a strap normally used for attaching small packs. The gun slipped inside it: It would hold if he moved smoothly. Putting his hands behind his head, he stood up slowly and began to move forward.

The woman swung the gun round, covering him.

"Gli altri!" she shouted. *"Dove sono gli altri?"*

He shook his head. "I don't know," he said in Hebrew. "I don't speak Italian."

He saw Yoel raise his head. The woman stared at him, not yet comprehending. She was surprising to him. Very beautiful and small, with short, crisp blond hair. Her hand on the gun was rock-firm. He had seen women like her among his own people in the West Bank, but had never thought to find one here. They had been inspired to great deeds by their faith. Could greed give courage as well?

She waved the gun at him, shouting instructions of some sort. He took a couple of steps forward. He had to be in range, near enough to make his first shot count. There would not be a second.

Suddenly, Yoel shouted in Hebrew, translating what the woman had said.

"She wants you to lift your hands higher. Slowly, she says. She says if you don't do it she'll shoot you and then shoot me."

He reached back for the pistol, but his fingers touched only air. The Browning's own weight had pushed it further down his back. He strained, but he could not get his hand to it.

The woman was shouting loudly now and gesticulating sharply with the gun. He lifted one hand, still straining with the other to reach the pistol. His finger grazed the butt. He would have to drop his arm and come at it from the side.

She saw his movement and guessed what it meant. A moment later, she had dropped to her knees and grabbed the boy, lifting him and holding him between herself and Yosef.

"Lasci cadere la pistola!"

"She wants you to drop your gun. Otherwise she'll shoot me. She means it."

He dropped his gun. He saw her raise her pistol. All gone, all finished. He closed his eyes and prayed quickly, without words.

There was a loud shot.

The boy did not know him at first. Yosef guessed it would take a long time for his nephew to understand what had happened. In any case, it was a couple of years since they had last met, a short lifetime at Yoel's age. His external injuries were unpleasant, but they would heal, and Yoel would learn to live with them in time. Yosef had replaced the bandage over the ear with a field dressing, properly applied: He'd patched up worse in his time.

What did worry him was the boy's state of mind. Yoel was in a state of shock, afraid of everything he saw or heard—the crack of a twig underfoot, the distant bleating of a mountain goat, the sudden flapping of a bird's wings as it rose ahead of them.

He had not asked about his parents, had not inquired when he would be reunited with them, had not cried for them. Even when Yosef had assured him that they would soon be home, the boy had shown no emotion, almost as if he had in a matter of days forgotten what home was or that he belonged there and not in a cave, cowering in the dark. Yoel walked with them, hunched up, his muscles knotted, as though bracing himself for the next blow or the next wound. Yosef watched him anxiously, as though he might at any moment explode. It was still much too early to tell how he would recover from his ordeal. But with Chaya in the state she was, Yosef feared that his nephew might withdraw yet further into himself and never come out again.

Matteo Deiana went ahead as before, guiding them along the narrow paths that would take them out of the Supramonte. His shot had taken the woman completely unawares, while her gun was pointed away from the boy. Up until that moment, he had been content to observe without interfering. The shepherds had been local men, ruffians for whom he had no liking, but he would not have fired on them all the same. The outsiders had been a different matter, but even then he would have left them entirely to the stranger, had it not been for the woman's cowardly attempt to use the wounded child as a shield.

Before leaving, Matteo and Yosef had done their best to hide the bodies in the thickest part of the *macchia* and clean up the area round the cave. By the time they left, a police unit looking for clues would still have had no difficulty in finding them, but a casual passerby would have seen little out of the ordinary. The locals were accustomed to stumbling across caves that had been used as hideouts: It wasn't even something worth reporting.

Twice on the journey back, Yosef stopped to pray; on these occasions he did not don his prayer shawl and tefillin, which were used for the morning service only. Matteo watched him from a distance with the same indifference as before. His sister had told him that the stranger was a Jew like the Levins, but it meant very little to him. In his youth there had been no Jews in Sardinia, none that he knew of. He had heard of race laws passed by the fascists in the thirties, and of the terrible things that had been done to Italian Jews later on when the Germans took control in the north. But that had been mainland business, nothing to do with him. The Levins paid his sister well, and she said they were good employers. That was enough for Matteo.

It was long after dark when they reached Matteo's cottage on the outskirts of Oliena. By then, they were all exhausted, and it was clear that Yoel could not go a step further. Matteo's wife took one look at the boy and whipped him straight off to her kitchen for hot food. It was cruel to think of taking him all the way home, she said. Before she would allow him to stir a step further, he had to be fed, washed, and given a good night's sleep in a comfortable bed.

Leaving the boy behind, Matteo and Yosef headed into the town. Maryam was waiting for them as arranged, in a little bar behind the church of San Lussorio. Yosef told her they had got his nephew back, but said nothing of what had happened in the mountains. She seemed genuinely relieved, although the tension between them remained. Yosef said he wanted to make a telephone call to Aryeh and Chaya.

The phone rang for several minutes, but no one answered. Yosef tried again, replacing the receiver at last with a feeling of unease.

"Something's wrong," he said. "They should be at home."

"The telephone's aren't always reliable," Maryam said. "Let me check with the operator."

It took some time to get the line checked, but when the operator came back on, it was to say that everything was working properly.

Yosef drove north with Maryam. Yoel would be safe with Matteo and his wife for the time being. Tomorrow, if all was well, Yosef would return to Oliena and bring him home.

As they drove, the atmosphere relaxed gradually. To avoid being drawn into a conversation about the kidnapping, Yosef asked Maryam about herself. An Israeli Arab, a Christian from Tiberias, she had made a new life for herself, first in Naples, then in Cagliari. She was a linguist, highly educated and highly ambitious, but in Israel there had been no work for her, or none that matched either her qualifications or her ambitions. She had a Ph.D. in artificial languages, and had tried to find work in computers. But all the firms involved in work of that kind had contracts with the Ministry of Defense; none would employ an Arab on the grounds that she might prove a security risk.

There had been the possibility of research work at Haifa's Technion Institute or at one of the universities, but she knew that would lead to a dead end. In over forty years, only one Arab had ever been appointed professor at an Israeli university, and Maryam had the added disadvantage of being a woman. She knew that, however good she was, however original her work, she would never achieve the things a Jewish colleague might take for granted.

As they drove, Maryam talked of her parents, of the home she had left behind, of her frustration at not being allowed to serve the land of her birth in the capacity for which she had been trained. Back in Israel, she would never have dared speak so openly of her grievances to a Jew, but here in Sardinia she owed no one any apologies. There were things on her mind, things it did her good to say.

Yosef listened with occasional nods and murmurs of assent. Most of the time, his mind was far away. He had heard Arabs griping before about how badly they were treated in Israel. He had a little sympathy for them, especially the educated ones like Maryam. But he was inclined to ask how well a Christian woman would fare in the average Arab country. And he could see the point of view of the computing firms. Arabs couldn't be trusted to serve in the army or the air force; it made no sense to employ them where they might have access to sensitive information, information they would pass on to one of the Arab intelligence agencies or to the international press. Maryam had done the right thing in leaving. It was a pity more Arabs didn't do the same. Yosef said so, and Maryam fell silent as though she was back in Israel again, in a country where she had no face and no voice.

It was nearly midnight when they reached Arzachena. The tiny town was silent, hidden in sleep. They passed a small church on their left, empty, bereft of light. Beyond it a road climbed steeply through a series of long bends, taking them past the graveyard and on to a quarter of modern villas.

An upstairs window was lit in the Levins' house, a pale steady light that suggested the couple were in their bedroom waiting for news of Yoel. All seemed quiet. Perhaps something had been wrong with the telephone after all.

Yosef parked about two hundred yards away from the house, in a spot that was neither lit nor overlooked. There was no sense in taking chances. He took out his Browning autoloader, checked it, and returned it to its holster.

"Stay here," he said. "If you see anyone acting suspiciously, hit the horn three times."

"My job was just to go with you as an interpreter," said Maryam.

"It's up to you," Yosef replied, "but you know what they did to my nephew. Now, my sister and her husband may be in danger. Call it your Christian duty, I don't care. But it would help me to have someone keep watch."

Maryam nodded. "Hurry up, then," she said.

Yosef opened the car door and slipped out into the darkness. The night was cold after the warmth of the car and the drowsiness of the long drive. There were no clouds, and the sky above staggered under the weight of stars. Yosef looked up, his eyes straining to see in the dark. It was a topsy-turvy world, he thought, whose God spun galaxies from light and left children to huddle without comfort in a cold cave. His thoughts disturbed him, and he turned to the task ahead of him.

The house appeared normal. Yosef skirted it once to check that all was as it should be. There were no open doors, no broken windows. Reassured, he went to the main door and rang the bell.

There was no reply. He rang again and waited, glancing round from time to time. The car and Maryam were out of sight, the street lay deserted like a road through a city whose inhabitants have slipped away by night. As he waited, and the seconds stretched into minutes, it came to him again, insidiously cruel, an old feeling, a feeling he had thought abandoned years ago on the streets of Beirut. It was no more than the knowledge that, whatever lay behind the door, it would leave him less human than before. A wave of nausea passed through his stomach, and then, abruptly, he felt cold, detached from what was coming, just a soldier in a foreign country doing his job.

The door caved in at his second attempt. No alarm sounded. Arzachena, like the rest of the Costa Smeralda, was protected by a special police force created by the Aga Khan, and security was normally not a problem—heavy doors and sophisticated alarm systems were left to the rich and the anxious.

Unholstering the pistol, he slipped the safety and stepped through the door. All silent, no one moving, no one speaking. He did not call out or tread heavily: the intruders, whoever they were, might still be here.

He found Maria Deiana in the kitchen, propped up in a chair, her mouth tightly gagged, tied with ropes just as Aryeh and Chaya had been. The intruders had cropped her hair and fastened round her neck a makeshift sign bearing the single word *traitor.* Her eyes were wide with fear, and at first she did not recognize him. The gun in his hand served only to increase her terror.

Bending down in front of her, he spoke calmly and slowly. She would not understand the words, but his manner reassured her until she was relaxed enough to remember the man who had come to the house the day before, the man who had come to rescue little Yoel.

He removed her gag, signaling to her to remain silent. He wanted to ask her if the intruders were still in the house, but he did not know how to. Stepping behind her, he started to untie the ropes that held her to the chair.

"*Il signore Levin ... La signora. Al piano superiore ... Va subito ...*"

He understood the reference to Maria's master and mistress, but not the rest.

"Where?" he asked. "Where are they?"

"*Gli hanno portato via ... di sopra, non so esattamente ... forse nella camera da letto ...*"

While she spoke, the old woman pointed upward. Yosef nodded. He finished untying her, then, motioning to her to remain where she was, he slipped out of the kitchen and started to climb the stairs.

He knew now where he would find Chaya and Aryeh. The light in the bedroom had been

69

left on like a beacon. He headed upward, his ears pricked for the least sound. But all he could hear was his own breath and the thumping of his heart. He pretended it was fear, as though ice had feelings, as though ice could feel afraid. It was better than admitting to himself what he really felt as he went in search of his baby sister.

He had to fight his way up the stairs against a tide of memories. Chaya in her cradle, Chaya at school, Chaya at his bar mitzvah, Chaya waiting for him when he returned on his first army leave, Chaya on her wedding day. At the top of the stairs, he stumbled like a blind man. They might have killed him then, if they had still been there. But he knew by now that they were long gone.

Someone had locked the door and sealed it up roughly with a quick-hardening foam, the sort of material builders use to fill wall cavities. He smashed the door inward with a single blow, and the next moment reeled back as a wave of gas took him in the throat and chest.

Staggering, he managed to drag himself away from the opening. He found himself beside the bathroom door. Tearing it open, he collapsed inside. Getting to his feet, he blundered about until he found a bath towel. He soaked it in water and wrapped it round the lower part of his head to use as a filter against the gas. Bracing himself, he went back onto the landing.

The bedroom door lay half-open, and gas was escaping into the rest of the house, odorless but deadly. Rushing forward, Yosef managed to shut the door before staggering down the stairs.

He hunkered down against the wall, coughing and wheezing. His head felt light, and his heart was racing inside his chest like a whipped dog. Minutes passed and he began to recover. His exposure to the gas had not been too intense or long in duration. He knew it was impossible that either Chaya or Aryeh were still alive in there, but he could not simply leave them.

He went inside again and brought Maria Deiana out, just in case the gas made its way to the kitchen. She was an old woman, and very frightened. Her lungs might not withstand even a small dose. Once she was settled on the doorstep, Yosef hurried to find a ladder.

There was a long one in the garage. He dragged it outside and found a hammer in a toolbox at the rear. The ladder slid up easily against the wall, its top end resting about two feet above the window. With the hammer rammed into his belt, Yosef started the ascent. His feet felt like lumps of lead, his chest was still abraded and burning.

He reached the sill and with an effort climbed the last few rungs. At first glance, everything in the bedroom seemed normal. The furniture stood in place, the pictures on the walls hung straight, scent bottles and makeup jars stood in rows on the dressing table. He caught sight of himself in a long mirror, a wild, uncanny creature suspended against curtains of darkness.

What Yosef saw next he saw in two distinct parts, each quite discrete yet inextricably linked to the other. On the wall above the double bed someone had painted a huge swastika in red paint. The execution was poor, the lines crooked, the direction of the hooks reversed. Paint had dribbled sloppily from each of the horizontal arms, as though they had bled.

Beneath the swastika, two figures lay on the bed, their bodies contorted, their limbs unmoving, their mouths wide-open in a vain struggle for breath. Their killers had shaved their heads and dressed them in striped suits. Yosef's first thought was that this was mockery, and then he saw that it was not, that it was something more cruel. It was re-creation.

Part 2
THE BOOKBINDER

9

In the weeks that followed, Yosef felt pursued. It was not that he thought anyone was coming after him in person—though the possibility could not wholly be dismissed after what had happened in the Supramonte—but that in that moment at the window he had felt himself transformed from an actor into an onlooker, from a hunter into quarry. He was no longer a person, he thought, no longer Yosef Abuhatseira, but a Jew, any Jew, watching his family dragged beneath a rough icon and wiped out while he looked on, immobile, at the top of a ladder from which there was no descent.

Israel was unnaturally cold, its northern borders choked with snow and ice, its skies leaden, its deserts barren. Rain fell in the day, a soft, uncomfortable rain that penetrated everything; at night there were no stars. A dead wind blew across the country from somewhere inexplicably remote. People shivered and stayed indoors. Yosef returned home like a man without a soul, his mind grown intricate with remorse, his heart suddenly barren.

Chaya and Aryeh were buried in Jerusalem side by side. The ceremony was presided over by both Ashkenazi and Sephardi rabbis. Yoel stood by the grave, mystified, unable to comprehend how, leaving the darkness of his cave, he had found himself in this greater darkness. He watched his parents go down to their graves as though from a great distance, without tears, without apparent emotion, seemingly without love. No one who saw him that day would ever forget. The boy had stood silently by the graveside, his head still bandaged, a black *kippa* resting on his hair, his small world shattered beyond repair.

On either side of him, his two grandfathers had stood rigidly, their hands holding his, their eyes focused on nothing. The two families prayed together, wept together, and ate together afterward in silence. They had no words for the enormity of what had happened, though. Thanks to Yosef, none of them knew the full extent of what had been done. It was, he told them, a kidnapping gone wrong. No more. They had been killed by the kidnappers as a warning to their next victims should they prove reluctant to part with the money needed to rescue their son or daughter.

He said nothing of the gas or the swastika painted on the wall above the bodies. That was a message all of them knew, and of which none needed reminding.

His own efforts to get to the bottom of the affair had been deeply frustrating. The police at the provincial capital of Sassari had been sympathetic, but he had sensed from early on that they were either unwilling or unable to investigate the murders properly. Partly, he was trapped by the unavoidable dishonesty in which he had felt it necessary to cloak his own activities. And partly there seemed to be a real reluctance to get drawn into an investigation that might lead to bad publicity for a resort area that depended so heavily on wealthy visitors.

Maria Deiana had backed his story fully, telling the police that Yosef had come to Arzachena in order to be with his sister and her husband after their son's kidnapping. Yosef, she said, had agreed to act as their *intermediario* following the unexplained disappearance of Michele Mannuzzu. She admitted that her employer had misled the police when he had told them Yoel was in Israel, but how else did the *ispettore* think he should have acted? Hadn't he been confused and frightened? she demanded. Hadn't the kidnappers warned him not to notify the authorities? Hadn't he been sent a severed finger and then an ear? What would the *ispettore* have done in his place? Didn't he have a mother, a loving wife, children?

Maryam had already decided with Yosef that their stories should match up. She knew she was already at risk of being arrested as an accessory to attempted negotiations with kidnappers without police permission. She still did not know what had happened up there in the Supramonte, but she didn't think it would be anything the police should know about. What happened to Yosef wasn't of much concern to her, but if she herself was implicated in something more serious, however innocently, the consequences could be serious: prison, deportation, or both.

She told the police she had accompanied Yosef to Oliena where they had met with two of the kidnappers and finally persuaded them that the sum demanded was out of all proportion to Aryeh's ability to pay. To their surprise, Yoel had been handed back to them, wounded but alive. Yosef and Maryam had left the exhausted boy with Matteo and returned to Arzachena, only to find his parents brutally murdered.

The gas used for the killings had been Zyklon B, a gas produced from hydrocyanic acid, manufactured by a company called Degesch for use in the Nazi death camps. The warning smell normally added to the gas had been removed by Degesch on the instructions of the SS in order not to alarm their victims before it had started to take effect.

Canisters left in the Levins' bedroom appeared to be genuine specimens dating from the 1940s. To Yosef, they were by far the most disturbing aspect of the case. How had the killers come by them? Why had they gone to such elaborate lengths—and, presumably, expense— just to mock their victims' Jewishness? Had the Zyklon-B canisters, like the swastika on the wall, been intended as a message of some sort?

"Believe me," the vice-questore in charge of the case had said, "the killers are simple brigands, nothing more. We have no *neo-fascisti* in Sardinia, least of all here on the Costa Smeralda. This business with the swastika—you can set your mind at rest, it's no more than a stunt to divert attention from the real motive for the killing."

"I can't believe that what you call 'simple brigands' can have access to Zyklon-B canisters," Yosef had retorted. He spoke through Maryam, who went everywhere with him now. The awfulness of the tragedy had broken down some of the barriers between them, and, in spite of themselves, they had become wary friends.

The vice-questore shook his head. "You would be surprised, *signore*, if you knew what some of our local criminals can get hold of. Ships come in to Cagliari from Naples every day. Some offload at other ports along the coast. Most we know about, others, the smaller boats, do not report themselves. And even the most honest ship's master will turn a blind eye to a little business between his crew and the port officials. If he showed too much interest in these goings-on, he would find himself in trouble, maybe very big trouble.

"Why trouble? Because some of his crew will belong to the Camorra and be under the protection of some important *mamma-santissima*. Those people can get you anything you care to name: drugs, weapons, women, children, politicians—whatever takes your fancy. A few cans of German gas would be nothing to them."

"But Zyklon B was last produced in the 1940s. It would be ..."

The vice-questore shrugged eloquently. "You do not understand," he said. "Fifty years is nothing to the Camorra. After the world war, they lined their pockets and their warehouses. If this gas had a use, they would have been sure to loot it and store it up somewhere. Believe me."

Yosef and the policeman had argued until it grew late, and it became clear that nothing the Israeli said would budge the other man from his position. There would be a hunt for the killers—a phone call from the Israeli embassy in Rome had already ensured that—but something told Yosef that it would be perfunctory. The victims had not been Sardinian or even Italian, their families possessed no influence with the *prefetto* or with anyone else who might move the hunt into a higher gear, and Yosef had no access to the system of *clientelismo*, through which it was possible to get things done on the island.

In a few months, the file would be closed, the whole affair forgotten. No one would take fright, no one would leave their villa on Romazzino Bay or cancel their mooring privileges at Porto Cervo marina, no one would buy so much as a new alarm system or a fiercer guard dog. The hotels and restaurants wanted it that way, the boutique owners wanted it that way, the police wanted it that way. Business as usual.

A week after the funeral, Yosef returned reluctantly to Qiryat Arba, where he had a business to run. This was a small bookbinding shop in the center of the *yishuv*, crammed with presses and cutters and rolls of vellum. Yosef had learned the art from his father, who had in his day been one of the finest bookbinders in the Jewish quarter of Fez. In Qiryat Arba, Yosef received orders from former customers of his father all over Israel, mainly from organizations of *haredim* or ultra-orthodox Jews who used large numbers of religious texts in the schools and seminaries where the next generations of the pious were being trained like hothouse plants.

Before Yosef's departure, there had been a heated and painful debate within the family about Yoel's future. Neither Aryeh nor Chaya had made provision in their wills for who would take responsibility for the boy in the event of their dying at the same time. Both sets of grandparents had offered to adopt him, and both had expressed severe reservations about his being brought up by the others.

To Aryeh's father and mother, their Sephardic relatives were lacking in culture, right-wing in their politics, and all too likely to turn their beloved grandson into a fanatic, an Arab-hater—the very kind of Oriental they had once thought to displace. To Chaya's family, the Levins, for all their piety and intelligence, were possessed of the flaws of Lithuanian *mitnagdim*—they were emotionally cold, logic-obsessed, stiff, more European than Jewish, unsuited to the climate and the character of the land they lived in.

The debate had gone on for days, now angry, now tearful, now repentant, now reheated by some chance remark, while Yoel moped in his room upstairs—they were all staying at the Abuhatseira's family home in Jerusalem—or was taken by a succession of aunts and uncles for endless walks through Independence Garden or the Biblical Zoo.

In the end, they had agreed to submit the matter to a religious court, the *beit din* of the Chief Rabbinate, whose decision both sides agreed to accept as final. Until a decision was forthcoming, Yoel would stay with one set of grandparents at a time, a month in Haifa, a month in Jerusalem. That such constant shuttling between warring factions might unsettle the boy further seemed to have occurred to no one.

Yosef had hoped for a day or two to himself, time to bring his business affairs up to date and to resettle himself mentally and emotionally. But Qiryat Arba is a tiny place, made up of only a few hundred Zionist families; word soon got round that he had returned. All the first day, his solitude was interrupted by visits from his neighbors, all of whom knew what had happened in Sardinia, all of whom were solicitous for Yosef and eager for news of Yoel, whom none of them had met.

Yosef welcomed them all, brought them inside, gave them mint tea—a Moroccan beverage on which he had been brought up—and listened for the most part in silence to their commiserations and their blessings for the future and Yoel's well-being. They meant well, he knew, even the mothers with marriageable daughters and veiled hints about how sad it was that he couldn't adopt Yoel himself, not without a wife. But he felt distanced from them all that day, as if something in him had changed during his absence.

He sat and watched the mothers make their pitches and expose their wares. The girls sat beside them, demure, embarrassed, shuffling on their seats, eager to be gone. How sickening, he thought, that we can sell ourselves and our families for so little profit. And he thought of the price that had been placed on Yoel's tiny head, and the price that had been exacted.

That evening, he visited the synagogue for the evening service. As he came out afterward, old friends greeted him, their manner sober, their curiosity evident beneath the conventional formulae. He spoke to a few, but made it evident he was tired and did not want to talk about recent events. Gradually, the little crowd around the door thinned.

Yosef stepped up to the notice board by the entrance and scanned the guard rota. His name was normally among those volunteering to accompany the children to school in the morning or back again in the afternoon, or to keep watch by the *yishuv* gate at night. There were several gaps for the following week, and he added his initials in each space, noting down the times in his diary.

"Yosef, *ma shelomkha*?" said a voice behind him.

He turned to see David Kushner standing with his arms folded, observing him. David was an American, a close friend who had served with Yosef in the Sayaret Matkal and come to Qiryat Arba around the same time.

"I'm all right, thank you, David."

"No need to put yourself down for duty yet. Take your time. You need a rest."

"No, I want to get back to routine. I can't just sit around."

They started walking away from the synagogue.

"How's the boy, Yosef? I hear you did a great job getting him out."

"I got him out, but that was just my training against theirs. When I got back ... Well, you know what happened."

"But the kid's okay?"

Yosef shook his head thoughtfully. "No," he said, "I don't think so. I don't think he'll ever be quite right again. He went through a lot, then he was rescued only to find his parents dead. Now his family is fighting over who gets to adopt him. It's crazy."

"The world's crazy, Yosef. While you were away, we had a little trouble of our own. Has anyone mentioned it to you?"

They walked on, past the community center, past the school, heading for Yosef's house. It was their custom to go there after *shul* two or three nights a week.

"No," Yosef answered, "nobody's said anything."

"It happened a couple of weeks ago at Shilo," David said, "just before you got back." Shilo was another West Bank *yishuv,* about forty miles north of Qiryat Arba, not far from Ramallah. "Some hotheads from al-Amari camp attacked the evening bus from Jerusalem. They killed the driver and injured several passengers. The guards onboard managed to kill one of them, but the rest got away.

"The army went into al-Amari the next day. Demolished half the camp, took most of the young men to prison. We're still waiting to hear if they charge any of them Of course, ACRI are making the usual fuss. 'The army ignored the civil rights of innocent Arabs.' Why the fuck can't those bastards spare some of their sympathy for the Jews who were on that bus? I don't know why they don't just clear out of here and let some real Israelis get on with the job."

Yosef had heard such sentiments often enough before, had expressed them himself many times. Tonight, they sounded stale.

"Did anything happen here?" he asked.

"No, things stayed real quiet. The night of the attack, a bunch of us went over to al-Khalil and knocked the troublemakers around some. Told them what it was for, said we'd be back if they got ideas in their heads. Guess those ACRI types would say we'd violated their rights."

"I'm sure they would, David."

They had reached the door of Yosef's house. Suddenly, he felt extremely tired. He couldn't stop thinking of the roughly painted swastika; it should have made him proud of what David was saying, that Jews could fight back, that there would never be a second Holocaust. Instead, he felt a little ashamed for his friend.

"Do you mind if I don't ask you in tonight, David? I'm tired. I think I need to sleep, I've a long day ahead of me tomorrow. There's so much to catch up on."

"Sure. You look bushed. I'll look in tomorrow after work. We'll talk. Don't worry. *Yihye tov.*"

It was a phrase for old men, thought Yosef; the young seldom used it. *Things will turn out all right, all will be well.*

He nodded and went inside. For a few moments, he wondered what he was doing there.

Instead of David, the next evening brought a stranger, someone from out of town. He asked for Yosef by name, asked if he could come in. Reluctantly, Yosef said yes.

"I'll get straight to the point," said the stranger before he had even sat down. "My name's Yossi Biran, I'm a desk officer with Mossad. We need to talk."

10

The stranger sat in Yosef's living room like a man who expects at any moment to be thrown out. Mossad officials were not welcome in the settlements, even if they told people their names and acted like regular human beings. The settlers knew that, sooner or later, they would become an impossible embarrassment for a future government, and their removal part of a deal between Israel and the Arab states. When that moment came, Mossad and the internal security service, Shin Bet, would be their most implacable enemies.

But Yossi Biran had not come to Qiryat Arba to make trouble for anyone. He wanted Yosef Abuhatseira to trust him, to like him if that was possible. But how was he to gain his confidence? He glanced round the small, sparsely furnished room. It was devoid of ornament, the walls white and free of pictures or photographs. But on a low sideboard stood a single concession to decoration, a discreet wooden frame displaying insignia that Biran recognized.

"Sayaret Matkal," he said, nodding in the direction of the insignia. Yosef said nothing. Biran looked at him. "How long did you serve with them?" he asked.

"Twelve years."

Biran pushed out his lower lip, nodding. "A long time. You must have seen a lot of action."

"Some. Like everybody else."

Biran nodded again. "More than most," he said. "We all had to work extra hard just to keep you guys in our sights."

Yosef smiled, catching the bait as he was supposed to.

"'We?'" he asked in his turn.

"Thirty-fifth Paras."

It was Yosef's turn to look impressed. "A tough unit."

"Hard enough. I got out after four years. Can't imagine three times that long."

Yosef found a chair opposite his visitor and sat down. Looking at Biran, he knew he could have stood twelve years if someone hadn't suggested he'd be more use working for intelligence.

"You said you needed to talk to me."

Biran nodded. "That's right."

"What about?"

The Mossad officer took a deep breath. "I want you to tell me what really happened in Sardinia."

Yosef looked at him blankly. His first instinct was to ask the man to leave. Maybe with somebody else he would have, but Biran was no desk jockey. He'd served with one of the toughest units in the Israeli army, and that gave him status in Yosef's eyes, enough to earn him a minute or so before he was thrown into the street.

"I don't understand," he said. "The Italian police have all the details. If your office wants to see them ..."

"We have seen them," Biran interrupted him. "But we think they're covering something up, and we want to know what it is."

"Isn't that a police matter?"

Biran shook his head. "There are aspects to this case that suggest it would be better handled by Mossad. In any case, our own police have extremely limited powers, and none whatever outside Israel. They are bound to accept whatever report the Italians pass on to them, even if they have their own doubts. My people suffer from fewer constraints."

"What aspects?"

"I'm sorry?"

"You said certain aspects of the case made it of interest to Mossad. I can't see what those would be."

Biran got ready to toss his second morsel of bait in Yosef's direction. "A few months ago," he said, "there was a similar case in Milan. A Jewish family—Italians, not Israelis—a father, mother, and two children, one fifteen, the other nine. All killed."

"A coincidence. Just because they were Jewish..."

"They were gassed. On the wall of the room where their bodies were found, someone had daubed a swastika. No coincidence."

Yosef shuddered. He stood and crossed to the window, shutting it. A chill had entered the room. Yosef turned and faced his visitor.

"Neo-fascists," he said. "It's what I already suspected. They choose Jewish targets at random."

Biran shook his head. "Neither case was random. In Milan, the police found blackmail letters, letters that demanded information in exchange for silence. The father, Ennio Pontecorvo, was an architect. He'd been making payoffs to city officials, and the anti-corruption investigators were breathing down his neck. The blackmailers knew enough to have him sent to prison on corruption charges.

"In the case of your sister and her husband, their son was kidnapped, there were demands for money, then information. So, what did Aryeh Levin know that this architect in Milan also knew? Whatever it was, it led to both their deaths."

"Aryeh knew nothing. He swore it. I believed him then, and I'm still sure of it."

"Why did he ask you to join him?"

"It's in the report."

"I want to hear it from you myself."

"Aryeh wanted me to negotiate with the kidnappers on his behalf. They use intermediaries. It's too risky to talk to the principals directly. He thought the police were watching him, that they'd stop any payments. So he asked me to help out."

Biran shook his head. The man was hiding the truth, he could see it. "Bullshit. You don't even speak Italian."

"I had an interpreter."

"That's clumsy, and you know it. Look, I know you went in after the kidnappers. I know you arranged for weapons to be supplied to you through Mivtzar Enterprises—don't look so surprised, you're well aware they carry out work for us as well. Part of our deal with them is that they keep us informed of any private citizens wanting to buy arms for their own use. I'm not interested in what you did to the kidnappers—frankly, I couldn't care less. But my guess is that you succeeded in setting your nephew free, and that the murders that followed were your punishment, and his. A punishment and a warning. That's what happened, isn't it?"

Yosef said nothing.

"Yosef, listen to me. Please. I'm not here to catch you out or shop you to the Italian authorities. Nothing you say to me leaves this room. That's a promise. I just want to know what really happened in Sardinia. Then perhaps you and I can talk about what's to be done next."

Yosef did not know what to think. The feeling of pursuit that had accompanied him to Israel was still there, like a shadow that would not leave him. Now he learned that Chaya and Aryeh had not been the only victims, that their deaths were part of a pattern, perhaps a much wider pattern than he could guess. If that was so, then he himself might genuinely be in danger, though he still could not think from what quarter. At the very least, it would make sense to listen to Yossi Biran, to find out what interest Mossad had in the business.

"No further than this room," he said. "Not even in a report."

Biran nodded. "You have my word."

Yosef told him how he had arranged for the arms to be made ready for him on arriving at Arzachena, how he had tracked down the kidnappers, and how he had dealt with them. Biran listened in silence, seemingly unmoved. Yosef's narrative was wooden, swept free of emotion, as though he had just returned from a mission and was delivering a verbal report to his commanding officer.

"Thank you," Biran said when Yosef came to a halt. "What you've told me sheds some light on a possible motive for the killing, but it doesn't get us any closer to what lies behind the whole business. You're sure there's nothing Aryeh told you that might give us some idea?"

Yosef shook his head firmly. "Absolutely not. He knew as little as you or I."

"Well, let's assume that's so. In that case, it's possible there was a mistake of some kind. Either

Aryeh's killers were mistaken in thinking he had this information or they took him for someone else. If it was mistaken identity, then we have to assume that it could all happen again."

Yosef felt the chill of the room pass through him. He thought of the bedroom in Arzachena, the swastika floating in front of his eyes. *We have to assume that it could all happen again....*

"Can't you do something?" he asked.

"That depends."

"Depends on what?"

"On you."

There was a silence. Yossi's heart was beating hard. He wanted Abuhatseira, wanted him badly.

"I don't understand. I've already done what I can."

"Yosef, I've talked about this very carefully with my superiors before coming here. We want you to go back to Sardinia. Ask questions, poke about, find out what you can."

Yosef stared at him, scarcely comprehending.

"You're crazy. What you're asking is crazy." He wanted to get to his feet, to throw the man out. You could never trust Mossad, never. But he was rooted to his chair.

"No, Yosef, not crazy. Very sane. You're the perfect man for this job. Your records show you had some intelligence experience with the army. You know how to take care of yourself if things get out of hand. Anyone else asking questions out there would invite suspicion, but for you it would seem entirely natural. You have the perfect excuse."

"I'm not a policeman, I'm not trained in carrying out investigations. What's wrong with the Italian police? If you point out to them the parallels with this case in Milan ..."

Biran sniffed contemptuously. "Yosef, please listen to me. We think there's more to this business than meets the eye. One of our tasks is surveillance of anti-Semitic and neo-fascist organizations wherever they make an appearance. In recent years, new groups have been multiplying like rats, and old ones have been recruiting new members by the hundreds. We suspect that the killings in Milan and Arzachena lead back to some activity of the Italian far right."

He hesitated. How much could he risk telling Abuhatseira at this stage? As little as possible, he had been instructed. The Sephardi was intelligent, brave, and dependable, but he was emotionally involved in this affair, and Biran could not divest himself of the notion that Oriental Jews were potentially unstable and easily inflamed, as irrational as the Arabs among whom they had lived for so many generations and whose culture they had at so many points imbibed.

"Yosef," he continued, "you should know that this possible right-wing connection is the reason we can't rely on the police. In the case of Arzachena, the questore with overall responsibility for police affairs in Sassari province is Dottore Fulvio Gui. Gui studied at the Police Academy in Rome in the 1950s, during the period when all police schools in the country were under the control of one man, Guido Leto. Leto had previously been the chief of OVRA, Mussolini's secret police. He and Gui were close friends until Leto's death. Gui's name has cropped up in various places, most notably as a contributor to a conference held in 1965 at the Parco dei Principi hotel in Rome. The conference was organized by the Alberto Pollio Institute, a leading right-wing think tank that had been founded in the previous year, partly with money from SIFAR, the Servizio Informazioni Forze Armate.

"Ezio Ortolani, the colonel in charge of the carabinieri in Sardinia, is equally unreliable. His brother is a deputy chairman of the MSI, Italy's leading right-wing party until it dissolved itself in 1995. He himself flirted with several extremist groups when he was a young officer, and he may have been involved in the 1964 carabinieri plan to launch a coup d'état."

Yosef threw up his hands. "You make it sound as if the whole Italian police system is riddled with fascists."

Biran smiled. "I wouldn't go that far. But a lot of money and effort were put into Italy after the war to ensure the communists never came to power. The police and carabinieri were major players in the power games of the sixties and seventies.

"All I'm saying is that we can't rely on the police to follow this through properly. Files may get misplaced, detectives reassigned, investigating magistrates given more important tasks. You, on the other hand, are free to follow any leads you get. Unless you actually break the law, there's very little the Italians can do to stop you, not without causing themselves some embarrassment. We can get you in there, supply you with money and light arms, back you up with what little information we have. After that, you're on your own."

"What you're asking is impossible. As you yourself said earlier, I don't even speak Italian."

"You got on well enough with an interpreter before. We'll provide you with sufficient funds to employ Maryam Shumayyil full-time."

Yosef's eyebrows went up. "You're willing to involve an Arab in an investigation like this?"

"Why not? If you've got no objections to her, neither do we. Her record's clean. There are no political suspects in her immediate family."

Yosef bit his lip. His room felt cold and damp. Spring seemed infinitely remote, summer an impossible dream. Maryam Shumayyil's face flashed briefly through his mind, momentarily warming him. She had helped him more than anyone in the days following the discovery of Chaya's murder. He suppressed the thought and turned to Biran.

"I'll have to think about it," he said. "I need a few days."

"If you insist. But please don't take too long. We may not have as much time as we'd like."

The two men shook hands and Biran left. Yosef listened to his car as it turned and growled its way out of the settlement. He stood at the window for a long time, thinking.

Early the next morning, a phone call woke Yosef from a troubled sleep. It was Biran. He sounded tired.

"Yosef? I thought you should know. It's happened again. A single man this time, a professor at Turin University. He was over eighty. An Auschwitz survivor called Alberto Cantoni."

Part 3
THE CAPTIVE

11

Sometimes he slept late, to eleven or twelve o'clock, and when he woke his back ached and he felt dizzy. It was an effort to drag himself out of bed, and he would feel wretched for most of the day afterward. Other mornings, he woke much too early, long before it was light, and lay in bed trying to get back to sleep, turning now and then to watch the progress of the digital clock on the low table beside him. The flickering green numbers seemed to be eating his life away in front of his eyes, inexorable and uncaring.

Either way, he suffered. There was no happy medium.

He had started to have dreams again. How long was it since he had last been troubled by them? Forty years? Fifty? He could not be absolutely certain that they were the same dreams, of course. Who could ever be sure of such a thing, even if they recurred night after night? There is, after all, no precise means of recording what goes on in that realm. Memory is a hopelessly unreliable guide.

A historian of dreams would have an impossible task, even more impossible than that allotted to those who seek to chronicle what we lightly term the real world. He thought his dreams were a species of record, but sometimes he woke up from them sweating and crying aloud. Not a record, then, but a kind of punishment.

His surroundings were pleasant, as pleasant

as they could be made under the circumstances. He had not been brought here under compulsion, and his keepers recognized that and gave it the recompense it deserved. He had a charming bedroom with an en-suite bathroom, a living room, and a little room where he could be alone to read or watch television or smoke or play patience. The ordinary television programs meant nothing to him, of course, since he spoke hardly a word of the language, but they had obtained a video machine and old films for him, and he indulged himself with them. Sometimes the time passed very slowly, sometimes it hurried by as though possessed.

The lawyer came once a week, on Wednesdays—not that it made the least difference to him what day of the week it was. It was the lawyer's job to go over everything with him, to prepare him for the trial. They didn't have a date and they had to be sure he was prepared for the sort of questions the defense counsel might put. So he and the lawyer went over it all time after time, week after week, until the last holes had been plugged. Everything hinged on his testimony, or so they told him. Sometimes the whole procedure would be followed using an interpreter, the way it would be when they came to the real thing.

"What is your name?"
"What is your date of birth?"
"What was your rank?"
"To whom were you immediately answerable?"
"What were your duties?"
"Can you elaborate?"
"How do you know that?"
"Do you have any evidence for that statement?"

"Can you elaborate?"
"Did you see that with your own eyes?"
"I find that hard to believe."
"Can you elaborate?"

He heard his own voice answering, staccato, dry, without emotion. Each answer drew behind it a train of memories, a long, lumbering train that came trundling toward the present through a burned and sterile landscape. Echoes of a distant country, reflections of a past buried so deeply he had thought it lost forever.

Inwardly, he knew he would never see the inside of a courtroom. There were too many people who wanted him out of the way, too many people he was willing to betray. He knew who they were, and what they were capable of. Sooner or later, they would find him.

Part 4
THE INTERPRETER

12

Porto Torres, Sardinia

He watched a gannet swoop, lopsided at first, then braced on perfect wings in wide, looping arcs through a cobbled sky. Others followed, their dirty white wings brilliant, now against the sky, now over the sea, foam-rough and struggling in the boat's broad wake. A deep blast of three notes on the ferry's horn sent the flock scurrying for height and distance. The notes were lost astern, but the silence was filled by a rumbling of heavy chains somewhere below his feet and a perceptible shift in the pitch of the marine engines. On the car deck, engines were being started in anticipation of the moment when the bow doors would open and unleash a small fleet of cars and trucks on the narrow roads of Sardinia.

The ferry had seen better days. A smell of diesel fuel hung thick and faintly nauseating on every inch of every deck like an old stain that nothing will erase. Rust scars defaced the white-painted bulkheads like the tracks of old tears beneath the rows of dirty portholes, and slowly corroded the great screws that held the capstans and davits and motor winches to the gray decks.

They had decided against flying him directly to Olbia, his previous port of entry to the island. Instead Yosef had flown to Rome from Tel Aviv, taken a taxi to Civitavecchia, and embarked there on the overnight Tirrenia ferry to Porto Torres on Sardinia's northwest coast. He was traveling under a false passport supplied by Mossad, using the name Yosef Katzir.

It had been a rough crossing and a dark sea. For most of the night, he had stayed below decks in his cramped cabin, sweating and unable to sleep. Outside, there had been the sound of high winds and waves smashing against the ship's metal sides. Once, he had fallen into an uneasy sleep and dreamed an ugly dream.

He was onboard a train, a steam train, crawling through a bleak country that he could see only through gaps in the wall. When he looked round, he saw that he was in a large wagon full of people like himself, the men unshaven, the women pale and anxious. He knew that they had been traveling for days, perhaps for weeks. And he guessed, or thought he guessed, the nature of their destination. As the train clanked through an empty station, he woke to the clangor of the boat's engine beating through the storm.

Going on deck, he had found himself lost in a great darkness, without moon or stars, and the sea lifting on all sides, black and empty and seemingly without limit, as though all shores had ceased. There had been no other ships in sight, no lights to mark a coast. Yosef had returned to his coffinlike chamber and remained there until well after daylight, huddled on his bunk.

The curious thing about his dream, he thought, was that no one in his family had had direct experience of the Holocaust, of deportation in cattle trucks, of the world slipping away through the slats of a wooden wagon. He had not been brought up as a child to stories told by grandparents or uncles. He had only known secondhand of the sufferings of European Jews, much as anyone of his age. And yet the dream had seemed not only vivid, but horribly real, and it left him now with a sense of deep despair.

As the ferry docked, he looked down toward the harbor and saw Maryam waiting for him, a small figure dressed in a red anorak and blue jeans. For the second time, her beauty took him by surprise as though death and distance had blotted it out. Even from a distance, she was prettier than he remembered. A second later, she moved, or the ferry shifted as it ground against the tires on the dockside, and the moment was gone. He turned and went back to the cabin for his rucksack, the only item of luggage he carried. Through the dirty porthole, he could see nothing but an expanse of gray sea on which an oil slick lay like varnish.

"How's your nephew?" Maryam asked as she turned her Volkswagen through the harbor gates. She had spent a lot of time with the boy following the murders, sometimes chatting—or trying to chat—in Italian, sometimes helping him out when his Hebrew was not up to a proper conversation with Yosef. The sessions in Hebrew had been the most harrowing, for Yoel associated the language exclusively with his parents and merely using it brought them to mind.

"Yoel? The doctors say he'll recover. But I don't know what they mean. He has scars that won't heal easily, and he's with people who'll destroy him just to show how much they love him."

"I don't understand."

He explained. It didn't take much imagination for her to grasp what was going wrong. Her own family, in their way, had similar problems. Extended families, whatever their virtues, can sometimes overwhelm the individuals within them.

"It's sad for him," she said, "whoever gets custody. I don't really understand why there's such rivalry. I thought all Jews were much the same."

He shook his head, and as he did so raised one hand unconsciously to straighten his *kippa*, a knitted circle held on the back of his skull by two thin hairpins. Even the style of *kippa* a man wore, he reflected, could speak volumes about his degree of religious devotion or his politics.

"Hook-nosed and avaricious, you mean?"

She glanced round at him, offended. "No, of course not. How stupid of you. I meant religiously. I know there's a massive difference between Reform and Orthodox, but I thought it ended there. You don't have sects the way we do."

"Not quite," he said. "But there are serious divisions all the same. And nowadays the *haredim*, the fundamentalists, won't even recognize other Jews as Jews. A lot of people get caught in these disputes. Yoel's just one more."

"That's a pity. He seems like a nice child."

"I hardly knew him," muttered Yosef, turning away to watch the street.

"I've booked a room for you at the President Hotel," said Maryam, changing the subject.

"What about yourself?"

"I'll be staying there, too, just down the corridor. I understood you needed me on call at any time."

He nodded. "I'm grateful to you for giving up so much time."

"That's all right. The students are on strike at the moment. It looks as though they may stay away from classes indefinitely if the right gets in at the election next month. Several of my colleagues are never on the campus as it is: half a dozen have jobs at other universities, a couple run private businesses, one has a government post, another is a member of the European Parliament. This is Italy, Yosef. They call professors here *baroni*, because of their influence outside the classroom.

"In any case, you're paying me more than the university does. I'm not a professor, just a humble *ricercatrice*."

They drew up outside the hotel.

"I've asked them to have your room ready," Maryam said. "You're bound to be tired after the crossing. I've done it myself often enough."

Yosef hesitated, then shook his head. "I'm not really tired," he said. "Let's just leave my bag here. I want to go to Arzachena."

"For anything special?"

"Yes. I want to look at my sister's house. I need it to focus on, to remind me why I'm here. Otherwise, this could be anywhere, and I could be just another tourist."

She nodded, though, looking at him. It was hard to believe he could ever be just "another tourist," or that anyone else would take him for one. It was not that she wholly understood his need for focusing, but she knew by now that he had his own reasons for the things he did, and that they were serious reasons.

"We'll take the bag in when we get back," she said, pulling out into the stream of traffic and narrowly missing a couple cutting past on a tiny Vespa. Within minutes, they had left the town and were on the road to Arzachena, little more than twelve miles away.

The village was set above high cliffs, as though it had grown there organically. The region was famous for its giants' tombs and stone temples, artifacts of a culture thousands of years old. But Yosef noticed none of this. His thoughts were fixed on remembering the events of that night, weeks earlier, when he had come here in the dark and found himself in an even greater darkness. In all his years of fighting and killing, it was the first time he had come face-to-face with genuine evil, and the thought of it still left him feeling weak.

They turned a corner into the street where Chaya's house stood. Yosef recognized the house at once, its blue roof and white stuccoed walls. Maryam drove closer. By the door, hidden at first by the trunk of a magnolia tree, stood a red and yellow sign. *In vendita*, it read. For Sale.

Back at the hotel, he slept for two hours. The dream returned, more unsettling than before. A child cried, inconsolable, while its tired mother tried to comfort it. There was no food, nothing to drink. Everyone suffered from the thirst. Sometimes they would stop in stations and hands would be stretched out, imploring help. But there were guards and dogs to keep the public away. He knew where they were going, but he kept it to himself: The others would find out soon enough.

Maryam was waiting for him downstairs in the lobby. He found her reading the files on the Milan and Padua cases, which he had left with her. They were, he had told her, Israeli police files: Half of the material was in Hebrew and the other half in Italian, taken from carabinieri and Polizia di Stato reports.

Seeing him approach, she stood up, putting the files down on a low table next to an empty cup that had held a *caffè ristretto*.

"How are you feeling now?" she asked.

"Rested," he said. "Ready to start. Did you get any sense from the lawyer?"

She nodded. The house sale was in the hands of Michele Mannuzzu's partner, with whom she had spoken an hour earlier.

"He says your father-in-law—Aryeh's father, that is—gave instructions for the sale. Apparently he has the right to do that as the chief executor of the will."

"I see. Well, it's not important. I just needed to know."

"I also asked him about Mannuzzu."

Yosef sat down. "And?"

"His body was found a couple of days ago in a shed near Oliena. The police are treating it as murder."

"Are they connecting his killing with Yoel's kidnap?"

"Apparently not."

"Nevertheless, any leads they get may help

109

us. Will Mannuzzu's partner be willing to provide us with any information he's given?"

"I'm not sure. The police may not tell him anything until their investigation is complete."

"It never will be if they don't link his killing to Chaya and Aryeh's. What about Mannuzzu's wife or his family? Can we get them to put some pressure on the police?"

Maryam shrugged. "I don't know. I'll speak to the wife. In the meantime, I have something else for you."

She reached for a file on the table beside her and passed it to him. Inside was a single sheet of paper on which Maryam had written a name and an address: Umberto Levi, 27 Via Nuraghe Albucciu, Arzachena.

"He's a Jew," said Maryam. "The family is originally from Naples. They own restaurants in Olbia, Porto Cervo, Liscia di Vacca, and La Moula. All of them very exclusive. Umberto has a wife, Rosa, and one son, a year older than Yoel. The two boys attended the Abbiadori school in Arzachena."

She looked up.

"Aryeh was right," she said. "Somebody made a mistake."

13

"Mr. Levi? This is Maryam Shumayyil. I spoke to you earlier this morning on the phone."

They were at Levi's gate. Maryam was speaking into an intercom unit while Yosef squinted through the close-set railings to see if anyone appeared at the door.

"Yes, yes," came a tetchy voice. "I remember. What is this about?"

"You said we could talk. I've brought a friend with me. He's an Israeli. His name is Yosef Abuhatseira."

"Yes, I'm sure. But I need to know what this is about. I'm a busy man. I don't have time to meet everyone."

Obviously, no one was coming to the door. They could not continue the entire conversation through an intercom system. Yosef gently eased Maryam to one side and bent his mouth to the grille.

"*Shalom,*" he said, and continued to speak in Hebrew, slowly and distinctly, using classical forms that a non-Israeli Jew might understand. "I'm sorry to trouble you, but I need to talk. I am the brother of Chaya Levin, the woman who was killed here recently. The brother-in-law of Aryeh Levin."

There was a long silence, punctuated by the faint sound of Levi breathing on the other side. Maryam looked up at the villa. It was a low, ocher-colored building, constructed, like so many of the more expensive properties around the Costa Smeralda, in a plain style designed to harmonize with its surroundings. Levi was not one of the super-rich, but he had money to spend. She guessed that four thousand million lire would be a manageable sum for him. It would hurt, but he could put it together.

"You'd better come in," Levi said at last. There was a buzzing sound and the gate swung inward. They went through and walked along a drive lined with holm oaks as far as the front door. Levi was waiting there for them, a slim man in his early fifties, wearing freshly pressed white linen trousers and a lavender cashmere pullover.

He led them to a pale arched room whose walls had been delicately stenciled in green and gold. Tall urns, griffins, and Greek gods stood in carefully balanced syncopation, now touching the ground, now flowing into the arches. A small fountain bubbled above a goldfish pool in one corner. Levi gestured toward a low divan. He himself took an armchair facing them.

"I know about the Levins," he said, speaking a little awkwardly in Hebrew. "My son and theirs were in the same school. What was the boy's name?"

"Yoel."

"Yes, Yoel. My boy is called Yigal. A year older than the Levin's child. I understand Yoel was kidnapped."

"Kidnapped and mutilated," said Yosef. He explained what had been done to his nephew. Levi listened in silence. He had heard of the killings, but he had not known of the cruelties inflicted on the boy. He thought of his own son, who was at school even as they spoke.

"Your family must be shattered by this," he said.

"It has destroyed our lives," said Yosef.

"But I don't understand what any of this has to do with me."

Yosef glanced at Maryam. It might be better coming from her; she was uninvolved.

"We think," she said, "that the kidnappers made a mistake. They took the Levins' son instead of yours, they demanded money from the Levins that was to have been demanded from you."

Levi sat upright. "Oh, no," he said, "that's quite impossible."

"I don't see why. Your names are almost identical, you live in the same small town, both families are Jewish."

Levi shook his head. "Nevertheless. These things are always planned carefully. There would have been ample opportunity to correct a mistake like that. The kidnappers have a certain code of honor. They depend on it for their own safety."

"There was a mistake," broke in Yosef. "The original demand for money was replaced by a demand for information. I spoke to my brother-in-law before his death. He knew nothing about this information. I swear he was telling the truth."

The blood had drained from Levi's face. "What was it they wanted to know?" he asked. His voice had altered, grown pale and insubstantial.

"The whereabouts of the shopkeeper," said Yosef. "*Il bottegaio.* I assume they were talking about an actual person. Does the phrase mean anything to you?"

Levi seemed suddenly exhausted. He closed his eyes briefly, then opened them and shook his head. "No," he said, "I don't know what it means. I know plenty of shopkeepers. Everyone does."

"Could it be a proper name or a title? Have you ever heard of someone called *il bottegaio* ? Perhaps as a sign of respect."

Again the tired swing of the head. "No. Never."

"What about Bianco?"

"No. Why are you asking me these questions? I had nothing to do with your nephew's kidnapping. I was not responsible for his parents' deaths."

"We're not suggesting you are," said Maryam. She could see that the man was frightened. "We merely think you may have information that would lead us to the killers. That's all we want."

"I'm sorry," said Levi, getting to his feet, "but I can't help you. You'll have to leave."

"Do you know how they died?"

"What?" Levi looked blankly at Yosef.

"Have you heard what they did to Aryeh and Chaya?"

Levi licked his lips. His color had changed, as though he were about to be sick. "The local paper said they were strangled. It's horrible, quite horrible. This is a quiet place, a good place to bring up children...."

Yosef interrupted, telling him what had happened, telling him about everything—the sealed room, the gas, the swastika.

"There have been other killings since," he said. "A family in Milan, a single man, a professor, in Padua. What's going on? I think you should tell me. I think you need help."

Levi flushed red, turning on Yosef. "Help? What sort of help can you give? Do you have any idea what you are up against, what sort of people?"

"Perhaps you can tell me."

Levi shook his head, resolute now, determined to give nothing more away. "I can tell you nothing. It is better for your own sake that I tell you nothing. You'd better leave."

He pressed a bell push set to one side of a white marble fireplace across which painted ivy clung in elaborate whorls. Moments later a man appeared in the doorway. He may have been nothing more than a gardener or a handyman, but he was well-built and obviously willing to have a go. Yosef could have broken his neck with very little trouble, but what would have been the point of that.

"I'm staying at the Hotel President," Yosef said. "You can contact me there."

"There'll be no need," said Levi. "Mr. Abuhatseira, please take my advice. Leave Sardinia. Leave Italy. Don't get drawn any further into this business. You can do no good, I assure you. Your sister and her husband are dead. Nothing you do here can possibly bring them back."

"That was never my intention. All I want is to stop it happening to anyone else. To find the people responsible and bring them to justice."

Levi raised his face and, for the first time, their eyes met. "Then you are wasting your time. Return to Israel. Otherwise, your nephew Yoel will lose an uncle in addition to a mother and father."

They walked back to Maryam's car in silence. On the other side of the road sat a small blue Fiat van with mirrored rear windows, the sort of inconspicuous *furgone* that can be seen bustling through the streets of any Italian town at any time. The lettering on the side read *La Nuova Sardegna*, the name of a left-wing newspaper published in Sassari.

They scarcely noticed the van, nor did they see the two men inside, one taking photographs, the other scribbling notes.

Maryam switched on the ignition and drove off. The car disappeared down the road, catching a puddle with its right wheels and throwing a plume of dirty water across the unfinished pavement. The van remained where it was for about half a minute, then pulled away from the curb, following them.

14

"He was lying," said Yosef. In the distance he could make out the sea, gray and without luster. The tires of the little Volkswagen hummed on the asphalt like a low wind across taut wires. "He knows what this is about all right."

"He's frightened," Maryam answered, taking a tight bend with little to spare. The sea vanished for a moment, then returned.

"I don't care. All the more reason to tell me what he knows. If he's in danger, I may be able to help."

"He doesn't know that. You aren't the fifth cavalry. And perhaps he knows better than you think. Maybe this isn't something you can help with. What are you going to do? Send in the Israeli army?"

He shrugged off the irony. "He might at least explain why. I'm going back. I won't let him turn me away like that. My sister and her husband were killed because somebody mistook them for Levi and his wife. He owes me an explanation."

"We'll go back this evening. Give him time to cool down and think it over. What you told him came as a shock."

Yosef shook his head. "No, not entirely. The details, perhaps. But I think he was expecting something like this. And I have an idea he already knew about the killings in Milan and Padua."

Maryam took a turning east, heading coastward to Porto Cervo. "He must know he's still at risk. If we were able to track him down..."

"Of course. But we had one advantage over the killers: We knew my brother-in-law didn't have the information they're after, that there'd been a mistake. Levi's safe until they realize what's happened. He may even be depending on the error to keep him safe."

"All the same, it's only a matter of time."

"Yes. I'll do my best to persuade him of that tonight. In the meantime, I'd like to speak to Mannuzzu's partner. What was his name again?"

"Sanguinetti. Gianadelio Sanguinetti. Why do you want to speak to him?"

"Mannuzzu knew something, I'm certain of it. The kidnappers had no reason to kill him if he was merely acting as Aryeh's go-between. From what I understand, the whole system depends on these go-betweens remaining untouchable. Is that right?"

"Yes, it's essential."

"My guess is that Mannuzzu knew or guessed what this was about and decided to cut himself in. Except that the people he found himself dealing with played a tougher game."

"What makes you think Sanguinetti will know anything?"

Yosef shrugged. "I'm not sure that he will. But he's the only link we've got to Mannuzzu and whatever it was he knew."

Maryam parked the car near the seafront at Porto Cervo. The hotel could wait until later. They needed a meal and a chance to talk.

It was the quiet time of day in Porto Cervo. The glitterati did not venture out of their villas until near sunset, when the up-market *passeggiata* of the Emerald Coast began. Out in the marina, the yachts of the rich and famous lay at anchor, bobbing gently in a slow dance. Everything seemed freshly painted. The streets, like the boats, were free of litter, gleaming, too good for mere human beings. Yosef felt nervous and out of place. This was not a world he understood. And something in it reminded him, strangely, of the railway wagon in his dream, with all its filth and squalor. They were connected somehow, he could not say why.

Maryam took him to the Hotel Cervo, whose beach restaurant overlooked the harbor.

"They make terrific pizzas here," she said. "You must be hungry."

"I can't eat pizza," he replied, not wanting to offend her, but unable to let it go. "They aren't *kasher*." He used the Sephardi pronunciation, but she understood. "Cheese and meat in the same dish isn't allowed."

"You can have a pizza without meat. *Ai funghi, carciofini,* or just a plain *margherita.*"

He smiled. "All right, then. But no seafood."

A waiter came up and Maryam ordered. Pizzas, a carafe of white wine, and mineral water. The waiter left, and she turned back to Yosef.

"Are you very orthodox?" she asked.

He shook his head. "Not really. Not like the *haredim*: They wouldn't even eat in a non-*kasher* restaurant. I know some people who won't touch food even though it has a seal of approval from the Chief Rabbinate."

She glanced at the marina. A tall, blond woman in a swimsuit waved to another across a short expanse of yachts. The second woman waved back, then called indistinctly to her friend.

"It all seems so complicated," Maryam said.

"It is. It can get much more complicated than that. Some rabbinical courts now employ scientists to determine whether the enzymes in food are *kasher*. I've no time for that sort of nit-picking. I try to be observant, but too much piety frightens me. Jewish extremists are as much a threat to Israel as Hamas."

She said nothing. Here was a man who lived in and fought for one of the most provocative Jewish settlements on the West Bank, talking about "Jewish extremists" as a threat. Whether he kept to the letter of the law or not was hardly relevant to the Arabs among whom he lived. The fine distinctions he was capable of making meant as little to them as the theories of higher mathematics or the laws of submolecular physics to the average high school student.

It occurred to her that, in spite of everything, this was a man she did not really know. She had made assumptions about him, most of them based on his Jewishness, fitting him to her own preconceptions as an Israeli Arab, or on his grief, modeling him to her inevitable compassion for what he and his family had suffered.

She looked hard at him, and wondered who he really was, what he believed, what he had done in his life. There were questions she needed to ask.

"Tell me," she said. "What really happened when you rescued Yoel from his kidnappers?"

In spite of his name, Inspector Enzo De Felice was not a happy man. Thirty-six years old and still in Sassari, still scarcely twenty miles from Bonnànaro, the farming village where he had been brought up and from which, like all his friends, he had escaped at the earliest possible opportunity. Thirty-six years old and still an inspector, as high as he was likely to climb unless he got out of here soon and showed what he could do in Rome or Florence or Milan.

Being Sardinian wasn't the problem. Eighty percent of the country's police officers were recruited from the south, six percent of the total from Sardinia. Half of his friends from police academy had jobs on the mainland, and several were already well on their way to important positions at the Ministry of the Interior in Rome.

His problem was simple: He had paid too little attention to the job of getting to know the right people, joining the most influential *consorterie*, and judging the ebb and flow of local politics. His biggest mistake had been in joining the Communist Party in the days when both the mayor and the prefetto had been PCI members. The 1993 elections had seemed set to put right-wingers in power, he had hastily joined the MSI, and the new mayor and prefetto had turned out to be moderate Christian Democrats. Now, the right-wing MSI had formally

120

disbanded itself, reemerging as the broader Alleanza Nazionale, and he didn't know where to turn.

The sound of traffic on the street below jolted him from his daily reflections on the unfairness of life. He'd been asking for double glazing for two years now, but Matteo Cambosu down in forensic records had somehow managed to have it installed in his office instead. Of course, Enzo knew perfectly well that both Cambosu and the glazing contractor were members of the same *confraternita*, a lay brotherhood that organized a procession through the streets of Sassari every Easter.

There was a knock on the door.

"Come in," muttered De Felice. He had not been expecting anyone. Unless ...

The man who entered was a young detective named Delitala. He'd been with De Felice's office for three months now, and was already looking for promotion over his boss's head. Enzo thought—not for the first time—that he should try to have Delitala transferred to other duties. On the other hand, Delitala's older brother Guido had connections with a state prosecutor at the Ministry of Justice....

"These are the pictures you asked for, *dottore*," said Delitala, dropping a thin file on the inspector's desk.

De Felice looked at the file, almost as though it meant nothing to him. The phone call from Sanguinetti had taken him by surprise that morning, and he had at first forgotten completely about the Arab woman and her connection to the Levin killing. Remembering, however, he had also remembered that the questore had

121

expressed a personal interest in the case, and that he had asked to be kept notified of developments. De Felice had wasted no time in putting a tail on her. He'd asked for photographs just to establish that it was the same woman he had interviewed.

"There was someone else with her, *dottore*," said Delitala as De Felice flipped open the file. "A man."

The inspector glanced at the photographs, taken while Maryam and Yosef left Levi's house. Yes, it was the same woman. But the man was a stranger to him.

"Where was this taken?" he asked.

"A private house on the outskirts of Arzachena, sir. I've got someone checking out the owners now."

Of course you have, thought De Felice. The little schemer never missed a trick.

"Let me know as soon as you get a name. I take it there's still someone watching them."

Delitala nodded. This job was still routine, but it had the edge he had already come to recognize, the edge that suggested it might slide into that area of so much potential, the irregular.

"I have two men still on their tail. They're having lunch at Porto Cervo."

"Fine. Keep me informed."

De Felice shut the file and slipped it into his desk drawer.

"Is that all, *dottore*?"

The inspector nodded. "Just let me know the minute something else comes up."

When he finished talking, a silence opened between them. Their pizzas, which had arrived ten minutes earlier, lay half-eaten and cooling on their plates. Above the harbor, a single gull screamed. The sea rose and fell like a gently beating heart. Out on the water, a tiny red sail marked the progress of a windsurfer as he moved from wave to wave, as though engaged in a hopeless quest for stability.

"Thank you," said Maryam at last. "You've been very honest."

"They would have killed him. You understand that."

She nodded. "Yes, I think I do. It's just ..." She forced herself to look at him. "I've never known someone before who ..." Her hesitation dragged into silence.

"Who kills people," he said, finishing her sentence for her.

She looked down at the table, at the uneaten meal for which she now felt no appetite.

"Yes," she whispered.

He nodded. "Then you're very lucky," he said. "I know too many people whose job it is to kill. And too many whose friends or family died because there was no one ready or able to kill on their behalf."

She looked up. "You mean the Holocaust?"

"Mostly that, yes."

"Did you lose members of your family?"

He shook his head. "We lived in Morocco. None of us was caught up in what happened in Europe."

"Then none of your own family died at the hands of the Nazis."

"Not my immediate family, no. But Aryeh's family, yes. Many of them. It's something very close to every Jew, something you can't escape."

She looked at him again, no longer flinching from his gaze.

"My mother's family was killed at Deir Yassin," she said, her voice soft and emotionless. "Her mother and father, an uncle, two aunts, two brothers, and a sister."

He did not reply. Deir Yassin had until that moment been nothing more than a name to him, an Arab village whose inhabitants had been massacred by Zionist terrorists in 1948.

"But we have not killed a single Jew in reprisal," she said. "Nor wished for the death of a single Jew."

He felt the wind come off the sea, cold and laced with salt. It made him shiver. He turned his face away from it and found himself looking directly at Maryam. She had not lowered her eyes. And he could think of nothing to say to her that would not seem trite or patronizing.

The vice-questore handed the photographs back to De Felice. The inspector had brought them straight to his superior, knowing that he had an interest in the case.

"Thank you," said the vice-questore. His name was Pierluigi Dessì, and, unlike De Felice, he had hopes of a serious improvement in his status while remaining in Sardinia. There were four questure on the island, one for each of its provinces, and each one had a questore approaching the age of compulsory retirement. Dessì had been given to believe that he might be in line for one of them. The only thing that could get in his way at the present time was the Levin case. The questore had spoken to him at length on the subject, and he had been left in no doubt as to its importance.

"The man is called Yosef Abuhatseira," Dessì continued. He spelled the name for his subordinate. "I suggest you check what name he is registered under at the hotel in Olbia—it's sensible to assume that he's staying under the same roof as the woman."

"I'll have that done immediately, sir."

"That's not the most important thing. I want your people to stay on their backs. Report back to me as soon as you know the identity of the person they visited this morning. And be sure to get the name of anyone else they visit or so much as speak to."

"Very well, sir," said De Felice, rising.

"Sit down. I haven't finished yet. I want you to stop them poking their noses into this affair. Do you understand me? Select two or three of your best men, men you can rely on. Frighten this couple off. If they get hurt, that's too bad. Nothing too rough, mind—we don't want trouble with their embassy. But see they get the message. See they're off the island by tomorrow night."

15

Gianadelio Sanguinetti was waiting for them in his office. Maryam had called earlier to fix an appointment, though she had not said that Yosef would be with her. As they entered, she noticed that the lawyer's eyes widened slightly, as though in recognition.

Sanguinetti stepped lightly round his desk,

holding out a hand in greeting. Maryam noticed how the hand was held at exactly the correct height, how the cuff above it had been expertly adjusted, how the smile on the man's face was set at precisely the right angles. Sanguinetti, like his gray Armani suit and the room in which he worked, was a product of the most careful calculation. In a nation of actors, where the whole of life is a theatrical performance, he had learned to play his role with all the fine adjustments necessary for success.

"We spoke earlier," he said, taking Maryam's hand with just the right amount of pressure. "But I don't think you mentioned your friend."

"This is Yosef Katzir," she said. "He was a friend of Aryeh and Chaya Levin, the couple who were killed a few weeks ago in Arzachena."

"Of course, of course. We were talking about their house this morning." The lawyer turned and applied his smile to Yosef. He reached out his hand as though to draw him into his charmed circle. Yosef took the hand and held it, not very hard, but with a measure of force that suggested he could crush it if he chose to. Sanguinetti's expression faltered briefly.

"I'm afraid Mr. Katzir doesn't speak any Italian," she said. "But he has mentioned a few points to me that he would like to clear up on behalf of the family."

"I see." Sanguinetti hesitated, then gestured to two leather upholstered chairs. "Please, why don't you sit down?" He skipped back behind his desk as though glad to put it between them.

"Mr. Sanguinetti," Maryam began, "before he died, Aryeh Levin instructed your partner, Michele Mannuzzu, to act for him as an intermediary to negotiate the release of his son, Yoel, from a band of kidnappers. Naturally, I understand that, since Mr. Mannuzzu's agreement to act in that capacity placed him outside the law, anything said about this matter must be off the record."

"Insofar as it affects the legal standing of this law firm, yes."

"Nevertheless, we know this is what happened, since Aryeh explained everything to his brother-in-law, Yosef."

Sanguinetti permitted himself a sideways glance at the man who had been introduced to him as Katzir. De Felice had already alerted him to the possibility that Abuhatseira might pay him a visit, and had warned him to be sure to keep his mouth shut. Not that Sanguinetti always liked doing what he was told, but in the present case ...

"I'm sure Michele would have done whatever he could to help a client in a time of need. Just as I am sure he would never have done anything improper or illegal."

"Whether or not he was breaking the law, your partner disappeared on the same night he went to meet with Yoel's abductors. Aryeh Levin was sent a photograph of his body. It was clearly intended as a warning, but Aryeh did not grasp its meaning."

"Oh, surely that was clear. He had not authorized Michele to pay the sum demanded. Therefore they killed Michele to drive their point home."

Maryam shook her head. "I have lived on this island long enough to know how things work. Kidnappers do not kill *intermediari*, that is a fundamental rule. The entire system would break down if that ever happened. No, Mannuzzu was killed for some other reason, and Yosef Abuhatseira thinks it was because he tried to cut himself in for a slice. The people behind the kidnapping didn't want money, they wanted information. But Mannuzzu knew they were willing to pay for that information, that a great deal of money was involved."

Sanguinetti shook his head. "This sounds highly implausible. Are you suggesting that Michele had access to this information himself?"

"It's possible that he came across it in the course of handling Aryeh's affairs. Aryeh himself was adamant that he knew nothing of what they wanted. We now think the whole thing was a terrible mistake. But your partner may have thought he had or could get what these people wanted. That implies he knew who they were and maybe had a shrewd idea what it was they were after. One thing we do know—he knew enough to get himself killed."

Sanguinetti shrugged. "So you say. But I still don't see how I can help you. Michele did not take me into his confidence in this matter. Whatever he knew, he took to the grave with him."

"Not necessarily. He may have kept records, memos. If you could give us access to those..."

The lawyer shook his head. "Absolutely not. His records will have information relating to other clients. Not even the police or the carabinieri could get to see those files without permission. If you think your suspicions are legitimate, I suggest you approach them and ask them to make inquiries on your behalf."

"That would be at the risk of exposing your partner's involvement in an illegal activity."

Sanguinetti shrugged again. "That will scarcely matter to him now, and it hardly inculpates me. Now, if you will forgive me, I have a client waiting."

They all stood. Maryam glanced across at Yosef, expecting him to say something, to come up with something more to ask Sanguinetti, but he remained silent, merely watching the lawyer as though he could read in his face or his gestures or his dress the answers he sought.

"Please," said Sanguinetti as he showed them to the door, "be sure to tell Mr. Abuhatseira that he and his family are constantly in my thoughts. Assure him that whatever can be done to track down the killers shall be done. But he should know that Michele Mannuzzu was an innocent victim, just like the Levins, and that he knew no more of this matter than they did."

He turned to shake hands again with Yosef. His palm was perfectly dry, his fingers supple. Again Yosef applied pressure to the lawyer's hand, and again he saw the flicker of fear in his eyes. As he took his hand away, he knew he had not yet finished with Sanguinetti.

They drove back to Olbia in silence. There was no sun and no sky. Maryam's manner toward Yosef had been cool ever since he told her about what had happened up there in the *macchia*. But he had known no other way to rescue the boy. Her approval or disapproval should not have mattered to him, but it did. He found himself caring about what she thought. It was a new emotion for him, and it left him uneasy.

129

She drove carefully, her eyes fixed on the road, as though thinking of nothing.

At the hotel they separated. Yosef said he wanted to rest. They planned to visit Michele Mannuzzu's widow that evening and he wanted to be fresh.

As they got out of the elevator, Maryam paused and turned.

"I'm sorry," she said. "It's just that ..."

"You don't have to explain. All I ask is that you take me as I am while I'm here. Once we've found the people I'm looking for ... Well, perhaps you can leave any judgements until then."

She nodded. She hadn't thought she was making judgements.

"I'll see you later," she said.

Once in his room, Yosef sat on the bed and made a brief telephone call. Half an hour later, there was a knock on his door. He opened it to see the same man who had brought him his weapons and ammunition to Aryeh's house. He carried a small case.

They had been sitting for almost three hours now outside the hotel and still the couple they were after had not made a reappearance. For all Vito Dettore knew, they were up in her room screwing one another silly. Lucky bastard, he thought, he wouldn't have minded a spot of the same thing for himself. His wife had lost interest in sex, and a police assistant's salary was hardly sufficient to keep a mistress. Still, with the overtime he and his team were getting for tonight's job, maybe he could at least afford a visit to one of the local *case di tolleranza*.

"Rough them up a bit," De Felice had said. "Tell them to make themselves scarce. And for God's sake behave like ordinary hoodlums."

The question was: Where were they going to do it? Out here in the street was much too public. He was hoping they'd come out and lead them somewhere quiet, a side road or a back alley. If they had to do it in the hotel, the whole thing could turn out messy. He looked toward the doorway again, praying to St. Michael for assistance. On second thought, perhaps Michael, who was the patron saint of policemen, wouldn't answer his prayers for such a business.

The car door was pulled open suddenly. Vito looked round to see his view blocked by a heavy man in a black suit.

"Right," said the man. "Clear off, you and your two gorillas. My boys are taking over."

"What are you talking about?" Vito could scarcely see the stranger, obscured as he was by the darkness and his own bulk. He made to reach into his pocket for his identification card, then remembered that he had left it behind on De Felice's instructions.

"I'm talking about this," the man said, thrusting two photographs under Vito's nose. "You're being replaced."

The photographs were identical to the two supplied to Vito at the *questura*.

"Who sent you? De Felice?"

"Yeah, De Felice. Now, get going."

"Let's see your badge," argued Vito. He wasn't going to give up the job without a struggle. It paid five times the normal overtime rate, and it was cash in the pocket.

"No badges," said the man. "Don't worry, you'll be paid. That's been taken care of. Now, clear out."

Vito opened his mouth to argue some more, then noticed the gun in the other man's shoulder holster. It wasn't a police revolver, nor was it carabinieri issue. The policeman closed his mouth and reached for the ignition key. He had lived on Sardinia all his life, long enough to know when to make trouble and when to shut up.

"Okay," he said, "we're going. I hope you enjoy yourselves."

"Don't worry," said the large man. "We intend to."

As the car pulled away from the curb, the man in black gestured to the driver of another car parked several yards further down the street. It drew up alongside him and he got in. Apart from the driver, there were two other men in the rear seat.

"They give you any trouble?" asked the driver.

The man in black shook his head. "No, they thought their boss sent me. Somebody called De Felice."

"I know him," volunteered one of the men in the back. "Small man, not too bright. Comes from Bonnànaro. Pulled me in three or four years ago on a drugs charge. It didn't stick, and we never met again. Is he on our list?"

The man in black shook his head. "Not for tonight. I'll double check just to be sure. For the moment, let's concentrate on the matter in hand."

The hotel was quiet. Not even the central heating made a sound. No elevators moving, no doors opening or closing, no room service carts being wheeled along the corridor. Complete silence. Maryam looked through her window. Still, silent streets the color of wet slate. No cars, no scooters, no pedestrians. As though she were stranded in a soundless bubble.

She had begun to realize that this thing she had allowed herself to get involved in might be dangerous. There had been a little risk from the start, she knew that, but with so many deaths to account for, Yosef must surely be a target. And, if he was at risk, then she too must be a potential victim should the killers strike again.

Yosef himself confused her. She had known that he had served in the army and, in all probability, killed people, but his account of the slaughter in the hills above Oliena had possessed an immediacy that left her troubled. However indirectly, she had been involved, and the knowledge seemed to taint her.

For all that, Yosef appeared to fit her definition of a decent man, whatever that was. He had risked his life to rescue his sister's child and he had returned to help track down her killers. In his conversation, she had sensed that he came to violence reluctantly, and that might have served to comfort her a little had it not been that he was so good at it.

A figure moved on the other side of the Via Principe Umberto, gray, entangled with shadows. A resident returning late from work, a doctor on his way to a woman in labor, a priest hurrying to administer the last rites? Or a watcher, snuggling deep down in the limitless gray shadows?

There was a knock at her door, then Yosef's

voice. It surprised her how much it reassured her to hear it. She opened the door and joined him in the corridor. He had shaved and was wearing a light suit and tie. Her face must have betrayed her. As she closed the door, he put one hand self-consciously on the knot of the tie.

"I'm taking you for dinner afterward," he said. "You deserve an apology for lunch. And you must be hungry."

"You might have told me," she protested. "I'm not dressed for going out."

"You look fine. Believe me."

She felt herself reddening. Against her own better judgement, she discovered that she did believe him, and that it flattered her to do so.

"Come on," she said in an attempt to cover her confusion. "We've got Mr. Levi and Michele Mannuzzu's widow to visit first."

He saw them coming, their faces illuminated momentarily in the light of the hotel entrance. They walked to a car parked nearby, a Volkswagen.

"That's them," he said. The driver turned the key in the ignition and waited until the Volkswagen had moved off before slipping into the road behind it.

He turned to his companions in the back.

"You can have the woman," he said. "Do what you like with her, but be sure she's not in a position to talk about it afterward. I want the Jew for myself."

16

There were lights in several rooms at the Levis' house, but no one was answering the door.

"He must have guessed we'd come back," said Maryam.

"Maybe." Yosef rang the bell again. He could hear the sound of a television program coming through a partly opened window on the ground floor. And still no one came.

"We could telephone."

"No," said Yosef, "it would only alert him. I wanted to take him by surprise."

"Perhaps he's at one of his restaurants."

Yosef nodded. She could just make out his head in the dark.

"I'd thought of that," he said. "But his wife and son would probably stay at home. And they must have a housekeeper."

"We'll call again in the morning," said Maryam. "We'll keep on calling till we find him in."

They turned to go. As they did so, a soft cry came from behind the gate. Maryam looked down to see a tabby cat sitting just behind the mesh. It opened its mouth and uttered another cry, louder and more pitiable than the first. Maryam bent down and stuck her fingers through the wire, murmuring to the animal in a calming voice.

"What's wrong, pussy?" she said. "What's wrong?"

The cat approached her nervously, brushing the side of its head tentatively against her fingers, then pulled back and cried again. Maryam felt her skin crawl at the sound.

"Something's wrong," she said. "He's upset."

"It's just a stray," said Yosef. "He's looking for food."

Maryam shook her head. "No, he's wearing a collar. This must be the family pet. He's worried about something. Believe me, I have several cats at home."

Yosef rejoined her at the gate. He knew nothing about cats himself, but he could tell that the animal was agitated, and he knew better than to ignore Maryam's concern.

"I think I'd better take a look inside," he said.

"I'll come, too."

He shook his head. "No, if something is wrong and I run into trouble, it's better you're on the outside. If necessary, you can go for help."

"Because I'm a woman...."

"No, that never even crossed my mind. I served in the Israeli army, remember. I'm going inside first because I have more experience at this sort of thing; you're staying outside because I need backup."

"You don't think—"

He cut her off. "Let's hope not," he said. "But I have to see for myself."

"How will I know what's happening?"

"You won't. I won't stay in more than five minutes, even if I haven't found anything. Go back to the car. Keep the engine running, but the lights off. I'll be back soon."

"Take care," she said. To her surprise, she realized she meant it.

Working late had grown to be a habit for Inspector De Felice. Worse than that, a vice. He told himself it was better than gambling or drinking, and like a gambler or a drinker he told himself he would give it up tomorrow, that he was in control of his problem, that the late hours would come to an end the moment his transfer to the mainland materialized. Maybe it would come sooner than he had hoped. Vice-questore Dessì had expressed himself pleased by De Felice's handling of the Levin case.

Of course, once he had seen how interested the vice-questore was in the affair, De Felice had decided to do some digging about on his own behalf. He had been impressed by what he had come up with so far. There was more to the murders than met the eye, and he already had a good idea of the direction in which further inquiries might lead him. He'd have to be discreet, of course, but then he had always prided himself on his ability to keep his mouth shut when it counted. If he could manage to compile a dossier along the lines he now anticipated, he had every reason to believe he would be in Rome by the summer, in a double-glazed and air-conditioned office.

He scrutinized the papers from the Levin file again, as though by committing their contents to heart he could assure himself of his passport to felicity. It was like an examination, he thought, only this time he was going to come out top of his class.

There was a knock on the door.

"*Avanti*," he called out without looking up.

The door opened, there was a sound of foot-steps, then the door closed again.

"Yes?" barked De Felice, still scanning the documents on his desk. "Can't you see I'm busy?"

There was no reply. Irritated, the inspector looked up. Two men were standing several feet away, examining him casually. He knew every-one who had any right to be inside the *questura*, especially outside normal office hours, but he recognized neither of the men in front of him.

"Who the hell are you?" he demanded. "What do you want?"

"Inspector De Felice." asked one of the men. He was solidly built, dark-complexioned, with wiry hair. De Felice might have put him down as a shepherd from the Barbagia had it not been for the sunglasses that hid his eyes.

"Yes, I'm De Felice. What are you doing in my office? Who let you in?" He would have to speak to Malagugini tomorrow. Malagugini was in charge of internal security, and from the looks of it he was doing a lousy job. De Felice allowed himself the luxury of supposing he might be able to use this incident as a lever with which to elbow Malagugini out of his post, installing himself in his place to initiate a comprehensive review and overhaul of the security system. Even a modest success, or the appearance of one, would serve to turn his colleague's misfortune into a springboard for his own appointment to Rome.

The man in sunglasses did not move and did not speak. Instead, he nodded to his compan-ion, a blond-haired youth with pockmarked skin. The younger man moved quickly across the room, ending up behind De Felice.

Before the policeman could react, the blond man swung his arms over his head, thrusting a thick strip of plastic tape over De Felice's mouth. At last the inspector reacted, lifting his hands to pull the other man's arms away. But the blond man was too quick for him. He grabbed De Felice's wrists and pulled his arms behind his back, pinning them hard.

De Felice's eyes bulged, and he squirmed frantically, his breath coming in tight, labored puffs in and out of his nose. But however hard he struggled, the blond man held him effortlessly, and he felt himself weakening, overpowered as much by his assailants' silence and malignity as by their physical strength.

The large man took something from his pocket. De Felice strained to see what it was, knowing that if it was brass knuckles or a blackjack he was only in for a beating, but that a knife or a gun meant death.

To his surprise and, for a moment, relief, it was only an aerosol spray, a large tin of deodorant or fly killer, the sort of thing they sold in bulk at his local supermarket. The ordinariness of it calmed him for a moment. And then, as the big man stepped toward him, he looked more closely and he understood. He would have screamed then if he had been able to. The aerosol contained glue, the sort of glue you could spray on cardboard or paper.

He felt his bowels and bladder shift and his legs become rubber. The next moment, the man in dark glasses was in front of him, pulling the tape away from his mouth. De Felice tried to scream, knowing this was the last chance he would ever have in his life. But it was useless.

The man in front of him had done this sort of thing before. He forced De Felice's mouth open, casually breaking his jaw as he did so, and into the gaping hole he inserted the head of the spray can. He pressed down hard on the nozzle at the rear, and as he did so he smiled at the blond man, and the blond man smiled back, conscious of another job well done.

Yosef scaled the fence without difficulty. He was not particularly concerned if he set off an alarm: any response would be better than the bleating of an unattended television set. At the same time, it would be foolish to reveal his location. If something had happened or was happening, those responsible might still be on the premises.

Using the holm oaks as cover, he crept to the half-open window. Inside, a large television set played to an empty room. A comedian went through his paces before a studio audience. Bursts of canned laughter erupted every few seconds, then the comedian would go into another routine. Yosef listened, consciously blotting out the sound of the television as he had been trained to blot out the crump of exploding shells or the whine of a jet. The garden behind him was still empty. Gently, he opened the window further until the space was wide enough for him to crawl through.

His chief fear was odorless gas. If the Levi family had been killed, that was the most likely method. The room in which he stood was safe, since the window had been open. But what would happen when he stepped through the door?

Holding a handkerchief to his mouth, he slipped from his pocket the handgun that had been delivered to him that afternoon, an H&K P7M8. With its squeeze cocker safety, it was a gun that allowed safe and accurate shooting in confined quarters. Trigger action could be light and even, since the striker was cocked by a separate device in front of the gun's handle. Sayaret Matkal recruits were normally trained to use Beretta pistols, but Yosef had developed a particular liking for the Heckler and Koch and used it wherever possible.

The door opened into a long corridor. A tentative sniff told him there was no gas in this area. Cautiously, he started to go from room to room on the ground floor.

By the time he started searching the next floor he had started to feel a sense of relief. The first bedroom he entered confirmed his suspicions. He took the handkerchief from his face and returned it to his pocket.

The doors of a long built-in wardrobe stood wide open, showing empty space and row upon row of coat hangers. It was the same in each of the bedrooms that followed. Umberto Levi had taken fright. Their visit that morning must have convinced him that his family was now directly threatened and that safety lay in flight. The Levis had packed what they could into any available bags and cases and by now, Yosef guessed, they would be on the first flight out of Olbia airport.

He put the gun away and started back down the stairs.

A match flared briefly as Maryam lit a cigarette. The red tip was just visible in the darkness. Outside the car, the air was cold and growing colder. She looked ahead into the night, as though expecting something or someone to appear. Once or twice, she glanced round, then back to the front again. She felt uneasy, as though someone was watching, but in the darkness everything was still.

There were watchers, indeed, but the darkness hid them perfectly.

17

Tina Mannuzzu busied herself with cups and saucers and little paper napkins. She did not know any other way to behave with guests, and since Michele's death she had found whatever comfort there was to find in this endlessly repeated ritual of genteel hospitality. Her days had become long rounds of entertaining as friends and family came to commiserate with her. She would not leave the house, not even to return calls, and word had got round to that effect, so everyone now came to her.

That was why, even at this unusual hour, she had opened the door so readily to two strangers, and why, once it was established that they, like so many of her callers, had a tenuous link with her husband, she had invited them inside.

"I used to see Mrs. Levin at bridge parties in Porto Cervo," she said to Yosef, who had been introduced to her under his assumed identity. Maryam translated. He nodded and smiled, balancing a cup of chocolate in one hand and a plate with amaretti in the other. "I knew Aryeh, too," Tina went on, "but not as well. He and Michele were good friends, of course."

Mannuzzu's widow was absurdly young for her new role, in her mid-twenties at most Maryam guessed. She was pretty, and it would not be long before a new man came into her life. But for the moment, it was plain that she was bewildered and in need of help. Death had taken her husband's life by a sudden, ugly gesture, and she was still unsure just where it stood in her simple scheme of things. Until now, it had been one of those things, like gray hair or incontinence pads, that lay much further down the road. And now, here it was, invading her ordered universe of coffee cups and Milanese tableware.

"Do you mind if we talk a little about Michele?" asked Maryam at Yosef's prompting. She felt uneasy sitting here, drinking coffee and making small talk, knowing all the time that she and Yosef were intruders into this woman's grief.

"No, of course not, I don't mind at all." Tina had been doing very little else for the past few days; in fact, she had talked more about Michele since his death than in the entire four years they had been married. It was funny, she thought: She talked about him incessantly, but she still hadn't cried, not even once, neither alone nor in company. Was that good or bad? she wondered.

"Mrs. Mannuzzu, before Michele died he was acting as the intermediary in connection with Yoel Levin's kidnapping. We're pretty sure he was killed by Yoel's kidnappers, or by some-

143

one more powerful one or two steps removed from them. Before he went out that night, did Michele say anything to you about what he was doing, who he thought he was going to see?"

Tina crossed her legs and straightened her skirt, pulling the hem a few inches below her knees, but not so far as to hide her long calves. Conservative at heart, she was dressed in black, even if the style of her widow's garb was far from what her grandmother in Macomer would have approved of.

"Michele never talked about work to me. He always said that a woman should never have to worry about such matters."

She herself, it was clear, had believed him. But when she looked up to see Maryam looking at her disapprovingly, she reddened slightly.

"Oh." She laughed. "He was very old-fashioned about such things. Well, I'm a little old-fashioned myself. Emancipation may be all right in Rome or Milan, or wherever it is you come from, miss, but here in Sardinia ... We like to go at our own pace."

"So Michele said nothing to you that evening?"

Tina frowned, as though trying hard to remember. "No, you're right, he did. Let me see.... It was just before he left. He said I shouldn't wait up for him, that he might be back late. I asked him where he was going and he said Oliena. He said he was going to drive there, in the Fiat. I was a little worried, because the car's been giving trouble lately and Michele isn't ..."

She caught herself, then continued as if it were no more than a correction of grammar. "Michele wasn't mechanically minded. I don't think he even knew where the engine was. But if you break down on that road at night ... Well, it wouldn't have been safe."

She stopped, as though newly aware of the irony.

"I see. Nothing else."

Tina shook her head, then her face brightened again. "Oh, yes. Just as he was going, he gave me a little kiss, the way he always did, and he said I might be able to have the new kitchen I've been wanting, the one from Snaidero, that we might be able to afford it sooner than we'd planned. I asked him why, and he said something had come up which might pay well."

"Did you ask him what it was?"

Tina frowned and shook her head mechanically. It was a gesture she used a lot.

"No, I told you—I never asked about his work."

Yosef leaned toward Maryam and made a brief suggestion.

"Tina, did Michele work at his office that day, or at home?"

"Oh, he worked mainly at his office. Sometimes he'd bring work home at night, though I told him not to. I read a piece in *Anna* once that said couples should keep home and office separate, otherwise ..."

"No, but that day. The day he met with Aryeh Levin. The day he went to Oliena."

"Oh, yes, you mean..." She stopped, frowning, realizing Maryam meant the day her husband had set out for his death, quite possibly the day he had died. "No, he ... Let me think. He was at the office, then I think he went to see Mr. Levin. Yes, he must have done, because I'd missed Chaya at our bridge party the day before, and I'd asked Michele to ask if she was all right. And then, I remember, Michele came back here that afternoon, and he went to his study and stayed there until a little before he left."

Maryam translated for Yosef, leaving out the digressions. Again Yosef muttered a few words.

"Mrs. Mannuzzu, has anyone been in Michele's study since then?"

"Well, I have, of course. And Adriana, our cleaning lady."

"Anyone else? Did the police ask to look at his papers or anything?"

Tina looked a little bewildered. Her hand shook slightly as she set down her cup of cooling coffee. So many questions. What exactly was going on? Had Michele been involved in something he shouldn't have?

"What do you mean?" she asked. "Why would the police ... ?"

Maryam shook her head. "There's nothing wrong. It's just that sometimes it's routine, when someone is killed. It's nothing to be worried about."

Tina pursed her lips and shook her head. The gesture comforted her. Saying no was a reflex that allowed her to keep a threatening world at bay.

"You mean the police didn't go in there?"

"That's right. They didn't ... I don't even think they went to his office."

"Do you think ... Would you mind if we had a look?"

"In his office?"

"No, his study here."

"Well, I don't know. Gianadelio said no one

was to tamper with anything until he had time to see to it himself. He's been very good. He's handling all the … business himself. I don't know what I'd do without him."

Maryam sensed the future even as Tina spoke. Thinking of Sanguinetti, she recoiled from the image it conjured up.

"Tina, we don't want to tamper with anything. We'd be happy for you to watch us. We won't take anything. All we're trying to do is find Aryeh and Chaya's killers."

"Well, I'm not sure. Gianadelio said I should check anything with him first. Maybe I should ring him."

"We spoke with him earlier," said Maryam hastily. "He said he wanted to help in any way he could, that we should have every facility. He was very helpful. A very kind man. But, then, I'm sure you know that."

Tina smiled. "Gianadelio's kindness itself," she said. "He's been such a help to me since… Michele died. But I still think I should mention it to him. You could come back tomorrow. I'll ring him at his office in the morning."

Maryam smiled again. She wondered how long she could keep this up.

"I'm afraid we have to be in Rome tomorrow. It's not something that can be canceled. We had hoped to finish our business here in Sardinia first."

"You're going to Rome in connection with the murders?"

Maryam nodded. "That and … There's also the question of little Yoel. You knew him, I suppose."

"Oh, of course. What a lovely child. Such a

147

poppet. And for such a thing to happen to him! Michele and I were never able to have children. Given time, perhaps ..."

She looked up pitifully, and there were traces of genuine tears in her eyes.

"It's for Yoel's sake that we're doing this," said Maryam. "He needs to know why these things happened. At the moment it all seems so pointless, and we're frightened he'll grow up thinking life has no meaning. But if we could find out who was behind the kidnapping and the killings, discover if they just wanted money, or if it was something else, we think it would help Yoel come to terms with it all in time."

Tina nodded. There had been a crazy moment, just after she heard of the Levins' deaths and what had been done to Yoel, that she had thought of offering to adopt the boy. But her best friend, Nicoletta, to whom she had confided her plan, had reminded her that Yoel was Jewish and that it would hardly be suitable to have someone like that in her family. What if she were to have children of her own later on?

All the same, little Yoel had been a favorite of hers.

"Of course," she said. "It's right he should know. I'll show you the study. You needn't worry, I won't breathe down your necks." She looked at Yosef, whom she treated as somewhat mentally retarded because he did not speak Italian.

"Ask him if he'd like another coffee, dear," she said to Maryam.

"I think we'd better just get down to business," Maryam answered, setting her own cup down on the table next to her.

Tina showed them to the little room that had

148

served as her husband's home office. Less mannered than Sanguinetti's workplace, this was nonetheless a well-planned and pleasantly appointed space. A long black desk held a small computer with a CD-ROM deck and a compact ink-jet printer, a telephone, various desk ornaments, a Berenice lamp, and nothing more. There was a single filing cabinet, also in black, a table with a fax, and built-in shelves holding lever-arch files.

"Call me if there's anything you need," said Tina before scuttling off to wash up and tidy.

"This looks hopeless," said Maryam, switching to Hebrew. "So tidy. It's not likely he left anything just lying around."

"Oh, I don't know. His widow says the cleaning lady paid a visit. If she was any good at her job, she'll have tidied up but not thrown any papers away."

"Unless they were already in the wastebasket. If he made any notes and tossed them in there, they're long gone."

"Well, we'll check when the cleaner was here, and what day the garbage is collected. In the meantime, let's see what's here. Why don't you skim the computer files? Your eye will be better than mine. I'll plod through the loose papers."

"Will you know what to look for? You could miss things just because you don't recognize certain words or abbreviations."

"Well, I'll try anyway. It may save time."

They set to work without really knowing what they were doing, guided by instinct more than expertise. It was alarmingly clear to them that they could find and discard clues without seeing them for what they were simply because neither of them had more than the haziest idea what they were looking for.

Every so often, Tina popped her head round the door in order to ask how they were getting on and if they wanted any more coffee or chocolate. Each time they smiled and thanked her politely, and each time they realized that it was growing later and later, and that before very long she would ask them to leave. Maryam's worst fear was that Tina would panic and ring Sanguinetti after all. If that happened, they were finished.

Maryam had been working at the desk for some time before she noticed the telephone. It was an Alcatel, a state-of-the-art digital phone complete with screen and keyboard. Maryam had once worked briefly as a foreign-language secretary in an office in Cagliari, where she had been shown how to use the phone and to make full use of its various capabilities.

One thing it did was to record the details of up to twenty-one calls made to other numbers. If they had been punched in, only the number, the duration of the call, and the time and date would show on the screen, but calls made through the built-in directory would also show the name of the person called. It was a simple matter to call up the information. She scrolled down the screen, finding a full twenty-one calls recorded. The last nine had been made on the day of Mannuzzu's disappearance: the twenty-first was the last call he had made, from his home phone at least. A few of the calls showed names, the others had clearly been made to numbers not recorded in the phone's directory. Maryam made a note in her diary of all nine calls, writing down everything including the time of day when each had been made.

It was nearly midnight and they had almost given up when Yosef stumbled on the first sheet of paper that contained any reference to the kidnapping. The paper was in a file he had already gone through several times, bearing Aryeh's name and containing various legal documents and records of sundry financial transactions conducted on his behalf. It was crumpled and dirty, with numerous brown rings made by several cups of coffee. There were also crumbs of what Maryam later identified as *sebada*, a local pastry dipped in honey: this had made it stick to the document next to it, causing Yosef to miss it on each of the previous occasions he had leafed through the file.

"Here," he said, passing the sheet to Maryam. "Can you make any sense of this? It has Yoel's name on it."

She took it from him. It contained irregular lines of handwriting, clearly jotted down at random, with several crossings-out and barely decipherable abbreviations.

Yoel L.: qcmmL richieste.
Sig.ra L. med. somma? Piu??   Calc. 10% Y., 10% la sig.ra.
20% ~~qcmmL~~ ocmmL   domanda 25%???
Bianco = W?? possibile. Controll. Moschetta? Procopio?
~~Pozzan???~~
(+ importante controll. incart. AR)
Levin err. per Levi?? ~~Controll. Buzzi.~~ Telef. viceq.
Bottegaio = K?   Controll. orig. Levin.

151

ted.?? Levi medess.

~~MSI~~ Altri nf? Relaz. ted.??

"This is hard to make sense of," said Maryam when she had studied the annotations for a little while. "But we're on the right track, no doubt of it. I think we should photocopy these notes and go over them properly later on. We may have to come back here to cross-check some of the names."

"We told Tina we were going to Rome."

Maryam shrugged. "We'll find an excuse."

There was a desktop photocopier in one corner. Maryam switched it on and ran off a couple of copies of the sheet. She handed the sheets to Yosef, who folded them neatly and slipped them into his jacket pocket. The original she returned to the box file in which Yosef had found it.

At that moment, Tina came in.

"It's terribly late," she said, yawning. It was obvious that even her patience was wearing thin. "Will you be very much longer?"

Maryam shook her head. It was important not to lose Tina's sympathy.

"I'm sorry," she said. "We hadn't noticed the time. I do apologize. But we're more or less finished in here anyway."

"Did you find anything?"

Maryam shook her head. "No, but at least we've eliminated your husband's papers from our search. It's just possible we may have to come back from Rome to look again, if something crops up there. I'd like to keep in touch, if that's all right with you."

"Oh, yes, you must. I want to know how little

Yoel's doing. He'll be missing his school here, and his little friends. If you ever want to bring him over for a holiday, you're more than welcome to stay here. It would be no trouble."

"That's very kind of you. I'll mention it to Yoel's grandparents. Now, I think we have to let you get to bed."

They left, still talking. Tomorrow, thought Maryam, Tina Mannuzzu will take her coffee cups back down from their shelf, and fry little *sebada* cakes with honey and curd cheese, and feed them to a succession of people she scarcely knows. And the honey will form a shell round her heart, a dark, sweet shell that will grow thicker and thicker until she no longer knows quite where all this began, or what grief was, or what her heart had once contained.

As they walked away from the house, the driver of a car parked opposite spoke quickly into a handset.

"They're leaving together. The Mannuzzu woman is staying behind. We'll follow the targets as before."

18

As they reached the car, Yosef asked Maryam for the keys.

"I'm not tired," she said. "I'm perfectly capable of getting us back to Olbia."

"I know you are. But I'd like a turn at the wheel. Please."

She glanced at him, catching his face in the light of a streetlamp. There was something in his expression that persuaded her not to argue. She handed over the keys and he opened the driver's door.

"You don't know the way," she said, climbing in beside him.

"You'll just have to guide me."

"It would be easier if I drive. Some of these roads can be dangerous at night if you don't know your way."

He switched on the engine and pulled away from the curb. She saw him adjust the rearview mirror and the side mirrors.

"I'm hungry," he said. "You must be starving, too. I didn't realize we'd be this late. Is there anywhere left open?"

"Plenty of places along the coast. Nightclubs mostly, where the smart set go. They only really get moving after midnight."

"Sounds terrible. Is there nowhere else?"

"Our hotel has room service."

"Then we'll go there," he said, glancing into the mirror.

"Is something wrong?" she asked, sensing a tension in him that had not been there before. "Why were you so insistent on driving?"

"There's a car behind us," he answered. "Don't look round, he'll guess we're on to him. He's been following us since we left Olbia. I think he was behind us leaving the hotel."

Maryam glanced into the side mirror on her side, catching a brief glimpse of headlights.

"I didn't notice anyone," she said.

"You're not trained to. And you haven't been trained in evasive driving either. The man behind us is fairly good, but not good enough. I can lose him quite easily, but I'm not sure I

154

want to. I'd like to know who he is and what he wants."

"How can you find that out?"

He shrugged, taking a sharp bend at speed, forcing them both to lean into the turn.

"It depends on what he's after. If he's just watching us, he'll clear off once he knows he's been spotted. But if he's after trouble, he'll try to stick to us. I need to make it hard for him, but not too hard."

He swung into the next bend at an even higher speed. The wheels spun, almost skidding on the poorly maintained tarmac. The Volkswagen was not an ideal vehicle for such tactics, especially if the car behind was well equipped. Yosef glanced in the mirror in time to see the flash of lights as their pursuer rounded the bend with ease.

"I need a side road on which I can get up some speed," he said. "One with bends and turnoffs."

"Why didn't you tell me earlier?" Maryam protested. "I could have looked at a map. This isn't exactly my home territory either! I only know the main roads."

Yosef swore beneath his breath. The driver of the car behind was certain to be local, in all likelihood familiar with every inch of road and track round here. That stripped away much of Yosef's advantage. The man would be hard to shake should Yosef decide to lose him: He would know the shortcuts and detours that would give him a reasonable chance of recovering his quarry were it to cut and run, all the more so since the quarry would probably be lost by then and wandering blindly in an attempt to get back on route.

They came to an unposted crossroads. Yosef swung left, changing down and up again with an exactitude born of long practice under hard conditions. As he felt the tires bite again, he gave the car its head, snatching a glance in the rearview mirror. If his pursuer wanted to drop out of the game, this was the moment when he would do so. And if not ...

He saw the long beam of the lights behind swing sideways, then converge into twin points as the car slewed, straightened, and picked up speed behind him. They meant business, then, thought Yosef.

He strained to make sense of the road ahead. It meandered without rhyme or reason through a patchy network of small farms, now diving between clumps of olive trees, now navigating a way through plantations of cork oaks, their gnarled and twisted trunks hurtling into sight like gargoyles. The road skirted a disused quarry, picking a tortured path through otherwise impenetrable swathes of *macchia*, now passing through winter-exhausted fields, forlorn and trackless.

Sometimes they would catch sight of a light in the distance, impossibly remote, as though beckoning to them from another universe. Otherwise, absolute darkness reigned beyond the narrow beam of their headlights. It was tempting to swing the Volkswagen suddenly into an open field and attempt to evade their pursuers that way, but Yosef preferred not to take the risk. If they got bogged down out there in the open, their chances of escaping would be slim. A capable gunman could pick them off as they stumbled through the rough fields.

The winding road made it impossible to get up to any real speed. Apart from their own car and that behind, the road was empty. That made it more tempting to take risks, to enter blind corners on the wrong side, to keep up speed regardless of what might lie ahead. More than once, Yosef missed coming off the road by inches.

He was driving to escape now. There was no way of knowing how many were in the car behind, nor whether they were armed, and he did not want to find out. But, in spite of his skill and his determination to get away, it was growing obvious that their pursuers were steadily gaining on them. Either the driver was better than he had at first seemed or the car had a more powerful and better tuned engine, better road handling abilities, and whatever else might be needed to give it such an edge. Yosef knew he could not hope to outrun his pursuers much longer.

"We need to make it back to Olbia," he said, "or to somewhere else inhabited. Have you no idea which way we should go?"

Maryam shook her head. She was growing frightened. Yosef's tension was palpable, and she knew they had been hopelessly lost for the past ten minutes.

Suddenly, Yosef caught sight of an opening on the left. They were already well past by the time it registered, but he slammed on the brakes, bringing them to a lurching, skidding halt, then threw the car hard into reverse. Steering with the help of the mirror and his reverse lights, he could see the headlights of the other car hurtling toward them. He pressed hard on the accelerator, fighting to keep the wheels in line. Along this stretch, the road was lined with densely planted trees.

The opening came in sight, and Yosef slammed into first, then second, turning into the gap and picking up speed as fast as possible. They were on a rough farm track leading across fields. He prayed the track would lead somewhere where there were people, to a farmhouse or a village, but it was dark ahead, and he began to think he might have taken them into a trap.

Moments later, he saw the lights of the pursuing car swing into view. His only hope, and the reason he had turned off the road in the first place, was that their pursuers were in a heavier vehicle that might be slowed down by the softer ground on which they were now traveling.

After about a thousand yards, the track began to narrow. Within moments they found themselves on a downward slope. The decline was gentle at first, then grew steeper with alarming rapidity. Yosef slipped into a low gear. Until he knew exactly what lay ahead, he could not afford to risk losing control.

Maryam wound down the window. There was something about this sudden descent that she did not like. She thought of the line of trees they had passed: They reminded her of something. A blast of cold air rushed in, stinging her face, pungent with a familiar smell.

"Slow down!" she yelled. "For God's sake, Yosef, put the brakes on!"

He responded, hitting the brake pedal in

controlled bursts, throwing the little car into a skid that took them right off the track and on to something that felt like grass. For a long moment, he thought the brakes were not going to hold, that the tires would not grip, that the car would topple on the steep slope and continue rolling until they reached the bottom. But he managed to pull the wheel round hard and get their nose pointing up the decline, using it as a second brake to slow them further. Without warning, there was a loud bang, and they were jerked hard against their belts as the car slammed to a complete standstill.

"What the hell was that?" asked Maryam, slumping back and rubbing her neck.

Yosef switched off the engine. The lights went dead.

"I think we hit a rock. Let me take a look."

A collection of large white rocks lay scattered across their path. The one they had struck was about two feet high and firmly wedged in the earth beneath. They had struck it full on and, from the look of things, it had smashed the front axle.

Yosef stepped up to the passenger window, which was still open.

"What was it?" he asked. "What did you see that made you shout 'stop'?"

"Nothing," she said, shaking her head. Her neck hurt from the jolt she had received. She'd heard of whiplash injuries. She hoped this wasn't serious. "I saw nothing. But you can smell it— we're near the sea. The trees back there were a windbreak." She stopped speaking. "Listen," she whispered.

He listened, and now he could hear what she heard, the sound of waves crashing on rocks somewhere close at hand.

"There are some steep precipices along this coast," Maryam said. "Not very high, but the fall would have been enough to kill us if we'd gone over. There's probably a beach down there, hence the track, but from the sound of those waves, I'd guess it's surrounded by rocks."

Suddenly, she felt Yosef grab her by the shoulder.

"Quickly," he said, "get out of the car."

He'd caught sight of the lights of the other car, bearing down on them in a straight line. Their pursuers must have seen them turn off the track and followed them over the decline, driving slowly enough to avoid any rocks that might lie in their path. The driver would have guessed already just where the track had been leading.

They reached a spot about twelve yards from the Volkswagen and stopped dead. Three men jumped out. The driver remained behind the wheel, ready to ram the Volkswagen if necessary. The car's powerful headlights remained lit, blinding Yosef and Maryam, pinning them where they were.

A voice rang out, speaking rapidly in Italian, in hard, peremptory tones. Yosef did not move a muscle. He kept his eyes turned very deliberately away from the headlights.

"He wants you to put your hands on the roof of the car," translated Maryam breathlessly. "And he wants me to get out."

"Just stay where you are. When I tell you,

160

open the door and roll out on this side. Make sure your seat belt's out of the way first."

The man called out again.

"You're trying my patience, Mister Fucking Jew," he said. "I told you to put your stinking hands in full view, and I told the bitch to get out of the car. I don't have time to waste. If you don't put your fucking hands where I told you, very slowly, I will take great pleasure in ripping your Jew cock off and stuffing it down your dirty little throat."

Maryam's translation did no justice to the text. Yosef calculated that they had half a minute or so before anyone started anything. Their would-be killers were jaunty, but they would not want to take chances, especially while their intended victims kept a car between themselves and any attack, and as long as it was unclear whether or not they were armed.

Yosef bent down again.

"Please tell him that if he and his friends do not get back in their car at once and drive away, I will kill them. Make sure he understands. If they open fire on us or attack us in any other way, they will die."

Maryam hesitated, then, seeing Yosef take something from inside his jacket, she glanced down. He held a heavy automatic pistol in his right hand.

"Where'd that come from?"

"I'll explain later. Now, please tell him what I said."

Maryam translated. She did her best, but her voice still shook. She was badly frightened. Even knowing that Yosef had not come unarmed, she did not feel wholly reassured. It had come home to her that she was, in all likelihood, only moments from death, and she felt unprepared and shaky. Yosef's warning was no more than bravado, and its implausibility caused the words to stick in her throat even as she spoke them.

All three of their attackers shared her estimation of the warning. They laughed together, invisible behind the vast beam of light. It was a good joke, this. The woman was—what? A schoolteacher? And the Jew was ... Well, that was it, he was a Jew.

The man in the black suit, unseen behind the lights of his car, drew back the bolt on his automatic. The others followed suit.

"Now!" hissed Yosef, throwing himself to the ground. Scared enough to do anything he said, Maryam pushed the door wide and rolled out, striking the ground hard with her shoulder, crying out in pain. Half a second later, a hail of bullets tore through the Volkswagen, shattering glass and punching ragged holes through the metal sheeting.

Maryam looked round desperately. She wanted Yosef to tell her what to do next, whether to move or stay, where to go, but he was nowhere to be seen.

It seemed like silence after the barrage of shots, but there was still the steady thrumming of the car's motor, the fall and fall of waves on eroded rock. Yosef's gun gave him one distinct advantage over his attackers: At his insistence, it had been fitted with a high-resolution night-vision scope.

Outside the beam of the headlights, the attackers would be all but blind. Yosef, his eyes carefully protected from the glare, was already in the shadows and circling. He had decided not to shoot out the headlights, even for the advantage that would provide: He and Maryam would need their pursuers' car to get back to Olbia.

All three of the men outside the car were available targets. Yosef was reluctant to kill them all, but he knew he might have no choice: A sustained hail of fire or even a random shot could kill Maryam, and he could not let that happen. Against his better judgement, he had started to care what happened to her.

He took aim at the man in the center and squeezed the trigger gently.

By the time the remaining two attackers had reacted, Yosef was well away from the position he had occupied. There were curses, then bursts of gunfire in the rough direction from which his shot had come.

"Maryam," he shouted. "Tell them again. I will kill them if they do not drop their guns and surrender."

She repeated what he had said, though she had no idea what was going on. This time, there was no laughter in reply.

Yosef scanned his opponents carefully. They were clearly flustered. Their victims did not usually fight back. But they still brandished their weapons. One had a submachine gun, the other a large handgun. The driver remained in the car. Yosef wanted to keep him alive, if possible. He needed someone who might have answers to his questions, someone who could tell him who was behind all this.

The leader of the attackers shouted again.

The killing of his *complice* had disoriented him, but he was in no mood to let himself be beaten by a Jew and a woman.

"He says he'll kill me if you don't give yourself up," shouted Maryam. "If you hand yourself over, he'll let me go."

"Do you want me to do that?" Yosef responded. "Tell me, and I'll do it if it's what you want. Otherwise I'll go on with what I started."

There was no hesitation and no uncertainty in her voice when she answered.

"No," she said. "Do what you have to do."

The attackers opened fire on the Volkswagen again. Maryam crouched down behind the rear wheel, but they were closer now and the bullets penetrated all the way. Only a few feet separated their line of fire from the spot where she huddled in a sweat of terror. She could try to make a run for it, but she knew they'd be ready for that now, knew they'd pick her off in the full glare of the lights before she got two yards.

And then, quite distinct within the cough and splutter of the submachine gun fire, she heard two shots, two seconds between them, no more. It was as if someone had pressed a switch. The submachine gun stuttered once, briefly, then fell silent. There was no more shooting. And in the silence she heard again the humming of the car's engine and the rolling of the loud sea.

19

Yosef crept forward slowly. The car, a large Mercedes, sat in front of him, its engine purring. Three men were dead, but the fourth still sat behind the wheel. Yosef wanted him alive. He had to find a way to make him talk.

He moved closer, keeping the driver in view through his nightscope. The man remained stock-still, as though frozen into immobility by the cold breath that had just passed within feet of him. The engine ran uninterruptedly, its voice lifting and falling gently as the driver's foot played with the accelerator pedal. Yosef came within a yard of the driver's window.

Suddenly, the engine was kicked to a crescendo, and without warning the car leaped forward. It crashed into the Volkswagen, halted momentarily, then, with renewed force, ground forward, carrying the carcass of the smaller car with it. The driver must have thought his only hope of escape must lie in pushing the car and anyone crouching behind it over the cliff.

Caught unawares in the lee of the Volkswagen, Maryam stumbled, tried to pick herself up, and rolled desperately in an attempt to escape being crushed by the car as it pushed toward her. As the cars gathered momentum, she found herself half-rolling, half-stumbling backward, the sharpness of the decline making it impossible to turn and jump clear of the Volkswagen's path.

Behind her, the roar of heavy waves pounding rocks grew in volume. How many yards, how many feet were there between her and the edge? The driver of the Mercedes did not let up. His foot remained pressed down hard on the pedal. Yosef fired, shattering the rear window and the windshield, but the bullet went wide, leaving the driver untouched. In the rear, the shattered window remained in its frame, frosted now, making a second shot impossible.

165

She never knew what saved her. In all probability it was an old root or a knot of sea grass. At one point she raised herself, twisting in an attempt to jump back, but as she did so her foot caught in something unyielding, throwing her sideways. Another roll took her afurther foot or two just as the Volkswagen pushed past, followed by the Mercedes, still picking up speed.

Seconds later, the clanking and crashing sounds that marked the Volkswagen's sideways tumble down the slope disappeared. The sharp hum of the Mercedes' engine lifted through the night air, pure and triumphant as a lark's song. It lasted an eternity of sorts, and then a double crash ended it forever. A moment later the darkness beyond the cliff's edge was lit by flame. And then the waves came, high and ruthless, and the light passed away.

Maryam looked up to see a figure standing over her. Still confused, she flinched and tried to pull away.

"Are you all right?" a voice said. It sounded familiar. The man spoke a language she knew from childhood. *"Inta bi-khayr?"*

She felt his hands on her arms, lifting her, as though the darkness had become animate and taken flesh. He was lifting her and all she could think of was her father's voice, long, long ago, when she had broken her leg and been taken to bed: *"Inta bi-khayr? A indaki alam?"*

"You could have been killed," he said.

She was on her feet now, her breath coming in great, salt-saturated gulps, her legs shaking, her heart flapping about as if on a loose string. She could have been killed over and over,

166

riddled with bullets or crushed by a car or thrown over a cliff onto angry rocks. She tried to speak, but no words came out. She could have been killed.

He held her while she shook. His own legs were scarcely his own. Better than Maryam, he knew how close they had both come. Holding her was as much to comfort himself as to reassure her. They stood like that for a long time while the waves below them moved on the shore unimpeded and a slow moon ached to find a crack in the clouds. The sound of shooting began to fade and Maryam gradually found herself again, as though she had been drifting far away.

More aware of one another now, their embrace became suddenly awkward. They could barely see one another, but that only served to enhance the growing physicality with which they were touching.

Yosef took his arms away and stepped back a couple of paces.

"Will you be all right?"

She nodded. The gesture was almost lost in the darkness. He wanted to touch her cheek with his hand, as though she herself was a lost thing.

"Yes," she said, finding her voice at last. She looked round. "Are they all dead?" she asked, already knowing the answer.

"I think so, yes," he answered. There was no hint of triumph in his voice. He did not gloat. All in all, he would have preferred there to be no killing and he recoiled at the thought of how it had been forced on him.

"What about the bodies?" she asked.

He knew what she meant. No pathologist would miss the bullet wounds. But there was a chance that adding the bodies to the mess below the cliff would delay the inevitable investigation. Had it not been for the Volkswagen, he and Maryam could have walked away from all this with no one the wiser. But the wreckage of the car lay there, immovable, her ownership of it providing ineluctable evidence of her involvement with the killings.

With the help of the nightscope, they found the three bodies. Each had been killed with a clean shot to the head. Maryam said nothing. All that needed saying had been said earlier in the exchange between Yosef and the leader of the would-be killers.

They lugged the bodies to the cliff edge. The salt wind had turned their skin prematurely cold and clammy. Maryam would not touch their hands or wrists, but held them by the ankles with the hems of their long trousers between her fingers and their flesh. Before they pushed them over, Yosef rummaged through their pockets for any papers he could find. He and Maryam could investigate them later for clues to their assailants' identities. The photocopies they had taken from Michele Mannuzzu's study were still in Yosef's inside pocket.

"What do we do now?" Maryam asked when they had finished. She felt tired beyond belief. It had been a long, exhausting day, she had eaten very little, and the events of the past hour or so had taken a heavy toll on her nerves.

"We go back up to the road, then we start walking. There's no other choice. We walk until we find a signpost or a farmhouse. I have money on me—we can pay for food and lodging, and for a car into Olbia in the morning."

"How long before ..." She came to a halt, glancing behind her at the cliff.

Yosef understood what she meant. He shrugged. There was not enough moonlight for Maryam to pick the gesture out of the dark.

"It depends," he said. "On how popular or deserted that spot is. On the farmer who owns this field and how often he comes down here. On whether any fishing boats pass this way close in to the coast. A day or two, I'd guess. Longer with luck. There'll be people looking for them, but they won't know where to look. We've got to get as far away from here as possible before that happens."

"Away? Where to?"

"At the moment, I don't know. Back to Israel perhaps."

She shook her head with vehemence. They were climbing the slope together, in the direction of the road. The sound of crashing waves was growing dull behind their backs.

"You know I can't go back there. And my name is known in any case. If the Italian police are looking for me, they'll find me there."

"You've done nothing," Yosef said. "I killed three of them, the other died while trying to kill you."

"We'd have to prove that."

"They were armed. The guns are down there with them. We have a case. When the time comes, we'll face a court with it. But not yet. We need to know who's behind all this first. Without that, nothing we say will make sense."

"And if we can't find out who's behind it?"

"We'll be given new identities."

She stopped and looked at him, dim beside her on the rough track.

"No," she said. "Stop right there. I want you to understand me. This is my life. I came to Italy to be myself, to get away from a country where all I could be was a shadow: a woman or an Arab or a Christian ... nothing of any value in itself, just another reason for someone to knock me down in the street. So I came here. I married an Italian, an academic from Naples, a man I'd met at conferences from time to time. It lasted three years, but in that time I'd got a new name, a new nationality, and some sort of identity. By the time I left him, I was beginning to be a person in my own right. Not just a daughter or a wife or a Palestinian with aspirations beyond her station, but someone with a career and a future.

"And now you're asking me to give that all up because I've got myself mixed up with you and something bad that happened to your family. I'm sorry for you, and I want to help, but I have my own life to lead."

"How will you do that behind bars?"

"Whatever happened, happened because of you, not me. I was with you as an interpreter, that's all. I'll tell the police that; they'll believe me."

"And the people who are after us?"

"Us?"

He paused. From where they stood, they could see the trees that marked the road, tall and evenly spaced in the middle distance. He listened for the sound of cars, but there was none. He had never felt so alone, never been in such a devouring darkness.

"Yes," he said. "They can't afford to let you go now. They have no way of telling what you know, but that makes no difference. It's as easy to kill two as one. Whoever these people are, whatever it is they want, you're in their way."

20

All stillness. Sometimes she could scarcely breathe in the tightness of the nights, sometimes she came to a dark place where there was only fear and loneliness. Since Michele's death, her singleness had been like a rope tied cruelly round her body, a rope that squeezed the breath from her throat and lungs. It slackened during the daylight hours, but only a little. The company of other people, and the myriad little things she found to do for them, were a space in which to breathe.

But at night in bed, hemmed in on all sides by the gross dark, the knots grew taut once more, and she would lie exhausted yet unable to sleep, tears streaming onto her pillow, wondering how best to die. Or she would awaken from a vile and useless sleep, her thoughts tainted, her mouth sour, her body shaken, to find it waiting for her.

Her sleep had been broken tonight by something familiar yet unexpected. She lay flat on the bed, feeling the cords tighten round her, not knowing what had awakened her.

Suddenly it came again, a shrill burst on the

doorbell. She froze like a trapped animal in the dark. The clock on her bedside table read 1:11. She had not been asleep very long, then. The bell rang again. She pulled herself out of bed reluctantly and drew on a long kimono, one that Michele had given her the previous Christmas, embroidered silk from Kyoto. She had read somewhere that they watched cherry blossoms in the springtime there.

For a moment the silk felt cold against her bare shoulders. There was a knot in her stomach now, as though all the ropes binding her had coalesced there into a matted ball.

Her first thought was that the Israeli couple had returned; perhaps they'd left something important behind. But she had told them she was tired, that she was going straight to bed. Surely they would have the good manners to call back in the morning. That meant it must be the police. Had something been found? Was someone else dead? Had they found and arrested her husband's killers?

The bell rang again. It was obviously someone who knew she was at home. She ran the last stretch, thinking it rude to keep them waiting.

At the door she paused. What if ... The bell sounded again, a long peal tinged with impatience. She put her hand to the knob and opened the door, stepping back slightly as she did so.

"Oh," she said, almost in a whisper, "it's you. I thought ..."

"Can I come in?"

"Come in? Yes, of course, why not? Though it's very late. I was asleep. I was in bed."

"I'm sorry. I didn't mean to disturb you. It's

just that this is important. Don't worry. It won't take long."

She closed the door. In the stillness she heard her heart beat like a tiny wooden drum. She started to turn, with an uneasy smile on her lips. It was the last thing she ever did.

21

In later memory, one thing merged with another until the sequence of events became blurred and it grew hard to disentangle them. They walked for what must have been miles, now in silence, now talking about nothing in particular. The moon glided in and out of clouds, showing them the road ahead and then as suddenly concealing it again. Once she grew agitated, and he quieted her by holding her hand. They walked like that for a long time, as if they had been lovers. It might have been idyllic but for what they had left behind.

The road seemed to wind forever, as if they had entered purgatory and had been condemned to wander there for an unknown period. They were never sure whether it took them alongside the sea or by stages away from it. The wind would change from time to time, sometimes bringing the smell of salt water with it, sometimes the freshness of the mountains.

At last there was a farmhouse, a little set off from the road on a steep hillside among groves of cork oaks. They were not exactly welcome, arriving unannounced in the middle of the night and waking the entire household, but money was brought into the conversation early and before half an hour had passed they were eating what remained of the family's evening meal and being shown to the best beds in the house. Their night's lodging cost almost as much as it might have at the Pitrizza or the Cala di Volpe a little down the coast.

They had, in fact, wound up somewhere along the rugged coastline north of Arzachena and had been walking inland since then, roughly in the direction of a small town called San Michele. On their arrival at the farmhouse, Maryam had explained that they had been taken for a drive by friends, that they had argued with them and become separated, and that they had finally lost their way entirely. This device, clumsy though it was, served perfectly well under the circumstances to explain not only how they had arrived in such an out-of-the-way spot on foot, but why they had no car of their own to return to.

They were not allowed to sleep late, and neither slept much nor well. Yosef's journey reached a terrible end that was no end: Men in black uniforms hustled him and his companions out of their cattle wagon onto the platform of a railway station lit by arc lamps and the headlights of long, black cars; a party of soldiers bearing the word *einzatsgruppe* on their uniforms used machine guns to mow down women and children from another wagon; loud orders were shouted in a language he did not understand, and he shouted back in Hebrew, warning his tormentors of the risk they ran, only to be greeted with shrill laughter; and somewhere there was a steep slope on which he slipped and slithered, knowing all the time that it carried him down to a bottomless pit in which he would fall forever.

Maryam dreamed of scuttling things on the sea bed, things that moved like crabs but looked like men. They had long arms, and tried to drag her down with them. She felt herself drowning in the open sea while all around her little boats were bobbing on the surface, just out of reach. She would wake and remember what had happened, then find herself pulled back against her will into the worst dreams she had ever known. Just once, before she woke finally in daylight, she found herself walking on a long beach in sunshine, holding the hand of a man who was not her father and not her husband. When she looked at last she saw Yosef beside her, and when she turned round the sea was calm.

They were driven to Olbia by the farmer's son, a taciturn man of around thirty who drove recklessly and turned from time to time to examine them as if they were beasts he was taking to market. He would remember them, Yosef thought. Once the police started asking questions about strangers in the area on that date, the quiet man at the wheel would start to talk.

Yosef asked him to leave them outside the town hall. No sooner were they on the pavement than he drove away without a word or a backward glance. But when the time came, he would remember, provided someone offered him a reward for doing so. Yosef had a shrewd idea that there would be a reward and that it would be a big one.

They found a small café on the corner of the next street, its small metal tables and frail chairs spilling chaotically onto the pavement like the furniture on some storm-tossed liner. They went inside and found a table near the back, out of sight, like lovers seeking seclusion. After a brief exchange of words, Yosef got up and left. As he went out the door, he turned and saw Maryam take out a cigarette and place it between her lips; he noticed that her hand shook softly as she did so. She saw him watching and smiled at him briefly.

There was a car with two men in it about twenty yards from the hotel. Yosef guessed that the disappearance of their attackers had already been reported to whoever had sent them. Until they called in, it would have to be assumed that the couple they had been following had given them the slip and that they might be stupid enough to return to the hotel.

The watcher at the rear was less conspicuous, and it took Yosef a little time to be sure of him. The alley running past the back door of the hotel was crisscrossed by telephone wires. A Post and Telecommunications van was parked several yards from the entrance, and a man in the uniform of a telephone engineer squatted on the flat roof of a building diagonally across from the hotel. He was repairing the junction where several strands of wires met, or so it appeared.

Yosef kept out of sight further down the alley and watched. After twenty minutes, he was certain: The engineer had not picked up a tool nor so much as touched a wire. He sat at his post, immobile most of the time, scanning the area leading into the rear of the hotel. Twice during the time Yosef was watching he spoke into a small intercom clipped to his lapel. Once, seeing a man approach the rear of the hotel, he scrutinized him through a pair of small but powerful binoculars.

Yosef slipped away and headed back to the café.

"We have a problem," he said. Quickly, he explained what was wrong. A waiter came, and he ordered a chocolate. Maryam already had a cup of *ristretto* on the table alongside her.

"Why do you need to get into the hotel?" asked Maryam.

"Most of my money's in there, plus my Katzir passport, two fallback passports, identity papers, another gun with ammunition, and some other items that were delivered to me yesterday."

"They may already have been in there," she said.

"Yes, I expect they have. But they won't have taken anything. They won't want to alarm us, and they won't want to take us in the hotel. It's possible they might try if we were together, but if only one of us goes in, they won't risk acting until we meet up again."

"What do you suggest?"

He shrugged. The waiter brought the chocolate, dark and thick and bitter. He swallowed it in three mouthfuls. He knew he ought to tell her to leave, but he found himself unable to do so.

"I've been busy while you were away," she said. From the corner of the table she drew forward one of the copies they had made the night before. Yosef had handed one to her earlier that morning. With it she now had three or four ruled sheets on which she had been making jottings. She took one of these and laid it alongside the copy of Mannuzzu's cryptic notes in front of Yosef.

Yoel L.: qcmmL richieste.
Sig.ra L. med. somma? Piu??   Calc. 10% Y., 10% la sig.ra.
20% ~~qcmmL~~ ocmmL   domanda 25%???
Bianco = W?? possibile. Controll. Moschetta? Procopio? ~~Pozzan???~~
(+ importante controll. incart. AR)
Levin err. per Levi?? ~~Controll. Buzzi.~~ Telef. viceq.
Bottegaio = K?   Controll. orig. Levin. ted.?? Levi medess.
~~MSI~~ Altri nf? Relaz. ted.??

"This is easier than it seems," she said. "Mannuzzu wasn't particularly trying to conceal his meaning, these were just notes to himself for future reference. Most of it is made up of abbreviations of standard Italian words, or of names. Look, here's my version." She showed him her copy.

Yoel Levin: quattrocentomille Lire richieste.
Signora Levin medessima somma? Piu?? Calcola 10% per Yoel, 10% per la signóra.
20% di ~~quattrocentomille Lire~~ ottocentomille Lire.
Domanda 25%
Bianco=Weiss?? possibile. Controlla Moschetta? Procopio? ~~Pozzan???~~

(importante di controllare l'incartamento
AR)

Levin un errore per Levi?? ~~Controlla Buzzi.~~
Telefona il vice-questore. Bottegaio=K?
Controlla se l'origine di Levin è tedescho??
Levi medessimo.

~~Movimento Sociale Italiano.~~ Altri
neofascisti? Relazione tedescha???

Yosef shook his head. "You're forgetting I
don't read a word of Italian."

"I haven't forgotten. This is just to show you
how the original can be expanded. Here's my
Hebrew version."

She handed him another sheet covered in
elegant handwriting. He had always thought of
Arabs as semiliterate and wholly antipathetic
to learning Hebrew. The grace of her hand took
him by surprise.

"My father taught me," she said, catching and
understanding his glance. "He's a schoolteacher.
He loves the Old Testament, so he learned
Hebrew and Aramaic in order to study the texts
in the original. I had more practical uses for
the language."

"Who taught him?" Yosef asked.

"He studied with a rabbi, a Sephardi from
Morocco. His name was Ovadiah Bar Yochai."

Yosef's eyes opened. Bar Yochai had been one
of the most respected Talmudic scholars of his
day, first in Morocco then in Israel. His *hilula*
on the outskirts of Haifa was a regular focus
for pilgrimages. In fact, Yosef's family had visited it three years before on Lag b'Omer. He
had a suspicion that Maryam's father had been
more than just a schoolmaster.

He began to read.

Yoel Levin: four hundred thousand Lire asked for.

Mrs. Levin the same sum? More?? Calculate 10% for Yoel, 10% for his mother.

20% of ~~four hundred thousand Lire~~ eight hundred thousand Lire.

<u>Ask for 25%</u>

Bianco=Weiss?? possible. Check Moschetta? Procopio? ~~Pozzan???~~

(important to check AR file)

Levin a mistake for Levi?? ~~Check Buzzi.~~ Telephone the vice-questore. Shopkeeper=K? Check if Levin's origins are German?? Ditto Levi.

~~Italian Social Movement.~~ Other neo-fascists? German connection???

"It makes some sense," Yosef said. "There's no question that Mannuzzu knew more than he should have done, and certainly more than was safe. It looks as though he was going to arrange for Chaya's abduction as well, then cut himself in on the deal. Presumably he could only do that in two ways. He could put pressure on Aryeh to reveal whatever it was he's supposed to have known and take his percentage as a reward. Or he could threaten to expose what he knew. At the same time, he was obviously aware of the possibility of a mix-up between Levin and Levi, which means he may have ended up trying to perform an elaborate double cross."

"It seems that way. He also seems to have known or guessed that 'Bianco' was a simple code for the German name Weiss."

"That seems odd. Why should someone who wanted to conceal his name do it so clumsily?"

Maryam shrugged. "He may not really have wanted it kept secret," she said, "just off the record. If Aryeh was supposed to know all these other things, then he might be thought able to guess who Bianco was—and perhaps knowing his identity was an essential part of the threat. Weiss may have a reputation for ruthlessness, and knowing Yoel was in his hands may have been enough to intimidate Aryeh into telling what he knew. Except that it was Levi who knew about Weiss, not Aryeh."

Yosef nodded. Maryam reached into her pocket for her pack of cigarettes. There was only one left. She held it out.

"No, thanks," he said.

"You don't smoke?"

"No," he said. "But go ahead."

She hesitated only briefly, then stuck the cigarette in her mouth and crumpled the pack, tossing it onto a heap of stubs in an ashtray.

"This MSI," Yosef said, "what is it?"

Maryam flicked her lighter and held the flame to the cigarette. Again he noticed the slight tremor in her hand.

"The Movimento Sociale Italiano—the official neo-fascist party until recently. It was founded just after the war in 1946. They had their first representatives in parliament by the end of the decade, and they did even better in the general election a few years ago. In 1995 they disbanded and became the National Alliance. Most people think it was a name change but little else."

"I thought fascism was banned in Italy after Mussolini."

"So do a lot of people. All that really happened was that the party faithful regrouped, the same way a lot of ex-Nazis in Germany moved into the Christian Democrat and Liberal parties after the war."

"And Mannuzzu thought they were involved in this business."

"That seems to have been his first assumption, but he obviously thought better of it. 'Other neo-fascists' could mean any number of groups. Every so often the MSI threw off a splinter group like Ordine Nuovo or the Avanguardia Nazionale. If there's a German connection, we could be looking at any number of illegal or semilegal organizations."

"You seem to know a lot about this."

She shook her head. "Not really. I just keep abreast of things. Fascism's still a hot topic in this country. The far right's been winning a lot of votes in recent years. A lot of people are worried."

"But none of this means anything in particular to you?"

"No."

"What about this 'AR file'?"

She spread her hands. "We have to assume that it's a file Mannuzzu kept, either in his office or at home. The initials mean nothing to me."

"What sort of file? A computer file?"

She shook her head. "No, that would be *archivio* or *file*. This is probably a box file or a spring binder."

"Did you notice anything like that on the shelves last night?"

"I don't think so. It may be in his office."

"Well, we'll have to think about how to get our hands on it. And I want to know who these people are he planned to check with. His address book would come in handy."

"The vice-questore may not be so difficult. I'm willing to bet it's De Felice, the man who was put in charge of the murder case."

"What makes you think so?"

"The way he tried to keep things under wraps, as though he was afraid he wouldn't be able to handle it if the case brought up too many issues. I thought he seemed on edge throughout his interviews with you."

"Yes, I remember that. But I don't want to let him know I'm here."

"We'll think of something," she said. She took a last, long pull on the cigarette and stubbed it out absentmindedly. A thin curl of smoke drifted from her nostrils like ectoplasm. She stared at the ashtray for a few moments, then looked up at Yosef.

"Do you speak German?" she asked.

"No, I'm afraid not. Why do you ask?"

"No particular reason. It's just that ..." She paused. "This thing about the shopkeeper—I noticed that Mannuzzu had some German books on his shelves, mainly legal dictionaries and a couple of texts on German commercial law. And then there was that thing about a 'German connection.' I wondered if he might not have guessed something on account of his knowledge of the language."

"What are you getting at?"

"'Bottegaio=K.' That's what the note said. 'Shopkeeper=K.' The interesting thing is that the German for shopkeeper is *Krämer*. And, just

183

like Weiss, Krämer is a proper name. I think Weiss wants to know the whereabouts of someone called Krämer. And I think Levi knows where he is and why Weiss wants him."

22

"We can't go in together," Yosef said. They were in a small church several blocks from the hotel. Yosef felt uneasy and out of place. It was the first time in his life he had ever set foot in a Christian house of worship. The candles and statues and burning incense troubled him. He sensed a preoccupation with the shadowy and the unreal, something he had never experienced in any synagogue or mosque. He felt that God might be anywhere but here. Yet they had come to the church because Maryam felt it was a safe haven, a place where they could whisper together unobserved, somewhere they could plan for the hours and days ahead.

"They'll be watching any couples that go inside with particular attention," he went on. "I don't think they know what's happened yet, and they may be under the illusion that we still know nothing and will be behaving as normal. That means one of us has to go in and get the bits and pieces while the other keeps an eye on the watchers at the front. Obviously, I have to be the one who goes in, since I know what I'm looking for, but I can't come up with a simple method. They may have other people in the lobby watching faces."

Maryam shook her head. They were in a dim

corner of the nave, and her face was half hidden in shadow. But somehow light from a nearby row of candles inhabited her eyes and made her seem incandescent, the only truly living being in a world of dead stone.

"I think I know a way," she said. "It means my going in and your watching, but I think it's safer than the reverse. All I need is a change of clothes and some makeup. And somewhere to change."

"Just clothes and makeup won't be enough."

She raised a finger as though to silence him. "Believe me," she murmured, "this will work."

On a nearby bench, an old woman turned and glared at them. She was dressed from head to foot in black and wore a long lace shawl over her head, a relic of the days when the Spanish had ruled Sardinia. A long rosary hung from her gnarled hand, its black beads worn by years of silent manipulation. With a grunt, she twisted back and resumed her prayers. Almost wordless, so long had they been rehearsed, they rose to the ceiling and were lost among the voices of pigeons.

They got up and walked silently to the door. Old wood worn and blackened by the fingers of generations. Maryam turned and looked back down the nave toward the light burning in the sanctuary. As though of its own volition, her hand made the sign of the cross. She genuflected, conscious of her own unbelief yet in need of what little reassurance the action provided. A prayer of sorts formed in her mind, a prayer for protection for herself and the man by her side. She glanced at him. The followers of her God had persecuted his people for centuries. What sort of protection could her prayers afford?

Coming outside, they walked on, blinded for a little time by the daylight, bright after the gloomy interior of the church. Yosef glanced up from time to time as though checking that his God had returned to the center of the universe. As he walked, he used shopwindows and car mirrors to ensure that they were not being followed.

Their undirected steps took them down to the harbor, where the Civitavecchia ferry was about to leave. The last cars were going aboard and passengers lined the rails, some waving to relatives on the ground. It went through both their minds that they might soon have to depart on the ferry themselves. They could not risk checking into another hotel. Their pursuers would have thought of that already and left photographs or descriptions, along with a promise of money.

Yet they needed a base, somewhere they could talk and rest and eat, a bolthole in the event of danger. A rented apartment was a possibility, but Yosef remained unsure: If he and Maryam could find one, so could their pursuers.

The solution lay a few yards further at a little dockside office. In its dusty window someone had stuck a sign reading *Barca da nolo*—Boat for hire. There was a faded color photograph below this wording, showing a twenty-foot diesel motor yacht. A hand-printed caption listed the boat's features, including a cabin large enough to sleep four and recently installed radar equipment.

The office was little more than a wooden shed,

dilapidated and salt-eaten. Inside, there was a long table and some rickety chairs that seemed to have been taken from a boat that had long ago gone to scrap. Surprisingly, there was someone behind the table, the surface of which was covered in stacks of paper, giving the place at least the semblance of a real office.

The hut's occupant was a grizzled creature of indeterminate age, a former sailor or docker forced into semiretirement here by drink or illness or a crippling accident. He wore an oil-stained cloth cap squashed down over his forehead, even indoors, and greasy overalls that had once been blue. He barely looked up when they came in, and replied to Maryam's question as to whether or not the boat was available by the merest nod.

"We'd like to see it," she said.

"I'm busy," he said.

"So are we. We want a boat this morning, not this afternoon or tomorrow. If you don't want to hire it ..."

"I only take cash," he said. He scrutinized them more closely. Not tourists exactly, but not the sort who usually came for a boat like his. "If you want something fancy, something you can pay for with plastic, you're wasting your time. Go to Porto Cervo or one of those places. They'll fix you up."

"Your boat looks fine to me. We aren't holding any yacht parties. If it's seaworthy, we'll take it."

The old man grunted. They didn't look as if they could tell a seaworthy boat from a tin of sardines, but if they had money, what did that matter? And the man had the air of somebody who knew what was what. Why they wanted the boat was none of his business. That was the sort of question you didn't ask round here, not if you wanted to stay alive. Drugs were the most likely thing. That meant only one thing to him: His customers would pay hard cash on the nail.

He took them to a mooring at the far end of the harbor. The *Eleonora d'Arborea* was a working boat that had been given a few coats of paint and fixed up to serve as a cheap day cruiser for people who couldn't pay the prices a bit further up the coast. They went onboard, and Yosef checked it over. Boats weren't his natural habitat, but he'd spent time with naval commando squads working along the Lebanese coast and he'd picked up more than a little seamanship from them in return for his own land-based skills. He wouldn't want to sail the Atlantic in it, but the little craft would serve for their present purpose and, if necessary, would take him across to the mainland. He was sure he could handle the boat single-handedly provided weather conditions remained favorable.

They left a deposit using what was left of the money Yosef had been carrying the night before and agreed to return with enough cash to hire the boat for the week. The hotel was still out of bounds, so Maryam found a branch of the Credito Italiano and drew out as much as she could without exciting curiosity or asking for authorization from Cagliari. It was just enough to cover the hire, which was made under one of Yosef's false names. The old sailor did not even ask for identification.

Back on the boat, Maryam disappeared belowdecks while Yosef busied himself checking the *Eleonora d'Arborea*'s equipment and making a mental note of the various items he might need to buy if he did decide to take her to sea. It would be easy enough to find someone to run it back again—if not a local, then somebody sent down for the purpose by Mossad.

When Maryam reappeared, he barely recognized her. She wore a platinum blond wig, high heels, black mesh stockings, a very short skirt, and a blouse that might have been and might not have been see-through. The funny thing was, she didn't look ridiculous. Confronted by such an apparition, Yosef's father would have averted his eyes and muttered invocations beneath his breath. Yosef did not find it so easy to look away. He blushed, every last ounce of his self-confidence torn away from him.

"Go on," Maryam prompted him, "say what you're thinking."

"I ..." He stumbled to a halt, as if mesmerized by the glossy lipstick and the multicolored makeup she had applied to her eyelids. "You look like a prostitute," he finally said.

She smiled and pirouetted. "Good," she said. "That's exactly what I hoped you'd say. Now, hurry up and find me a taxi." She giggled, unable to remain serious in spite of herself. "I'm charging by the hour."

23

The taxi drew up outside the hotel. Yosef had already got out at an intersection further down the street and was in place to watch Maryam slip inside.

189

She had noticed the prostitutes the day before while waiting in the lobby for Yosef to sleep off his tiredness. At least three had come in during the time she was there and gone straight up to rooms on other floors. Staff on duty at reception had given them no more than a cursory glance. They were as much a part of the hotel's daily comings and goings as the bellboys and chambermaids.

She guessed that Olbia, like one or two other cities in Sardinia, had experienced a growth in prostitution during the late eighties. In the past, and no doubt still, there had been the traditional *case di tolleranza* for the benefit of local men. But with the development of the nearby Costa Smeralda and the steady influx of tourists and second-home owners, women from several countries had started coming here in search of some of the loose cash that was rattling around the resorts. Round here, loose change could be as good as a small win on the lottery. The Costa liked to keep its act clean on the surface, so a lot of the sleaze ended up here, in the hotels and bars of what was already one of the island's brasher towns.

The man at reception gave her the once-over and bent his head back to the desk. A new girl on the game was nothing to gape at. In any case, he would know perfectly well that his bosses had already been handed regular sums to make sure their staff looked the other way. One or two people in the lobby cast glances in her direction, some of the men with more than passing interest, but no one really saw her. She had joined an invisible tribe, a tribe that inhabited the real world yet connected with it only in secret and behind shadows.

She reached the third floor, where their rooms were located. The hotel had recently introduced plastic cards to allow guests to carry their keys with them at all times. She went to her own room first and took a few items she could not do without; they went into the enormous handbag she had bought at the same time as the clothes.

She opened her door and looked out. The corridor was empty. Taking a deep breath, she slipped out, closing the door behind her soundlessly. Yosef's room was to her left, five or six doors further down. She started toward it, listening for the first sound of someone coming.

Muffled in the distance, she could hear the hum of a vacuum cleaner. A door slammed shut, followed by the rumbling of a cart's wheels. An elevator traveled between two floors, then stopped. Someone knocked on a door and a voice answered dully from inside. The morning round of room cleaning was still underway. For some reason, it reminded Maryam of her honeymoon, of late mornings in bed, of discreet knocks and footsteps moving away again, of sunlight lost among bleached sheets. She reached Yosef's room and slipped inside.

It took a few moments for her eyes to adjust to the dimness. Yosef must have closed the curtains before leaving the previous evening. Or perhaps he had closed them when he took his morning sleep and they had remained that way since then. She found the light switch and pressed it. Only the bedside lights came on.

She thought she screamed, though in reality

her lips remained closed and the sound was in her head. Later, she realized that her silence probably saved her life.

The body moved slightly, not of its own volition, but because the rope on which it was suspended kept trying to recover some pristine straightness. It kept twisting, now left, now right, a few millimeters each time, just enough to produce the tiny electric motion. They had tied one end of the rope to a ring in the ceiling that had originally been used to hold the heavy central lamp. The other end was knotted hard round the corpse's ankles, trussing it in midair like a carcass in an abattoir. Someone walked across the floor above and the boards transmitted further motion to the rope, sending the body into another partial twist.

It was a very white corpse, like paper or milk. Maryam stared at it while minute after minute passed, unable to tear her eyes away, as though she too had been caught by the ankles and tied. It was a woman's body, the breasts curiously distorted by hanging upside down, the long hair pooled on the carpet as though spilled there. The wrists, like the ankles, had been tied together then split open in two great gashes. They had drained her of blood, drained her until she was white. Two large buckets stood by the bed. Both were empty, but they were stained a dirty brown color.

Seeing her from this angle, Maryam did not recognize her at first. It could have been anyone. The thought passed through her mind that Yosef had been responsible, that he had brought the woman here and tortured her to death in his search for information. And then she noticed the rings on the left hand and looked more closely. It was Tina Mannuzzu, her pretty face dimmed and closed.

The recognition stung Maryam into life. She felt hot and on the verge of throwing up. The room seemed to spin round her. Gasping, she made for the bathroom, keeping close to the walls, as far from the dangling body as possible.

She leaned against the bathroom door until her head cleared and the spinning sensation slowed down. The nausea was still there, but under control. She still felt hot, as though her temperature had suddenly risen to dangerous levels. Stepping to the washbasin, she made the mistake of looking into the bath.

It was not a lot of blood, but it was enough to animate a woman's body. It lay in a congealing pool on the bottom of the bath. What most horrified Maryam was the sense of tidiness, the care with which the blood had been poured, leaving the sides and edges of the bath immaculate.

She vomited into the sink, thinking, as she did so, that it was a good thing she hadn't eaten much the day before. The absurd thought was something to cling to, as though it made sense of the horror surrounding her.

Her stomach emptied itself at last. Gasping, she ran water into the sink, snatching handfuls from the tap to splash on her face and neck.

At that moment, someone knocked loudly on the outer door.

24

The chambermaid had already inserted her pass key in the lock and was about to come in when

Maryam got to the door. She grabbed it and held it firmly so that it did not open more than a few inches.

"*Chiedo scusa*," said the woman. "I'd like to do your room up now, if you don't mind."

Maryam shook her head. She tried to look ill and to conceal as much of herself as possible behind the door.

"I'm sorry," she mumbled, "but I'm not feeling very well." It was not a lie. She could feel her stomach slipping and sliding inside, her heart walloping blindly against her chest. "Can you come back later? Or just leave the room until tomorrow?"

The maid gave her a disdainful glance. "I'm not supposed to do that. They're very strict here. Every room has to have a daily bed change and clean-out."

"Well, that's too bad. I have a migraine, and I've just been sick. I want to spend the day in bed."

As if seeing Maryam for the first time, the chambermaid's manner changed. She pushed forward slightly, trying to see round the door. Maryam had not had time to switch off the lights. The corpse was still in full view.

"Here, are you a guest or just here on business?"

"A guest."

"You're not dressed like one."

"It's none of your concern how I dress. Or do you want me to mention your nosiness to the management? They get paid well enough to leave guests alone."

The maid shrugged and backed away. No

point in getting herself in hot water over a *puttana*.

"Next time," she said, backing off, "why not remember to put out a *Non Disturbare* sign? That's what they're for."

"Thanks. I'll do that now."

Maryam closed the door hurriedly. Her stomach was still churning. Moments later, she threw up on the floor, a sparse, thin vomit that burned her throat but left her unrelieved.

There was a "Do Not Disturb" sign on one of the bedside tables. She opened the door again and hung it over the knob outside. How long it would keep intruders out was anybody's guess.

Yosef would be getting worried by now. She did not want him taking risks in order to find out what had happened to her. The sooner she got back to him, the better. But first, she had to get the items he had asked her to find: There might not be a second chance to get into the room. Steeling herself to ignore the body swinging from the ceiling—she could not bring herself even to think of cutting it down—she looked in the places Yosef had mentioned. Everything was where he had said it would be, even the cash.

Opening the door a few inches, she glanced out nervously. The door of the room diagonally opposite was partly open, and she could hear the sound of a vacuum cleaner coming from inside. The corridor was still deserted. Slipping out, she closed the door firmly, leaving the *Non Disturbare* sign where it was.

Yosef did his best to suppress his feelings when Maryam strode up to him, taking him by the

195

arm in a direction away from the hotel, but the signs of relief on his face were unmistakable. He kissed her lightly on the cheek, but he wanted to do more than that, to hold her, to reassure himself that she was safe. And then, pulling back, he saw that, beneath the makeup, something was wrong. She had started to cry, and he drew her aside, torn between his wanting to comfort her and the need to avoid a public scene.

There was a narrow alleyway a few yards away. He took her there, conscious of one or two people staring at them, drawing their own conclusions. As long as no one tried to interfere, he couldn't care less what they thought.

In the semiprivacy of the alley, she broke down completely, clinging to him without restraint or embarrassment, her fear and horror combining in a single cry of pain. He held her silently, not knowing what had brought her to this state, almost ashamed that it gave him pleasure to have her so close and in such need of him. He told himself that it meant nothing, that anyone would have done the same thing, that when the tears passed she would pull away and regain her customary aloofness.

But in that very thought lay the germ of something else, the knowledge that he was fooling himself, or trying to. The uncomfortable fact was that he loved her, and that he could not bear it if she returned to herself and dried her eyes and said, "I can manage quite well without you, thanks."

He held her more tightly, knowing this, and as though by instinct she pressed in against him more closely. He closed his eyes and the sound of traffic from the street faded and was almost gone. The pluck of her sobbing and the irregular coming and going of her breath were all he could hear.

It was like a long sleep, this embrace that was not quite an embrace, this awkward, almost paternal holding and comforting of the woman he had not wanted to love, but whom he did love in spite of everything. There was room in it to dream, and space enough to let a lifetime's thoughts disentangle themselves. He held her unself-consciously in the end, as though the dreamwork was done, and waited for them both to waken, sleepers out of night.

She came round slowly, her dreadful, half-comic makeup smeared and ruined, her eyes swollen. She looked at him, then looked a second time, sensing what she was almost afraid to sense. His heart gave a crippled leap, as full of pain as joy seeing the recognition in her eyes, that unrehearsed knowing, that almost gloating certainty. They loved each other then, though the impossibility of it was uppermost in both their minds. He kissed her all the same, and he was gentle in doing it; he let his lips graze hers, taking the bright, greasy lipstick from the surface as a restorer lifts varnish from an old canvas and gives it life again. Her lips moved against his, a mere fluttering, and he sensed her tongue laid behind them, coiled like a spring of unimaginable strength, full of inexpressible sadness.

He touched her cheek with his bare hand, smearing tears and mascara across the vaulted curve of her cheekbone, as if in apology for the touch of his lips on hers and the wordless, deaf appeal in his eyes, the crazed look that told her he loved her while he struggled to hide it from them both. She looked up at him again and it all poured out, the body swinging from a chiseled hook, the blood settling in the bottom of a low bath, and the horror that she was still in there, that she could not get out, that doors had closed all round her, that she was there forever with the body and the blood and the knock on the door.

"It's all right," he said gently, still holding her. "It's over now, you're here with me, you're all right."

And over and over again, words to soothe and comfort, all the time wanting to say "I love you," and knowing he could not, not now, perhaps never.

She calmed down at last and he helped her dry her face.

"I look a mess," she said.

"I think I prefer you like this," he answered, blushing at the presumption in the words. But she blushed, too, just a little, and he felt secretly pleased he had said it after all.

"I'll have to redo it all the same," she said. She took a small mirror and items of makeup from her bag. He bent down and helped himself to things he needed. They were returning to normal now, in a moment their intimacy would be a thing of the past.

A boy passed by, looking in at them, and whistled. Yosef glared at him, and he ran away, laughing.

"What are we going to do?" she asked. They were fully awake now, he thought, the long sleep was over.

"We have to get her body out of my room.

You're sure it was her, that it was Mrs. Mannuzzu?"

She nodded. There had been no mistake.

"If the police find her there ..." He paused, not needing to expand. "The 'Do not Disturb' sign won't keep the staff out forever. And our friends outside may get impatient and decide to phone the police themselves."

He glanced at his watch. It was nearly noon.

"I'll have to get it over with," he said.

"Yes," she answered bleakly, not having the right words to say. He was running an appalling risk, she understood that. Was it really possible that they loved one another, she asked herself, that this strange man had become more than a passer-by for her?

"How will you get in?" she asked. "They're still watching. I saw them when I left."

"I know a way," he said, and fell silent. There was a way, a quick way, but he had not wanted to use it. It meant killing a man. But he had no choice now, they'd taken that from him, just as they'd taken Tina Mannuzzu's life, casually, with no real thought.

He stepped to the opening of the alleyway and looked out. The street was unchanged, they'd been forgotten. Her face was fixed now, but she had lost confidence in her role. Going to the hotel had been easy, there had been a purpose in it. Now she had to play the same part while just waiting. And someone loved her now, that made it different. He wanted her to go back to the café, to wait for him there.

"If anything happens to me, I want you to get Mannuzzu's note to Mossad, that and anything else we know." He gave her a name and a number to ring. "Wait for me in the café," he said, all emotion suppressed. "I won't be long."

He was almost gone when she stopped him.

"Yosef," she said, barely whispering his name. She stepped up to him and kissed him, once on the lips, while her fingers brushed his cheek.

"Take care," she said.

Yosef knew he would have to move quickly. Apart from the fact that the chambermaid could return at any moment and insist on gaining entry, there was the problem of communications between the watcher at the rear and the team at the front. Yosef needed to put the man at the back out of action, but as soon as he failed to make his regular call-in, his colleagues at the front would come to check. If he timed it well, that gave him fifteen minutes at the outside.

The man Yosef had seen masquerading as an engineer had been replaced by a second. Yosef surveyed the alley carefully, confirming that the watcher on the roof was the only one posted at the rear. Fortunately, it was lunchtime and the alley was quieter than it had been.

There was a flat roof about fifty feet down from the one on which the engineer kept his vigil. It bristled with television antennas and satellite dishes, and in one corner a large water tank stood against the wall like a circular buttress.

Jutting out from the side of the building next door was a rusted fire escape. The escape was separated from the edge of the flat roof by a gap of about four feet. The jump would have been easy if he could have done it from above, but the only reasonable point of takeoff dictated an upward trajectory of about fifteen degrees.

He climbed quietly to the spot he had chosen and waited until a couple of young men in shiny suits passed by underneath. The watcher had his eyes fixed on the hotel. Getting on to the rail of the fire escape and balancing for the jump was difficult, but the jump itself was one of the hardest he had ever made. A few inches more, or a sharper angle of ascent, and he would not have made it. As it was, he had to scramble for a grip on the edge and pull himself bodily up the side of the building.

He remained there without moving until he was sure the watcher had heard nothing. Bending, he removed his shoes and carried them the short distance to the water tank. Sure of his cover now, he settled down to observe the fake engineer. Twice the man raised and lowered his glasses. He was vigilant in a quiet, untaxed way that suggested he had received proper training. Yosef thought of the men he had killed the night before. They had made mistakes, but not too many. He was sure that they, too, had been trained by people who knew what they were doing.

Suddenly, the engineer lifted his lapel and spoke into the little mouthpiece. This was the moment Yosef had been waiting for. The gap between calls was the maximum time available to him in which to carry out all he had to, here and in the hotel. He reached into a pocket and took out a large metal catapult. It looked like a larger version of a child's toy, but it was not a toy: In the right hands, it could serve as a weapon every bit as deadly as a gun. A gun would have been more certain, but Yosef knew that, even with a silencer, a shot could give him away.

The watcher lowered his lapel and returned to his surveillance of the alleyway. Yosef placed a heavy metal pellet in the pouch of the catapult and raised it, aiming through the fork at a spot on the side of his target's head. He held his hand perfectly still, feeling the strain through his wrist as the powerful elastic came back. It took great skill and endless hours of practice to fire one of these well, but the hard work paid off in terms of silence and safety. With a snap, he released the pellet, and half a second later the watcher fell sideways in a heap.

Wearing his shoes again, Yosef hurried to cover his traces. A long jump took him to the roof from which the watcher had been spying. Yosef bent and checked for a pulse; there was none. He lifted the body and bent it into a posture that mimicked sleep. Any casual passer-by would decide that the man was dozing on the job.

The engineer's ladder took Yosef back down to ground level. He checked quickly for signs of someone paying him undue attention, decided that no one was, and headed for the back door of the President.

The door led straight into the kitchen. Yosef had timed things well. It was the lunch hour, and the kitchen was buzzing with activity. Everywhere cooks and waiters were running, cooking, bawling orders, snatching dishes, cutting bread, slicing vegetables, stirring pasta, heating sauces, boiling water, cleaning, rinsing, wiping, bellowing, skipping expertly round each other. Nobody had time to spare to scrutinize a new face, much less to question what he was doing there at all.

He went through like someone who knew what he was doing and found himself in the hotel restaurant. Within seconds, he had transformed himself into a guest, smiling at a friend at a table next to the wall, shaking his head and shrugging, then making for the door that led to the toilets. As he expected, it also led to the lobby, since the toilets served both the restaurant and the other public rooms.

He was at the door of his room half a minute later. The key card slipped into its slot without a murmur, and the door swung open.

Tina Mannuzzu was where Maryam had said, still white, still naked, still dead. Like Aryeh's and Chaya's deaths, this one too had been rigged for the purposes of terror and contemplation. Yosef had no time to stand and stare and think. With the door firmly bolted, he found a chair and cut her down. It was not a long drop, and she fell almost soundlessly in a heap on the floor.

He found the light fitting and replaced it. The buckets he left in the middle of the floor. He could feel the minutes ticking away. Any moment now, the watchers at the front would be expecting their third man to call in, and when he did not they would start to move.

The bath was a real problem. He could not afford to leave the blood, but it had coagulated and even caked in places. It would not be a simple matter of just flushing it down the drain. Instead, he scooped it up, using a fruit bowl from the bedroom, and threw it into the toilet. When he had scraped out as much as he could, he flushed the cistern. He ran hot water into the bath, poured in copious amounts of shampoo, and scrubbed hard with a towel. When he had finished, he knew there was still more than enough blood left in the bath to hang a man, but he hoped the chambermaid, already pressed for time, would not give it more than a cursory glance.

Leaving Tina's body and the blood-soaked towel out of the line of sight from the open door, he crossed the corridor and knocked on the door opposite. No one answered. He knocked hard a second time. Again no answer.

Opening the door was no problem. It didn't matter that a police investigation would find the lock forced: This was meant to look like a crime anyway.

Returning to his own room, he threw the towel over his shoulder, then picked up Tina Mannuzzu by the armpits. They were cold and smooth to the touch, as though freshly shaven not long before her death.

With time only for a quick glance into the corridor to make certain that no one was coming, he dragged her across and directly into the next room. He left her on the freshly-made bed and threw the towel into the bathroom. It took another twenty seconds to fetch the buckets and leave them near the body.

He closed both doors and started for the elevator. At that moment, sharp above the background hum of traffic from the street, he heard the wailing of police sirens. They were heading in his direction.

25

Half a dozen policemen were entering the lobby as Yosef reached it. He caught sight of the two watchers from the front at the same moment. They were walking alongside a policeman, talking to him as though explaining something. Yosef took note of the fact for future reference. He stayed behind a pillar until they had passed, then slipped out onto the street. No one called after him.

He rejoined Maryam at the café. The relief on her face when she saw him come through the door was so transparent that he felt he wanted nothing more than to stay here with her for the rest of his life. He wondered if Tina Mannuzzu had loved Michele this much, or been loved by him, but the thought of her snatched away his joy and he thrust it from him. It was not easy to come to terms with what had happened to him. Love had never played a serious role in his life, and he had no skill with it. Just a little thing, a look or a word, was suddenly enough to throw him into the deepest confusion.

He told Maryam how things had gone and they left the café shortly afterward. At the boat, she changed back into her everyday clothes. Yosef was tempted to cast off and head for the mainland, but one thing held him back: the file marked "AR" and the thought of what it might contain.

If it was at Mannuzzu's house, this might be Yosef's last chance to get his hands on it. The police would take some time to identify Tina's body, unless someone reported her missing. If, on the other hand, it was at the office, getting hold of it could prove time-consuming, and Yosef knew that too much of a delay at this point could be fatal.

He decided to try the house and if he drew a blank there, he would abandon the file and leave Sardinia directly. Mossad could send someone else to break into the office. They probably kept a list of local criminals in the desk drawer the way other people have the names of plumbers and electricians.

He waited for her on the flying bridge, watching the movement of boats in and out of the harbor and a plane headed east, high up, slipping into a bank of low cloud. Some of the time, he thought about the file and how to get it, but mostly he thought about Maryam.

She appeared suddenly in the cabin doorway and called his name softly. He turned and his heart, which he had been trying to harden against this moment, softened at the sight of her. She was not what he had expected, not what he had been promised.

That he would marry and have children one day had always been part of his deal with the small world to which he belonged. It was just another one of those things that made life bearable. God and His laws set the world in order and all man had to do was to love God and observe His laws. Love was dangerous. Love could subvert everything, cause a man to leave his parents or his wife, tempt a woman to stray from home, weaken the bonds holding the very fabric of society together.

He realized that it was love's unpredictability that made it so threatening. His world was one where everything possible was done to reduce the stress of life in a universe governed by chance. There was a right way for doing everything: how to dress, how to eat, what to eat, how to transact business, whom to marry. He had expected marriage to someone carefully chosen by his family, someone attractive, intelligent, and good-hearted, someone who would be his companion and a mother to his children.

But not this. This took your breath away.

She came up to the bridge and stood beside him, much smaller than he was, her head barely reaching to his chest. Without the gaudy clothes and the heavy makeup, he felt he was seeing her for the first time.

He looked at her in the full light that was billowing across the open water. She was like a dream, he thought, the sort you can't find in sleep, however hard you try.

"Tell me about your husband," he said. It was not what he had meant to say, but the words had come out as though of their own accord.

She shook her long hair pennantlike into the wind, squinting a little against the light.

"What about him?" she asked.

"You told me how you met him, and that you left him a couple of years ago. Why was that?"

She looked down at the water for a long time before answering. Her eyes were focused on the waves as they rode in from the deep sea beyond the harbor, but her mind was elsewhere. This was all happening too quickly, she thought.

She hardly knew this man, and much of what she knew she did not like.

She was trying not to be simplistic. It wasn't hard to see that he was everything she had been brought up to hate: an Israeli, a Jew, even— for God's sake—a hard-liner, a West Bank settler. So she tried to ignore all that, to put it aside as prejudice. And still he disturbed her. She had seen him kill, had listened to him describe other killings he had carried out, and she knew there would be many others about which he would say nothing. If there were killings, she thought, what else might there be in his past? Beatings, assassinations, torture, rape?

"He started beating me," she said, as though prompted by her thoughts. "A little at first. A few slaps when we quarreled. We would make up afterward. He would cry and say it was all right, that it would never happen again. We put it down to nerves, to pressure at work, to the beatings he'd had from his father when he was a child. But it happened again, and soon it became regular, and I stopped believing his promises."

"Was he drunk when he ... did this?" There was something in Yosef's voice. She did not know exactly what, but it both frightened and reassured her. Rage, she thought, but not directed at her. She shook her head. A motorboat passed carrying a plume of white water in its wake. It turned and headed seaward.

"No," she said. "He didn't drink much. Always, whenever he beat me, he was cold sober. He never shouted, he never swore. When he beat me, it was always a silent business. But something changed in him all the same. He accused me of all sorts of things, though none of them were true. Of wanting other men, even of sleeping with them. I told him he was the only man I loved, but it didn't matter. I tried to run away twice, to friends, but both times he found me and brought me back."

"What about the police? Didn't you go to them?"

She nodded. "Of course. In the end I had to. But they didn't do much. I could see they didn't take it seriously. Sardinia's not a very emancipated place. Men are supposed to keep an eye on their women, make sure they don't stray. Knocking your wife around isn't that unusual. It's even expected, so long as it doesn't get out of hand. I realized I'd exchanged one male-dominated society for another."

A sentence came to her from the opening chapter of Deledda's masterpiece, about the four daughters of don Zame: *soppratutto, non dovevano sollevar gli occhi agli uomini, né permettersi di pensare ad uno che non fosse destinato per loro sposo.* "Above all, they were not to raise their eyes in the presence of men, nor to allow themselves to think of anyone whom they were not destined to marry." Not much had changed here in almost a century, she thought despairingly.

"I'm sorry," he said as though apologizing for himself. What for, she wondered? Because he was a man? Because he too belonged to a male-dominated culture?

"What happened in the end? Did you leave him?"

She shook her head. What horrified her most about her own narrative was its banality, as though it were impossible to escape the mute, endlessly repeating misery that everyone else endured.

"I planned to get away, the way wives always do. But ... He met someone else, a student from Naples." And that was banal, too, she thought. Tawdry, cheap, predictable. What must he think of me? she wondered.

"He went back to join his family. The girl is the daughter of friends of theirs. They're living together now, but he has hopes of an annulment. If he gets it, they'll marry. Then he'll start beating her."

He did not say anything. She looked at him and, to her surprise, she found herself shaking. He did not touch her. Slowly, the shaking passed. She looked at him again. There had been an expression in his eyes. She had not been mistaken, it was still there. Not tenderness exactly, something stronger than that. She understood. Whatever else he might do, Yosef Abuhatseira would never lift his hand to her in anger.

He was thinking about Tina Mannuzzu. Had they beaten her before killing her? Raped her, perhaps? He wanted to find them and make them suffer, whoever they were. And he wondered if that too was not part of the same sickness.

"I have to go," he said. "Do you mind staying here to keep an eye on things?"

"It's all right," she said. "I'm feeling a lot better now. Let me come with you."

"You don't even know where I'm going."

She smiled. "Of course I do. You want to look for the 'AR' file at Mannuzzu's house. If it's there you won't find it without me. Remember, I'm the one who speaks Italian."

"It could be dangerous."

"Tell me something I don't know."

26

From outside, all was quiet. A few children, not long back from school, rode bicycles up and down the street. Oblivious of them, an old man pushed a cart piled high with fruit, trudging despondently with the air of one who only wants to get each day over, until there is no more cart to push and no more fruit to sell. The children watched him pass, a little in awe of his grizzled beard and desolate eyes, but the moment he had his back to them, they trailed along behind him, half mocking, half terrified. From time to time, he called aloud, hawking his produce, and a few housewives came out to pick over the cart and buy fruit for the evening meal.

They had hired a car, and Yosef told Maryam to drive past several times before halting on a gentle slope a little down from the house. It was quiet, but not too quiet. If unfriendly eyes were observing the Mannuzzus' house, they were well hidden. There were few hiding places on the other side of the street, and the houses opposite were not well positioned to serve as vantage points.

They broke in through a back window, at a spot where they could not be overlooked. Yosef had been confident that, whatever alarm system was in use, Tina's killers would not have reset it before leaving. That would have been the last thing on their minds.

Nothing seemed out of place at first. So far,

the house bore no visible signs of break-in or violence. And yet they both knew Tina Mannuzzu had been taken from here and dragged to her death not many hours before. The kitchen had been recently cleaned, just as she would have left it before retiring. Her killers had not come immediately then. But she must have let them in. There were no visible signs of a forced entry back or front. That suggested that she had known them or, at least, thought she had reason to trust them.

The stillness in the house was almost hypnotic. Yosef felt as though the air itself resisted his passage through it, as though the dead couple who had lived here stood, one on either side, holding him back.

He went directly to the study, and here, suddenly, all thought of stillness vanished. The room had been turned upside down: papers, files, books, and folders sifted and thrown in heaps; drawers pulled from desks and cabinets and their contents turned out onto the floor; pictures ripped from the wall as though someone had been looking for a safe.

The living room was much the same, though the damage was less extensive. They found the safe upstairs in the main bedroom, the door open, the interior swept clean. Cash and bonds lay strewn across the floor. Someone had wanted to make it clear that this had not been a common burglary.

They went downstairs again. Had the intruders been after the same thing as themselves, Michele Mannuzzu's "AR" file? Or had there been something else, something the intruders alone knew about? There was no way they could ever know, nor could they easily discover if the file they had come to look for was already gone or still hidden somewhere.

"This is useless," said Yosef. "We don't even know what it is exactly we're looking for."

"There's always Mannuzzu's office."

"It won't be easy getting in there."

"All the same, we could try. I think we should tell Sanguinetti what's happened and ask him to reconsider whether he knows anything or not. It depends on how much he really does know. My guess is not too much. Which means he'll be frightened. That means he may cooperate."

"It's a long shot."

"It's still worth a try."

She found a telephone and rang the office number. A secretary answered.

"I'd like to speak to Signor Sanguinetti, please."

There was a short pause.

"I'm afraid Signor Sanguinetti hasn't come in to work today." The secretary sounded worried.

"Can you get him at home?"

"He isn't there. There's no answer. It's most unlike him. And today of all days."

"I'm sorry?"

"We had a break-in last night. They broke into his office and Mr. Mannuzzu's. I can't even start to tidy up until he gets here. You'll have to call back tomorrow. But I doubt very much if he'll be able to speak to you then. Maybe next week, when all this has died down. Who shall I say was calling?"

"That's all right. He doesn't know me."

Maryam put the phone down and explained to Yosef what had happened.

"They're cleaning up," he said. "Tidying the mess that got made when someone confused Levin for Levi. Somebody has given orders that no traces are to be left, no trails for the police or anyone else to follow."

"Where does that leave us?"

"We're unfinished business. If we stay in Sardinia, they'll get to us sooner or later."

It had come to that, then, she thought. She would have to make a decision sooner than she had feared.

"I can go back to Cagliari," she said. She had sat in an armchair, facing him. All around her, books lay in disarray, hauled down from shelves next to the fireplace. Idly, she started to tidy them, putting them in small heaps.

He shook his head. "Not now. They know who you are. You wouldn't survive a week. I'm sorry, but that's how things are. I'm willing to take the blame for getting you involved. But that won't help."

She knew he was right, though she found it hard to admit it. Saying so would mean the end of the life she had started to construct for herself here. She had friends, colleagues, students to teach, a dog and two cats that were currently lodged with her neighbors. In Cagliari she had a job, a career structure (however rickety), an *equo canone* flat near the town center, and hopes. Elsewhere, nothing.

For some reason, it came to her that this was how so many Jews had been trapped in Germany and the rest of Eastern Europe by the rise of fascism. They had seen it coming, they had sensed the threat, but each had feared to give up something: a job, a home, a table at a favorite restaurant. The instinct that prompted her to stay where she was in spite of the danger was the same one that had persuaded so many to linger just a bit too long, the same one that had caused her parents and many of their friends to remain in Palestine after it became Israel. They had not been rounded up or put in camps or gassed, but they had paid a price all the same. She realized that reason could not provide a solution to her dilemma.

"I'll think about it," she said. "Give me time."

"Time is what we don't have. These people aren't amateurs. They won't give us the luxury of thinking it through."

She lifted another heap of books and set them on top of a pile she had straightened earlier. Was it even worth the effort of running? she asked herself.

"We'd better go," Yosef said. "The police could be here any minute. Once they identify Tina's body ..."

Maryam got to her feet. She felt tired, so tired that even the thought of rest did not comfort her.

Just as she got to the living room door, she stopped.

"Yosef ... Can you remember? When we were talking with Tina last night ... I can't remember whether I translated or not. We were talking about what Michele did on that last day. She said something about his planning to drive to Oliena. But I'm sure she said she was worried about it, that he couldn't drive very well or ..." She halted, the memory coming at last. "No, that wasn't it. 'Michele wasn't mechanically minded. I don't think he even knew where the engine was.' That's what she said."

"Yes, I remember. You must have translated."

"But ..." She took his hand and drew him back into the room. "Look," she said, pointing to the heap of books she had been arranging. Yosef looked down.

They were not books, properly speaking, at all, but tightly packed loose-leaf folders, the sort used for a series of weekly magazines that collect into an encyclopedia. But these had been published just as they were, in a series. They were manuals for a range of motor cars: Saab 9000, Volvo 480, Lotus Elan, Rover 200 Cabriolet, Nissan 300ZX, Subaru SVX, and others such as Bugattis, Lamborghinis, Maseratis, Ferraris, cars Michele Mannuzzu could only have dreamed of owning.

These were not manuals designed for wanna-be owners, full of lush photographs and well-honed prose. They had been written for people who liked to get their hands dirty. There were no glamorous shots of full-leather trim or sleekly styled spoilers, just line drawings of engine parts with numbered instructions on how to take components apart, clean or repair them, and put them back together again. Not the sort of thing you might expect to find on the shelves of someone who drove a Fiat and did not even know where the engine was.

Yosef picked up a Nissan manual and flipped through it. Only the front and rear pages belonged to the original manual. The rest were loose-leaf sheets inserted by Mannuzzu himself. Typewritten pages, photocopies, photographs in color and black and white, newspaper cuttings pasted to larger sheets, handwritten notes.

He handed the file to Maryam.

"What do you make of this?"

She leafed slowly through the sheets, then closed the file.

"At a guess, I'd say this provides us with the lowdown on goings-on within the Communist Party in Sassari province. Let's see one of the others."

Yosef picked up a file at random. It was labeled "Jaguar XJ6." He handed it to Maryam, who flipped through it carefully.

"This has material on the police."

Other files contained material on the carabinieri, the Christian Democrat Party, a local crime consortium, journalists, and, not surprisingly, lawyers. Michele Mannuzzu had been a busy man. Even if only a little of the dirt he had raked over ever proved damaging, there must still have been a lot of people he could have hurt.

"There still doesn't seem to be one labeled 'AR,'" said Maryam.

Yosef bent down and went through some files they had not yet looked at, then lifted one out of the heap.

"Here," he said.

It was a manual for an Alfa Romeo. Maryam nodded and opened it. She read for a while, then looked up at Yosef.

"Yes," she said. "This is the one we're after."

"Let me see."

He took it on his lap and opened it. It contained much of the same sort of material as the other files, but it soon became apparent that the subject matter was somewhat different. It was the photographs that told most of the story: men in black uniforms raising their arms in the fascist salute; men in civilian clothes standing in front of photographs of Mussolini or Hitler; young men photographed perhaps fifty years ago alongside much older men, photographed recently, with notes indicating that they were one and the same person; a shot of soldiers with the bodies of men and women they had shot, and next to it a photograph of a bishop giving his blessing to a private military reunion.

Yosef closed the file. He could feel his heart beating uncomfortably. These were not his memories, not his family's memories, but, like his dream, they haunted him.

"Come on," he said. "It's time we got out of here."

Part 5
THE POLICEMAN

27

Inspector Antonio Nieddu swore volubly and then, for good measure, let fly another mouthful of well-ripened adjectives. He had long ago persuaded himself that, up here on the stygian top floor of the Sassari *questura*, it did not matter in the least what oaths or imprecations were allowed to wander the corridors or pollute the already stagnant atmosphere. In his cubbyhole of a room, swearing loudly and often was one of the few outlets he had. When he ran out of oaths in Italian, he would switch to Sardo for a while, entertaining his neighbors with snatches of obscenity forged by generations of Barbagian shepherds.

He swore most days, on and off, but today he really had reason. First of all, his lunch hour had been completely ruined by a homicide that showed all the signs of giving him a long-term ache in the balls. And now Dessì, the vice-questore to whom he was immediately answerable, had been in here in person, telling him that, as of this afternoon, he was in charge of all De Felice's outstanding cases. He was not being transferred to them, they were being transferred to him, in addition to his own load. "Budgetary constraints" had been the only response to his expressions of disbelief. And when he had countered with a string of "bugger the budgets," Dessì had merely shrugged and walked out.

What had De Felice wanted to kill himself for anyway? Surely he hadn't given up hope of getting to Rome before his retirement? There'd been a note, apparently, but that would probably tell them precious little. "I'm sorry, I fucked up, I can't live with myself anymore, life has lost all meaning...." That sort of thing. You could write them in advance and seldom get them wrong.

But why worry about that? Internal affairs would untie whatever knots had twisted Enzo De Felice's sad life. The case might even get referred to the Ministry in Rome, as such matters often did. That would be a sort of posthumous triumph for De Felice. He'd have been pleased as punch to know his name had got that far. In the meantime, the living would have to plow on with the work he had left behind.

Before Nieddu could even think about that, however, there was the little matter of the homicide and how to get it on its way. An artist had prepared an impression of the dead woman fit for publication in the evening papers and for transmission on the local television news. That should get some responses, maybe even a firm identification before it was time to knock off. If he got to knock off, which he doubted.

The couple they were holding downstairs would have to be released soon, before the British consulate got involved. They were middle-aged tourists from a place called Ayr in Scotland, didn't speak a word of Italian beyond a barely recognizable *buongiorno*, *per favore*, and *grazie*, and were unmistakably bewildered by the whole business. All the same, a dead body had been found in their hotel room, so the formalities had to be observed. Not even the consul could object to that.

Nieddu was more interested in the whereabouts of the inhabitant of the room opposite, number 316, a certain Yosef Katzir, an Israeli citizen. Katzir had checked into the hotel the day before, but he'd eaten no meals there so far, including breakfast this morning. The booking in his name had been made by an Italian woman, Maryam Longhi, who had given a home address in Cagliari. They were already checking up on her down there. Longhi had also failed to show for breakfast, and her room, like Katzir's, had not been slept in. They had both left luggage, but nothing essential. No passports, money, travelers' checks, or other papers.

Traces of blood had been found in Katzir's bath, and forensics were carrying out an analysis of it right now. Nieddu did not need their report to be ninety-nine percent sure that the victim had died in Katzir's room, or at least spent some time there after death.

So far, so good. All the same, Nieddu was worried. Things didn't add together. Why, for example, had someone called the police and told them they would find a body on the third floor of the President? Who would stand to benefit from that? Not Katzir, obviously. His girlfriend, perhaps? He thought that unlikely. A dutiful citizen who was afraid to give his name? True, some people were willing to speak out nowadays in order to combat organized crime, but he doubted that he was about to uncover an Israeli connection to any of the syndicates on the island.

He closed the file, swearing beneath his

breath. If this went on, he'd run out of obsceni-
ties before the day was over. Sighing, he crossed
to the already cluttered table on which Dessì
had dumped De Felice's files. Maybe he'd better
see what his colleague had been working on.
There might be something there that would
repay his efforts more than this body in the bath
stunt.

Part 6
THE *MAFTIR*

28

They crossed by night on a rough dark sea, and in the morning when they woke, the sea was like glass, bloodred at first as the sun rose over it, then purple. And no waves, as though night had brought them to a lake between hills without wind or currents. They took turns manning the wheel, and each time one woke the other, it was with an uneasy sense that waking intersected dreaming and that a careless look or a misplaced touch might leave them foundering in deeper seas.

Sailing obliquely, they passed from Sardinia past Elba and so into the Ligurian Sea, reaching landfall finally at a small fishing village called San Fruttuoso, on a headland not far south of Genoa. Within an hour of their arrival, the *Eleonora d'Arborea* was at sea again, manned by two young fishermen whom Yosef had paid well to return her safely to Olbia. To ensure they did not make off with the little craft and sell it in Genoa or La Spezia, Maryam sent a telegram to the owner in which she gave details of the young men, their names and their addresses.

They took the regular boat to Camogli, then a local bus to Genoa. From there, they left on the first *rapido* train to Milan, where they bought tickets to Rimini. They chose a *diretto* which stopped at Piacenza, Parma, Reggio, Modena, Bologna, and Forlì. Getting off at Bologna station, they had a short wait for a bus to Florence. In Florence, they bought train tickets to Rome, but left instead on a late afternoon flight to Turin. It was dark when they arrived, and colder than it had been in Sardinia. The darkness wrapped them like a thick mantle, as though to hide them, yet Yosef could not rid himself of the sensation that he was being followed, step by circuitous step, along a narrow road without exits.

The next day was a Saturday, dark and marred by drizzle from a slate-gray sky. Yosef woke early after a night of unremembered dreams that left him sad and pensive without reason. They were staying at the Vecchia Lanterna, a hotel on the Corso Re Umberto, near the center. To help divert inquiries about a couple answering their description, they booked in separately, leaving more than an hour between them.

The night before, after *shabbat* prayers alone, Yosef had inquired at the desk about local synagogues. The receptionist had clearly not had such a request before, but she searched in her guide under "Places of Worship" and found that there was just one, the Tempio Israelitico in the Via San Pio Quinto.

After an early breakfast, he took his prayer shawl and tefillin and set off to find the synagogue with the help of a tourist map. The details given to him at the hotel had been blandly uninformative, describing the place of worship as a *sinagoga* and no more. It might be Orthodox, it might be Reform, it might, for all he knew, belong to the Turin community of the Lubavitcher Hasidim—he had no way of knowing. And he was not quite sure whether Italian Jews were Ashkenazim or Sephardim, with all the differences that could make in points of ritual and language.

The service was already underway when he arrived. To his confusion, the interior of the synagogue was different from the style he was used to, having two rows of benches along the northern and southern walls and the *bimah*, the reading platform, on the west wall, facing the Ark, rather than in the center. He slipped in to a bench near the rear on the north side, his phylacteries already in place and his tallith lifted loosely over his head, and silently offered up the prayers that had been said before his arrival.

He was almost unobserved at first, but as the service wore on, men opposite took notice of him, and on his own side one or two heads started to turn. Without visible means of communication, awareness of his presence passed through the hall like a contagion.

He grew uncomfortable, sensing that he was not welcome, that, for some reason, the congregation suspected him, even that a few of them were frightened. It was then that it occurred to him how thoughtless he had been. His features had always seemed more Arab than Jewish, and back in Israel, like other Sephardim, he had occasionally been made to feel uncomfortable on that account. He realized that some people here might have taken him for an Arab, a terrorist perhaps, a lone gunman on a mission to avenge the massacre at the Tomb of the Patriarchs in Hebron, or a suicide bomber sent by Hamas to settle the score for Qana.

Prayer followed prayer, and benediction

229

succeeded benediction, and throughout them Yosef tried to concentrate on the words, to find himself again. It was more difficult than it had ever been, even on those occasions when he was newly returned from the battlefield or an assignment that had taken him outside all ordinary human sense of right and wrong. The Hebrew words, recited in the strange accent of the Italian liturgy, seemed suddenly alien, and his own presence in the synagogue almost monstrous. His thoughts kept turning to Maryam, and without his wishing it, they quickly grew lascivious and he felt a sense of shame, as though he had become a visible defilement.

From the *shema*, they passed to the silent benediction, and thus to the *kedushah*. As the leader of the service chanted aloud the repetition of the silent benediction, an old man approached Yosef with something in his hand. It was a small card, printed with the Hebrew word *maftir*. As Yosef reached out his hand to take it, puzzled that it should have come to him, the old man leaned toward him and whispered something in Italian. Yosef shook his head, indicating that he had not understood. The look of alarm in the old man's face was blatant. Quickly, Yosef guessed what was wrong.

A *maftir* is a member of the congregation called up to hear the last Torah lesson and to recite from one of the Prophetic books. An Arab terrorist, presented with a card like that, would not have known what to do.

"I'm sorry," he whispered quickly in Hebrew. "I don't speak Italian. Say that my name is Yosef bar Baruch."

The old man's expression lightened, and he resumed his original seat near the front. A few minutes later, the doors of the Ark were opened, the Torah scroll was lifted out, and the doors closed once more. Two men carried the scroll to the *bimah* and laid it down.

A voice called out, "Stand up, Yosef son of Baruch, *maftir*," and Yosef, who had been waiting for this, stood and went to the podium. He made the blessing, and a man with a black beard stood beside him and chanted a passage from the Torah. Yosef made the second blessing, and after a short silence the scroll was raised and removed from the podium.

He was alone at the podium now. He could see both ends of the synagogue, could feel every eye on him, as though he had been stripped naked before a room full of medical students. But already he could sense a lifting in the atmosphere. He was passing the test they had set for him, proving himself one of them. He felt no joy of return, only an inexplicable sadness that they had doubted him in the first place. And even here, he thought of Maryam, though without lust.

He read from the Book of Isaiah, a passage selected for him:

"'Remember the former things of old: for I am God, and there is none else; I am God, and there is none like me,

'Declaring the end from the beginning, and from ancient times the things that are not yet done, saying, My counsel shall stand, and I will do all my pleasure:

'Calling a ravenous bird from the east, the

man that executeth my counsel from a far country: yea, I have spoken it, I will also bring it to pass; I have purposed it, I will also do it.'"

A chorus of voices, rising and falling in a singsong lilt that seemed at once familiar and foreign to him, joined him in the recitation of the final words. As he chanted the concluding blessings, he saw their faces, relaxed now, some smiling, as if in welcome. But he felt a stranger among them, a man from a far country come for a purpose they would not understand. Bitter at heart, he left the *bimah* and returned to his seat.

The *Musaf Kedushah* followed, it being a *shabbat* service. Yosef followed the words as if they were letters recited in a foreign alphabet, aware of the approving glances that passed over him from time to time. His heart had never been empty like this at a time of prayer, and he felt as though a sudden sickness had entered him, a mortal stillness deep at his heart.

When the service ended, the congregation broke up rapidly as its members hurried to get home in order to rest before lunch or to spend time with their wives and children. Yosef returned the *maftir* card to the old man, who thanked him warmly in stilted Hebrew. As they shook hands, Yosef was startled by a firm touch on his shoulder. He spun to see a tall, bearded man in a black suit, his hand held out in greeting.

"*Shabbat shalom,*" the man boomed. "You've come from Eretz Israel, am I right?" He spoke in Hebrew, fluently, and with little trace of the Italian accent that flavored the language here. It was colloquial Israeli Hebrew, too, not the liturgical form learned by rote and seldom understood.

Yosef nodded. The stranger beamed.

"My name's Leone Mortara," he said. "I'm the *Rosh Ha-Kahal* here. And you're Yosef ...?"

"Elbaz," said Yosef, giving the surname he was currently using. "From Haifa."

"What a coincidence. I lived there for six years, between 1985 and 1991. You've just come over?"

Yosef nodded. "On business. I have a small printing firm."

"You're on your own?" Mortara glanced up at the gallery. Was there, perhaps, a wife waiting?

"Alone, yes. This is just a short trip. I'm staying at a hotel."

"Oh, that's no good, no good at all. Especially on *shabbat*. Do you speak Italian?"

Yosef shook his head. "I do all my business in English."

"All the worse. That settles it. You've got to come home with me. My wife makes a wonderful lunch on *shabbat*, and there's always room for half a dozen more. We have other guests, you won't be alone."

Yosef tried to protest, but not too strenuously. This was exactly why he'd come, after all.

Mortara took him by the arm and led him outside. A throng of men stood on the pavement, talking vociferously in Italian. Mortara was greeted warmly by everyone and drawn immediately into the group. Yosef was not surprised by his new friend's popularity: as *Rosh Ha-Kahal*, he was the elected head of the community, the chief lay official of the synagogue. He brought Yosef across and introduced him to each of the others in turn. The rabbi, a small man called Lattes, took Yosef's hand with a smile.

"We thought you were an Arab, you know. You should have let us know in advance that you were coming."

Yosef smiled in return, though inside he was far from feeling at ease. For a matter of minutes, he had been an outsider, an enemy among his own people, and he still felt chilled by the experience.

People started to say good-bye to one another. Mortara said it was time to go. As they turned from the doorway, Yosef glanced up and noticed a plaque beside the door. Seeing him look, Mortara halted.

"It's in honor of the Jews who were deported from Turin, mainly in 1943. It was never as bad in Italy as in other parts of Europe, but a lot of people died all the same. My grandparents were killed at Auschwitz. And now ..."

He stopped.

"It's *shabbat*," he said. "Not a day for gloom."

Yosef smiled and said nothing. But inside the chill had deepened.

29

Maryam had slept late and eaten a scrappy breakfast in her room. Her head hurt, and she still could not rid herself of the sensation of being at sea. She had only ever sailed on large boats before, and that not often, and the motion of the little *Eleonora d'Arborea*, even on a calm sea, had been unsettling.

Yosef had told her the night before that he planned to attend morning service in the synagogue and that he hoped to meet some members of the local Jewish community afterward. It was quite likely he would be away several hours, perhaps even until the evening.

They had gone to their beds early, but before that, over a meal in the hotel restaurant, he had outlined his plans to her. His primary aim in coming to the mainland was to discover, if he could, what Ennio Pontecorvo, a Milanese architect, Professor Alberto Cantoni, a professor of Greek from Turin, and Umberto Levi, a Sardinian restaurateur, had had in common. Cantoni had died here in Turin, and Yosef hoped he might have left behind family or friends who could help him make the right connection. According to Mossad, the professor had been an observant Jew and a regular attendee at the synagogue.

Throughout the meal, she had sensed a growing distance in him, as though he was retreating from her back to some image of himself in which he had no need for her. Perhaps it was necessary, she reasoned. Perhaps he could not convince others of his sincerity if he did not altogether believe in himself. To do that would mean excluding her from his thoughts. She herself had no such place to retreat to. That part of her that was most real, the part on which she depended whenever her identity was threatened by external forces, was the very part in which she loved him above all other considerations.

There was a small library on the ground floor, and she went there once she had dressed, taking with her the file they had found in the Mannuzzus' house. Yosef had asked her to look it over while he was away. She ordered a coffee and *biscotti* and found herself a table where she would not be disturbed.

It was not easy to make sense of the file. She tried at first to establish on what principle it had been compiled, only to find herself more bewildered. In the end, she concluded that it had been put together at random, more as an *aide-memoire* than a finished text. Its purpose was clear from the outset, however, and by the time she had read through everything three or four times, she had begun to form a vivid impression of how names and faces fitted together.

Mannuzzu had been clever. By a constitutional quirk, membership in the MSI or the National Alliance was not, in itself, illegal, but overt plans to bring back fascism were. In a country that had experienced more than one extreme right-wing attempt to launch a coup, fears of conspiracy were ubiquitous. But by the same token, plotters were subtle and experienced in the art of laying false trails.

The file took all this into account. Mannuzzu had compiled his materials from a wide variety of sources: newspaper and magazine articles, legal reports, police files, comments by journalists with whom he seemed to have been well acquainted, transcripts of summary preparatory sessions held by public prosecutors in several cities, summaries of formal preparatory sessions initiated by examining magistrates, and even snippets of information lifted from the files of the SISDE, the Servizio per le Informazioni e la Sicurezza Domestica, Italy's civilian secret intelligence service.

No one item was ever damning in itself. But by following circuitous paths, it was possible to bring to light hidden links and to trace patterns among the tangled web of evidence and hearsay. Maryam remembered a book of 3-D puzzles she had once seen. She had stared for ages at meaningless pages of colored shapes until, suddenly, she had been rewarded with recognizable pictures in three dimensions. It seemed like magic, yet she knew that, underneath it all, every line and every dot was informed by the coldest logic.

Here, for example, was *l'onorevole* Mauro D'Ambrosio, the Christian Democrat prefect of Sassari province, opening a small factory in Alghero where components were to be manufactured for the Olivetti factory at Ivrea. A local newspaper editorial attested to D'Ambrosio's democratic, anti-fascist credentials and praised him for his opposition to Vallarino La Mattina, a Sardinian neo-fascist leader.

But here was a photograph of Dottore Mario Buscetta, the owner of the computer components factory, attending a meeting of the MSI in Porto Torres. And here he was again, smiling benevolently in the background while D'Ambrosio gave a speech at a local school. A few pages further, there was a police report mentioning a series of meetings between Buscetta and Renato Lussu, a small-time criminal from Pozzomaggiore. That, too, might have passed if not for innocence, then at least for careless involvement in petty crime. But here was Lussu

237

at a meeting of the Porto Torres branch of the far-right Ordine Nuovo terrorist organization in 1974, and again at a gathering of Avanguardia Nazionale, another extremist group, in May 1993.

As in a simple math exercise, things added up. And, as in a drama, plot and characters mingled to form a coherent, if partly told, tale. A bit player might appear only once or twice in the entire performance, but, by dint of his relationship with the principal actors, still steer the onlooker to surprising conclusions.

She recognized names from the coded note left by Mannuzzu, which she still had by her. Moschetta, for example, turned out to be a National Alliance deputy in the Italian parliament, and Procopio was a left-wing journalist who worked for *La Nuova Sardegna*, a Sassari-based paper. The name Pozzan occurred several times: once in a transcript of a deposition made before Examining Magistrate Graziano Vinciguerra of the assize court at Sassari, frequently in a carabiniere report on the 1975 bombing at Lucca, and again in a summing-up by judges for the Court of Cassation in a case involving Ordine Nero, an offshoot of Ordine Nuovo. From these references, Maryam deduced that he was either a police informer or an agent provocateur employed by the SISDE and, before that, by the SID, the Servizio Informazioni Difesa, the military intelligence organization active in the 1970s.

Buzzi was not mentioned, but there were several references to a Mario B., who had been involved with more than one kidnapping, usually in Sardinia and a few times on the mainland. Maryam guessed that fuller details about him had been kept by Mannuzzu in another file. It was, however, clear from the present material that, apart from his criminal activities, he had close neo-fascist connections.

All of these and others were linked in an intricate web that involved neo-fascist extremists; National Alliance deputies from Sardinia and several mainland cities; several right-wing members of the European Parliament (including a former deputy chairman of the Group of the European Right); high-ranking police and carabinieri officers; SISDE officials; a general holding an executive post with SISMI, the Servizio per le Informazioni e la Sicurezza Militare, which had taken over the role of the SID following massive changes to the system in 1977; and a sprinkling of employees in various ministries.

Mannuzzu's own motives—and hence the scope of his inquiries—had been severely limited: He had compiled his dossier mainly as a guide to local *uomini rispettati*, men of influence from whom he might from time to time solicit favors. It was, after all, no more than what anyone else did in a society rife with corruption, in which a man might advance, if he advanced at all, according to the pull he could exert on those in a position to further his interests. Up to a certain point, Michele Mannuzzu had been a skilled practitioner of the art of winning friends and influencing people.

But his horizons had been limited as far as Maryam could tell, not just to Sardinia but to

Sassari province, and when she tried to expand the picture much beyond that, the edges grew blurred and then faded to nothing.

Nevertheless, she had two questions that she continued to ask herself. What had led Mannuzzu to think he was on to something big in the wake of Yoel Levin's kidnapping, an event that, on the surface, seemed to have no connection with the contents of this file? And what had gone wrong?

Her most important discovery concerned the man who had identified himself to Aryeh Levin as Bianco, and whom Mannuzzu called Weiss. The name first appeared in a press cutting taken from an obscure Italian-language newspaper published in Switzerland, *Il Corriere del Ticino*. The interview had been given early in 1981 by Abu Ayad, at that time Yasser Arafat's deputy within the Al-Fatah organization. According to a note by Mannuzzu, the article followed an interview granted the paper several months earlier, arranged through Colonel Stefano Giovannone, SISMI's representative in Beirut, and a close acquaintance of Abu Ayad's.

Ayad had already revealed that the PLO had arrested several German neo-fascists while undergoing training at a camp near Aqura, run by the Christian Falangist militia. The Germans were members of the Sportsgruppe Hoffman, a right-wing terror organization whose leader, Karl Heinz Hoffman, had already been linked to the Bologna train bombing of 1981.

In his second interview, Ayad testified that the Germans had confessed while in PLO hands to involvement in the Bologna bombing along with a like-minded French group working in conjunction with Italian extremists. Not only that, but Hoffman himself had been taking orders from someone more powerful, a shadowy figure whom they knew only as Weiss.

There were several references to behind-the-scenes influence from a German right-wing leader, named only by his initial, "W." These occurred in a *Riservatissimo* ("Most Confidential") report drawn up by SISDE and included in the documents lodged with the Moro Commission. Although the commission had rejected the idea of right-wing interests in the kidnapping and subsequent murder of Prime Minister Aldo Moro in 1978, evidence presented to them linked the mysterious and powerful Herr "W" to several Italian political figures, including the current prefect and questore of Sassari province.

Next to this report, Mannuzzu had pasted a page from a far-right Italian magazine called *Quex* (named, Maryam guessed, for the hero of the popular Nazi film, *Hitlerjunge Quex*). The page contained an article by someone using the *nom de guerre* Cola di Rienzo. At the head of the text was a depiction of the symbols that had graced the original di Rienzo's flag: the figure of Rome seated astride two lions, one hand holding the globe, the other a palm, and underneath the legend *Roma caput mundi*— Rome, the head of the world.

"In recent months," the article read in part, "we have had cause to celebrate the close bonds that we have forged with our northern brothers. We stand together in the struggle for liberty and truth, just as our fathers stood shoulder to shoulder in the dark days of the last war. But whereas they were betrayed from within by an international conspiracy of Jews and communists, we struggle today in a Europe virtually rid of the Jewish plague, a Europe from which the Communist tyranny has been eliminated.

"Last week our committee, along with representatives from Ordine Nuovo and Ordine Nero, traveled to Belgium for the annual rally at Diksmuide. While there, we held meetings with comrades from across the continent, and in their company raised aloft the banner of racial purity and Aryan supremacy. The FN, FNE, and PNFE were there from France, and from Belgium itself the WNP and VB. Spain sent a contingent made up of members of CEDADE and the Fuerza Nueva, the British sent seventeen heroes of their National Front and BNP, and the Germans, flushed with so many recent victories in the battle against immigration, sent luminaries of the REP. We met Danes and Swedes and Norwegians, and a host of new faces from the newly liberated lands of the east, from Czechoslovakia, Poland, and Romania, all heirs of the great anti-Jew and anti-Communist struggle.

"So many letters, so many names; but they all spelled one thing: POWER. Together, united in a single vision, we talked late into the night, honing the pan-European strategy that will take us to certain victory in the months and years ahead. The forces of light are on the march, and the battalions of darkness are already quailing before the sound of our tramping feet.

"Those of you who have been in the movement long will understand me when I say that our cup ran over on the second night, when our camp was visited by Herr W., whose guiding hand and enlightened mind are never far from our deliberations. He spoke with us, listened to our problems, and made suggestions from that inexhaustible fund of knowledge and experience that he has always placed at our disposal.

"On the following day, he made a private visit to the Italian contingent and spent three hours in a frank and full discussion of our current strategy. What he told us must, of course, remain confidential for the present time. But suffice it to say that he reaffirmed his commitment to our long-term plans and promised his undying support for our endeavors in the coming year."

When she finally looked up, it was after three o'clock. Her eyes were tired, and she felt hungry. Yosef still had not returned. She looked round the small, empty room. Books on the shelves, newspapers and magazines strewn across an oak table. From outside came the diminished, hollow sounds of a hotel on a Saturday afternoon. Laughter came from another room, then a burst of applause: a wedding reception drawing to a close.

She closed the file and put it to one side. On the table was the copy she had made of Mannuzzu's note. It all made more sense now. Had Mannuzzu contacted all these people in the end? She looked for the slip of paper on which she had recorded the lawyer's last telephone calls. Moschetta was there, and Procopio. He had called the deputy's office at 4:17 that afternoon and spoken with someone, probably Moschetta himself, for seven minutes.

His call to Procopio had lasted longer, a total of sixteen minutes and twenty-three seconds.

There were two other names that had not been mentioned on the note, but which did crop up in the file: Guido Pomarici, a lawyer who defended right-wing clients, and Sereno Loiacono, a former civil servant in Mussolini's short-lived Salò Republic. Mannuzzu had spoken to them for three minutes and fourteen minutes respectively. Pomarici had a Rome number, Loiacono one in Bormio, a picturesque ski resort several miles from the Austrian border.

She collected her papers and went back upstairs to her room. One by one, she rang the five remaining numbers. Each time, when someone replied, she apologized for having dialed a wrong number. One was Pozzan, another was a woman called Sciascia. Not recognizing the name, Maryam had conversed briefly with her, pretending that she was looking for another Sciascia, and had discovered that the other woman's first name was Rosita and that she lived alone. She was Sardinian, with an address in Nuoro: Mannuzzu's mistress, perhaps?

Two did not reply. The last number rang several times before anyone answered. Maryam was about to put the phone down again when a man's voice came on the line.

"De Vuono."

"I'm sorry," she said. "Who am I speaking to?"

"This is Guglielmo De Vuono. Who is this?"

Maryam paused, her heart in her mouth. Surely it was not possible.

"I ... I wanted the Ministry of Justice," she stammered.

"This is the Ministry. Where did you get this number?"

"I'm sorry," she said. "There must be a mistake."

She put the phone down. Her hand was shaking.

Guglielmo De Vuono was the new Minister of Justice. He had taken office three months earlier following the assassination of his left-wing predecessor, Amico Fiamminghini.

30

Lunch with the Mortaras was less a meal than a rite of passage, an initiation into the life, not just of a family, but of an entire community. It passed through several cycles, and at times Yosef thought it would be perpetually renewed, that he would remain in the family's city-center apartment forever, eating Sabbath food and listening to a torrent of conversation in Italian. Family and guests would eat, then leave the table to talk in groups or use the bathroom, then return to eat some more, then talk, play chess, read, or listen to music.

There was a casualness about everything that pleased him greatly. He could remember solemn *shabbats* at home, days when everything that might be construed as impiety had been strictly banned. Here, the emphasis was less on the Law and its observance than on friendship and its cultivation, and any form of leisure activity seemed to be allowed. People came to the door and stayed for a little, now joining in the meal as fresh bowls appeared from the kitchen, now mingling with a group talking politics or books or sports. Meanwhile, others made their farewells and left. Yosef sat among it all, perplexed yet delighted by the vitality that surrounded him.

Leone introduced him to everyone. With most of the guests, Yosef would exchange little more than perfunctory greetings, or hold a brief, stilted conversation mediated by Leone. A few spoke Hebrew well enough to talk at greater length, and one or two, summoned expressly by telephone, possessed a fluency acquired after several Ulpan courses and years of residence in Israel.

The conversation drifted, as though drawn by a deep, invisible current, to the continuing Middle East peace talks and, inevitably, to Israel's role in them. It shocked Yosef to find almost everyone in that softly lighted room vehement in his or her opposition to the settler movement and to all policies and parties that threatened the rights of Arabs. The settlers and those who backed them, everyone agreed, had become the chief obstacle to a lasting peace, or at least as great a cause for division as Hamas or Islamic Jihad.

Yosef, afraid of betraying himself by an incautious remark, either remained silent or feigned agreement with the others. They were decent people, he could see, and unflagging in their support for Israel. Perhaps they were not as religiously observant as most of the people he knew at home, perhaps they were more than a little naive in their understanding of political issues. But, faced by their warmth and cheerfulness, it disconcerted him to realize that they had kept alive something that had almost died in Israel itself, that, in a fragile world, it was harder for them to be Jews than it was for him and his friends in their robust citadel of Qiryat Arba.

"The real problems are here in Europe again," said a young man on Yosef's left, an engineer from Moncalieri. "What happens in the Middle East is a sideshow now."

"I can hardly agree with that," said Yosef. "If there's another war, we could lose everything, all we've ever fought for."

"Perhaps you would," said the engineer. His name was Bruno Frezza and he had long pale hair, soft and well-cut, like a girl's. But his features were masculine, and the look in his eyes troubled Yosef. "But we'd still be here," he went on, "in the Diaspora. The Diaspora is never-ending, don't you see? With or without Israel, there will always be an exile. There are already more Jews in America than there are in Israel. You can't change that. Nor can I. But we can work to change the conditions of our exile. That's why Europe is important. It's where the Holocaust took place. If we can't find a way to make Europe turn its back on race hatred for good, then nothing else we hold will ever come to anything."

"But that's absurd.... If we lose what we have in Israel, if we let the Arabs drive us into the sea, it will be a second Holocaust."

Yosef was reminded of his own days at the Netiv Meir yeshiva high school in Jerusalem, when he and his study partner had spent entire mornings arguing Talmud together while others held their own disputations or watched theirs for entertainment. There, he had felt himself on home ground; here, he felt as though traps were being set for him at every juncture, and that he was being humored only to be trounced and mocked.

Frezza shook his head. Others watched him, their eyes on his face.

"No," he said, "you just don't understand. You can't, you don't live here, you don't see what is happening. If the Arabs drive you into the sea, that's because they want their land back, nothing more. It's not because they hate the color of your skin or the shape of your nose or the fact your hair is black and curls. Racially, you're both the same, both Semites. Whatever hatred they feel for you, it isn't racist."

"What is it, then?" demanded Yosef. During the *intifada*, he had heard young Arabs taunting him and his fellow soldiers, crying, "Go home, dirty Jews!"

"I told you: it's territorial. Religious sometimes. But never racist. Islam isn't a racist religion. Your Muslim enemies may despise you as unbelievers, but that's all. You share the honor with Christians and anyone else who isn't a Muslim."

Yosef's distress was mounting. He was being attacked by someone on whom he felt he should be able to depend.

"I don't understand," he said. "Why do you keep saying 'you'? Surely we're all Jews in this room."

"Of course we are. But you're an Israeli and we're Italians. To the Arabs, that makes you different from us: a Zionist, a usurper, a cog in an international conspiracy."

"But that's just the point," said Yosef excitedly. He was disturbed by the direction in which the engineer's arguments were heading. "They see you as part of this international conspiracy as well—not just us Israelis."

"Of course they do. But the conspiracy isn't just made up of Jews. The whole Western world is part of it. It's the latest Crusade. Christians, Jews, atheists—we're all waging war on Islam and the Arab world. But it's an imperialist war, nothing to do with race."

"You mean that when an Arab singles out a Jew and kills him, he isn't being racist?"

Frezza shook his head. "I don't think so, no. If the Jew converted to Islam or left Israel, he wouldn't be targeted. Not for being a Jew anyway. It's the opposite of what happened under the Nazis."

"Rubbish, it's exactly the same. Hitler wanted Europe *Judenfrei*, the Arabs want the Middle East free of Jews. If they ever succeed in pushing us into the sea, the end result will be identical."

"No," protested Frezza, using a series of gestures utterly foreign to Yosef. "Don't you see, it wouldn't be identical. They would stop at the sea. The Nazis wouldn't have stopped until every last Jew had been exterminated. For them, it was a war against a vile disease and they could see no other solution than to eradicate us from the face of the earth for good. Before they came to power, a Jew in Germany or Poland or elsewhere had choices. He could become a Christian or an atheist. He could consider himself a German or a Pole or an Italian or a Frenchman. His citizenship didn't depend on his beliefs or his race.

"The Nuremberg Laws changed all that.

249

Being Jewish was suddenly a racial thing, something it hadn't been before. You couldn't convert from being a Jew. If your grandparents had been Jewish, you were Jewish, even if you thought Moses was a pain in the neck and the laws of the Torah were a heap of antiquated nonsense. You could scream 'I'm a German atheist' all you liked, but the SS would still drag you off to Auschwitz."

"But surely that's just the point. Over here in Europe, you're Italians or whatever you want to be again. In the Middle East, we're Jews, and we're surrounded by people who refuse to recognize our country, much less our citizenship in it."

Leone Mortara broke in. "Bruno, stop giving our guest such a hard time. He won't come back if you make him so uncomfortable. In any case, he's partly right. Jews may have been tolerated in Islamic countries, but they never had the right to full citizenship. And there were pogroms in places like Iran long before Israel came on the scene." He turned to Yosef. "I hope you're not upset."

"Of course not. I enjoy a good argument."

However, Mortara could sense Yosef's discomfiture. "Whether it's good or not, it's hardly fair when you've just arrived here. You can't be expected to understand why Bruno is so worked up."

Yosef shrugged. "It's just my bad luck," he said, "to run into a room full of peaceniks. Back home, I try to leave you guys alone."

"You're mistaken," Leone pressed. "Not all of us here are doves. Certainly not Bruno, I assure you. We all care what happens to Israel,

250

even if we don't always give that impression. But things are taking place here that have a more immediate significance for us. The extreme right-wing is getting stronger all across Europe. There's not much chance they can get back into power, but they can do a lot of damage all the same.

"Here in Italy they've actually been in government again since 1994. When Berlusconi's government collapsed scarcely a year after he came to power, it looked as though the entire system was about to disintegrate. That gave the right a further chance to infiltrate themselves. So far attacks on foreigners have been fairly limited, but the harder the far right pushes for extreme measures, the more tempting it is for the center parties and the moderate right to introduce legislation in the hope of keeping things under control. Every time there's an attack on an immigrant or a gang of thugs burn down a hostel, a supposedly moderate politician will appear on television to condemn the violence and ask for a ban on further immigration.

"You may think this has nothing to do with us, but surely I don't have to tell you that the stronger the fascists become, the more we're at risk."

Yosef sensed that the moment had come for him to turn the conversation into the channel he had been hoping to steer it all along.

"I heard something about this before I left Haifa," he said. "Weren't there some killings here not long ago? One of them was here, I think. An elderly Jew. And two others, in Milan and Sardinia. I heard they were all killed by neo-fascists. Is that true?"

Glances were exchanged. It seemed as though an unseen hand had summoned winter back to the room. No one moved. Mortara looked at Frezza, then at some others, then back at Yosef.

"Yes," he said. "There have been killings. Alberto Cantoni was found dead in his apartment in Turin a few weeks ago. He was a professor of Greek at the university here. It was a tragedy for all of us. He worshiped at our synagogue, he was a regular guest at these lunches."

"I'm sorry. Have they found his killers? Do they know what the motive was?"

Bruno snorted. Mortara looked sharply at him, then back at Yosef.

"No," Mortara said. "There are no leads. No one has been apprehended."

Bruno leaned forward. "For God's sake, Leone, you might as well tell the man the truth." He turned to Yosef. "Look, the fact is that the police don't give a damn who killed Cantoni. He was a Jew, a kike, a yid, and that means it's worth more than their jobs to haul somebody in who might have had a hand in his killing. The same thing happened in Milan. An entire family, people called Pontecorvo, wiped out by fascists. But no one gives a damn. No leads, no clues, no arrests. And all the time, they know only too well who did it."

"You mean they know the killers?" Yosef could feel his heart straining. Surely it could not be this simple?

"Not by name, no. But they know as well I do that they were neo-fascists. Even you'd been told that. But the police say, no, the killings have nothing in common, just burglaries gone wrong. Ignore the swastikas, they were just daubed there to put us off the scent."

"You mentioned a killing in Sardinia," said Leone. He seemed uneasy, like someone who knows he is about to hear bad news yet cannot quite believe that it is happening. "I don't think we've heard of it. When was the murder, do you know?"

"I'm not sure," lied Yosef. He glanced casually round him. Whispered remarks in Italian were being exchanged. One or two people seemed particularly interested in what he had to say. "A while ago, maybe around the time of Professor Cantoni's murder, maybe a few weeks earlier."

"Is that all you know?" asked Bruno. His eyes were bright with interest.

"I think it was a couple," said Yosef. "A husband and wife. Their name was Levin, if I remember correctly."

"Levin?" asked Leone. "Are you sure?"

"I'm not certain...."

"Could it have been Levi?"

"I can't be absolutely sure. It's possible."

A worried look passed between Bruno and Leone.

"And you say they were killed by fascists?" Leone asked.

Yosef shrugged. "That's what I was told. Do you think the killings are linked in any way?"

"Yes," said Bruno. Leone shot a glance at the younger man, as though warning him to be quiet, but he went on as though unaware. "A group of fascists is amusing itself killing Jews. That's what makes the connection. It could be one of a number of gangs—'Ludwig,' 'Falange,'

'Brigata Goebbels,' who knows? Or perhaps a new group we don't yet know the name of."

Mortara visibly relaxed. Whatever he had feared Frezza might say had clearly not been said. The engineer was giving nothing away. If there had been a stronger link between the killings, it was not about to be paraded before the eyes of a stranger.

"You think it's a single group?" asked Yosef, trying to keep the conversation moving.

Frezza shrugged. "Here and in Milan, yes. But Sardinia ..." He shrugged again. "I don't know. I'd need more details. I don't think any of the groups I mentioned is active over there."

"You seem to know quite a bit about these people."

Frezza was about to answer when Mortara chipped in.

"We all know a lot about them. It pays to stay informed. Perhaps the Jews in Italy didn't suffer as badly as those in the rest of Europe during the last war, but we still lost thousands to the death camps when the Germans took control here in the north. We've remained vigilant ever since. The fascist movement in this country wasn't snuffed out overnight after the Allied invasion; it just went underground. And now it's coming out into the open again. We've had our share of graves desecrated, we've all received hate mail and pamphlets through the post, there have been attacks on synagogues. And now these killings."

"Not to mention the Pacchia affair," said a man on Mortara's right. Yosef could not remember his name. He noticed that Mortara seemed uneasy.

"What's that?" he asked.

Mortara answered for the other man. "It's a trial," he said. "A man called Pier Maria Pacchia, a right-winger even within the National Alliance, a deputy from Florence. He goes on trial this Monday on a charge of denying the Holocaust."

"And does he?"

"Deny the Holocaust? Oh, no question of that. He wrote a book called *L'Olocausto che non era mai*—'The Holocaust that Never Was.' There's nothing fresh in it, he bases everything on all the standard denial literature—Irving, Faurisson, App, Carto, all that crowd. The thing is that, like Faurisson in France, Pacchia has a certain support in this country. He is a member of parliament, after all, and his party has stood behind him on the issue. They claim, as they always do, that it isn't a matter of right or wrong, of historical fact or inaccuracy, but of basic freedom of speech.

"Pacchia has even managed to get some left-wing writers behind him, arguing on the grounds that no book or article should ever be banned, that censorship sucks the air out of serious public debate."

"The thing is," Frezza broke in, "that if Pacchia and his publisher win, it will set a precedent for God knows what kind of hate literature. People will claim freedom of speech to argue that blacks are mentally inferior to whites, or that homosexuals are disease carriers, or that sterilization of the mentally defective would be a good thing. Some of those things can be said already, but only in a backstairs sort of way. The Holocaust is such a basic concept that victory on that front would be a green light to every species of nastiness you can imagine. It could be the issue that will take the right to the point where they can make or break the next coalition government."

"There's another problem," said Mortara. "I don't know how familiar you are with Italian politics. Does the name Alberto Luzzatto mean anything to you?"

Yosef shook his head.

"Luzzatto is head of the new Progressive Alliance Party. It's a broadly left-to-center party which has grown in popularity in the past couple of years, and they look poised to win a majority in the election month after next. Luzzatto could well become the next prime minister, if it weren't for one thing. He's Jewish."

Yosef nodded. Even if he could not yet understand quite how they fit together, he could almost hear the pieces of the puzzle falling into place.

"Is that likely to be a problem?" he asked.

"It shouldn't be, but it is. His opponents are using it against him, some subtly, some rather crudely. A lot of people see the Pacchia trial as the crucial political event in postwar Italy. If Pacchia loses, it will be enough to break the anti-Jewish lobby and bring Luzzatto into power. If that happens, he has the breadth of support to implement real reforms. In particular, he has promised to act against two of the most dangerous forces in our society: the extreme right and the Mafia. If Luzzatto carries it off here, it could have repercussions throughout Europe."

"And if he doesn't win?"

Mortara was silent for a moment. When he spoke, his voice was strangely altered.

"You may be looking at a room of dead men," he said.

Part 7
THE *GRUPPENFÜHRER*

31

Gorbitz
Dresden, Germany

The cold here was unlike any other cold, the damp unlike any other damp. The locals had a name that covered them both: ice in the soul. It had nothing to do with temperature. Gorbitz was no colder than any other part of Dresden or Saxony, its people were scarcely more poorly clothed. But all a visitor had to do was cast his eye down those long concrete vistas, those gray streets with their high-rise blocks growing from the pavements like giant stalagmites in the most desolate of cabins, and he could already feel the ice forming in his heart.

Dresden had risen from its own ashes into a world only a little less dreadful than the one that had witnessed its destruction. What flocks of British bombers had failed to do with fire, some forty years of Communist rule now accomplished with ice and concrete. The city was rimmed with gaunt cement towers, choked by roads that existed only to join housing estate to factory complex and factory complex to housing estate. There was no joy. The sky above was black with smoke and yellow with the fumes of industrial chemicals.

Gorbitz was Dresden's largest housing project. Size apart, it was identical to the neighboring *neubau* developments of Johannstadt and Hauptbahnhof, identical to the high-rise sprawls of East Berlin, identical to the gray urban expanses of Saarlouis, Zittau, Halle, Greifswald, Hünxe, and Cottbus. Externally, little had changed since the collapse of the Democratic Republic and the reunification of Germany. The concrete was a little blacker, perhaps, the streets were a little dirtier, the faces of the people were a shade more downcast. They had hoped for so much and received so little, and deep inside, far down where the ice had fastened on their souls, they were afraid and angry.

A small crowd had gathered on the street three hours earlier, just as it was growing dark. Now it had swollen, and every minute brought new arrivals. The main body had collected around a five-story residential complex set back behind a low wall and ringed by a thin line of police. This was a former GDR *Ausländerwohneheim*, a dormitory for workers from socialist countries now transformed into a hostel for refugees. It stood a few doors from the *Espeklub*, the old East German youth center, now deserted for more attractive pursuits like taunting and killing foreigners.

Inside the hostel tonight were fourteen Angolan and eight Vietnamese families. They had barricaded themselves inside their rooms and hidden their children beneath the beds or in cupboards. As they sat, huddled together, trembling with fear, they could hear the sounds of the growing crowd outside. Those that spoke German could understand the repeated chant: *"Ausländer aus! Ausländer aus!"* that rose up from the street.

The crowd was diverse, and growing more so by the minute. Around the fringes stood local residents, drawn here in spite of the cold in the hope of a bit of excitement or entertainment. Already, a ragged band of camp followers had set themselves up to make the most of the event. One resident had wheeled in his sausage stand and was frying and selling bratwurst in rolls to hungry onlookers. Someone else was offering beer and soft drinks, and beside him a girl in jeans had opened a stall stocked with cheap knitted hats and scarves. It was going to be a long night, and a cold one, and she reckoned on making a respectable profit before morning.

Young men in bomber jackets moved among the crowd touting copies of the right-wing DVU party's newspaper, *Die Deutsche National Zeitung*. It only cost one mark, and more than one on-looker handed over a coin and took a copy. Why not? He could read it later, when all this was over. Maybe he'd join the party himself one of these days. Why not? Germany for the Germans wasn't such a bad idea, was it?

Meanwhile, others with more developed thoughts on the subject were standing closer to the action. Little knots of skinheads stood around, each group marked out from the others by small differences in their clothing. Near the fringes were several clusters of the less political skins: Mode-Skins, Oi-Skins, Edel-Skins, and Schmuddel-Skins. Closer in were the Nazi-Skins, and at the front of the crowd fully fledged neo-Nazis, some in brown shirts and black ties. They had come from Gorbitz, Johannstadt, and Hauptbahnhof—in twos and threes at first, then in larger groups.

These were the most vociferous, choosing and directing the slogans shouted at the hostel: *"Fidschis aus! Kohlen aus!"* The slogans echoed graffiti already scrawled across the walls of the building: *Türken aus! Juden aus!* Above the door, someone had written with a spray can: *Hoyerswerda—Ausländerfrei stadt* and *Rostock-Lichtenhagen—immer Deutsche,* calling up the memory of two major racist incidents that had followed Germany's reunification.

Already, the first contingents of neo-fascists from other towns and cities had started to roll up in cars and buses. There were *Deutsche Alternative* members from Dresden and Leipzig, *Gubner Front* activists from nearby Guben, and from elsewhere in Saxony, representatives of *SS-Osten,* the Union of Saxon Werewolves, and the *Nationaler Widerstand Deutschland.* Others from further afield were already on their way, summoned by telephone and even fax from bases throughout the country.

Down near the edge of the crowd, a few of the new arrivals could be seen speaking into mobile phones and walkie-talkies. Several had brought radio-jamming devices, and one was monitoring the police wave bands from a clear position further down the street. A van had arrived from Cottbus bringing petrol and bottles, and inside it two young men belonging to the *Wiking Jugend* were busy preparing crates of Molotov cocktails—"Mollies" for short—in calculated anticipation of an escalation in the violence.

Overhead, two police helicopters cut the cold air in shreds, patrolling the district with apparent disinterest. On the ground, the authorities had sent in ambulances and fire engines in case things got out of hand. But things were already out of hand and the crowd was swelling to such proportions that, unless someone acted quickly, it would soon be impossible for either the ambulances or the fire trucks to get through. Yet nobody was going to act quickly, in the naive hope that, by holding back, they might avoid another riot.

Off from the crowd stood a small knot of *faschos*, the elder brothers of the Nazi-Skins. These were the elite of the extremist activists, and it was from their ranks that instructions were being sent into the crowd. The police captain in charge of the situation was relatively new to the job and thought the real troublemakers were the shouting mob leaders his men were confronting from behind their toughened glass shields. He could not have been more wrong.

Nguyen Truong Chinh stood at the window of his small apartment on the third floor of the hostel and contemplated the crowd thirty feet below. He had never been so scared in his life, not even as a child during the war in Vietnam. Then the enemy had never reached within a hundred miles of his home village, except with bombs dropped from planes too high to see. Now they were so close he could make out their faces in the light of the torches they held, could hear their voices, could feel their hatred rise up like a foul stench and settle in his lungs.

In Vietnam he had been just a child, with adults to take care of him and keep him safe from the aggressor from across the seas. Now he had a wife and children of his own in the room behind him, cowering and quaking, expecting him to save them and knowing he was as powerless as they were.

He had been in Germany for ten years now, first under Communist rule, then under capitalist. As far as he was concerned, there was little difference, except that under the GDR he had been safer. He had been hated then, too, but the state had kept much tighter control over its thugs. On his arrival in East Germany, he had been one of hundreds of foreigners drafted to take over the menial labor at the Schwarze Pümpe electric power plant outside Hoyerswerda. After the racist violence there in 1991, he had been transferred to Dresden, a city of 500,000 which then had a foreign population of only 10,000 and which the authorities had fondly imagined would be largely immune to racist tension.

He had met his wife soon after his arrival, married, and started a family. The federal government recognized his GDR work contract and gave him a job in a factory in Gorbitz manufacturing processed food. Things were going to be better in the new Germany, he thought. But he was soon to be disabused of his fantasies.

After unification, he had applied for and obtained the status of political refugee. Even under the old regime, he had made little secret of his opinions, and had been in trouble with the Stasi secret police more than once. To return to Vietnam would have invited risk, and he had thought it prudent to take his chances in his adopted country. But his adopted countrymen had wanted none of him and his family. They had been spat at regularly in the street, pushed and jostled in the supermarket, cold-shouldered in the factory canteen and the local café.

The children, a boy of six and a girl of four, were terrified out of their wits. They were in the small bathroom, as far from the trouble as he could get them, but every time there was an outburst below or a stone or bottle crashed against the building or smashed through a window, they screamed and cowered against the wall. When were the police going to come to take them out? Someone had blared instructions through a megaphone, but Nguyen had been unable to understand most of it. A few of them had tried ringing police headquarters from the phone in the lobby, but the wires had been cut. Unless the police or fire brigade came for them, they were trapped.

He looked round. On a chair near the back wall, his wife sat trembling uncontrollably. He had tried to talk to her, to reassure her, but she had been unable to take anything in. Word got round among the guest workers. She knew what had happened in Hoyerswerda, Rostock, and elsewhere, and she was just waiting for the surge of fire that would kill them all.

She looked up and their eyes met. They knew they were going to die. Worse than that, they knew their children would die, too. And neither could find the words or the gestures to communicate their fear and their longing.

At that moment, there was a shattering of glass as a bottle, hurled from below, came crashing through the window. It rolled across the floor and came to rest at Nguyen's feet like a grenade primed to go off.

On the street, a black Mercedes glided to a halt beside the quietly watching knot of *faschos*. A man dressed in a thick cashmere overcoat stepped out. The little group parted to let him through, then closed in again. One of the *faschos*, a man in his forties with thinning hair and an unattractive profile, stepped forward and greeted the newcomer.

"*Grüß Gott*, Gerhard. I'm so pleased you could make it."

"*Grüß Gott*. I'm sorry to be a little late, Rainer."

"You're not late at all. We've just been waiting for you to arrive before deciding how far to let this go. Otherwise, everything's under control. We'll be ready for action once Heinz's people get here."

The new arrival nodded. "They're on their way," he said. "I spoke with Heinz on my way here. He had to pick up some equipment before leaving. What about our friends from the *Nationalistische Front*?"

"They're the group down at the far end singing German folk songs. Willi has told them to hold back until they receive orders."

"And the NPD?"

"Over there by the youth club. They're just back from two weeks' training at the Hünxe camp."

"Good, they'll be on form. What about the police?"

"We can handle them. They haven't mobilized enough men. All those remarks in the leftist press about police provocation have made them jittery. The man in command doesn't have a clue what's really going on here. Willi's lads are ready to set up a diversion round the corner. Then we move in. Provided you give the go-ahead."

At that moment, a younger man in his late twenties slipped through the crowd and approached Rainer. He saluted his superior, raising his forearm and bringing his heels smartly together. There was nothing sloppy or tentative about his bearing or his manner. Rainer returned the salute briskly. Not many yards away, the crowd was baying and jeering like a beast without reins. But here, within the little knot of hard-core activists, all was sober and well-mannered. Here, though the beast was for the most part unaware of it, were the reins that could turn its many heads and direct it in whatever direction suited its masters.

"Sir, the *Wiking Jugend* say everything's ready down their end. They have enough Mollies now for three attack waves. It should be enough."

"Thank you, Jörg." Rainer took the younger man's arm and led him before the newcomer.

"Gerhard, let me introduce my lieutenant, Jörg Thierse. Jörg has been the movement's most constant support here in Dresden for over a year." Pausing, he turned to Thierse. "Jörg, this is SS Gruppenführer Gerhard Weiss. You will have heard of him, of course."

Thierse saluted again, this time with a sharpness and intensity that betokened the high degree of respect he felt for the man to whom he had been introduced.

"Herr Gruppenführer, I'm honored to make

your acquaintance. Rainer is quite right: I have heard a great deal about you and your loyalty to the Reich."

They spoke for a few minutes, then Thierse was dismissed and ordered to return to the *Wiking Jugend* sector and to tell them to start distributing the Molotov cocktails. Weiss and Rainer walked off together, out of earshot of the others.

"Gerhard, I'm a little worried. Do you think this is a good moment to escalate things here? The situation in Italy hasn't been resolved yet. A thing like this could still swing opinion there against us."

Weiss shook his head. "I don't think so. Our prospects there are better than ever. But a lot of people are wavering, which is why we have to send out the right signal. They're tired of compromise more than anything else, fed up with coalitions, power-sharing, and hung parliaments. They want to know that like-minded people in other countries are willing and able to take hard, decisive action, especially on issues like immigration. This will stiffen their resolve, you'll see."

"I hope so. But the trial in Milan could still go either way. What if the Jews really do bring—"

"It won't go that far, I promise you. I have people on the job twenty-four hours a day now. We'll find him, don't worry."

"And the Israeli—what about him?"

"Abuhatseira?"

"I don't know. Whatever the fuck he's called. How much does he know?"

"He knows nothing. All he has is guesswork. He's poking around in the dark."

"Nevertheless, he may get lucky. The yid is dangerous. And I've heard that he's slipped out of Sardinia."

"You heard correctly. My information is that he's using a false name, Katzir or Elbaz. He got out on Thursday night aboard a boat called the *Eleanora d'Arborea*. It anchored at a place called San Fruttuoso on Friday morning and was returned the same evening to its owners in Olbia. My people are on his trail already. They'll find him. You have my word."

"Very well. If you're sure you have things under control. I want to keep things simple. But if this shit from Israel starts poking his nose into this business any further ..."

"Trust me, Rainer. He's as good as dead."

A figure detached itself from the cluster of *faschos* nearby and came across to them.

"Sir, Heinz Felderer and his team have just arrived in Gorbitz. They can be in position within three minutes. He wants instructions."

Rainer looked at Weiss. "Well, Gerhard—do we go ahead? I'm in your hands?"

Weiss contemplated the scene before him: the singing, swaying crowd, the thin police line, the emergency vehicles parked where they could most easily be disabled, the water cannon in the wrong place. He looked the hostel up and down, and a thin smile crossed his lips. Once, he thought he saw a face at a window on the third floor, caught briefly in the light of the torches below.

"I want them all dead," he said. His voice was flat and unemotional, as though he were asking for a packet of cigarettes or some other everyday commodity. "Don't leave a single Jew

271

alive in there. Burn the place down round their heads."

Rainer looked at him oddly. "They aren't Jews," he said quietly, thinking Weiss had misunderstood the situation. "Just *Fidschis* and *Kohlen*."

Weiss looked at him. Age lent him an air of dark authority. He had supervised mass executions before Rainer Ehrenburg had been born. His eyes glistened in the light of the torches.

"I know what I said, Rainer. Believe me, when it comes to the crux, they're all Jews—black Jews, yellow Jews, white Jews, it's just one thing. There's only ever been one answer to a plague of vermin—exterminate them before they outnumber you."

He paused and looked up at the hostel again, unconsciously seeking out the pale face in the window.

"Tell your boys to get to work," he said. And for a moment there was silence.

Part 8
THE SCHOLAR

32

It was after nine when Yosef got back to the hotel. He had stayed on at Mortara's for a second meal after all the other guests had gone. Mortara and he had reminisced about Haifa, and Yosef had learned a little more about the hopes and fears of Italian Jews. Once or twice, he had tried to nudge the conversation back to the theme of the trial, but each time Mortara had steered away from it again. In the end Yosef had concluded that to show too much interest could prove counterproductive. He had arranged to meet Mortara and some Hebrew-speaking friends later in the week for lunch at a restaurant called Del Cambio.

Maryam was waiting in her room. She seemed tense, her manner both distant and irritated.

"Have you had anything to eat yet?" he asked.

"It's quite all right. I had some sandwiches from room service. Don't worry, I'm not hungry."

"What about a coffee? I'm told there are good cafés on the Piazza Castello. My friends recommended a place called Mulassano. We ..."

"Why didn't you ring? Why didn't you leave a message? You could have let me know you'd be back late. I've been worrying myself to death, thinking something...."

She caught herself just in time before bursting into tears. Seeing the astonished look on his face, she realized how like a nagging wife or mother she must have sounded. Somewhere

275

in her brain, the words she had been about to utter hung half-born, repeating themselves rhythmically and almost without meaning: "thinking something had happened to you ... happened to you ... happened to you."

She tried to smile, to wipe away the trite impression she had just made, but she could not. Her lips seemed to belong to someone else. To her dismay, she realized that she was shaking, that not only her lips, but her entire body had passed out of her certain control. She did not know what ruled her now, whether anxiety or fear or, beyond and above them both, love. Her skin felt hot, and she knew her cheeks had grown red. There was nothing she could do to prevent it. Still the smile would not come; instead of it there was the trembling, and all the time she could not take her eyes from him.

This time, when he put his arms round her, he knew there could be no pulling back. His need for her was urgent and overwhelming, sweeping away with it everything he had thought himself to be, all the arguments his mind had summoned up over the past few days to resist her and to deny everything he felt for her.

In the same moment that he took her in his arms, the trembling left her and a great shudder passed through her, leaving her utterly still as though she stood unmoving at the heart of a vortex or a hurricane. She felt herself half lifted, cradled, sealed by the knot of his embrace, and she heard herself cry out as though he had hurt her in some way. Suddenly, her body belonged to her again, and she raised her arms, pulling him to her, to hold him there forever.

"I love you," he said, and he realized that, although he had said the same words to other women in the past, he had never really understood their power or their worth until now.

"I never thought I'd hear that said in Hebrew," she answered. Her voice was very small and frightened.

He bent close then and whispered the same words in her ear in Arabic, and for a moment she rested like that, letting the words settle, Hebrew and Arabic mixed. Deep inside her she could feel her past and her present collide, small planets out of orbit, but she did not dare think of the future or whether it could have any meaning. Then she raised her hands to his face and turned his head until they were looking into one another's eyes, and she repeated to him what he had just said, first in Arabic, then in Hebrew. She drew back a little just to see him better, to let him draw her close again with his hand behind her head until their lips met and there were no more words.

Afterward, they lay in bed and talked, and it was as if they did so for the first time. In between, they would fall silent for long stretches at a time. The silences did not matter. It was enough to be able to turn and see that the other was there, or to lay skin to skin and know there was no more solitude. They made love again at midnight, more slowly this time, but with an increased passion that was almost frightening. After that, they slept for a time.

Yosef had never known such unmingled happiness, had never found it so easy to abandon his defenses in another's presence. All his life, he had been obliged to construct faces for himself, with gestures to accompany them and moods and attitudes to fit. In Morocco, he had been compliant, a Jew who knew his place and would never make trouble; in the army, he had acquired some of the brashness of his colleagues, to show that an Oriental Jew was as good an Israeli as one whose grandparents had come from Europe; and on the West Bank, he had adopted the role of a hard-liner because that was how settlers were supposed to be.

Here, with Maryam, none of his many faces fitted, and he found himself naked, stripped of artifice, knowing he wanted only one thing: for her to love him as he was. If she did, he thought, perhaps it might help him find his true identity.

She woke and watched him as he slept beside her, unaware of her attention. A soft glow came from a nightlight on the bedside table, enough for her to see him by, enough to commit to memory every inch of his face and body. She had never scrutinized her husband like this even once in the years they had been together, never stayed awake watching him breathe, wondering what he was dreaming about. Yet here she was, sleeping with a man who should have been her enemy, a man who stood for all she had learned to hate and despise, watching over him as though over a sleeping child.

She fell asleep again soon afterward and was taken by dreams, brought down deep into their world and held there against her will, beyond the passing of time. She dreamed of them both together, herself and Yosef, and she dreamed of them both naked and in a strange place with-

out walls, a place that seemed to go on forever. Her dream shifted and shimmered about
her, and their nakedness, that had been so pleasant a thing when she was awake, became all at
once a cause of unease, as though the dream
was poisoned. When she looked at him in the
dream, his body was thin and his head was
shaved. There was a tattoo on his left arm; when
she looked at her own arm, it was tattooed as
well. When she ran the palm of her right hand
across her head, it was shaved like his, and she
felt ashamed and frightened.

The dream ended and she passed into a sleep
without dreams.

There was a light, a light that moved back and
forth then came to rest on her eyelids. And a
voice, a harsh voice barking at her in a foreign
language. She fought them both for as long as
she could, then her eyes came open and she
saw that this was not a dream, that someone
was shining a torch in her face and snapping
at her in Italian, telling her to get up. Beside
her, Yosef was also half-awake. Another unseen
figure was next to him, pulling the bedclothes
away, forcing him to rise. She could just make
out a gloved hand, and in the hand a pistol
pointed straight at Yosef's head.

33

Yosef knew three things with certainty: first,
that he was sitting on a hard chair of medium
height with a high back; second, that he was
not dead; third, that he could not see.

Little by little, he tried to add to his fund of knowledge, but with each fresh addition his certainty diminished, leaving him with speculation in the end. He sensed that he was in the center of a large room of uncertain dimensions. From time to time there came the echoes of footsteps and the voices of his captors, whispering or speaking out loud in Italian. There was a door somewhere on his left that opened occasionally to let someone in or out. He could see absolutely nothing because someone had placed a thick black hood over his head. They had tied his hands behind him, round the back of the chair, so that he could not reach the hood.

Except at the beginning, when he had been ordered to dress and to accompany his assailants out of the hotel, no one had said a word to him. Maryam had translated their curt instructions at first, but when they took him from her room she was kept behind in order to assure his continued compliance. He had known that she had been frightened to death, and he had tried to reassure her, but they had pulled him away abruptly. He thought he might never see her again.

He had made no attempt to escape or draw attention while they crossed the long, high lobby, watched only by the bored gaze of the night porter, and he had climbed without protest into the large car that waited by the curb outside, its engine purring gently. There were three men with him, all dressed in suits. They kept behind him, as if to make sure he was given no opportunity to get a proper look at their faces. The moment he got inside, a man sitting on the rear seat had thrust the hood over his head.

The others had climbed in and they had driven off.

No one had spoken throughout the journey. They had driven for an hour or so, although Yosef had found it impossible to keep an accurate track of time. Knowing nothing of Turin or its environs, he had failed miserably to preserve a sense of direction. He did, however, suspect that they had traveled in circles and that they were still in the city: He had not experienced the cessation of noise that might have been expected had they headed into the countryside.

One thing he did know. They were deep underground, having come to where they now were by means of several steep flights of stairs and a long winding passage that had sloped at an acute angle for several hundred yards. The air was stale and damp, as though long trapped beneath the earth.

He himself did not speak. Not in the car, not in the room once they reached it. He knew who they were, he knew why they had come for him. It surprised him that they had not killed him already. There was nothing he could tell them, nothing he knew that they did not already know better than he. Unless they thought he was privy to the one secret that so consumed them, the whereabouts of the man called "K," whom Maryam guessed to be a German named Krämer. Yosef clenched his teeth hard against the thought, for if indeed they imagined him to know where they might find Krämer, then he would take a very long time to die.

Every so often, footsteps approached his chair and he knew that someone was standing in front of him or behind him, staring, watching, perhaps waiting for an order. Those were the worst moments, when he thought a blow would suddenly send him reeling or a gunshot would crack his skull from side to side. Worst of all was the knowledge that he feared the former most, that to imagine a slow beating in the darkness had more power to terrify than the thought of oblivion.

He thought often and with pain of Maryam. He had sharp, painful memories of their lovemaking earlier that night, of his return to her and her trembling and his taking her in his arms. Above all, he felt guilty for having involved her in this business knowing that he should have sent her away long before, but that his selfish need of her had prevented him from acting. Now, it was too late, and he feared she might already be dead or worse.

There was a long silence and for a time he was sure the room was empty. The room was cold, and he felt himself shiver. He felt light-headed from a mixture of fear and lack of sleep. It was difficult to breathe beneath the hood, and his skin itched from prolonged contact with the rough cloth. Thinking that his captors had perhaps retired for the night, he let his head slump forward and tried to snatch a little sleep.

Just as he felt himself begin to drift off, there came the bang of a door closing, then quick footsteps crossed the floor toward him. His head lifted and he braced himself for the blow or shot that might follow. Someone scraped a chair along the floor, a metal chair dragging across cracked tiles.

"I am told you do not speak Italian, Mr. Elbaz. Or is it Katzir? Or something else perhaps?"

The voice of his interlocutor was, Yosef guessed, that of a man in his forties, educated, calm, and neutral. The man spoke English with an American accent and, as far as he could judge, the fluency of a native speaker. He said nothing in reply.

"Well, let us call you Mr. Elbaz, then. Yosef Elbaz. We can establish your real name in due course, but let Elbaz do for now. Tell me, Yosef, who sent you to Italy?"

Yosef said nothing. The cold seeped into his bones and the silence into his heart.

"There is very little point in not talking, Yosef. My friends out there are much less gentle than I. And they have reason to be angry with you. You have prejudiced their safety and compromised the security of a very important undertaking. So, you see, they have a right to be told why you are here and who sent you."

"Go to hell."

"Well, that's an improvement. At least I know now that you've not been struck dumb."

"Please, take off the hood."

There was a brief silence, then his questioner said, "All right."

He felt a hand touch the top of his head, then the hood was lifted and light flooded his eyes, abnormally bright. That was the worst moment, for he knew with certainty then that they did not care if he saw their faces, that they had already decided to kill him once the questioning ended.

It took several minutes for his eyes to adjust to the brightness. Slowly, a room formed out of raw light: a low-ceilinged chamber divided by square pillars at regular intervals, bare concrete walls, a floor of ocher-colored kiln-fired tiles, cracked and caked with the grime of many years. The light, once he grew accustomed to it, was not particularly bright at all. It came from a group of fluorescent tubes above the section in which he was seated, and a steadying rise and fall in the brightness suggested that these were powered by a small generator rather than from the regular supply.

The man sent to question Yosef sat watching patiently from a chair some three feet to his left. He was dressed in corduroy slacks and a thick woolen sweater, he wore thin gold glasses with strong lenses, and he had thin sand-colored hair brushed back carefully to reveal a high forehead. Yosef had expected someone brutish and threatening, but this man seemed intelligent and no more dangerous than a boy fresh from school.

"May we continue?" he asked.

Yosef nodded.

"What is your interest in the Pacchia case?"

So he'd been right, thought Yosef: There was a connection between the killings and the forthcoming trial.

"I knew nothing of Pacchia or the trial until this afternoon. You have to believe me."

The stranger shook his head. "No, I don't have to. I know next to nothing about you. For example, you say you've just arrived in Italy from Israel. And yet you know about the deaths of Ennio Pontecorvo and Alberto Cantoni, not to mention the other killing in Sardinia. None of those murders was reported in the international press, not even in Israel. They were played down here in Italy. So perhaps you can explain just how you came by your information."

Yosef knew he had been trapped. He could not begin to guess how his captors were so well informed about what he knew, but he could not let them know that Mossad was aware of what had been happening here and was trying to intervene.

"I have business contacts in Italy," Yosef said. "Jewish contacts. They'd read about the killings in the local press, and they thought I might be interested."

"You made no mention of those contacts yesterday when you chatted about your affairs at Leone Mortara's."

A chill went through Yosef. If they knew what he had said not many hours previously at a private gathering, there could be only one explanation: They had managed to infiltrate the Jewish community of Turin. Was that why Professor Cantoni had met his death? Had the old man said something incautious in the course of a lunch at Mortara's and been killed in consequence following a report from an unsuspected fascist informer? An informer who was still doing his job.

"I saw no reason to mention them," he retorted.

"You're lying. The question is why. If you are an Israeli, then you can hardly be working for Pacchia and his friends. Unless, of course, you're actually an Arab like your friend Miss Shumayyil. Which brings us back to the question of who sent you."

Yosef did a slow double-take. What had the

man meant by that phrase, "Pacchia and his friends"? Surely he was himself one of Pacchia's henchmen, or at least an admirer. Why would he distance himself from his own group in such an awkward way? Yosef looked at him, wondering if it had been an attempt to trick him, but his questioner showed no obvious sign of waiting for him to fall into a trap.

"No one sent me," he said. "I'm here on my own, for my own reasons."

"And what are they?"

Yosef had been thinking hard. He knew that he was not going to come out of this alive whatever happened, but he still hoped it might be possible to save Maryam at the very least. If they thought she knew nothing of what lay behind the killings, there was a chance—a very slim chance—that he could persuade them to let her go. It was all he had left to cling to, and he did so desperately.

"Very well," he said. "I'll tell you what I can. If you don't like it, that's too bad. My name is Yosef Abuhatseira. I'm an Israeli Jew from Qiryat Arba in Judea. I had a sister called Chaya. She was twenty-eight years old, and she had a son called Yoel. Yoel was kidnapped just over a month ago, and after that Chaya was murdered along with her husband, Aryeh. They were murdered by your people or your associates. In cold blood and for no good reason. The killings were the ones that took place in Sardinia. Their name was Levin—I'm sure that means something to you."

The man beside him shook his head slowly, as though it hurt him to do so. He appeared honestly not to recognize the name.

"No," he said. "Their names mean nothing at all to me. Tell me the rest."

Yosef explained as concisely as he could the circumstances under which he had originally been brought to Sardinia, his hunt for Yoel, and his discovery of the bodies of Aryeh and Chaya on his return to Arzachena. He had gone back to the island for no other purpose than to track down their killers, he said. The police had been dragging their feet and he had lost all confidence in them. Maryam Shumayyil had been hired by him as an interpreter; she knew nothing more than the bare minimum, nothing the police did not know.

Yosef's story came to an end. A long silence followed. His questioner did not immediately pursue any of the things he had said, but instead sat quite still, his head resting on one hand as though deep in thought. Yosef prayed that his explanation of Maryam's role had been sufficient to make his captors think twice about hurting her.

The man raised his head and looked at Yosef, and for a moment it seemed that he was afraid of something.

"Yosef," he said. His voice had undergone a change and was no longer the confident voice in which he had spoken before. "A little earlier, you said that your sister and her husband had been killed by my people or my associates. I did not understand you. What exactly did you mean?"

"Surely that's obvious."

"No, it isn't. When you said 'your people,' whom did you mean?"

"I don't know exactly. I know very little about

287

your organizations and their factions. Alleanza Nazionale, Avanguardia Nazionale, Ordine Nuovo—you could belong to any or all of them, how would I know? But it all boils down to the same thing in the end. My sister and her husband were killed by fascists, and for no other reason than that they were Jews."

The interrogator stared at Yosef as though in disbelief. The silence between them now was wracked by more than fear. Something was very wrong.

"Yosef," asked the other man, "is what you've just told me true?"

Yosef nodded wearily. His features and his gestures both were clear of guile, like a wild place scraped free of all but sand or the underpinnings of sand, the bare rock and the gravel. His eyes held no deceit.

"Do you dream?" asked the man. He too seemed tired, stripped down to something utterly bare.

"We all dream," answered Yosef.

"But what do you dream of when you dream?"

And somehow Yosef understood. It did not make sense, it contradicted his sense of what was happening, but he understood.

"I dream of wagons," he said, "long wagons of wood filled with sleeping people, and with people past sleep, people who have no dreams. I dream of men in black uniforms, and dogs like wolves, and wire to make the limits of the world. And behind the wire faces and bare hands shivering with cold. And in my dreams sometimes I am naked, and my head is shaved, and the men in black uniforms are pushing me into a small room that smells of carbolic. That's all.

My dreams end there, and I know nothing more than that. You may know more. You should know what follows in that little room."

He stopped speaking. The narrow chamber shook with his voice, and a long silence followed. It was hard to break it, for it was the deepest of all silences.

The stranger said nothing. Yosef watched him sit there, inert, as though shocked or defeated by what he had told him.

"Wait there," he said finally, as though mocking the ropes that held Yosef to the chair.

He went out and was away a long time. Yosef sat without moving. Why had the man asked him about his dreams? Did fascists dream of the same things? Were he and his captors locked together in a senseless nightmare of their mutual construction, just as the same blood flowed in all their veins? Time passed in a silence like ice, as though a glacier moved soundlessly through the room, slipping to oblivion with Yosef in its maw.

The door opened and the interrogator came back in. He was followed by a second man. As Yosef looked up, he caught sight of the second man's face, and he knew at once that he recognized him. It was only as the man stepped toward him that he was able to put a name and an identity to the face. He saw again the long, pale hair, the troubled eyes; he was taken back to that afternoon, to the conversation that had followed the *shabbat* lunch at Leone Mortara's, and he knew that the informer who had betrayed him to his abductors had been Bruno Frezza.

34

He looked at the bedside clock and swore loudly. His wife stirred in her sleep, and he swore again, this time under his breath, fearing that he had woken her. She grunted, then rolled over. He felt her right arm graze his chest.

"Antonio," she murmured, *"che hai? Non puoi dormire?"*

He squeezed her hand and released it.

"Non ho niente. Dormi pure, dormi."

She murmured something incomprehensible and rolled back on her left side. He sighed and glanced at the clock again. It was after two and he was on duty again at eight.

He'd been uneasy all day, tormented by a growing host of inconsistencies and contradictions in the case he was handling, the homicide at the President Hotel. Too much was happening too fast, and he was already feeling out of his depth.

The artist's impression of the dead woman that had been released to the press had brought in an immediate response. Several people had contacted the *questura* to identify her as Tina Mannuzzu, the wife of a lawyer from Arzachena. Each of Nieddu's contacts had made a point of mentioning that Tina's husband, Michele, had been found murdered not long ago near Oliena.

The inspector had remembered the case, but he could not at first recall whether it had been dealt with by his own *questura*—which covered

290

the region in which the victim had lived—or that of Nuoro province, where his body had been found. A quick check showed that Nuoro had passed the affair on to Sassari, and that the case had been handed to De Felice. That should have meant that he himself would now have a copy of the original file, but when he looked, there was nothing. Discreet inquiries revealed that there was no record of Michele Mannuzzu's murder anywhere in the Sassari *questura* building.

His principal contact, Tina Mannuzzu's sister, Silvana, had given him whatever details she possessed of the circumstances in which Michele had met his death. He had, she explained, been acting as *intermediario* for clients whose son had been kidnapped. She had not known the name, but she had remembered that they were Jewish. And she did know that the boy's parents had been killed in Arzachena soon after Michele disappeared.

Another contact, a member of the bridge club to which Tina had belonged, confirmed the story of the kidnapping, although she claimed to have known nothing of Michele's role in the negotiations. She was able to identify the murdered couple as Aryeh and Chaya Levin, and their son as Yoel. Another thing she remembered—the Levins had been visited by a relative from Israel, a man called Abu-something. He'd taken the boy back to Israel with him along with the remains of Yoel's parents, who were to be buried in Jerusalem.

Nieddu had been puzzled. A kidnapping followed by a double murder ought to have attracted a great deal of attention, especially in a place like Arzachena, which prided itself on its security. That, of course, would be good enough reason to keep the whole thing under wraps. Both the tourist trade and the long-term rental business could be badly affected by a thing like that. But it was still peculiar that someone in his position, an inspector in the homicide division at Sassari police headquarters, should be so completely in the dark.

He had checked central records for a second time, and for the second time he had drawn a blank. No murder of people called Levin was listed anywhere.

Half an hour in the local library had brought to light only the briefest of references to the deaths of Aryeh and Chaya Levin in the local paper. Their son Yoel, the piece had noted, had been taken home to Israel by relatives. He had made a note of the fact that the Levins were originally Israelis. One murder in Sassari province that involved Israeli citizens was unusual. Two within not much more than a month could not be coincidence.

There had been no mention in the newspaper piece of an abduction or a ransom demand. Back at the *questura,* Nieddu had checked the central registry. There was no record of Yoel Levin's kidnapping nor of his parents' murders.

It seemed fair to assume that, if there had indeed been a kidnapping, the boy had been taken south into Nuoro. That would explain the later appearance of the *intermediario's* body near Oliena, and possibly the lack of a reference to the abduction in the Sassari files.

He had telephoned the records department at the Nuoro *questura.* The conversation was still etched on his brain, and in the darkness of his bedroom, it played and replayed itself, denying him sleep or comfort.

"We have no record of a kidnapping under that name," said the clerk. "Just a minute, though—something's coming up here. Give me a second. Yes, we had a report a couple of days ago that some bodies had been found buried up in the Gennargentu. An item of clothing was found in a cave nearby, a child's jacket. There was a name inside. Yoel Levin. The bodies have been taken to the mortuary for examination. No results as yet."

He had put down the phone and thought long and hard about what was happening. No doubt now about the kidnapping or the murders, but his thoughts kept returning to the unidentified Israeli who had visited the Levins before their deaths. A call to passport control at Rome's Fiumicino Airport confirmed that an Israeli citizen named Yosef Abuhatseira had passed through a few days after the disappearance of Michele Mannuzzu. A faxed photograph gave the man a face, and a trip to the President Hotel provided immediate confirmation that Yosef Abuhatseira and Yosef Katzir were one and the same person.

The real bombshell had burst later that afternoon. On his way out of Olbia, he had listened to a local police broadcast and heard that two cars had been found wrecked at the foot of a cliff in the north of the island along with the bodies of four men, three of whom had gunshot wounds. The report had not especially interested him, but all the way back to Sassari something about it had nagged at him.

It was only as he was climbing the stairs up to his office (he was on weekend shift) that it clicked. One of the cars had been a red 1993 Volkswagen. Five minutes later, he had what he wanted in front of him: a Volkswagen of the same year and color had belonged to Abuhatseira's associate, Maryam Shumayyil. He had picked up the phone and verified the report with the station at Olbia, whose officers had investigated the wrecks. The license plate of the wrecked car corresponded to that belonging to Shumayyil.

Nieddu now had a series of incidents, none of them related on the surface, yet all linked through one person, the Israeli, Abuhatseira. It occurred to him that if Abuhatseira had really come to Sardinia in order to help his sister and brother-in-law, then it was entirely possible that the later murders had been carried out by him in revenge for their deaths. Michele Mannuzzu must have betrayed his clients in some way, and it was not impossible that his wife had been involved. The bodies in the Gennargentu would, he guessed, turn out to be those of Yoel Levin's kidnappers. And once the men found at the foot of the cliff alongside Maryam Shumayyil's Volkswagen had been identified, it would doubtless be shown that they, too, had had a hand in the Levin murders.

The most pressing problem, however, was why so many files were missing. The kidnapping he could discount: If the Levins had had any sense, they would have kept the affair to themselves and involved a third party—which is what they appeared to have done. But the killings had not been solved, which meant that someone at the *questura* must have been given responsibility for them. He could have gone round his colleagues one by one, asking if anyone knew of the case, but something made him hesitate. Police files did not disappear by accident, which meant that someone had meant them to disappear.

A phone call to the Israeli embassy had produced the unsurprising information that the office was closed until Monday morning. His bridge club informant had been more helpful. She had told him that Aryeh Levin had been in the hotel trade. Guessing that if the Levins had been targeted for a ransom demand, they must have had a little money, Nieddu had concentrated on the larger establishments first of all, and half an hour later he was on the line with Aryeh's former partner, Fabio Quintavalle.

Their conversation provided little more than confirmation of the Levins' deaths. Quintavalle had been told nothing of a kidnapping and knew nothing of Mannuzzu's involvement in the affair, although he did know that the lawyer had acted for Aryeh in the past.

"You might try the Levins' housekeeper," he said, just as he was about to put the phone down. "Her name's Maria Deiana. I think she comes from Oliena or near there originally."

A call to the Levins' nearest *droghiere* produced the information that Maria had returned to live with her brother after the tragedy. No, they had no telephone, but she had left a neighbor's number in case anyone needed to get in touch. The shopkeeper found the number after a short search, and twenty minutes later Nieddu was speaking with the former housekeeper.

She told him everything about the kidnapping and the events that had followed it. Naturally, she omitted all mention of the expedition into the Gennargentu and Yoel's rescue, sticking instead to the "official" version, whereby Yosef had acted as *intermediario* and Maryam as interpreter, ending in Yoel's handover and the return to Arzachena, where they found Aryeh and Chaya murdered.

They talked for a very long time, and though he tried his hardest, he could not get the old woman to budge from her story. It was only at the very end, quite inadvertently, that she told him what he wanted to hear.

"I don't see why you're asking all this," she had said. "You've got it all on paper anyway."

"I'm sorry, I don't understand. We've not spoken before."

"No, but the other policeman made notes. He has it all in his little book."

"What other policeman was that?"

"The one that visited me after the murder, of course. He was an inspector like yourself."

"Can you remember his name?"

A silence had followed. Then her voice, thinned by distance, had said, "De Felice. That was it. Inspector De Felice."

He lay in the silence, and beside him his wife's soft breathing sounded as though it came from another world. The events of the day passed through his head like quicksilver in a narrow channel, bright and shining and dizzying. He wondered if De Felice had put up much of a struggle. And he wondered how long it would be before they came for him.

35

Palazzo di Giustizia
Milan
Monday morning

The Palace of Justice lay beneath a marble gray sky, a bauble set down without consequence among other baubles. Its high, striated facade carried words and emblems proclaiming the virtues of the law and the benefits of justice, but the scene unfolding on its steps mocked them like dirt thrown in the face of a benefactor.

A long line of police formed a wavering wall between two distinct groups of protesters, right-wingers on one side, everybody else on the other, divided like rival crowds at a football match—the sort of match at which one can smell the scent of imminent tragedy. It was a very poor symbol of society at large, or of local or national politics, and yet almost every group of any significance in Italian life was represented, and almost every sentiment found its focus and expression somewhere in the swaying multitude.

There had been an impressive turnout by supporters of Pacchia and his codefendants. Not only were there representatives of the extreme right, immediately recognizable by their shaven heads, black jackets, or flagrantly fascist badges, there was also a large contingent of self-proclaimed "ordinary citizens." These were disenfranchised Christian Democrats who had not yet taken the step of voting National Alliance, but who considered themselves financially and morally imperiled by a wave of illegal immigrants brought to their shores by a complex cabal of Jews and atheists and Communists. They had come to add their voices to the clamor defending Pier Maria Pacchia from his persecutors, and if that meant rubbing shoulders with skinheads, at least the skinheads held something sacred and were willing to stand up for what they believed.

Facing them was a mixed array of the presumed persecutors, ranging from liberal Catholics and frightened Jews to anarchists and left-wing extremists with their own agendas. While the anarchists tried to shout down a group of youths in black shirts who sang old fascist songs and lifted their arms in imitation of their grandfathers, most of those in the liberal camp simply stood and watched the drama unfold, their faces worried, helpless, and afraid.

Some held placards, others candles, pale in the morning light, and many wore on their arms the yellow Star of David. Not all who wore it had Jewish blood in their veins. They knew that if Pacchia won his case, it would not be long before the line of police that now protected them and their right to be here would step aside and let the men in black shirts turn their rage on them and their friends. The hot rage would turn in days to cold fury, their candles would be snuffed out, and the stars they wore as armbands would once again become a badge of suffering.

From his vantage point in a helicopter circling above the palazzo, carabiniere captain

Bernardino Mei could see the scene on the ground unfolding like a pageant: the police like a narrow, constantly moving stream, the crowds on either side like trembling banks of earth shaken by an earthquake—each threatening to fall, all at once, upon the other. In the center, flanked by police, stretched a narrow passage through which a steady flow of lawyers, reporters, witnesses, and others with business in the courts was struggling to enter the building.

He saw another television van approaching from the southern sector of the ring road and radioed ground control to prepare for its arrival. The van could not approach down the Via Guastalla, which was blocked off in order to protect the Jewish temple at the bottom of the street. This meant rerouting it before it reached the Via San Barnaba.

Raiuno, Raidue, and Raitre were already at the Palazzo, each preparing to cover the trial with its own political bias. The van was from Canale 5, their main rival, but there were also crews from several foreign news networks. In a few hours' time, excerpts from the trial would be broadcast on millions of TV screens.

Two blocks away, in front of the university, a line of armored vehicles, Fiat 55–13 armored buses and personnel carriers, stood ready to move in the moment the demonstrations showed signs of getting out of hand. The APCs were equipped with water cannons and breech-loaded smoke-grenade launchers, and the men in them were provided not only with riot shields and body armor, but also with tear-gas grenades, mace canisters, and Schermuly antiriot guns chambered for firing plastic baton rounds.

From the helicopter, everything seemed to take place in a curious, strained silence, as though in a dream. The shifting of the crowd was at times almost balletic, all cries and imprecations muffled or wiped out by the chopping of the rotors.

On the ground, however, it seemed that pure bedlam had erupted onto the streets of the city. The baying of the crowd was matched by the cacophony of sounds produced by the police and carabinieri—the sirens of patrol cars, the raucous voices of megaphones issuing incomprehensible instructions, the strutting flap of the helicopter overhead.

As though from nowhere, a long black car flanked by police motorcycles drew up outside the palazzo. Pier Maria Pacchia had arrived. Within seconds, the police presence at the curbside had miraculously thickened. The nearside rear door of the car was flung open and Pacchia stepped confidently out onto the pavement, his face wreathed in smiles.

He stood and faced the crowd, a tall, suave figure wearing a long black overcoat that had been draped negligently over square shoulders. His suit was newly pressed, his discreetly striped tie held in place by a diamond-tipped pin. For a few moments, he stood by the car, smiling at the press and television cameras, broadcasting a message of serenity and confidence, almost of nonchalance in the face of so much hostility.

A reporter from the conservative RAI 1 channel managed to squeeze through the knot of spectators, thrusting a microphone in his direction.

"Signor Pacchia, how do you feel at this moment?"

"I feel very well, Roberta, very well indeed. Why shouldn't I? This is a basic matter of human rights. There are extremists in this country who wish to suppress my right to speak freely on an issue of vital concern to the public. I have every confidence in the judicial system, and I know that justice will be done. If it is not, we shall take the matter before the European Court of Human Rights. I am not here today to defend myself, but to fight for the rights of the downtrodden. Now, if you'll excuse me, I have to be in court."

Cheered loudly on one side and booed on the other, he made his way quietly down the precarious human tunnel, preceded and followed by an armed police guard. At the steps, he turned once more to the crowd, raised his arm in what might have been the polite wave of a parliamentarian or the long-proscribed salute of a defeated tyranny, and smiled one last time for the cameras.

On the street, a second car had drawn up. It carried Enrico Butti and Guido Gentileschi, the publisher and bookseller who were Pacchia's codefendants. Known to only a few in the crowd, their reception and their passage to the court was less clamorous than that of their predecessor. Unlike Pacchia, they betrayed their nervousness by their hunched postures and anxious glances. They ignored the microphones thrust before them and averted their faces from the cameras as best they could. Unlike Pacchia, they had no bodyguards, only a couple of regular policemen appointed to the task of escorting them as far as the courtroom.

As Butti reached the steps, he turned to let Gentileschi catch up with him. Just then, there was a movement in the crowd. An elderly man with long white hair leaned out from a clump of demonstrators calling for an end to fascism and, as though by a miracle, succeeded in aiming a gob of spit directly at Butti. It caught the publisher in the face, just below the eye, and he jerked back, raising one hand too late to defend himself. Gentileschi made it to the steps, and both men turned to walk the last few yards into the palazzo.

There was a popping sound, then another and another, each time muffled by the crowd. Butti staggered forward, his arms lifting, and fell facedown on the steps. A broad crimson stain had already appeared on his back. Gentileschi, though hit twice, managed to turn as though trying to run back to the safety of the throng below, a look of fear and confusion on his face. A fourth shot rang out, distinct this time, hitting him full in the chest. He did not cry out or stagger or clutch his wound, but simply crumpled where he stood, his head striking the steps with a loud crack, his blood mingling with that of his companion.

It was not until much later that witnesses established that the shots had come not from that part of the crowd made up of the victims' opponents, but from a knot of right-wingers connected to the Ludwig action group. Mysteriously, the gunman had managed to drop his weapon, an Uzi pistol, and make his escape. By then, however, it scarcely mattered where he had come from or where he had run to. The rumor had already spread that Butti and Gentileschi had been killed by a Jewish assassin, a hit man sent by Mossad to silence them and Pacchia.

36

On the television screen, Yosef watched Butti stagger and fall, then Gentileschi slither in his own blood, cough, and die. The crack of the fourth shot still hung in the air, as indelible as blood on linen. He listened as silence engulfed the crowd and continued listening as the occasional cries of shock turned to mingled horror and rage. He looked again and watched the crimson stains on the victims' clothing spread like red ink on blotting paper. Somewhere, a megaphone blared, the words clipped and indistinct. A stream of blood gathered and rolled with what seemed like deliberate solemnity across the steps of the palazzo, mocking the very purpose of the place.

The camera moved in and hung for several moments above the blood as though to fix it as an emblem in the viewer's mind. Later, pious hands would dip articles of clothing in the stream and carry them away as relics. Now the picture faded and the face of the newscaster appeared again on the screen. Yosef lifted the remote control and turned down the sound.

It was the fifth or sixth time he had watched the film of the killings. The scene had been played and replayed at every opportunity throughout the day, keeping viewers tuned in with morbid intensity to Raiuno and its hourly bulletins.

Yosef put down the remote and turned to the man beside him, Bruno Frezza.

"The shots came from the right, I'm sure of it," said Yosef. "But we could do with film from one or two other angles."

"I've got people working on that. The video recorder will be here soon. I've asked for one with slow motion, jogging, and freeze-frame facilities. But we may not need it. We're getting eyewitness reports that confirm the gunman was in the fascist section of the crowd."

It had taken time and effort to confirm Yosef's story. Messages and photographs had been sent to Sardinia and Israel, discreet but businesslike inquiries had been made at the Israeli embassy in Rome, and by Sunday evening he had received a clean bill of health. He was who he claimed to be, and he had been sent to Italy by Mossad, if only unofficially. The same process had been gone through for Maryam with similar results.

Bruno Frezza and his companions were founding members of Azione Ebrea, a Jewish organization set up in 1992 to combat the recrudescence of anti-Semitism within Italy. The organization operated openly, holding public meetings, publishing a monthly news and features journal, and generally drawing attention to the problem of verbal or physical attacks on Jews or Jewish property.

Following the decision to prosecute Pier Maria Pacchia, Bruno and two friends decided to set up a secret committee, initially to monitor the trial and later to take action to secure a conviction. Since most of the leading members of the original action group were by then fairly well-known, they invited a number of less prominent individuals to help. Ennio Pontecorvo, Alberto Cantoni, and Umberto Levi had all been members of the committee. Yosef had been told about Azione Ebrea, but not about the committee handling the Pacchia trial.

It had, however, quickly become apparent that Yosef possessed skills and experience the others lacked. They were well-equipped intellectually, but, although they had guns and the will to use them, none had police or military experience or the know-how that went with it. In the situation now developing, Frezza realized that Yosef's arrival might prove more than fortuitous.

Maryam came into the room just then. She and Yosef had spent a tense day together on Sunday, aware that their abductors were not fascists as they had assumed, but still not knowing whether their stories would be believed or not. Once their identities had been confirmed, however, they were told both the identity of their captors and the nature of the place to which they had been taken.

This was a complex of rooms located deep beneath Turin, part of a wider network of tunnels and chambers burrowed beneath the city over some three centuries. The first tunnels had been excavated during the great siege of 1706 and added to over the years for all manner of reasons, not all of them legitimate. It was reputed that covens of Satanists used these man-made caverns as venues for their midnight masses, but they had also served more mundane functions.

During the Second World War, at the height of the Allied bombing raids on the city, a section of the tunnels had been converted into air-raid shelters, provided with their own water supply and electricity. Forgotten after the war and the collapse of the Mussolini regime, they had been rediscovered with the help of Alberto Cantoni, who had himself sheltered there before being denounced and sent first to the internment camp at Fossoli and then to Auschwitz with the convoy of February 22, 1944.

Frezza and his colleagues had been using the old shelter for several months now. They had found a way to provide electricity by means of the original oil-fired generator, returned to working order by a colleague. In the back of Bruno's mind had been the notion that, one day soon, they and other members of the Jewish community might well need a hiding place once again.

Maryam went up to Yosef and kissed him gently but affectionately on the cheek. He blushed, but smiled at her. He had still not grown accustomed to the idea of having a lover around, much less to revealing the fact to others. But since nobody else seemed even to notice, he relaxed a little and followed her with his eyes as she sat down near him. He found it hard to believe that she had any time for him at all, much less that she had said she loved him.

"Keep the TV on," Maryam said. "Lazzarini's due to make a statement any minute." She had been in another room, listening to a radio report on the killings.

"I'm sorry," said Yosef, "who's Lazzarini?"

"The prime minister, silly. Don't you know anything about Italy?"

"Of course I do. It's just that you seem to have new prime ministers every week or so."

"That's an exaggeration," said Frezza. "Most of them last around a month now."

"Has the assassination film been on again?" Maryam asked. She shuddered. The morbid interest shown in the subject had depressed her.

Yosef nodded. "I'm afraid so, yes."

"No new film?"

"Not yet. I'm beginning to think the police may have confiscated film from the other crews covering the event. The Raiuno footage is all they've been showing."

"Have you tried the other channels?"

"Yes," answered Frezza. "They all use the Raiuno footage."

"Well, it's probably the best available. They were in an ideal spot, and they got everything in close-up. It's what people want to see. All the same, a different viewpoint would be a relief. I don't think I can bear to watch the Raiuno film again."

"Bruno says there are reports that the shot was fired from inside the fascist crowd."

Maryam turned to Frezza. "Is that correct?" He nodded.

"But surely they'd have caught the gunman. They wouldn't have let him out alive. The last radio report said the shots came from a group of Jewish protestors. There's some idea that the killer was Jewish."

"I don't like the sound of it," said Bruno. "It's starting to look like a setup. Butti and Gentileschi were the weakest links in Pacchia's defense. They threatened to bring him down

307

with them if they crumbled. And there was a good chance of that happening. At the very least, it's made our job much harder. I think the fascists had them shot and now they're trying to kill two birds with one stone by pinning the blame on the Jews. It wouldn't be the first time."

"Could they get away with that?" asked Yosef. "With a setup, I mean?"

"You must be joking," answered Bruno. "This is the country of setups. The right got away with it in the seventies when they carried out a series of bombing campaigns and made it seem like the work of left-wing extremists. They've done it before and got away with it. This would be nothing by comparison."

"Shhhh," whispered Maryam. "Lazzarini's just coming on."

Yosef turned up the volume. The prime minister had already been speaking. He looked gray and anxious, like someone who has just found himself in a trap from which there is no escape.

"...this morning. I have asked General Mario Danti of the carabinieri to launch an immediate investigation to ensure that the assassin is apprehended and brought to justice without delay.

"Today's proceedings at the assize court have, naturally, been adjourned. However, following a discussion with the minister of justice and the presiding magistrates, it may be possible to commence the trial tomorrow morning. Steps have been taken to ensure the safety of parliamentary deputy Pier Maria Pacchia, and security in and around the courtroom will be increased.

"I want to assure all of you that everything

humanly possible is being done to ensure that the perpetrators of this criminal act will not be allowed to make a mockery of this country's legal system or the concept of justice itself. Whoever carried out this cowardly deed will be hounded, caught, and punished. Favor will be shown to no one, whether they be Jews, Catholics, or atheists. And if it is found that whoever pulled the trigger was acting on instructions from others, let there be no doubt in anyone's mind that they, too, will be hunted down and made to answer for their crimes."

There was a pause during which Lazzarini said nothing, but sat wide-eyed staring at the camera, a man in limbo, the object of the attention of millions of people to whom he was tied neither by love nor by affection, but by the bonds of custom and negligence. Maryam translated the gist of what he had said for Yosef.

"He's losing control," said Bruno. "Just look at him—he's scared. He knows this could finish him and he doesn't know what to do next."

The picture faded and the newscaster returned to the screen. Yosef lifted the remote to kill the sound, but Maryam interrupted him.

"Just a moment. I think Pacchia's coming on."

"Pacchia?" Bruno looked at her. "What's going on? He was instructed not to make statements to the press. The magistrates said it would prejudice the trial."

Suddenly, the screen flickered and Pier Maria Pacchia appeared in front of a backdrop of the Duomo, suggesting he was in another studio.

"I have asked and received permission to say a few words to you," he began. "As you already know, my codefendants, Enrico Butti and Guido

Gentileschi, were gunned down this morning in a cowardly attack that happened as they were on their way to court. Their voices have been silenced forever. They cannot now defend themselves from the unfounded and inaccurate charges that had been laid against them.

"It now rests with me to clear their names. I have been advised that my own life is at risk, and I have every reason to take that warning seriously. It has been suggested that I should go into hiding or that the trial should now be held in camera, at a more secure location.

"I have rejected both suggestions. To do either would be to bend to the pressure of the international Jewish lobby, whose only wish is to see me gagged, as the mouths of my codefendants were so permanently gagged this morning. The trial will continue under the scrutiny of the press and television, in the full glare of publicity, and under the eyes of the public. There will, of course, have to be restrictions on both press and public access to the Palazzo di Giustizia, but under the circumstances, I am sure those concerned will prove both tolerant and understanding.

"The trial will go ahead, and I will be exonerated. The issue at stake here is nothing less than the sacred right to freedom of speech and opinion, and I am willing to put my own life at risk in order to fight for that right. For myself, I ask nothing but your prayers, that right may triumph over wrong and freedom over tyranny. And I ask your prayers for the souls of Enrico Butti and Guido Gentileschi, peace-loving men who paid this morning with their lives that others might live in freedom and in truth."

The picture returned again to the main studio. Yosef lowered the sound while Maryam summed up for him what Pacchia had said. He listened in disgust and astonishment, hardly believing it possible that anyone should want to twist reality to such an abnormal degree.

Without asking, Bruno reached out and snatched the remote control from Yosef. He turned the sound up and Maryam fell silent.

"We have a further item relating to this morning's tragedy. An official spokesman for the ministry of justice has just confirmed that the trial of Signor Pacchia, originally scheduled to begin today, will instead commence tomorrow, although a precise time has not been set. Protestors will be barred from the area around the Palace of Justice, and entrance to the building for reporters and members of the public will be severely restricted.

"The ministry has also confirmed that a change will now be made to the panel of magistrates hearing the case. It is understood that two of the three judges have been granted leave to stand down. Dottore Giambattista Tacca and Dottore Mariotto Palmerucci are to preside over unrelated cases next week. In their place, judges Agostino Fo and Ettore Della Robbia will sit at the assize court."

Bruno almost leaped from his seat.

"What the hell's going on?" he demanded. "That means all three magistrates hearing the case will be right-wingers. They can't do this."

"Can't you stop them?"

"We'll have to do something. This whole thing's being manipulated. First the press, now the judges. It's a disaster."

311

"Just a second," said Maryam. She had caught sight of something on the screen. The newscaster was unfolding a note that had been passed to him. He looked up.

"We have just received word from the carabinieri that a suspect has been named in the Palazzo di Giustizia killings. He is a Jewish male, aged thirty-seven, and only recently arrived in this country. The Polizia di Stato have confirmed that a man answering his description is already wanted in connection with a number of killings in Sardinia.

"Our source states that the suspect is an Israeli citizen. Since his arrival in this country he has been using a number of false identities. His real name is Yosef Abuhatseira, and he has also been calling himself Yosef Katzir and Yosef Elbaz. It is understood that Abuhatseira is a trained assassin, and it is thought likely that he was sent to Italy by a foreign intelligence agency with the object of eliminating the defendants in the Pacchia trial.

"We hope to have more information about the suspect shortly. In the meantime, we have just been sent the following photograph. Anyone who thinks they have seen Abuhatseira is requested to make immediate contact with either the carabinieri or the police. On no account should members of the public approach him. He is armed and dangerous."

A photograph of Yosef was flashed on the screen. The quality was poor, but it would be enough to trigger recognition in more than one viewer. Yosef turned to Bruno.

"You're right," he said. "This is a setup."

312

37

"Come in, Inspector Nieddu. Sit down." The vice-questore sat behind his desk like a Buddha who has just found a flaw in nirvana. Nieddu had only been in Dessì's office two or three times before, and each time it had been like a hand grabbing him by the balls and twisting hard. He wiped his brow with a grubby tissue and sat down.

"Are you making progress with the President Hotel killing?" Dessì asked.

"I have leads, yes, sir."

"What about Katzir? Have you managed to track him down yet?"

Nieddu shook his head glumly. Katzir or Abuhatseira or whatever his name was had covered his tracks well. The search for him had led to the mainland, and recent reports suggested that the Israeli had finally headed north, possibly to Milan or Turin. Nieddu himself had spent most of his time working on the more problematic aspects of the case, particularly the presumed links to other killings on the island. He still could not understand how it all fit together, and more than anything he was puzzled and worried by the systematic effort to lose police records.

"He's somewhere in Piemonte or Lombardia, sir, I'm almost certain of it. Most probably Milan or Turin: We've got leads to both cities. I expect to hear more any day now. If you like, I'll get on to it right away."

A look of contempt crossed Dessì's face.

"You'd be wasting your time. Here, take a look at this. It's just come in from the ministry in Rome."

The vice-questore passed a sheet of fax paper across the desk. Nieddu picked it up as though it might explode. In a way it did.

The suspect currently sought in connection with the murders of Enrico Butti and Guido Gentileschi in Milan this morning is Yosef Abuhatseira, an Israeli citizen from Qiryat Arba. Abuhatseira entered Italy through Fiumicino Airport on the 17th of March using the assumed name of Yosef Katzir. He has since used the name Yosef Elbaz and possibly other identities.

The suspect is wanted in Sardinia for the murders of Michele and Tina Mannuzzu, both of Arzachena; of Paolo Satta, Giacinto Ledda, Loddo Ciusa, Sardus Cambosu, and Matteo Padedda, all shepherds from the Gennargentu in Nuoro province; of Raffaella Carra, an accountant from Oliena; and of Filippo Biasi, Cesare Turiddu, and Andrea Lussu, all residents of Olbia.

Although these killings appear to be directly linked to the recent deaths of Abuhatseira's sister and brother-in-law in Arzachena in January, there is reason to suspect a political motive for the assassinations carried out this morning. In the ...

Nieddu stopped reading. He felt stiff and sore, as though someone had been pummeling him mercilessly. Something was badly wrong.

"I'm sorry, sir," he said. "I don't understand."

314

"What don't you understand? It's self-explanatory."

"Well, I'm not sure, sir. This information about the links to these other killings—how did the ministry get hold of it? I've been keeping all that in a separate file at home. I didn't want to release it until I had some hard evidence tying Abuhatseira in. It's all conjecture at the moment. Or so I thought. But I've told nobody else about it."

Dessì frowned. He seemed displeased about something. Or worried—it was hard to tell the difference.

"Just what have you told people about this case?" he demanded. There was a note in his voice that warned Nieddu to be careful what he said next.

"The same as in any case. I've interviewed witnesses, given instructions to my men. But I still don't understand how any of this got back to Rome."

"Inspector, this isn't just 'any case.' I've just spoken with Scarpa in the Administrazione di Pubblica Sicurezza. Their Office for Prevention has received information from SISDE that Abuhatseira is a Mossad agent. That means that the pursuit of this case will now pass out of your hands. It also means that any information you or your men have gathered about the suspect will be classified secret. You'll be asked to pass everything you have over to the Office for Prevention and to keep your mouth shut about what you know."

Nieddu had been blocked more than once in the pursuit of a conviction, usually for reasons of local politics, and each time he had put up with the interference as part of the natural order of things. But this time he felt an unprecedented sense of outrage. It seemed too good to be true that Yosef Abuhatseira had turned up in Milan as a political assassin. Something stank, and Nieddu was determined to find out what it was.

"I'm sorry, sir, but I'm not happy about this. The Office for Prevention or SISDE or somebody else has been messing about with files in this building. We should have files on the deaths of Aryeh and Chaya Levin and the murder of Michele Mannuzzu, Tina's husband. There should also be a file on a kidnapping that took place in Arzachena in January: The victim was the Levins' son, Yoel. His jacket turned up in a cave near the spot where the shepherds from the Gennargentu were found."

"That's very interesting. Have you approached anyone else about this yet?"

"Not yet. I was waiting until we had Abuhatseira in custody. I want to hear his story before I try to get the files back."

"I see. And where do you think he is now?"

"I told you, sir. Turin or Milan. From the look of it, Milan."

"Perhaps. More likely he's far away by now. What about Turin? Have you any leads there?"

Nieddu nodded. "A few, sir."

"Fine. Let me have them. I'll pass them on. And bring me all your files at the same time. All of them, mind."

Nieddu could see he was being dismissed. He was still unhappy, but he didn't think he would get far with Dessì. And after what had happened to De Felice, perhaps it was better he didn't try.

"I'll have them sent up right away, sir."

As he was about to leave, Dessì called after him. "Inspector, this has been a private conversation. Do you understand me?"

"Yes, sir. Perfectly."

He went into the corridor and closed the door behind him. To his surprise, he found he was no longer sweating. His skin was stone cold, as though he were already dead.

38

"Who is Krämer?" asked Yosef. "And why is he so important? Why is Weiss willing to kill so many people in order to find him?"

Yosef, Maryam, Bruno, and the man who had interrogated Yosef were sitting round a table in a makeshift dining room. The latter's name was David Rich. He was an American, a Harvard professor who had specialized in the study of the Holocaust after completing his doctoral thesis. His dissertation had been devoted to the genesis and consequences of the Wannsee Conference of 1942 at which Heydrich and others had set afoot the Final Solution. Published in the following year by Harvard University Press, it had received enthusiastic reviews in several academic journals and a mention in the *New York Times Book Review*. As a result, David had achieved a little recognition as an authority on the destruction of European Jewry.

In the late eighties, David, like many others, had been disturbed by the "historian's debate" in what was then West Germany. Some historians, including respected academics, were arguing, among other things, that more Aryans than Jews had died at Auschwitz and that the motives of those who denied the Holocaust were "often honorable."

David had smelled something in the air, and he did not like it. Out of the best motives, men and women he had previously respected for their scholarship had started to give moral support to anti-Semites. His growing fears had prompted him to return to the sources in order to demonstrate that, whatever quibbles might exist about the details, the basic facts of the Holocaust were incontrovertible. Since then, most of his time had been spent responding to the work of writers like Pacchia.

David was Bruno Frezza's brother-in-law. They had met while David was in Turin researching Italian anti-Jewish legislation under German occupation. Bruno had introduced David to his sister, Amelia, and three weeks later they had surprised everyone by announcing their engagement. Now David and Amelia divided their time between Cambridge, Massachusetts, and Turin, where he held a part-time teaching post.

He and Bruno exchanged glances.

"How did you hear of Krämer?" asked Bruno.

"I hadn't heard of him until this moment," answered Yosef. "Until you told me, I couldn't be sure he really existed." He paused and turned to Maryam. "Perhaps, you'd better explain."

She did her best to describe the circuitous route by which she had come to guess that the "shopkeeper" sought by Weiss must be a man called Krämer. Without Mannuzzu's cryptic message and file and the notes she had made from them, it was difficult to make things perfectly clear. Yet David and Bruno listened carefully and without impatience.

When she reached the end, Bruno nodded.

"Thank you. This file could be of use to us. Would you object to letting us see it?"

She shook her head. "You have as much right to it as we did. Perhaps more. I'll go back to the hotel in the morning."

"I can send someone."

"They might not be allowed into my room. I can get the papers and settle our bills at the same time. I take it that you'd prefer it if Yosef and I stayed here for the moment."

David smiled. "If Weiss's people are looking for you, this is the only safe place you can go."

Yosef leaned forward. "You still haven't told us who Krämer is. I think I have a right to know."

Bruno and David exchanged glances again. Bruno nodded, and David stood. He went to a cupboard at the back of the room and rummaged about inside it for about half a minute. When he came back, he was holding a video cassette.

"This is a tape of a television documentary we had made recently. It was filmed by a production company based in Rome. Funding came from a number of Jewish organizations in the United States and Israel. All any of them know is that their money has gone toward public relations work designed to repudiate Holocaust denial in Europe.

"The film can't be shown anywhere in the world until the Pacchia trial finishes. Once it's over, however, we expect enough publicity to guarantee the documentary airtime round the world. One or two deals are in the pipeline already. Again, the buyers only know we're selling a documentary on Holocaust denial. It makes little difference whether Pacchia wins or loses, since there are no specific allegations directed against him."

He paused and stepped to the TV set. Bending down, he inserted the tape.

"This is a Hebrew version. The head of Israeli television has given us his personal assurance it will be transmitted whatever happens. But even he hasn't seen it yet."

He sat down and pressed the "play" button. The screen jumped, then a sequence of numbers appeared, followed by Italian titles. Underneath, in smaller Hebrew letters, Yosef read: "Architect of the Holocaust. The Story of Otto Krämer." Somber music played. Yosef recognized it as Górecki's *Third Symphony*, his *Symphony of Sorrowful Songs*.

Behind the titles, blurred images flickered and swam like ghosts. Yosef caught glimpses of familiar scenes: barbed wire, sentry towers, the gaunt faces of the damned. The titles faded at last, and the images coalesced into a face. A child's face, a boy's. Gradually, the features of the little boy slipped and grew into those of an adolescent, then those of a youth, then a young man, and so, shifting through all the tricks of electronic manipulation, through all the stages of life to old age. The images shifted and separated, but it was always a single face that looked out from the screen, always one man staring at the camera.

"*This is the face behind the greatest crime of*

the twentieth century," began a voice, speaking low in carefully phrased Hebrew. *"Not the best-known face, not the best remembered, but once you know the man behind it, the hardest to forget."*

The old man's face dissolved, and in its place there emerged a street scene, jumpy and flickering, taken from a very early film.

"Munich, 1910. In the month of August, a first child, Otto, was born to Ernst and Winnifried Krämer. Ernst came from a farming family, but had received a good education and embarked on a career as a grammar school teacher.

"When young Otto was four, his father was seriously wounded at the second battle of Ypres."

The scene shifted to stock footage from the trenches of the First World War.

"Disillusioned by his own wasted sacrifice and Germany's humiliation in the peace talks of 1918, in 1925 Ernst became a member of the still insignificant National Socialist Party. He went on to play a leading role in the Nationalsozialistische Lehrerbund, the Nazi Teachers' Association. By his teens, young Otto—" a picture flashed on the screen *"—had received a thorough grounding in right-wing ideology. On his twentieth birthday in 1930, he, too, joined the party. To mark the event, his father had a traditional Bavarian outfit made for him at Bechler's, the leading Munich tailors."*

Yosef watched as a photograph of young Otto in his lederhosen was overlaid by film of Hitler Youth marching. The choral voices of Górecki's lament faltered and were swamped by a thousand young voices singing the *Horst Wessel Lied*. And, as they watched in silence, the *Hitlerjugend* became grim-faced SA men marching behind banners emblazoned with the swastika. In the next photograph that came on the screen, Otto Krämer seemed to have grown up suddenly.

"By then Otto was studying economics, first at Munich University, then at Mainz. He'd originally planned to become a teacher, like his father, but when the Nazis came to power in 1933, he was encouraged to think in terms of a career that would be of more direct use to the Reich."

In the background, film of the new Germany: autobahns, housing for the masses, work for all. Górecki's music returned, poignant and somber.

"At that time, the Nazi party had very few trained intellectuals. They'd plenty of support from the teaching profession and the universities, but they needed men with brains to work in the organizations of the new state. While students burned books on the Unter den Linden, the party apparatus went in search of trained minds who would prove loyal to the Reich."

Maryam felt a terrible anger and a terrible sadness as she watched the screen turn white with flames and saw the cheering faces of young men hurrying to the bonfires, their arms filled with books and pamphlets.

"In June 1935 an ambitious former naval officer called Oswald Pohl became the Head of Administration on Himmler's personal staff."

A photograph of Pohl came on the screen. In spite of the black uniform, he had an ordinary, almost kindly face, and warm, human eyes.

"He started to build up an administrative system within the SS which eventually grew into one of the wealthiest and most powerful institutions within the Third Reich. But first, he needed men— above all, men with brains.

"Otto Krämer had already been encouraged by his father to consider a career in the SS. The administrative section seemed ideal, and he started to make approaches in order to find a post. A close friend of his mother already held a senior position within the SS Central Office, and he managed to secure young Otto a place in Pohl's office."

Otto again—this time in the black uniform of a junior SS officer. His bland, easygoing features contrasted with the ice in his eyes.

"In addition to his growing administrative responsibilities for the SS in general, Pohl was also head of the Directorate for Budget and Buildings. Pohl quickly realized that Otto Krämer possessed special talents that would make him particularly useful in running the Directorate and its increasingly complex financial concerns, so Otto was transferred there with the rank of SS-Untersturmführer."

Suddenly, the screen changed to color. An elderly woman appeared, speaking in German. A caption declared her to be Sophie Sternbach. Her real voice faded almost to nothing, and an Israeli woman's voice took over, speaking in Hebrew.

"'Untersturmführer Krämer was always kind to me. I would be typing in my office, which was next to his, and he'd come in with little presents. Chocolates or biscuits. At first I thought he was particularly fond of me, but I soon found out he was like that with all the girls. He was a good-looking young man, of course, so I think we all rather fancied our chances with him....'"

She smiled, feeding on her memories of a time that, for all that it had ended badly, had been fun. The color drained from her image, the sound changed, returning once more to

323

Górecki's solemn incantations, and on the screen there appeared footage taken at the early concentration camps. No overt images of death or suffering, but a gray world full of the premonition of what was to come.

"Otto Krämer might never have become involved in the more sinister side of Nazi life if his boss hadn't been so ambitious to expand his own influence. The Directorate's finance section had a subdivision dealing with concentration camp labor."

Yosef leaned forward to read the captions on a chart showing the relevant divisions and their relationship to the overall SS command structure. Behind the bright lines and letters of the chart, the images of the camps continued, as faint and tenebrous as winter shadows.

"From September 1941 the entire Directorate became part of the Inspekteur der Konzentrationslager, the Concentration Camp Inspectorate.

"Otto Krämer probably had very limited objectives in joining Pohl's office, but Pohl himself was, as we know, busy building an empire of his own. One of the key elements in this empire was his ability to make use of slave labor, which meant control of the labor and concentration camps."

Bruno and David watched the set, but their attention was focused on Yosef and Maryam, conscious that their reactions might prove a barometer of wider feeling once the documentary was shown to the public. On the screen, an old Polish man talked of the years he had spent as a slave of the Reich. In his face were still visible the fear and humiliation that had broken his spirit. His back still bore the marks of the beatings and whippings that had been part of his daily existence.

More old footage followed, film of SS guards brandishing guns and riding stocks. All familiar, all chilling.

"Two things happened within a short time of each other early in 1942. First, in February, Pohl merged his administrative organization with the Buildings Directorate to form the SS Economic and Administrative Office."

"In March, Himmler reorganized the chain of command for the camps, placing them under direct control of the new SS office."

A new, incredibly labyrinthine chart appeared. Its innumerable tentacles grew and spread across the screen, lines crossing and intersecting again and again like tangled threads.

"The camps had become a massive operation. Even for an intensely bureaucratic regime, the situation had grown out of control. Pohl needed the camps if he was to keep his slave labor enterprises running smoothly, and he wanted to have them run efficiently and economically.

"One man had the knowledge and experience to make the camp system work—Otto Krämer. Pohl made him a full colonel and appointed him coordinator of the concentration camp division within the SS Economic and Administrative Office. In simple terms, Otto Krämer ran the Reich's one hundred and sixty-five labor camps."

Another photograph of Krämer, this time in the uniform of a Standartenführer. Self-confidence seemed to emanate from him. He was one of the world's new masters, invincible and capable of anything.

"All written and oral extermination orders for the camps went through the Economic and Administrative Office, mainly via Pohl. But Pohl's agenda

differed from that of his rivals in the Nazi hierarchy. He was eager to ensure the survival of as large a number of prisoners as possible, and even to see that they were relatively well treated, since they formed the chief reserve from which his labor battalions were to be drafted. You cannot run a slave empire without slaves.

"There was a basic contradiction involved in the running of the concentration camps and even the death camps. The Final Solution, designed to rid Europe permanently of its Jewish population, was already well under way by the time Otto Krämer took over effective control of the camp system."

Stock footage of Adolf Hitler, his strident tones declaring his intention to destroy the Jewish race. Yosef felt a shiver run through him.

"But the war effort demanded increasing supplies of labor just to keep the whole machine going. It was a dilemma the Nazis never solved, and it may have lost them the war.

"Responsibility for the extermination of the Jews lay with a separate branch of the SS, the Central Security Directorate. In May 1942, three months after Krämer took charge of the camps, the Directorate came under the command of a notorious hard-liner, Ernst Kaltenbrunner. Kaltenbrunner was determined to see through the Führer's wish to wipe the Jewish race from the face of the earth, and he used his extensive powers to rush through the extermination program.

"The result was a lengthy battle between the Central Security Directorate and Pohl's Economic and Administrative Office, with the former pressing for the immediate massacre of all Jews and the latter preferring to work them to death. Kalten-

brunner had the advantage that he was working to carry out the express wishes of the Führer, and Himmler was, of course, scarcely well disposed to the Jews.

"But Pohl was not without resources. Himmler hated Jews, but he also had a desperate need to produce armaments for the SS, and Pohl was able to provide him with the factories and the slaves to work in them. It wasn't long before a compromise was reached. The go-between was Otto Krämer.

"Krämer understood the logistics of the camp system better than anyone, and he knew better than Himmler the costs and delays that too rapid an implementation of the extermination program would incur. When Pohl and Himmler sat down to discuss how many should go to the gas chambers and how many should be worked to death, Krämer was always there, pencil in hand, columns of figures in front of him. On a few occasions, he accompanied them for consultations with Hitler, sometimes at the Reich Chancellory in Berlin, sometimes at Berchtesgaden. He had become a very powerful man indeed."

An old man appeared on the screen. He was sitting in an armchair beside an open window through which sunlight streamed. A caption said that he had been Adolf Hitler's adjutant at Berchtesgaden.

"'I remember Otto Krämer very well,' he said. 'He was more intelligent than some of the SS people we entertained. The Führer had a high opinion of him, thought he understood the real needs of the economy better than anyone. He once said to me he thought Krämer would make a good minister for economics, but that he was still too young for the job.

"'One thing I remember very clearly. We were all on the terrace, waiting for tea to be brought in. Krämer had just arrived from Berlin. He knew I had a young lady and that I wanted to marry her, but she wasn't sure. While no one was looking, he slipped me a package. It contained six pairs of silk stockings, something you just couldn't get for love or money in those days. "I hope this softens her up a bit," he said. I remember he gave me a huge wink. The next moment, he was chatting away to the Führer. She never married me, of course. Her name was Anna. A very nice looking girl ...'"

Film of young German women dancing with Wehrmacht and SS officers. Nazi propaganda film of blond-haired girls on a farm, smiling and laughing as they brought in the hay. Film of Jewish women and children, their heads shaved, their faces gaunt with fear and hunger, herded like cattle into waiting trucks.

"Not only was Krämer directly involved at almost every stage of the extermination process, but he had firsthand experience of Hitler's views on the subject. He himself was a key figure in expediting the slaughter of Europe's Jews. Without his organizational skills, far fewer might have died."

They all watched numbly as a camera swung through black iron gates into the empty camp at Auschwitz, past barracks, across roll-call yards, alongside crematoria. Snow lay on the hard ground, icicles hung from roofs, and in the distance freezing fog curled about the trunks of leafless trees. The melancholy notes of the symphony seemed to hang in the icy air as though fashioned there. The camera panned through a room packed with glass cabinets in which the striped uniforms worn by former inmates hung, inert, yet somehow alive. In another room, other cases held mounds of rotting hair, shoes, eyeglasses, suitcases with the names of the dead.

"Today, there are increasing numbers of right-wingers who deny that the Holocaust ever happened. Others have argued that Hitler knew nothing about the annihilation of the Jews and that the Final Solution was the brainchild of Himmler and Heydrich. They would like us to believe that the Third Reich was nothing more than a well-planned welfare state in which all men were happy, contented, and free.

"Otto Krämer is one of the few men still alive who knows such statements are lies. He is an old man, but his mind is as sharp as it ever was. His memory of events fifty and more years ago is vivid. Otto Krämer knows the truth behind the Holocaust. He was an eyewitness to the daily round of death in the camps. And in his possession is a file of written documents in Hitler's hand, documents that give specific orders for extermination to continue at the killing centers. His testimony, given freely after a lifetime spent in hiding, brings the wheel full-circle. He knew the men who ordered the slaughter of millions, he helped them build their empire of death.

"However hard the deluded and the embittered fanatics of the far right deny that the Holocaust took place, there is one voice that can silence them. It is the voice of Otto Krämer."

The images of death shivered and dissolved, and an old man came on the screen. His long white hair, his emaciated features, and his stillness all combined to imbue him with the qualities of an Indian swami.

He looked into the camera and began to speak.

39

Yosef helped himself to more pasta. The meal was kosher and had been prepared by Amelia, David's wife. She had eaten quickly, then slipped away to relieve another member of the team monitoring developments in the Pacchia trial and the hunt for the presumed assassin of Butti and Gentileschi.

David poured some more wine from a bottle of Lachryma Christi.

"Why is Weiss so desperate to find Krämer?" Yosef asked.

"I should have thought that was obvious. Krämer represents an enormous threat to the entire neo-fascist movement. When the time comes, he'll be the key witness for the prosecution against Pacchia. I'm absolutely certain that his testimony isn't just going to crush Pacchia, but that it'll more or less finish the whole Holocaust denial business. That's why Weiss and his friends want to get their hands on him so badly, and why they'll kill anyone who gets in their way. Krämer can hurt them in ways you or I can't begin to. Believe me— once he appears in that witness box, people are going to sit up and pay attention."

"How did Krämer manage to avoid arrest after the war?" asked Maryam.

"And how the hell did you persuade him to testify against Pacchia?" added Yosef.

Bruno twisted a forkful of linguini into his mouth and chewed before answering.

"He got out along a ratline," he said at last, "just like hundreds of other war criminals. During the last month or so of hostilities, before the Russians arrived, he managed to put together a dossier of all the top secret papers he'd kept. He hid them at a farmhouse at Klosterfelde, not far from Oranienburg. He'd no idea which way things might go once the war was over and the Nazi hierarchy was dead or dispersed, but he had a shrewd notion that papers like the ones he'd salvaged might provide a bargaining chip if he needed one. They'd been his insurance while the Reich lasted, now he had a chance of getting it extended for the same premium.

"All the same, things went a lot faster than he'd anticipated. He was forced to leave his treasure trove behind for the time being. His first priority was to get himself out of the eastern sector, which was about to be swallowed up by Soviet forces, and into the west, where the Allies were taking control.

"At that point, you could still get into Austria fairly easily. From there he slipped over the border into Italy. He wasn't alone, and border controls were very lax. No one challenged his right to leave one country for another, since the entire area was under Allied rule anyway. He headed down through Udine to Treviso, then west to Milan, where one of his former colleagues, Walter Rauff, had managed to set up the first stage of an escape network designed to smuggle Nazis out of Europe. Rauff, Skorzeny, and a few others had made plans for these ratlines as soon as they realized the war was lost, and word had got about on the SS grapevine that this was where people should head once the time came.

"Rauff had been head of the Milan SD, which made him de facto SS security chief for the whole of northwest Italy. He'd been arrested after the war and held briefly in San Vittore prison, but the secretary to the cardinal of Milan succeeded in having him released. He changed his name and got hold of false papers so he could set himself up in a small flat without fear of being betrayed to the Allied authorities.

"Rauff sent Krämer on to a German theological seminary in Rome, the Pontificio Santa Maria dell' Anima in the Via della Pace. The rector of the Pontificio at the time was a notorious Nazi sympathizer, Bishop Alois Hudal. Hudal was an Austrian by birth, but he supported the German Reich as though God Himself had told him to. He was, incidentally, a Jew hater of the first water.

"Hudal used his contacts with Vatican charities to get fake ID papers and a Red Cross passport for Krämer. This wasn't a special favor for Otto, of course. The bishop was already supplying a steady stream of war criminals with false documents under the cover of the help he was giving to legitimate German and Austrian refugees. In those days, all you needed was a valid Red Cross passport and you could be out of the clutches of the Allies in a matter of days.

"Krämer was told to head for Genoa, where another priest, Archbishop Siri, arranged passage for him on a ship bound for Argentina, the *Stella Maris*. Once he got to South America, it was a simple matter to join the local German community and to make his mark within the SS old comrades association. He'd changed his name to Siegfried Kraus, but his real identity was an open secret in the circles he moved in. Things started to settle down after the war, and he and his friends gradually set up a regular system of communications with old Nazis in Europe and the Middle East.

"With qualifications and connections like his, Krämer had no trouble finding employment. President Perón was in desperate need of skilled financial advisors. He gave Krämer a post as consultant on economic affairs to the government. Even after Perón's overthrow, Otto managed to hold on to his position. You can chuck out presidents, but men like Otto Krämer aren't exactly littering the sidewalks.

"He married for the first time, to a much younger German woman whose family had been living in Buenos Aires since the late nineteenth century. There's no need to go into the details of his life there. He started a family, he became reasonably wealthy, and he continued to take an active interest in National Socialist politics. A number of charitable organizations, all designed to assist former Nazis or to provide funds for the extreme right in several countries, were run by him, and his investments ensured a steady supply of finance for them.

"Quite a success story. I don't have to tell you how different things were for Krämer from how they turned out for most survivors of the Holocaust. Or at least ..." Bruno paused and looked at David. "David, maybe you'd better explain what happened later."

David took a sip of wine and set his glass down carefully on the table. His plate of pasta was almost untouched.

"Things went smoothly enough for Krämer until a few years ago," he said. "Just like a dream. Power, money, a beautiful wife, a loving family. He'd never suffered pangs of conscience, he had no remorse about what he'd done under the Reich. That was all in the past, he could afford to forget it. None of it had any connection to what he was now.

"Then his life changed overnight. Literally. His wife, his son Heinrich, his daughter Marina, Heinrich's wife Anna, Marina's husband Jürgen, and their children were all on a pleasure cruise off Mar del Plata. It was the start of the school holidays, and this was to be a short break before their proper vacation a few days later, when Otto himself would be free to travel. He wasn't on the pleasure trip because the minister of finance had called him in order to go over a new budget.

"The boat in which Krämer's family were traveling capsized and they were all drowned, right down to Marina's three-month-old baby. It doesn't take much imagination to understand what a calamity like that could do to a man. Speaking for myself, I don't think I could survive a loss on that scale. Krämer was desolate, utterly and singularly bereft of all that had mattered to him. He spent over a month locked up alone in his house. He didn't eat, he refused to answer the doorbell or the telephone, he was unwashed, unshaved—more like an animal than a human being.

"In the end, some friends forced their way in and got him out. It didn't do any good. He still wouldn't eat, he couldn't sleep, he wouldn't touch anything the doctors prescribed for him. All he wanted was to die, but he had a horror of it and could never steel himself to the act, to face the moment when it would all be over. Something was holding him back, and that something was the knowledge of who and what he was. Overnight, he had become connected to his past."

David paused and took another sip of wine. For a few moments, he sat with his head bowed, as though putting his thoughts in order. When he looked up, he seemed preoccupied, as if his meditations had led him into places he would rather not have visited.

"The man who saved him was a local priest, Father Ezequiel Sarmiento. Ironically, Sarmiento was a Marxist, a political radical to whom the fascism of Perón and his successors was anathema, yet he visited Krämer every day for six months and talked to him in the garden of his friend's house, just the two of them together, a young man and an old man, almost without barriers between them, and yet very separate, each one extremely, irredeemably alone. Sarmiento knew exactly who Krämer was, of course—if not in detail, at least in broad terms. He was under no illusions, he had no particular hopes.

"Krämer had never been a religious man, although in his youth he had, like his father, been a *gottgläubiger*, a member of the neo-pagan German Faith Movement promoted by the Nazis. In Argentina he had formally converted to Catholicism to please his wife's rather conservative family, but for no other reason. His own children had been brought up as churchgoers, if only to teach them respect for tradition, something that had become terribly important to Krämer, and he had accompanied them to mass on a regular basis. That was all. There had never been any spark in him of real spirituality.

"Sarmiento never tried to ignite such a spark, never attempted to turn Krämer into a pious man, but he succeeded in demonstrating to him that, if he did not resolve the dilemma he found himself in, death would be the least of his problems.

"I can't say what happened between them. Krämer has told me a little, and there's a lot I can guess, but most of what went on did so deep inside Krämer himself, in places where I can't follow him. There's a lot he won't speak about, or can't.

"In the end, however, Sarmiento achieved something with Krämer. I don't think you can call it conversion. Krämer still isn't a religious man, at least not as I understand it. And yet in a curious sense he has almost become holy. I don't mean that to sound arch. Otto Krämer has been touched by something, above all I, think, by a consciousness of exactly what it was he and his colleagues did to the human race, a sense of the burden they laid on everyone who has lived since then.

"We have talked at length about the Holocaust, always without embarrassment, in order to put together his testimony and to prepare him for questions in court. It was he who approached us, when he read about Pacchia and the lies he'd published. He was put in touch with me by a group of Jewish lawyers working on the case. They wanted an expert to go through his testimony.

"He told me when he first came to this country that, reading a translation of Pacchia's pamphlet, he wept for hours. The reality of what had happened all those years ago is something so tangible for Krämer that the mere denial of it hurts him, as though it threatens to unmake him. He'd been at the center of a very great evil, you see, at the heart of something utterly merciless, wholly without pity, and to see it swept away as if it had never happened was like witnessing the deaths of his family again and again, without acknowledging them."

David finished speaking. The room was vibrant with his account of Krämer's horror. Everyone had finished eating. Silence permeated the stained concrete walls and seemed to penetrate beyond, into the bare rock. The city above had ceased to exist, and with it the world, all but this tiny chamber.

"I would like to meet Krämer," Yosef said.

David and Bruno looked at one another. They still did not really know Yosef.

"I have a right," he said. "You know I do."

"A lot of people have that right," Bruno answered. "But we can't let just anyone see him who wants to. He's not an exhibit."

"That's not the right I mean," Yosef answered. He was tired now, pushed to an extremity, and he needed to speak to the man who stood so silently at the center of all this killing as he had stood, unmoving, all those years ago.

"I have a special reason. My sister and her

husband died because they'd never heard of Krämer and couldn't have betrayed him whether they wanted to or not. I have a nephew who still has nightmares, who may have nightmares for the rest of his life. My whole family is in mourning because of that man and what he knows. I want to ask him if any of that was worth it. I'd like to speak to him, maybe ask him a few questions, try to understand, if that's possible."

They said nothing. The only sounds that could be heard were those of water in pipes nearby and the hum of the heating.

"Very well," said David. "I'll take you to him."

"Where is he being kept?" asked Yosef.

David smiled and looked at him. "He's next door," he said. "He's been in the next room ever since you got here."

40

The room into which Yosef was shown was part of a small suite hastily reconstructed from four storerooms that had once been used to store bottles of vermouth. A faint smell of sweet alcohol still hung in the air, not quite there, not quite evaporated, like the odor of flowers after a wedding when the dancers have gone or a funeral when the mourners have departed.

Krämer was expecting him. He sat facing the door, an old man with white hair, yellow teeth, and sagging skin, for whom the world had shrunk to a narrow opening in a wall. To Yosef, he seemed spent, a confection of sallow flesh pressed hard against old bones, a death's head set atop kindling.

But as he drew nearer, Yosef saw what he had at first missed, that Otto Krämer was wasted not by coming death but by an inner fire or a beautiful torment that ran through him like sap in high branches. His eyes were furious with feeling, his gaze animated by an untamed and confident intellect. Suddenly, he was less an old man than a young man caught unawares, a stranger trapped in his own flesh as though a lifetime had flashed by in moments with neither warning nor pity.

He sat upright on a high-sprung sofa, his legs crossed and his arms on either side for support or symmetry. He motioned to Yosef, drawing him without words to a chair next to him. Yosef sat down, aware that, in spite of himself, he was nervous and even a little frightened. It was the first time he had met a war criminal from his parents' era, and the meeting carried with it heavy burdens of myth and horror and unassuaged outrage.

"I am sorry," said Krämer. His voice was surprisingly soft, a little hesitant. He spoke in English, diffidently. "Your sister. Her husband. Your nephew. It is a great tragedy for you, for your family."

"They died because of you. Because they didn't know who you were."

"Yes, I understand. David has explained it all to me. I am deeply sorry. But I can do nothing."

"I don't expect you to do anything. Nothing can bring them back."

"And you? How do you feel about their deaths?"

"How should I feel? How do you expect me to feel?"

"Angry. Ashamed. Helpless. Guilty, perhaps."

"Why should I feel guilty? I wasn't responsible for their deaths. You were more to blame. They died because of you."

Krämer shook his white head slowly. "No, not because of me. I had no more to do with their deaths than you. I can feel no responsibility or guilt."

"Yet you ask if I feel guilty."

Krämer nodded. "Guilt is a natural reaction. You were not there to help, you might have saved them if you had got back sooner, you should have thought about their protection before you went off to search for the boy. Your unconscious mind can invent a hundred and one reasons to feel guilty."

He paused, uncrossing his legs and running a hand through his hair. His skin was paper-thin and mottled, almost translucent, like the dried calyx of an iris. The veins showed underneath like something precious under glass.

"When my family drowned," he continued, "I felt the most terrible guilt. I know you will find that difficult to understand. You will think, this is a man who has helped to kill millions, yet he feels only guilt for the deaths of his own family. That is true, it is what I felt at first. I should have delayed their trip, I should have checked on the quality of the boat they had chosen, I should have joined them, perhaps something would have happened and they would not have drowned. I was preoccupied with such thoughts for a very long time.

"When Father Sarmiento first came to me, that is how he found me—a creature of guilt. It was the first thing he taught me, that it is useless to feel guilty for acts in which I have been powerless. If I am to feel guilty, it must be for things I have done or left undone. Not for the deaths of my family, which I could not have prevented, but for the deaths of the millions that I helped to organize, for which I had never felt any real guilt to speak of."

"Could you have prevented them?"

The old man raised his head, looked at Yosef, and smiled.

"That is the first question we all ask ourselves. It is the hardest of all to answer. And it is the wrong question. Sarmiento taught me that as well. I know that nothing I could have done would have prevented what happened. I was not Himmler, not Kaltenbrunner, not Hitler. I had no power over events at that level. Like Eichmann, I was just another bureaucrat.

"But even bureaucrats have control over their lives. It would have been simple for me to have taken myself out of what I was doing, to have found other employment. No one forced me to work in that department, no one put a gun to my head and insisted that I do my work so well. My life was not at risk."

"And now it is. Is that why you are here?"

Krämer nodded. It was the simplest of gestures.

"Yes," he said. "I am here to make amends. To be found guilty at last."

"Do you think my dreams are caused by guilt?" asked Yosef.

"I don't understand." Krämer sat on the edge of the sofa, his hands clasped in front of him. Yosef felt almost cheated, as though denied some obscure opportunity to take revenge or to unburden himself of an unfocused hatred.

"I dream I'm in a train being taken to a concentration camp," Yosef explained. "Or arriving there. Or being taken to a gas chamber. But I never dream of living there, of the daily pain and misery. And when I wake, it's as if it had all happened to someone else."

"And you think this is somehow caused by guilt?"

"Guilt, yes. My family never suffered, we were not European Jews. Given time, I'm sure they would have been swept up as well, but it never happened. Yet I've spent most of my life with people whose entire families were wiped out. I live in a country built on the ruins of your Holocaust."

"And you feel guilty?"

Yosef spread his hands. "I don't know what I feel," he said.

Krämer nodded. It was hard to imagine this old man calculating the deaths of millions down to the last shoelace and bar of soap.

"I dream of the camps, too," he said. "You may think it a strange thing, but I never did at the time, nor for long afterward, not until my family was wiped out, not until Sarmiento spoke to me. They started then, a flood of dreams, dreams that would go on all night as though they had been stored up, stack upon stack of them, like films on a reel, for all those years.

342

"My dreams are not like yours, however. I am never a victim, always a guard, in the uniform of the Totenkopfverbände. You understand, of course, that I never wore such a uniform under the Reich. I thought of myself almost as a civilian, even though I worked for the SS. My visits to the camps were rare. It was a duty I disliked and that I delegated as much as possible. From time to time, however, inspections were necessary, and I would travel to this camp or that. I would spend a day, at the most two, then return, eager to get the stench out of my nostrils.

"But now I dream I am there forever, that I shall never leave. It is my hell. The strange thing, the thing I cannot properly explain, is that I want to join the prisoners, to tear off my uniform and put on the striped suit of a prisoner. I suppose that is my need to expiate my sins."

"Then you believe in sin?"

Krämer shrugged. "I believe in right and wrong, and I know that what I did was wrong, however it may have appeared to me at the time. Whether it was also a sin—that is something I do not think about."

"What did Sarmiento have to say about that?"

"About sin? He never used the word in my presence. I think ... no, I know I frightened him. He often told me that when he was with me he came close to losing his faith in God."

"Why was that?"

"Because I was alive, because I still had the hope of salvation. He was a priest, it was his duty to save my soul, and yet he could not bring himself to do it."

"I don't understand."

"He explained it to me once. He said that the camps destroyed all meaning for salvation in Christ. It was his constant thought. Here, he said, is a Jewish child, two years old, a little less, a little more, it doesn't matter. He does not believe in Christ, he has never heard of Christ. Yet, when his body is taken from the gas chamber and thrown into the crematorium, his soul is already in hell. It is in hell now, it will remain in hell forever, undergoing all the tortures of the damned.

"And here am I, one of those who sent children like that to die, still alive, still conscious, still capable of choosing Christ. And if I do, if I embrace him and enter the Church, my sins will be forgiven, and when I die my soul will enter paradise and will remain there for all eternity, in bliss. If that Jewish child holds out his hand for a drink of water, and I refuse him, it will not even cloud my conscience or intrude for a moment on my state of bliss.

"The horror of that would keep Sarmiento awake at nights. Either there is a God who could rule over His creation with less pity or conscience than Hitler, or there is no God at all. There is, of course, a third alternative: The Jewish child, along with every other soul who has never heard of Jesus Christ, is allowed into paradise anyway. In that case, there is no need for Christ, no need for his death on the cross, no need for the Church, no need for priests like Sarmiento. That is why I frighten him. That is why I do not pray, why I do not ask forgiveness for what I have done."

41

"Maryam, I don't think it's such a good idea for you to go back to your hotel after all."

Bruno and she were drinking coffee together while David took Yosef to meet Krämer. Amelia had joined them, bringing a box of *amaretti* and the latest information on the trial and manhunt. Someone had managed to find a photograph of Yosef, and this had now been flashed across the nation's television screens. Details of his background had been provided, together with what were transparent falsifications, such as the implication that he had been working for Mossad since leaving the army.

"But if we leave Mannuzzu's file there," Maryam answered, "it won't be long before someone finds there was a connection between Yosef and myself and lays their hands on it. We booked into the hotel separately, but I think the people chasing Yosef know perfectly well we were together."

"That's what I'm worried about. They could be waiting for you there. On the other hand, we need the file. Our organization is building a database on neo-fascist activists and sympathizers in this country, and Mannuzzu may have collected information that would be of help to us. We have almost nothing on local officials in Sardinia. I'd also like to see what he has on Weiss. And the telephone number for De Vuono—that is especially important. We've had our suspicions about him for some time, but this could be the first piece of solid evidence connecting him to the extreme right.

"We'll have someone check into the hotel this evening. He can assess the situation and, if the coast is clear, he can break into your room and take the file."

All the paperwork had gone up to Dessì an hour earlier, and now Nieddu felt himself almost bereft. He had other cases to follow up, some of them important ones that had been on his desk for too long already, but none of them held the slightest interest for him. In spite of everything, he wanted to pursue the President Hotel killing through all its ramifications, but the chance had been taken from him. Experience and a nose for intrigue told him that Yosef Abuhatseira had been set up for the Palazzo di Giustizia killings, and that should have been enough to warn him off. But dislike of Dessì on the one hand and an innate stubbornness (for which his wife had other names) on the other made him rebel against the very thought of backing away.

He'd kept copies of his case notes, together with one or two documents that he thought might come in useful. The question now was, what was he going to do with it all? Send it to a higher authority with a request that they investigate the whole thing? Pop the file in the post, addressed to the internal affairs section in the ministry of the interior in Rome? Lock it in a cupboard marked *Non Disturbare*? Soak it in petrol and burn it? Crush it into wads and choke himself to death on them?

Nieddu had no reason to care a damn what happened to Yosef Abuhatseira. He still had ample reason to think that the Israeli had killed at least some of the people on his long list, including Tina Mannuzzu. But if Abuhatseira had not killed Butti and Gentileschi, someone else had, and perhaps a lot of others were standing behind them, waiting for whatever it was they expected to happen when Abuhatseira was captured or, as was more likely, gunned down by the security forces.

"Don't hang about, David. Get in and out as quickly as possible. They won't be looking for you, but they may be watching the hotel."

"The radio said they're looking for Yosef in Milan."

Bruno shook his head. "Don't depend on that. He says he covered his tracks well, and I believe him. But they seem to know he's in the north somewhere, and it won't be long before they trace him to Turin, if they haven't done so already."

"Okay. I'll be quick."

"Take care."

"Tell me about Weiss." Maryam was alone with Amelia. David's wife was young and very pretty, dressed in the sort of clothes Maryam could only have dreamed of owning, and possessed of that all-embracing northern Italian self-assurance that Maryam still found hard to cope with. Yet in the brief time they had been together, mainly on Sunday, the two women had found much in common, and Amelia had shown a genuine concern and friendliness for her new acquaintance. She had brought her fresh clothes, makeup, and a huge box of toiletries.

Amelia taught English at a *licèo classico* situated near the Palazzo Carignano. Her family disapproved of her working, or at least working in what they called a "real job." They would have preferred her to be a model or a dress designer, but Amelia had insisted on her right to a serious career and—another bone of contention at first— a serious husband.

"You'd really have to ask David about that," Amelia said. "Weiss is a particular interest of his. I know a little, enough to make me pray I never meet the man. Krämer, for instance— he's quite human, really, you can almost pity him. I thought I'd hate him, but when I first met him I found it impossible. I'm not so sure about Weiss.

"His real name's Emil Luders. SS Gruppen-führer Luders, to be exact. David's told me a bit about his war record. If anyone deserved to be hanged as a war criminal, it's Weiss. He was in charge of extermination squads on the Eastern Front to begin with. It seems he enjoyed his work. Even the SS had to issue warnings about his behavior. He liked to hurt people." She paused, and Maryam saw her flinch from her own words. "He still does."

"How come he was never arrested?"

"Oh, you'd have to ask David the details. He was in Italy by the end of the war, I know that. I think he was responsible for rounding up Jews here in the northwest. His own mother was Ital-ian, which is how he comes to speak the language fairly well. One way or another, he got a new name and made his way back to Germany. He's been there ever since.

"Nobody had the slightest idea that Luders and Weiss were one and the same person, not till Krämer let it slip one evening. But Weiss knows we've got Krämer, and he knows Krämer can hurt him, maybe even put an end to him. So he's determined to find Krämer and kill him before that happens. Krämer and anybody he's spoken to."

There was a knock on the door, somewhere between tentative and peremptory.

"Come in," Nieddu called. He wasn't expecting anyone and all the offices on his floor were already empty.

The men who entered seemed familiar, possibly because they had modeled themselves on popular images of what they wanted to be. The large man in sunglasses appeared almost surprised by his own heaviness, the blond youngster seemed to have difficulty keeping his face straight.

The older man locked the door and turned.

"Nieddu?" he asked.

"Who wants to know?"

"I asked if you were Nieddu."

"This is my office. I ask the questions."

The youngster looked at the older man.

"The fuck is fucking us about. His name's on the door. Let's go."

Without waiting for further comment, the boy moved like a crab past and behind Nieddu's desk. He and the older man had perfected the act together, they moved through its stages with grace and coordination. Nieddu felt the long arms come over his head, felt the tape press over his lips.

Unlike De Felice, he had been waiting for the visit. He hadn't known exactly what they would do, but he had been ready for them to act, and he acted first, before they had a chance to overpower him. He pushed back, smashing his chair into the blond man's knees, sending him staggering hard against the wall. Before the youth could recover, Nieddu was on his feet. He hurled the chair out of the way and moved in, hitting his assailant in the stomach with a hard fist, and, as the boy slumped, he kicked him with all his strength on the side of the head, smashing his cheekbone.

When he turned, the older man was barely two feet away from him, holding a knife. Nieddu took a deep breath and lifted the pistol he had taken from the desk, where he had kept it under a file, ready for the attack he had known would come.

"The answer is 'yes,'" he said, "my name is Nieddu. And unless you let go of the knife, I'd say you have about four seconds to live."

The hotel was quiet. David arrived with a small suitcase and a British passport. At the desk, he explained in deliberately broken Italian that he'd been unable to make an advance reservation, but that he needed a room for the night. The receptionist smiled and replied in good English that, since it was out of season, there would be no problem. He could have a suite for a reduced rate if he wanted.

★ ★ ★

When his attackers had been taken away, one to the hospital, the other to the holding cells in the *questura* cellars, Nieddu put his chair back behind his desk and sat down again. Like someone who knows he has passed the stage when thinking will do him any good, he picked up the phone and punched in a number.

"Hello, Alisarda? I'd like to book a single ticket to Turin, please."

David slipped out of Maryam's room and shut the door behind him softly. There was no one in the corridor, no sound anywhere. He carried Mannuzzu's file and Maryam's notes in a briefcase. His suitcase could stay in his own room until he had a chance to return for it; it contained nothing but rags and bits of scrap Bruno and he had gathered together at short notice.

Outside the hotel, a slow drizzle peppered the night. Men and women passed in pairs or singly, their pace a little faster than usual. There was a vigil for Italy's new right-wing martyrs somewhere in the center of town, and word had gone round that there would be a protest against Jewish intrigue, but nobody took it that seriously. It was raining, and they wanted to get home from the shops or out to the cinema, so let them protest if they wanted to.

In a black Mercedes parked opposite the Vecchia Lanterna, a man sat speaking into a radio handset. David's entry to Maryam's room had not gone unnoticed. The room had been wired with a silent alarm system the day be-

351

fore, and the hotel security staff instructed to keep an eye on things. They hadn't objected—why should they when the men in their office had shown them a warrant signed by the justice minister in person?

"This is unit one. Hotel security say he's coming down now. He's carrying a briefcase. We have no ID as yet, but there is a negative on Abuhatseira. I'll follow him from here, but I'll need backup."

The information from Sardinia had been spot on. A pity that the policeman responsible for tracking their target to Turin had had to be eliminated, but with the coup only days away, they could hardly afford to take chances.

David appeared in the doorway and stepped into the street. There were no taxis anywhere in sight. He shivered and started to walk.

42

Gerhard Weiss folded and unfolded his hands, flexed and unflexed his long, supple fingers. The signs of age were growing unmistakable on his skin, yet he kept decrepitude at bay as best he might by a strict regime that had altered little since his days in the Hitler Youth. He rose at six, exercised religiously for one hour, ate only vegetarian food, and attended no doctor but his private *heilpraktiker*.

For almost eighty years he had taken care of his body, and in return he expected it to serve him well. His task in life was not yet over, and he had vowed not to weaken or abandon the struggle until he had set the movement back again on its course to victory. In a few years he could afford to relax, confident that all he had set out to achieve had been achieved and that nothing would be able to turn back the tide of history. Communism had been defeated and would never again pose a threat, the democracies were flabby and corrupt, on the verge of inward collapse. Men and women everywhere were crying out for change, for real leadership in an age of despair, and in increasing numbers they knew where they could find it.

A red light flashed on his desk console. Weiss pushed a small button and spoke briefly. A male voice answered, speaking in Italian.

"Signor Weiss? *Sono Giancarlo*. Am I free to speak?"

"Go ahead. This is a secure line."

"We think we've found the Jew."

"Abuhatseira?"

"Yes. One of our men followed an associate of his from the hotel where he'd been staying. The trail led to a *farmacia* in the Via Pietro Micca, near the Teatro Alfieri. We've had the *farmacia* checked out. It belongs to a Jew called Montemezzo. He's not a member of Frezza's group, but he does turn up regularly at Mortara's. We think they could be hiding the Israeli there."

"Why do you say the man that was followed is an associate of Abuhatseira's?"

"He used a key to get into the woman's room. We think he came for the papers she left behind."

"You left them untouched?"

"Yes, of course. You said we should do nothing to excite suspicion."

"Fine. What makes you so sure Abuhatseira's at the pharmacy?"

There was a brief silence.

"It's a hunch, that's all. Why not just take the papers and head on home with them?"

"Do you know who the associate is?"

"Not yet. It was dark, we couldn't get a good look at him."

"All right. Keep a close eye on the place, back and front. Follow anyone who leaves, but don't let them see you. Report back to me the moment you have anything more."

"You don't want us to go in, sir?"

"Not until you're absolutely sure. If there's no one there, we'll only be giving them a warning. Remember that Abuhatseira isn't our chief target. I want Krämer. And I want him alive."

"I'll remind my unit." The speaker paused. "Do you have any further orders, sir?"

"No, that's all. Don't do anything else without checking with me. If necessary, I'll fly to Turin tonight." There was a brief silence. Weiss reached out his hand again to break the connection. Then, as though unsure of something, he drew it back again.

"Giancarlo—where did you say the *farmacia* is?"

"In the Via Pietro Micca."

"There was something else."

"Near the Alfieri Theater."

"That's not far from the little puppet theater, is it?"

"The Gianduja, sir. No, sir, it's a couple of streets away."

Another silence followed, a much longer one. At last, Giancarlo spoke again.

"Are you still there, sir?"

"Yes, yes … Listen, Giancarlo, there's something I want you to do."

"Yes, sir?"

"I'd like you to ring Taddeo Maciachini. Ask him if he remembers an air-raid shelter somewhere in that area and whether it connected to the tunnels under the city. It used to be one of his duties, making sure there were no Jews hiding down there."

"You don't think …"

"It's too early to think. But if I'm right, we may have found Krämer at last."

It was good to be aboveground again, if only briefly. David had returned an hour earlier with the file and notes, and he and Bruno were still going through them, following a briefing from Maryam. Amelia had gone to bed, and so had Krämer. Other members of the group would remain awake all night, some to continue monitoring the situation, others to stand guard. Maryam and Yosef had asked for half an hour in which to get some fresh air. The streets were almost deserted now, and Bruno had agreed, though reluctantly.

Yosef held Maryam's hand tightly as they walked. He still found it hard to believe that they had become lovers, that somewhere, outside all this craziness, a new life was waiting for them both. Above all, just as he no longer had confidence in himself, so he found it hard to understand why someone like Maryam would show him any love at all.

Neither of them minded that it was still raining lightly; it was just good to breathe some fresh air and feel the city fall asleep around them.

"What's he like?" Maryam asked.

He knew she meant Krämer, but he did not answer at once. Her hand was warm, as though it belonged to an entirely different world than the one he had just been in. Krämer had unsettled him, left him feeling naked and defenseless, precisely because he did not know how to guard himself against the knowledge he had gained that night. That his enemy was as human as himself, and as flawed, and as open to wounds and grief. He had gone to Krämer's room wanting to despise or hate the old man, but had found himself incapable of either emotion. The connection was impossible to make. His demons, the demons that haunted the dreams of Bruno and David and Amelia, were young men in smart black uniforms and shiny jackboots, not retired bureaucrats with soft white hair and the lines of bereavement and human pain on their faces. It was not that he pitied or loved or understood Krämer; it was just that he could not sit in judgement of him, and that he knew Krämer alone could not bear so much guilt.

"Like? Krämer's like no one I've ever met. In a way, he reminds me of my father, and then I look at him and he isn't like him at all. And I wonder which of them it is that I've never known, Krämer or my father...."

They talked for a long time, huddled in the doorway of a puppet theater like teenage lovers who know they must soon be home yet seek to squeeze all they can from the minutes remaining to them.

"It's getting late," said Yosef at last, glancing at his watch. "I promised Bruno we wouldn't be back late."

They made their way back to the *farmacia*. As they passed a shop selling electrical goods, they caught sight of a bank of brightly lit television screens, all tuned to the same channel. As though the entire nation had not grown tired of seeing it, the film of that morning's assassinations was being replayed. They watched for a few seconds, then turned and walked away into the rain and the darkness.

"Signor Weiss. I have something for you." Giancarlo's voice sounded elated, full of a delighted tension. "The quality isn't good, our man had to use a parabolic microphone from a distance, but you can make out what they're saying. The language is Hebrew, but I've had it translated."

There was a silence, then a whistling sound like wind, the sound of traffic growing then fading away, and a sound of footsteps.

"What's he like?" Maryam's voice was broken, but the words could be made out clearly. Giancarlo read the translation over the sound of the tape. A long lull followed, punctuated by further traffic sounds and something that might have been light rain touching glass. And then, rumpled and fluctuating, Yosef's voice came across a field of static.

"Like? Krämer's like no one I've ever met. In a way, he reminds me of my father, and then I look at him and he isn't like him at all. And I wonder which of them it is that I've never known, Krämer or my father...."

357

43

The darkness expanded and contracted all around Yosef like a thick black cloth drawn close over his eyes. Down here, where there could never be anything but artificial light, where sunlight had never penetrated and would never penetrate, the darkness was of a special quality, as though stored up and strengthened since the beginning of time.

He blinked and pulled himself upright in bed. Beside him, Maryam was fast asleep. As he moved, his flank grazed hers and she turned with a murmur onto her other side. He wanted to wake her and make love as an incantation against the darkness, but he could not bring himself to disturb her sleep. He himself had snatched only a few minutes of slumber since coming to bed. His thoughts were too confused to allow the relaxation necessary for anything but the shallowest doze. His conversation with Krämer played and replayed itself as though engraved deep in his mind, each word and gesture tooled there like glyphs carved in hard stone.

He sat, propped up against his pillow, listening for sounds of life outside the room. He had no idea what time it was, but guessed it was very late. The first thing he heard was a drumming of quick footsteps, then the sound of a door opening. Silence returned, but only briefly, to be broken by a man's voice crying out, sudden and angry. He sat forward in bed, listening intently. More footsteps, a loud cry, and then, bleak and ugly, the all too familiar sound of two pistol shots in quick succession.

He reacted quickly, placing his hand over Maryam's mouth as she woke, hushing her with a few hurried words whispered directly in her ear.

"They're here. Get up and be ready to make a run for it. I'm going to find Krämer."

They rolled out of bed, snatching handfuls of clothes from the floor, and crawled to the opposite wall beside the door. Yosef had no weapon, the room held no means of defense. He struggled into his jeans, huddling against the wall. There was another burst of gunfire, more shouting, the cry of someone badly hurt, Amelia's voice pleading, suddenly cut off.

The door crashed open, throwing a band of light across the floor and bed. Yosef stiffened, knowing that what happened in the next few seconds would decide not only his fate and Maryam's, but that of countless others.

A man stepped into the room, dressed from head to foot in black and wearing a black balaclava over his head. He held a submachine gun stiffly in front of him, tight against a strap round his neck. Yosef let him take a second step, threw a shoe under his line of sight against the far wall, and, as the man turned, threw himself on him. The intruder twisted in an attempt to toss him off, but Yosef already had an arm round his neck. He pulled back and up hard in a smooth motion. The gunman's neck started to give and suddenly cracked as crushed vertebrae gave way. He fell limply and crashed to the floor. Yosef ripped the gun from his grasp and turned to face the doorway.

In the confusion outside, no one had noticed what had happened. Yosef half turned and motioned to Maryam to wait.

"Stay here," he hissed. "I'll see what's happening."

He did not know whether they would want Krämer alive or dead, but he was sure that was who they had come for. If Krämer was already dead, the most he could hope to do would be to get Maryam and himself out. Weiss would have sent in a properly equipped team with orders to wipe out everyone in the shelter, and Yosef was in no position to prevent them.

The shelter was symmetrically shaped, with only one proper entrance and exit through the pharmacy. A long central corridor was entered from stairs leading up to the rear of the shop, and it would have been through here that the raiding party had got into the complex. At either end of the central corridor, and in its center, shorter passages branched off, each terminating in a long rectangular room like dumbbells. There were four smaller rooms directly off the central corridor and entered from it.

At the far end, the long corridor continued for several yards before ending in a low, plastered wall on the other side of which, so Bruno had said, lay the first of the older tunnels to which the shelter had originally been connected, in the event of their proving necessary for additional accommodation.

Krämer's quarters had been created by dividing one of the long rooms at the far end into four, making a bedroom, sitting room, kitchen, and bathroom. He had called it his *konzentrationslager*, without irony, and above one door

360

he had erected a small handwritten notice that read *"Wahrheit macht Frei"*—The Truth Shall Set You Free—not so much in mockery as in sorrow.

The room in which Yosef and Maryam had been sleeping was at the end of the furthest branch corridor corresponding to the one leading to Krämer's quarters. As Yosef slipped through the open door, he saw two men dragging Krämer round the corner into the main corridor. Like the first man, they were also hooded and dressed in black. Krämer was wearing pajamas, his hair was ruffled, and his feet were bare.

Yosef ran to the end and followed them. Sporadic shooting was still coming from the rooms at the other end of the corridor. Yosef could see that if they got much further, Krämer would be with the main group, beyond all hope of rescue. He set his gun to fire single rounds, raised it, and shot the man on the left in the back. He stumbled, pulling Krämer down with him. The third man had been quick enough to let go of Krämer at the last moment. He half turned, lifting his weapon, but Yosef already had him targeted. A second shot entered his left temple, dropping him where he stood.

Yosef ran to Krämer and helped him to his feet.

"Are you all right?" he asked.

Krämer looked at him and smiled. His face was curiously calm, his eyes more puzzled than afraid.

"You're wasting your time," he said. "I'm grateful to you for trying, but it's too late. There's only one way out of here. We won't make it as far as the stairs."

"I'm not planning to go that way."

Yosef picked up the submachine gun that had been dropped by one of Krämer's abductors.

"Can you use one of these?" he asked.

Krämer shook his head.

"But surely you had training," protested Yosef. "You were in the SS, they gave you military training."

The old man smiled. "I was in the SS," he said, "but I was a desk officer. I had the right to wear the uniform, but no one ever expected me to fight. I'm sorry."

"All right. Let's get going before someone comes." Yosef slung the gun over his own shoulder and helped Krämer back down the corridor.

The shooting at the other end still continued, but it had grown thin and scattered, as if only one person were holding several at bay. For a moment, Yosef felt an urge to hurry to the assistance of the sole survivor, but he knew it would prove a needlessly heroic gesture. His duty was to get Otto Krämer out of here if he could.

They hurried to the corner. Maryam was standing in the branch corridor, dressed and ready to join them.

"Get the flashlights!" Yosef called. They had been given two flashlights to use in the room or in the event of a power failure, since Bruno wanted to save fuel for the generator by switching off any lighting that was not strictly necessary.

Maryam ran back into the room and reappeared moments later with the flashlights.

At that moment, two more raiders entered the long corridor and caught sight of Yosef and

Krämer. They hesitated just a moment too long, afraid to contravene orders by opening fire on the old man. Yosef pushed Krämer behind the wall, crouched, flicking the switch on his weapon as he did so, and squeezed off two bursts of automatic fire before his opponents had a chance to take stock of the situation.

One man went down, the other dropped his gun, bent to pick it up, thought better of it, and scrabbled for cover in the branch corridor he had come from.

Yosef waved Maryam across.

"According to Bruno," he said, "the wall at the end here is just lathes and plaster. The tunnel used to go on further, into a maze of older diggings, and Bruno had the wall put in to make this area self-contained. I can probably break through without much difficulty, but I need someone to hold off our friends back there. Can you handle a submachine gun?"

She shook her head. "You may remember," she said, "that your enlightened government wouldn't let me serve in the armed forces. If I'd been a Jewish boy, I'd have been allowed to shoot and kill with the best, but all we Arabs are good for is throwing stones at soldiers."

He almost smiled. "All right," was all he said. "You'll just have to learn fast." He held out the second gun he had captured. "This is set to fire on automatic. It has quite a kick, so use something to pad your shoulder. Don't bother about aiming, what you're trying to do is keep them as far away as possible. Fire in short bursts, leave time in between to check what they're doing. And be sure to tuck yourself hard behind the wall."

They ran to the final turn. Behind them, three raiders had already started down the central corridor. Yosef turned and fired on them. Their return fire was badly aimed. As they reached the corner, Yosef flicked back to single-fire mode. Using the wall as cover, he fired two careful shots, dropping two of his attackers and forcing the other to scramble back to the far end. It was obvious that the attackers had not expected to meet with more than token resistance.

Maryam took his place at the corner. The plaster wall was only a few yards away.

"What will you use to break the wall down?" Maryam asked.

Yosef pointed to a heavy fire extinguisher, one of several positioned at the ends of corridors throughout the shelter. With only one safe exit, fire safety had been a primary consideration in the refurbishment of the complex.

Krämer sat down beside Maryam, cradling the other gun.

"Are you all right?" asked Yosef.

Krämer nodded and smiled. He patted the gun.

"I may not be much use, but I can point it and fire it if I need to. I won't let them take me alive. It's what Weiss wants, to haul me before some ridiculous tribunal in order to humiliate me and give everybody else a warning. I'd sooner die down here."

Maryam glanced back down the corridor. It was still empty, but the sounds of harsh voices and running feet echoed and reechoed along the concrete. Opposite her, a long brown stain caused by rust from a leaking pipe lay vivid against the rough gray wall. Krämer handed her his pajama top, and she rolled it into a pad to minimize the force of the recoil, slipping it between her shoulder and the butt of the gun. Her throat was tight and dry and her hands shook. She wanted to be sick.

Yosef checked that she was as well covered as she could be, then turned and started to beat against the wall with the extinguisher. Each blow took a chunk of plaster with it, then there was a cracking sound as he broke through a row of lathes. A dozen more blows and he'd created a hole large enough for them to climb through. Behind him, Maryam fired a quick burst, raking the corridor.

Heavy firing followed at once from the other end, sending a swarm of bullets thudding against the back wall, tearing lumps from it and narrowly missing Maryam. She pulled back, shaking, letting the gun fall with a clatter to the floor. Her shoulder ached and her arm was numb. She had never been so terrified, never felt so vulnerable. But as the firing from the other side faded, she picked up the gun and stepped back to the corner. Taking a deep breath, she glanced into the corridor.

In the interval, one man had made a dash as far as the first branch corridor. He caught sight of Maryam and opened fire. Under the cover he now laid down, three more made the short run and joined him. They were only yards away from the rear of the corridor now.

Yosef took the gun from Maryam.

"Take one of the flashlights and help Krämer through. Just keep going until you find a way out of here."

He had absolutely no idea what they would

find in there, but he knew that their only hope—slim as it was—lay in losing their pursuers in the network of tunnels beyond the wall.

"Take him to Mortara," he continued. "You'll find him through the synagogue. Get him under cover and keep him there until he appears in court. If necessary, contact Baruch Caplin at the Israeli embassy in Rome—he'll give you any assistance you need."

"What about you?"

He could not look her in the eyes. His hands could not touch her. He wished he were anywhere but here, wished he were dead. He would not say good-bye, would not listen to her say it.

"I'm staying here to hold them off. The important thing is to get Krämer out."

"I won't leave you."

"Don't make me plead with you," he said. "All we've gone through has been for this one thing, to get that old man in front of a bench of magistrates. It's why my sister died, and Aryeh, and all those others. Please don't make me ask you again."

They were gaining now, only yards away, creeping down the corridor, and he knew that the longer he delayed, the more chance there was of killing her and Krämer as well as himself. He saw her looking at him, saw tears in the corners of her eyes, saw anger collide with grief.

He turned his back abruptly on her and stepped up to the corner, holding the gun as if it were anything but a weapon. Armed, he felt more defenseless than he had been naked in her arms. He stood stiffly by the wall, drawing breath tightly into his lungs. It was more than he could bear, not to see her again. He glanced round and looked at her, and her head was haloed momentarily by the light she held. The next moment, she was gone.

44

About ten yards past the wall, the corridor ended at a T junction. Its twin branches each ran into darkness, with no indication as to which had been the more used or was more likely to lead to the outside. It was immediately clear that this section of the network had long ago fallen into disuse. The walls, unlike those of the corridor from which they had just come, were roughly cut, unplastered, and unpainted. They seemed never to have been intended for anything as sophisticated as human habitation. The ceiling here was lower, and all life appeared to have been taken suddenly from the air, as though no one had breathed in here for centuries.

Maryam hesitated. Without help, Yosef would be unable to find his way or decide which opening to take. Beside her, Krämer was already showing signs of physical distress. The stale air, on top of the sudden shock of his seizure and rescue, was making it hard for him to breathe. When they stopped, he leaned against the wall, taking deep breaths that sawed through his lungs like old saws. Maryam wondered how much farther he could go.

She was still stunned by what had happened, unable to take in the fact that she might never see Yosef again. All she did know for certain was that she might not come out of these tunnels alive. She looked at the old man in front of her, at his gray skin and hollow eyes, and she wondered why he was worth so many lives. It would have taken almost nothing to snuff him out, like a candle that had burned too long and with too little light. Yosef was worth a thousand Krämers, she thought, and yet he was throwing his life away in order to ensure the old man's safety. She sighed. A sound of shooting echoed behind them.

Making her mind up, she bent down and scrabbled on the rough floor for a lump of rock. Finding a suitable piece, she used it to scrape hasty, ill-formed letters on the wall. The writing was faint, but visible, and she prayed Yosef would pause here long enough to see and read what she had written, all in Hebrew, so only he would understand: *Gone to the right. We need help.*

Throwing down the stone, she bent and took the old man's arm gently.

"We have to go," she said. "Lean on me."

Yosef eased back on the trigger. He was still firing single rounds, aimed carefully at any of the raiders foolish enough to make himself a viable target. One man had been winged in the left arm, another in his upper leg, and they were now back in the third branch corridor, nursing their wounds.

Yosef knew he could not keep this up indefinitely. If the attackers decided to make an all-out onslaught on his position, there was little he could do to stop them short of emptying his magazine in a sweeping defensive action, an action that would come to an end as soon as his last bullet had been fired. From that point on, he would have no resources other than his bare hands. He'd have to hold them off as long as possible, and then perhaps draw them into the tunnels.

The silence grew gentle until it seemed almost loud, as though it had been a roaring in his ears and every least sound an explosion. Yosef edged back to the corner and glanced into the corridor. A tall man was standing at the far end. He wore no hood and carried no gun, and one hand rested on the head of a polished stick.

As Yosef drew back, the tall man spoke in a loud voice, perfectly audible in the narrow confines of that place, with its peculiar acoustics and unbalanced echoes.

"Mr. Abuhatseira, allow me to introduce myself. My name is Gerhard Weiss. I think you know of me, or that you guess at my existence. Excuse me if I speak in English, but I speak no Hebrew, and I am sure you speak no German or Italian."

There was a short pause, as though Weiss were collecting untidy thoughts. The silence returned, but pregnant now with the possibility of what Weiss was going to say.

"I imagine you are at this moment in the frame of mind of those ancestors of yours who died at Masada rather than surrender to the might of Rome. That was not a dishonorable choice. My own Führer and his companions in the bunker at Berlin made the same decision, and for much the same reasons.

"But it is not always the wisest choice. Already too many people have died to protect a single man. All of them have thrown their lives away for a chimera. Otto Krämer is worth nothing to you or to the Zionist cause. My people already have witnesses ready to appear in court, men and women of impeccable character who will testify that the man you call Krämer is an impostor, that the real Otto Krämer died years ago in exile.

"These witnesses are not Nazis or Nazi sympathizers. One or two of them are Jews. It doesn't really matter whether their testimony is true or not or whether Krämer is the genuine article or a substitute. What matters is this: By the end of the trial, sufficient doubt will have been sown to make the verdict inevitable. Pier Maria Pacchia will be acquitted. Questioning the Zionist myth of the Holocaust will remain perfectly legal. And when we have won our case in Italy, we will take the issue before the European Court of Human Rights, and I assure you we shall win again.

"That is, of course, assuming you succeed in getting this Krämer of yours to court alive. At the moment, that seems very unlikely. Within the next few moments, my men will attack in force. You will die. Miss Shumayyil will die. Krämer—or whoever he is—will die.

"I would prefer to bring this matter to an easier conclusion. Hand Krämer over now and you and your woman friend will be free to go. You have my word. And thirty seconds in which to make up your mind."

In answer, Yosef stepped out into the opening and loosed a volley of automatic fire in Weiss's direction. But the German had already stepped back behind cover and the bullets hit nothing but concrete.

Yosef stopped firing. Weiss's long speech had had absolutely no effect on him. Certainly, he did not for a moment believe that Krämer was an impostor. Weiss would never have gone to so much trouble to track down and kill a man whose identity could so easily be challenged in court.

Krämer's credibility, even the outcome of the Pacchia trial, were not what mattered now. Perhaps they had never been the chief issues. What was important was that one man, from his own conscience, had had the courage to speak and the strength to affirm, after so many years, all that he had once been. That mattered, and the fact that others had willingly risked or given their lives for him to do so.

From nowhere there came a whooshing sound, followed by a loud crash. Suddenly the air was filled with acrid, choking fumes. They were firing CS gas in an attempt to overpower Yosef without further risk to themselves. Unprotected, he staggered back coughing, almost dropping his gun in the overwhelming need to raise his hands to his eyes in order to ease the stinging.

Half blind and still choking, he stumbled through the gap in the wall and down the tunnel, pausing only to pull a handkerchief from his trouser pocket. He slung the machine gun over his shoulder and ran on, holding the handkerchief tight against his mouth. With his other hand, he switched on the flashlight and played its wide beam over the floor and walls.

The tunnel stretched out darkly ahead of him,

a narrow passage of old rock and compacted clay shored up by wooden struts, blurred by the haze that clouded his vision. Holding his breath, he wiped the cloth over his eyes, then returned it to his mouth. It was important to be able to see as clearly as possible in the darkness, but it was even more important to keep his lungs free of the gas. A single cough or an accidental splutter could give him away to his pursuers.

He staggered forward, blinking hard in an effort to see through the film of tears with which his eyes, still smarting violently, attempted to flush away the last traces of the gas. The walls of the tunnel swam in front of him, the light split into thousands of bright fragments transforming the circle of his vision into a swirling kaleidoscope. He could hear voices behind him, harsh voices calling, and the sound of running feet.

Taking another deep breath, he wiped his eyes once more. His vision cleared long enough for him to see a wall ahead. He swung the flashlight to the right, then left. Side tunnels branched off, each as dark as the other. He had no idea which way Maryam and Krämer had gone. When he looked back at the wall, the rock face was already blurred. The sound of approaching feet grew louder. His attackers were already in the tunnel and gaining on him.

He turned and fired into the blackness, three short bursts. His magazine would soon be empty. If only he knew which opening Maryam had chosen, he could lead the attackers in the opposite direction.

Bending, he wiped his eyes and looked hard at the ground, first on one side, then the other.

As his vision started to blur again, he noticed two sharply incised footprints at the entrance to the right-hand tunnel. Quickly, he scuffed them out, then turned and headed into the other opening. He'd wait until they reached the wall, then open fire on them. He would play the pied piper and draw all the rats after him. It didn't matter if they did not drown, just as long as they followed him.

45

The world was a beam of white light. They stumbled through the tunnel, harried by the sound of shooting behind them and by the demons each carried inside, past walls of clay packed tightly and held in place by wooden struts, ceilings made from oak beams caked with dust and the webs of ancient spiders, floors marbled by the footprints of men long dead.

Maryam caught a whiff of something ugly in the air. They were using some sort of gas, and faint tendrils had made their insidious way toward them. She glanced at Krämer hobbling beside her, his hand clutching tightly at her arm for support, his chest straining with the effort of moving quickly. She realized that if the gas grew much stronger, his lungs might not hold up. If only Yosef would hurry, she thought. She was not sure she could get Krämer out of here alone.

The tunnel narrowed, imperceptibly at first, then quite dramatically, shrinking around them until it forced them to bend, then crouch, and finally get down on their hands and knees to crawl. There had been no side openings, no suggestion of an alternative route. Maryam knew they had no third choice: They could either go on or go back.

"Wait here," she said, seeing that Krämer was finding it hard to keep up with her, partly on account of the simple effort involved in crawling, partly because the gas-tainted air was growing thin.

She crawled ahead, holding the flashlight in one hand, hoping against hope that the tunnel would start to widen out again. Several yards later, her hopes were finally shattered. The tunnel came to an abrupt end against a wall of solid clay in which the marks of tools long cast aside were still visible. There was no way out.

Yosef tripped and picked himself up. The tunnel wound its way forward as though following some natural course, whether to find a passage between outcrops of rock or to avoid one or the other of Turin's four main waterways he could not guess. He took advantage of the turnings, keeping the flashlight switched off until he rounded a corner, then shining it briefly ahead in order to make sure of the next section. It was an awkward means of progress, but he could not risk his pursuers identifying his position by means of the light.

He could hear their footsteps and, from time to time, their voices somewhere behind him. They were still at a distance, but gaining steadily. One wrong turn, one long hesitation would be all they needed to give them the advantage they sought. He pressed on harder, praying that Maryam had found a way out by now.

A side tunnel appeared on his right, lower and narrower than the passage through which he was running. He paused only briefly, but instinct warned him against taking the risk. Better to stick to the main route, which was more likely to lead directly to an exit.

The tunnel turned right after that, then left, before continuing straight ahead. A few yards further along, the light picked out an opening on his left. At first he thought it another side tunnel, but when he shone the flashlight inside, it turned out to be nothing more than a disused storeroom. The floor was littered with small wooden crates, many of them broken and covered in mildew. Rotting sacks lay in crumpled heaps, and in one corner Yosef could make out a dust-covered stack of corked bottles.

Without further hesitation, he slipped inside. It took only moments to strip half a dozen moldy sacks from one of the heaps. Lying with his face toward the opening, he covered himself with the sacks, leaving only a narrow aperture through which to see. An idea had begun to form in his mind.

There was no point in using the gas again until they knew they had the Jew and his friends cornered. Weiss had warned them against firing CS rounds too liberally in such a confined space: There was a risk that the traitor, Krämer, might be overcome, and that was something Weiss did not want. He wanted the old man alive, wanted to make a lesson of him, and it was their task to see his wishes carried out.

They were sure they were gaining on their quarry. Their leader, a man called Vitale, had brought them to a halt a couple of times in order to listen, and once they had heard the distinct sound of hurrying footsteps ahead, then silence had returned. Vitale was sure Krämer was weakening by now, and if he could convince the Jew that it was useless trying to get any further with the old man, the whole thing could end without more bloodshed. Of course, Vitale was not sure what Weiss would want to do with the Jew or the Arab woman once he got his hands on them, but that wasn't his business anyway. He'd been trained to obey orders, and that was what he intended to do.

Vitale—a university lecturer in physics in everyday life—stopped and raised his hand. The entire party halted, and a sudden silence filled the tunnels that almost took their breath away. Vitale shone a flashlight into a little chamber on the left, a shallow room hollowed out of the earth and walled with rough wood planks. Old boxes, sacking, a heap of bottles. He swung the beam up and down the little chamber, but nothing moved.

"Come on," he said, "there's nothing in here."

They went on, moving slowly in single file, their breathing loud in their ears, trapped in the antiflash hoods and gas masks they wore.

Maryam lowered Krämer to the ground. His breathing was labored and she was growing increasingly anxious for him. Coming back to the spot where the tunnels forked had been the worst bit. The concentration of gas had been heaviest there, and Krämer had been forced to hold his pajama top against his face in an attempt to block as much out as possible. In spite of that, he had inhaled more than was good for him. For the moment, he could go no further.

Maryam knew that Yosef must have headed down the opposite tunnel after all. Krämer's only hope was in her finding him. She left the old man propped up against the wall and set off down the passage.

Yosef waited until the last man passed, then slipped out into the tunnel again. He knew what he wanted, but thought of the risk almost persuaded him to turn back and head the other way.

In the dark, it was difficult to gauge either space or distance. He could hear the sound of the raiders just ahead, and when he turned the next bend he suddenly saw the glow of a flashlight as it swung in an unsteady arc across the ceiling. Moving on bare feet, making as little sound as possible, he quickly covered the distance between himself and the last man. He had seen the hoods and masks when they passed the entrance to the storeroom and knew his approach would be undetected, but the same masks prevented him from silencing his man quickly and effectively by means of a hand across his mouth.

He was bare inches away from the other man when he sensed him grow aware of his presence. The raider paused in his stride, half turning. An instant later, Yosef struck, clamping one arm over the man's face to bring him to an abrupt halt. At almost the same moment he sliced sideways with the side of his free hand to strike the carotid artery. The sharp, expert blow cut off the flow of blood to the man's brain. He went limp and his body fell back onto Yosef, who took the weight, snatching his gun as it started to drop from his lifeless fingers.

Yosef pulled the hood and mask over the dead man's head. The hood was not really necessary, he decided, but the mask was essential. It was a lightweight respirator, a Schermuly or SES model with the filter to the left, familiar to him from his days in antiriot work. He slipped it over his head and felt an immediate improvement in his breathing.

The man was wearing a black shirt and trousers, and wore a belt to which several extra magazines were attached. Yosef unbuckled the belt, listening all the time for the sound of the dead man's colleagues returning. Suddenly, he noticed that as well as the magazines the belt carried a pouch containing a hand grenade.

His original plan had been to drag the body back to the side tunnel and to leave it there while he hid in the storeroom again. That way, his pursuers might have headed down the side passage, leaving Yosef free to make his way out through the main tunnel.

Now a better idea suggested itself. Leaving the dead man where he had fallen, he hurried back to the storeroom. Working frantically, he tore apart one of the sacks under which he had been hiding. As he had expected, the sack itself was half rotten and fell apart easily, but the cord with which its edges had been sewn was made of more durable material. It took only moments till Yosef had a length of twine in his hands, about six feet long and just about strong enough for what he had in mind.

Back in the tunnel, he listened anxiously for the sound of returning footsteps. There was only the old silence, rendered more intense now by the absence of any sounds but those of his own breathing. His pursuers must not yet have discovered that he was no longer ahead of them, but it could only be a matter of time before it dawned on them that they were chasing a phantom.

Several yards along from the storeroom, two wooden struts held a beam across the ceiling. It was not too difficult to wedge the grenade behind one of the struts, with its body rammed into the clay wall about one foot from the ground and the pin facing into the tunnel.

He tied one end of the cord to the pin and the other to the strut facing it. The twine was just taut enough to yank the pin from the grenade the moment someone tripped across it. There would be a delay of a few seconds before the grenade exploded. Now, if his pursuers came back this way, they would bring the roof down, trapping themselves and leaving Yosef free to make his way out through the other passage.

He started to make his way back along the tunnel, one machine gun in his hands, the other across his shoulders. Now that he felt almost secure again, he allowed himself to relax a little, and as he did so felt himself assailed by a bizarre and sudden sense of loss. The thought that he might never see or hear or touch Maryam again entered his veins like a poison. All about him, the darkness seemed to deepen, and all the silences in it multiplied until they became one silence, and himself a heart in it, beating all alone in the dark and quiet.

Rounding the next corner, he stopped, every muscle tense, straining to hear. Footsteps were coming from the direction of the bunker. He could not guess how many, but he knew he could not risk going straight ahead. He had not yet come to the side tunnel, so his only choice was to turn back again to the storeroom.

It took him half a minute to return to the opening, and moments to cover himself with the sacks again. He lay waiting, his heart pounding, knowing he might himself be trapped if this second group of raiders hit the tripwire before he could slip away.

The footsteps came faintly along the passage, growing louder every second until he could distinguish clearly that they belonged to only one person. Could it be Weiss? Yosef realized that it might be safer to kill this newcomer than risk being caught in a collapsing tunnel. He tensed himself, watching the opening. The faint glow of a flashlight became visible, then grew rapidly as the footsteps approached.

"Alla sinistra o alla destra?" They had reached a second fork. Their map showed that either direction led to an exit, but they had to know which way their quarry had chosen.

Vitale listened intently, but he could hear nothing. His second-in-command, Marco Nucci, was at the entrance to the other tunnel. He had taken his hood off in order to hear more clearly, but seemed to be having no greater success than his leader.

Lelio Buonconsiglio, a metalworker from Pianezza who had belonged to the party's bodyguard corps for five years now and whose opinion Vitale valued, stepped forward.

"Sir, I think we've been tricked. I don't think they all came this way. Krämer and one of the others could have slipped down the side tunnel we passed a while back."

"What makes you so sure?"

In answer, Buonconsiglio pointed at the ground.

"There's quite a bit of damp around this section, sir. I think we're close to the river. You've left some footprints over there, and Marco's left a few in the other opening. I don't see any beyond that." He shone his own flashlight into the passage to make his point. "They'll get away if we don't turn back now."

At the very last moment, as he was about to spring out, he realized that it was Maryam. For a stunned few seconds, he paused, then, horror-struck, scrambled to his feet after her.

He rushed into the corridor, shouting, warning her not to go any further, but his voice was muffled and changed by the gas mask and what emerged was scarcely intelligible.

Too late, he realized what he had done. She half turned and caught sight of him, a tall man in a gas mask carrying a machine gun yelling at her. There was no time for her to think, no time for anything but flight. Unhesitatingly, she turned and ran, ran as fast as she could down the tunnel.

He tore the respirator from his face, but she already had her back to him. As he opened his mouth to call again, he saw her trip and fall against the cord.

"Run!" he shouted in Hebrew, then again in Arabic. "Run!"

She started to pick herself up, started to run, her body acting before her mind could even grasp what was happening.

He saw her lift herself to her knees, and at the same moment saw something move behind her, further down the tunnel: a light, swinging wildly as though someone were running with it in his hand.

A man's voice called out and was at once snuffed out by a loud roar as the grenade exploded. The explosion sounded like a clap of thunder, briefly sharp, then muffled by the earth as it absorbed the blast. Yosef watched in horror. As the sound of the explosion rippled away into a series of dull echoes, another sound replaced it, the sound of falling earth as the roof started to collapse.

46

Even in the light of what happened later, Yosef would always regard those moments as the worst in his life. By the time the crashing and roaring had stopped and the great cloud of dust and debris that filled the tunnel settled enough to let him see, he felt as though he, too, had been crushed beneath tons of rubble.

The cave-in had been only partial, apparently limited to the sector between the struts where the explosion had been set and those next in line, but the entire tunnel had filled with rock and earth, and it was impossible to know just how far the collapse extended in the other direction.

He was not sure how long he stood by the

wall of settling earth, for his thoughts were not his own and his body seemed to belong to another being, something not quite human. More than anything, when the silence came, he could hear his heart beating, and it seemed the loneliest thing in the universe, each beat as distinct as the striking of a bell in a high tower whose toll reaches beyond all expectation.

Later, he realized that he must have scrabbled at the earth for a time, for his hands were filthy and bleeding and his nails torn. At some point, he must have known it was useless, that no human hands could tear their way through those untold feet or yards of solid earth and rock. He was sure she had been buried beneath that grotesque, immovable mound of rubble, and with her all that had been resurrected, however briefly, in him.

He found Krämer sprawled on the ground not much further down the tunnel, where Maryam had been forced to leave him. The old man was conscious, but weak and barely able to move. Yosef took his pajama top from his face and replaced it with the gas mask. Within a few minutes, the old man's breathing started to grow more normal.

"How do you feel?" asked Yosef.

In reply, Krämer shook his head softly and held up one hand, asking for time.

At that moment, Yosef heard a sound from the direction of the fork where the short tunnel went down to the shelter. Someone was coming at last to investigate the explosion.

"We've got to get out of here," said Yosef. "Can you hold on round my neck? I'll carry you."

Krämer nodded. Yosef bent down and helped the old man climb onto his back. With his arms tight round Yosef's neck and his legs supported by his hands, he hung limply, like the old man of the sea or a doll of immeasurable value who might at any moment be broken by a careless or impetuous gesture.

There was not enough height for Yosef to straighten up in order to use his legs properly. Instead, he staggered forward, bowed down less by the old man's weight than by the strain that carrying him at all produced in his tendons. The sound of approaching footsteps grew louder every moment, and Yosef's heart went cold when he realized he had left both submachine guns in the storeroom.

They would never make it that far. Their only chance was to get to the side tunnel and hope that the men behind them continued through the main passage in search of the source of the explosion. Yosef could hear Krämer's voice in his left ear, harsh through the respirator filter. He wondered how long the old man's lungs would hold out without fresh air, even with the help of the mask. His own lungs, exposed once more to the all-pervasive CS gas, were burning, but he dared not stop, even to use the respirator briefly.

The tunnel seemed to go on forever. He still had his flashlight, tucked into the ammunition belt round his waist, and from time to time he would switch it on to gain an impression of the section immediately ahead. The darkness seemed interminable, the distance between himself and the opening a constantly expanding measurement without proper meaning or borders. Behind them someone called out in a loud voice, a cry that bounced off the walls and came to them broken.

"Have they seen us?" Yosef asked.

"No," wheezed Krämer. "Keep going."

Yosef pressed on. His legs felt as though they were about to give way, and he dared not wonder just how much longer they could support him and Krämer.

"Please," came Krämer's voice, distorted by the mask, "don't ... let Weiss ... take me ... alive."

"I'll do my best," panted Yosef. His voice was unexpectedly weak, thinned by the gas and the exertions that had brought him thus far.

"No. Not that. You ... have to ... kill me."

Yosef felt himself hesitate, for it was unthinkable to kill someone who posed no threat to him. Yet he knew Krämer was right, that it would be the height of cruelty to leave him to Weiss and his thugs. Once, in Lebanon, a wounded comrade had asked the same thing of him, and then he had unhesitatingly agreed. In the end, it had not come to that, and he had been able to bring his friend out alive. But he had known then that he would have killed both his comrade and himself had it been necessary. Weiss was right. The spirit of Masada was still alive.

He said nothing in reply, but saved his breath to carry Krämer the remaining ten yards that brought them to the smaller tunnel. Yosef wanted to lie down and recover his strength before continuing: The side passage was much narrower and lower than the one they were in, and it would be impossible for him to carry Krämer through it. They would have to crawl on hands and knees, and if there was no way out at the end, they would die like that, slowly, unable to turn around, unable to crawl back.

The sound of nearing footsteps made up his mind for him. Hurriedly, he turned on his back, facing Krämer.

"Can you manage to crawl behind me?" he asked. "If you hold on to my hands I'll pull you."

"I'll try." Some of Krämer's strength was returning with the improvement in his breathing. "But let's not waste any more time."

Yosef crawled into the opening backward, using his heels to propel him on his backside. Krämer came after him, half crawling, half sliding on his knees as Yosef pulled him in short, gasping stretches along the earth floor.

Gerhard Weiss hesitated at the entrance to the side tunnel.

"What's down here?" he asked.

"I'm not sure," said his local *comandante*, a small man called Umberto Gui. "Let me have a look."

Gui fumbled in his pocket for the map of the tunnels he had obtained earlier. With a nervous finger, he traced the route he and his men had taken to enter the old air-raid shelter, then established the position of the tunnel they were in.

"*Sì, sì, è essatamente qui. Eccola.*" He stabbed his finger at a short line on the map. "It's an old overflow tunnel, *una galleria di troppopieno*. They were built to drain off rainwater into the Dora Riparia River in the event of a flood."

"Is there a way out?" asked Weiss.

Gui shook his head. "I don't think so. There

used to be outlets above the river. I can remember seeing them when I was a boy. But the Consiglio Comunale had them all closed up years ago as health hazards. You don't think they can have gone down here, do you?"

"I don't know. Anything's possible."

Weiss shone his flashlight into the opening. The beam showed a flat surface of beaten earth, rough wooden walls, and ceiling beams at regular intervals. There was no sign of movement, no sound, nothing to suggest that anyone had passed through here recently. On the ground there were indentations and abrasions that could have been left by human beings, but no footprints. Weiss was on edge. He wanted to trace the source of the explosion. Going down a narrow tunnel like this would hold them back.

"Umberto," he said, "I think I saw some cans of gasoline back there. Can you send a man to bring one here? Have him soak the walls. Once this wood catches fire, the rest of the tunnel should go up like tinder. We'll set light to it on our way out."

Yosef lay on the ground, gasping for breath. Next to him, Otto Krämer was curled into a tight, fetuslike ball, struggling to stay warm. Yosef himself was cold to the bone, and he knew that if they did not get out of here quickly, they might very well die from exposure.

He was sure their pursuers had gone past. No sounds had come from the opening to the tunnel, and he was confident they were no longer being pursued. But that was scant comfort. They could still die in here of cold, thirst, or hunger. If there proved to be no way out other than back the way they had come, then death would find them quickly enough. Yosef could see that Krämer might not last very much longer. The strain he had been under had taken its toll, and any prolongation of it might finish him.

Getting Krämer out was all that mattered now. Even the possibility of getting the German to testify at the trial seemed unbelievably remote. His own life meant nothing to him now that he had lost Maryam. They would rest a little longer, then set out again along the tunnel. It had to come to an end somewhere, it had to have been built for some reason.

Something tugged gently at his nostrils, a teasing, nagging smell. It seemed familiar, yet so faint was it that he could not begin to identify it. He sniffed hard, and even as he did so the smell altered and became another smell, equally faint at first, then growing in strength. For a moment, he thought it might be more CS gas, but a second and a third inhalation brought it home to him. This smell was smoke, and before that he had smelled gasoline. Weiss had set fire to the tunnel.

She felt dizzy, and something in her head had gone insane. It was thrashing about inside her skull as though desperate to escape, and doing as much damage as it could on the way. She scarcely noticed the cuts and bruises on other parts of her body, extensive as they were.

She opened her eyes and looked up. A bright light stabbed her mercilessly and she closed her eyes again, lifting one arm in a vain attempt to ward the light off. Someone grabbed the arm and pulled her to her feet. She cried out in pain.

Cuts and bruises were not the only injuries she had sustained.

"Where's Krämer?" someone shouted. She wondered what language they were speaking. It seemed foreign, yet strangely familiar. The voice jabbed at her again. "Was he with you when the ceiling collapsed?" She wondered how she could understand this foreign speech, then realized the man was speaking Italian.

"Krämer? I don't ... remember. Where ... am I?"

Another hand snatched her. She tried to open her eyes again, but the light was still unbearable.

"If he was caught in that, he's dead. We can question her later. Now, let's get the hell out of here before the rest of the roof caves in."

The smoke was growing thicker by the minute. At least Krämer would be protected by the respirator, but Yosef knew that if he himself were overcome by the fumes, the outcome would be the same. By the time the fire reached them, it would be more or less redundant.

He dug his heels in hard and dragged himself another few feet, holding Krämer tightly by the wrists. The old man did what he could to ease the burden, crawling on his knees to bring himself close to Yosef. They moved in silence. Words had ceased to matter, even thoughts were useless. The only thing of any importance now was the will to crawl another foot, to drag aching flesh and bones another inch.

Yosef pushed again. Soon, he thought, all that would be left would be the will to survive, without the physical strength to move any further.

He let go of Krämer and twisted until he was on his belly. Now he could see ahead, but there was only darkness. His hand fumbled for the flashlight, then brought it up. The beam played on the endless floor and walls like a lantern lowered into a grave. And then it moved a foot to the right and he saw something different. He moved the beam again, straining to see more clearly. The tunnel ended in a large metal grille, its bars thin and rusted, beyond it darkness.

The first visible wisps of smoke came swirling through the light. He summoned up his last strength and crawled the last few feet. He put his hand to the grille. It seemed solid, its bars set hard in mortar. But what lay beyond it? He reached through with one hand and his fingers touched the hard surface of a metal bulkhead.

47

Yosef would never know it, but he and Otto Krämer would owe their lives to a corrupt local businessman called Andreo il Truccatore ("the Fixer") Laguardia. Laguardia was a welder by trade and the owner of a small Turin-based company that carried out freelance work for Fiat. GuardiaCo. also had an ability to win local government franchises, largely due to its boss's reputation for charming manners, disarming politeness, and a readiness to send in large men carrying welding equipment should a little firm persuasion ever prove necessary.

Several years earlier, Andreo had paid *tangenti* amounting to several million lire to a local politician eager to make his mark on the national scene and in desperate need of funds to do so. Among numerous tokens of gratitude had been a contract to cap and seal the outlets to several disused rainwater outlets on the Po, the Torrente Stura di Lanzo, the Torrente Sangone, and the Fiume Dora Riparia. Simply welding metal covers across the existing grilles had been the cheapest and least time-consuming option, and Laguardia had cheerfully embraced it. The work on the Dora section had taken two days in all. The grateful politician, by a curious twist of fate, had been Pier Maria Pacchia. Laguardia was one of the chief contributors to his defense fund.

Yosef discovered the flaw in Laguardia's system the moment he put his back to the grille. The original bars, deeply rusted by years of exposure to wind and water, snapped like twigs. Since the metal cover had merely been set against them and welded tight at the edges, the moment the bars gave way, it went with them and fell with a loud splash into the water below.

Outside, a sickly dawn had come to the city. Birds sang as though weary of the ritual, and the first cars and buses were snarling and grinding their way through gray, early morning streets. The first flight of the day had just left Turin airport and was leaving a vapor trail in the wet air.

Yosef leaned out and reached up. His fingers touched the bottom rung of an ancient ladder of stanchions that climbed to street level. He looked up at a pale sky that still swarmed with stars, and took the deepest breath he had ever taken in his life.

48

They arrived as though shipwrecked, on a deserted embankment overlooking a gray canal that wound its way between steep banks and looming buildings. Neither man knew where they had come from nor where they had emerged, only that they were somewhere in Turin with no one to help them. They had no money, almost no clothes, and no friends to whom they could turn. Krämer was ill, and Yosef knew that if he stayed out much longer on the streets, he would die. He considered giving himself up to the police, if only to secure hospital treatment for the old man, but on reflection, he realized that he might as well sign Krämer's death warrant.

They staggered along the embankment, half naked, filthy, shivering in a sharp wind that came off the water like a knife: Jew and Jew-killer thrown together at the end of the world; Edgar, posing as mad Tom, leading his blind father to the precipice's edge. Now and then the driver of a car or a moped rider would stare at them, but no one stopped. The light grew in the sky and the sleeping city slowly came awake, but neither sunlight nor bustle brought comfort.

They came to a halt by the embankment wall. Krämer could go no further. His breathing was harsh and wheezing, he shivered uncontrollably. Yosef tried to think, but his mind was as numb as his body, his thoughts scarred by despair and loss.

Slowly, he became aware of voices somewhere to his left. He looked round and saw a trailer parked by the side of the road and a line of men leading to it. He went closer and saw that the line was made up of old men and down-and-outs. The trailer was some sort of soup kitchen, and they were serving breakfast to vagrants who slept on the embankment.

Yosef joined the line. Hot soup or coffee would be of some help. He shuffled forward, oblivious to the looks of disgust the other members of the line cast at him. At last, his turn came. A young man stared at him from behind the counter of the van. Yosef raised one hand and lifted two fingers, pointing all the time at Krämer, who still lay against the wall. The boy stuck his head out and looked at the old man.

"E il tuo amico?" he said.

Yosef did not understand. He shrugged and repeated the gesture, adding the word *"due"* from his tiny Italian vocabulary.

"Tuo padre?"

Again Yosef shrugged.

"E malato?"

"We need food," Yosef said in English. "We're cold. My friend is dying."

The young man understood enough to know that something out of the ordinary was going on. Despite angry cries from the men in the line, he climbed down from the van and went to where Krämer was lying, shivering and helpless. Yosef followed him. The youth bent down and touched Krämer's forehead.

"Quest' uomo è gravemente malato. A bisogno di calore e di un medico. Dobbiamo chiamare un'ambulanza."

Yosef grasped only the last word, and he guessed the boy's meaning.

"No," he said. "No ambulance. No hospital."

The boy looked at him strangely. He was accustomed to the ways of down-and-outs, to their distrust for authority, but this man seemed more agitated than made sense under the circumstances.

"*Morirà*," he said. "*Senza attenzione medica, morirà. Ha capito?* Your friend die. Need medical treatment."

At that moment, a small car drew up alongside. The driver got out and came across to them. He was a gray-haired man of about fifty dressed in a long overcoat. Yosef caught a glimpse of a dog collar, then the newcomer pulled the lapels of his coat together against the cold.

He spoke briefly to the young man, who explained the situation to him rapidly in Italian. Yosef looked on, feeling increasingly helpless, aware that control over the situation was slipping from his fingers. The priest nodded, glancing down at Krämer every so often, then back at the youth. When the boy had finished, the priest bent down and examined Krämer carefully.

"*E semimorto. Chiama un'ambulanza subito.*"

Yosef took the priest's arm. "Please," he said. "He will die if he goes to a hospital."

The priest raised himself and looked directly at Yosef for the first time. Yosef could see that he was angry, that he thought he was endangering the old man's life for some whim or obsession of his own. The priest opened his mouth as though to scold Yosef, then closed it again.

Yosef saw the dawning glimmer of recognition, then the certain knowledge in the priest's eyes. He let his hand fall from his arm.

The priest turned to his assistant.

"*Roberto, gli altri vi attendono. Sono freddi. Lasciami occuparmi di questo.*"

The young man looked at him curiously, surprised by the sudden shift. The priest's eyes were fixed hard on his, and he knew argument was pointless. He nodded and returned to the trailer where the line had grown much longer.

The priest turned to Yosef. "Help me get him into the back of the car," he said, speaking in English.

Yosef felt a weight lift from his heart. Something told him the priest was not about to turn him or Krämer in. He bent down, and together they lifted Krämer onto the rear seat of the little Fiat.

"Get in," said the priest. He himself climbed into the driver's seat. He switched on the engine, put the heating on to full, and pulled out into a stream of early morning traffic that had started to fill the embankment.

The priest's name was Father Innocente Tambroni. He ran a refuge for the city's *emarginati* in the crypt of his church, San Giambattista, in the Montebianco district. He was a radical, both religiously and politically, who had given refuge over the years to all manner of men, women, and children: down-and-outs, illegal immigrants, political refugees, unwed mothers, defrocked priests, drug addicts, and southern workers cast on the dust heap when the northern motor industry contracted.

His relations with the Vatican were far from good, although he had so far escaped the fate of other dissenting priests who had been drummed out of the Church for supporting divorce or contraception or abortion or gay rights. His own arms were open wide, but unlike those of more than one bishop he had known, his embrace did not include right-wing extremists or mafiosi.

He helped Yosef carry Krämer to a private room behind the crypt, where a pallet bed had already been set out. This was the sick room, where some of those seeking sanctuary could receive medical treatment without risking arrest or worse in a hospital. As soon as the old man had been warmly wrapped in blankets, Tambroni made a telephone call. He spoke for about half a minute, then replaced the receiver. Only then did he pay any attention to Yosef.

"We have a doctor who attends to our sick without charge. His name is Dr. Zaganelli. You can trust him. As for yourself, you may share my quarters until we can decide what to do with you."

"You know who I am?" asked Yosef.

Tambroni nodded. "Your face is better known than any other in Italy at the moment, Mr. Abuhatseira."

"You aren't planning to hand me over to the police?"

Tambroni shrugged. "Perhaps. This is not a refuge for murderers or assassins. Are you a murderer, Mr. Abuhatseira?"

Yosef hesitated. "I have killed men, yes."

"That is not what I meant."

"I did not kill Butti or Gentileschi."

"No, I didn't think you did. The right wing here in Italy have tried that trick too often. They carry out shootings and bombings, then pin the blame on their enemies. It has become such a habit that when something like this happens we professional skeptics like to think twice and three times before we reach conclusions."

"And what conclusion have you reached about the assassinations?"

Tambroni pushed out his lower lip. "The shots came from the fascist sector of the crowd. If you had been there, you would not have escaped alive. In a situation where the accused is a Jew and the crime involves right-wing bullies like Pacchia and his friends, I tend to give the benefit of doubt to the Jew. That may not always be wise. I have given shelter to many Palestinians in my church, and I know what your countrymen get up to. I am under no illusions. But Pacchia is an evil man, and I would want better evidence against you before handing you over."

"I'm not the only one they're after," said Yosef. "That old man is the real target. He could bring you serious danger."

The priest shrugged. "I have been in danger before."

There was a knock on the door. A woman in nun's clothing came in.

"*Il dottore Zaganelli è arrivato. E permesso?*"

"*Sì, sì, farlo entrare.*"

The doctor entered, followed closely by the nun, who carried his bag. He was a dapper little man of around sixty, complete with an oiled mustache and a bow tie. He shook Tambroni's hand and spoke urgently with him for a couple of minutes. Meanwhile, the nun was bending over Krämer, preparing him for the doctor's examination. She paid no heed at all to Yosef.

Tambroni finished explaining the situation to the doctor. He took Yosef's arm.

"I think it's time you and I had a proper talk, Mr. Abuhatseira. And I think you could do with some breakfast."

Later that day, Yosef asked if he could make a telephone call.

"Not from here," said Tambroni. "We have to assume that the line from this church is regularly tapped. When I want to make what might prove to be a compromising call, I find a phone booth, the further away from here the better."

Leaving Krämer with the nun, Sister Consolata, Tambroni drove Yosef across town to a phone booth in a deserted part of town. He warned Yosef not to spend long on the call, since a trace could be put on a line in moments. If there was a regular tap on the number he was calling, he was running a serious risk of discovery.

"If necessary," he said, "we can go from booth to booth. But I suggest you just keep your call brief and to the point."

Yosef nodded. He was still in a state of shock. Everything that happened to him now seemed only partly real, and he himself an unreal creature, devoid of feelings or memories or regrets. Like a robot, he had a task to perform, that was all that mattered now. And when his task was finished? He tried not to think about that.

He rang the Israeli embassy in Rome.

"I want to speak to Baruch Caplin," he said. "It's urgent."

Caplin was the Mossad station chief with overall responsibility for operations in Italy. Before leaving Israel, Yosef had been given his name and an assurance that, if he needed to get out of Italy in a hurry, Caplin would arrange things.

"I'm sorry," answered the switchboard operator, "but what is this in connection with?"

"Tell Caplin this is Maroc. M-A-R-O-C. My operation has been compromised. I need help desperately."

There was a pause, then the operator responded.

"I'm going to put you on hold, sir. I won't be long."

"No, I can't risk that. I'll call you back. Ten minutes."

They drove to another part of town and found a phone in a small café. Tambroni handed over more tokens.

"Take care," he murmured.

Yosef dialed the number again. "This is Maroc," he said. "Put me through to Caplin."

"I'm sorry, sir, but there is no one of that name at the embassy."

Yosef felt himself go cold inside.

"There has to be a mistake," he said. "Caplin is Mossad Chief of Station. I'm an active agent and I'm in trouble. He has a duty to help me."

"I'm sorry, sir, but we have no one here belonging to Mossad. Perhaps you should contact their headquarters in Jerusalem."

"Listen, my name is Yosef Abuhatseira. Tell Caplin that. Make sure he understands. Abuhatseira."

"I'm sorry, sir. I can't help you any further."

There was a click, and the phone went dead.

49

He knew now why Mossad had chosen him. He was deniable, as easily repudiated as an Arab wife, a maverick acting on his own out of a desire for revenge. They had not calculated on the assassination attempt. As a result, he had become a serious liability, for if a Mossad agent were to be linked to the deaths of Butti and Gentileschi, it would destroy Alberto Luzzatto's chances of being elected prime minister. If that occurred, the opportunity for fostering stronger relations between Israel and Italy would have been lost indefinitely. Far better that Yosef was deemed not to exist.

They drove back to the church in silence. Yosef watched the city pass like a dull, gimcrack film set, a place with neither heart nor substance. He felt desperately alone and frightened. It was not capture he feared, or death, but the possibility that, in the heart of all this, there might be no meaning whatever.

On arriving at the church, he inquired about Krämer and was told by Sister Consolata that the old man was starting to rally. He had been through a great deal, but some sort of fighting spirit had finally surfaced and now he seemed on the way to recovery. Yosef breathed a sigh of relief. To have lost Krämer at this stage would have been the final blow, the unavoidable confirmation that it had, indeed, all been worthless.

A room had been prepared for him and he went there now, exhausted and in need of sleep, though he feared his dreams more than anything. Sleep came, and dreams came, but he did not wake for a long time.

Two days passed. His dreams were of one thing now, a closed and endless circle of horror. He saw her go ahead of him into the gas chamber, naked and helpless as a child, and he made to reach her, to pull her back or enter with her. It was all the same, but a great metal door slammed shut between them and he could not see or hear or touch her.

On the third day, Father Tambroni went to Leone Mortara's house, dressed as a door-to-door salesman.

"Thank God you've come," said Mortara, once the situation had been explained. "Is Yosef safe?"

"For the moment, yes. But I'm not easy about keeping him at San Giambattista too long. It's too well-known as a refugee sanctuary, and a thorough search would bring him to light."

"What about Krämer?"

"Krämer is well. It was touch and go for a while, but the doctor thinks he'll be on his feet in a few days.'"

"Will he be able to attend court?"

The Pacchia trial was well under way, but the public mood was sympathetic to the defense. Pacchia had managed to assemble a panel of "expert witnesses" ready to testify that established theories concerning the Holocaust might legitimately be called in doubt. The state prosecutor had so far proved inadequate to the situation, letting too many of Pacchia's experts off the hook. Several prosecution witnesses had decided not to appear at the last minute. It was turning into a one-sided affair. Only Otto Krämer's appearance in court could turn the tide.

"I think so, yes. He says he wants to go on with it."

"You understand why he is so important?"

Tambroni nodded. "Absolutely. I'll do everything I can to keep him safe. I've already been speaking with some of my best contacts, without mentioning any names. I can find other safe houses for them both."

"Good. Our key people were wiped out in the raid on the shelter. I don't have the resources to handle this on my own. And there is a major problem."

"Yes?"

Mortara hesitated. What he had to say was not easy.

"It concerns Yosef. He was with a woman called Maryam Shumayyil. I believe he thinks she was killed during the raid."

The priest nodded. "That's so," he said. "There was a cave-in. She was buried under the rubble. Yosef was there—he saw it all."

"Apparently she's still alive. I haven't spoken to her, but I'm told it can be confirmed. She was on the other side of the cave-in. Apart from some cuts and bruises, she's perfectly well."

"That's wonderful news. Yosef will be overjoyed."

Mortara shook his head. "Not altogether. She

is alive, but she is in the hands of a man called Weiss. Has Yosef mentioned him to you?"

Tambroni took a deep breath. He knew what was coming.

"Yes," he whispered.

"Weiss is holding Miss Shumayyil until he has confirmation that Krämer is dead. If he has proof of that, he will let her go. If, on the other hand, Krämer is still alive, then Weiss is prepared to exchange her for him and the papers that were in his possession. In the event of Yosef refusing these options, she will be killed."

"How does Weiss know Yosef is alive?"

"Yosef left some equipment behind on the embankment near where you found him. It contained an ammunition belt, and the finder handed it over to the police. Needless to say, Weiss was told about it within an hour." He paused. "He has given Yosef until tomorrow either to tell him where to find Krämer's body or to hand him over."

50

Otto Krämer was moved that afternoon to a private sanitarium run by a Jewish doctor called Momigliano. Yosef was sent to stay at the home of Tambroni's brother, a liberal investigative journalist on whose discretion they could rely absolutely. His room was concealed behind heavy bookcases on the second floor and was virtually impossible to detect without ripping the house apart. More than one political refugee had found shelter there over the years. Ironically, several of them had been Palestinians.

They met that night on the outskirts of town in a house belonging to a young Jewish couple who had been close friends of Bruno Frezza's. Mortara was there, nervous and out of his depth, along with Yosef, Tambroni, the lawyer responsible for providing Krämer's testimony to the state prosecutor (and ensuring that Krämer took the stand), and two surviving members of Azione Ebrea. The latter were armed.

They talked for over three hours, until they had gone over every option at least a dozen times, and dismissed most of them as either too dangerous or unworkable. Much to Yosef's frustration, the conversation lapsed frequently into Italian, and wherever possible he tried to encourage the others to use English or Hebrew. It was vital to him that he understood everything that was discussed that night. Maryam's life depended on it.

By prearrangement, shortly before eleven o'clock, Yosef was driven to a phone booth several miles away. He dialed a number that had been supplied to Mortara by Weiss. Weiss himself answered, his voice surprisingly soft now that it was amplified by nothing more powerful than a telephone earpiece.

"How good to hear your voice at last, Mr. Abuhatseira. You're to be congratulated on your resourcefulness. For a Jew, you've shown singular cleverness. But I regret that the initiative still rests with me. I have someone who must mean more to you than Otto Krämer ever could. It's a simple enough equation. Her life against that of a man who was responsible for the deaths of millions of your people."

"So you accept that what Krämer says is true?"

Weiss's shrug was almost audible. "Why ever not? It happened, and it was not a mistake. Thanks to the defeat of the Reich, international Jewry has gone on to extend its sinister influence round the world. And as a result things are ten times worse than they ever were. The white race and Western civilization are in imminent danger of extinction. That is why there must be another Holocaust, and another after that if necessary."

"Let me speak to Maryam."

"Certainly. I shall have her brought to the phone."

There was some shuffling in the background, then a woman's voice came down the line. Maryam's voice. He could not have mistaken it.

"Yosef, it's true. I'm sorry, but I got clear of the cave-in only to walk straight into the arms of the raiding party."

"Are you all right, love?"

He could hear the catch in her voice as she struggled to answer.

"Yes, I'm all right. They haven't hurt me ... or anything. Weiss is telling the truth, though. He will kill me. But you mustn't worry about that. You thought I was dead already. Just go on thinking it. Krämer has to be allowed to testify."

"I can't do that. You know I can't. You're all that matters to me. I've just found out you're alive—you can't expect me to let them kill you now."

"You have to, Yosef. They'll kill Krämer, and Pacchia will be free to spread whatever lies he likes. I'm not—"

The receiver was snatched from her abruptly. Weiss's voice came back on the line.

"I think you and I see eye to eye, Mr. Abuhatseira. She's a very beautiful woman. I'd hate to see her abused in any way."

"How do I know you'll let her go?"

"Ask for advice from whoever is looking after you. I suggest the traditional handover venue: Turin has dozens of bridges, the choice is yours. The moment we see Krämer coming in our direction, we will let your woman go. She will have a gun aimed at her back the whole way. You are free to do the same with Krämer. Once he and his papers are with us, you can take her wherever you like."

"And what guarantee do I have that you won't notify the police where to find me?"

"That's a risk you will have to take. I'm a man of my word. I prefer not to have the police around either."

"Very well. I'll call you later."

"Remember, you have until noon. No later. Be very sure you do exactly as I have told you."

"The decision has to be yours, Yosef—no one else has the right. None of us will judge you, whatever you decide. Believe me."

Mortara spoke gently, as though cajoling a child to eat. Yosef sat staring at the floor. He knew that whatever decision he arrived at, at least one more person would die.

It was eight o'clock in the morning. None of them had slept properly. Their red-rimmed eyes and sagging faces showed the strain of the past hours.

Yosef shivered. He would have to live with his decision, live with it every day from now on. He could enter the gas chamber at last and bring out someone he loved. But he could do so only at the price of dragging another victim with him and leaving him there, along with all those faceless, nameless others.

He raised his head.

"How long will it take to get to the sanitarium?" he asked.

51

The choice of bridge was almost thrust on them. A city center location was out of the question, but all the main bridges crossing the Po on the north and south carried highways thick with traffic. They might have set up some sort of fake diversion and kept cars away for a short time, but in doing so they would be running a serious risk of bringing a squad of traffic police to the spot.

In the end, Tambroni identified the perfect spot. In the south of the city, the Italia '61 gardens flanked the river, and one of the many paths turned right onto a footbridge. This short structure led directly onto the Corso Moncalieri, a main road that led directly in the south to the S.S. 29 to Savona and in the north half a dozen major arteries. On the other side of the corso, the city gave way at once to a vast region of open land dotted with villas and small housing projects.

Their first thought had been to go in shortly after dawn, when all would be quiet and they could effect the handover without much likelihood of being observed. But a moment's thought had shown that such a plan held too many dangers. Weiss still bore grudges, notably against Yosef, and given the chance of taking revenge without being seen, he might just go ahead.

Only yards from the west end of the footbridge, a car would be waiting on the road that ran straight down the center of the park, the Corso Unità d'Italia, ready to whisk them away into the early morning traffic. Any sign of another car parked nearby and the deal would be off.

The location and the time—ten o'clock exactly—were communicated to Weiss, and they set out for the park. Mortara had suggested that Yosef remain behind rather than risk his own life in an ambush, but Yosef had refused.

"I made my decision," he said, "and I have to see it through. Anything else would be cowardly. I have to be there."

There was a second reason for his presence. Earlier that night, Tambroni had obtained a weapon for him, a sniper's rifle equipped with a bipod and high-magnification sights. It was a weapon he had used before. Holding it, he felt it possible that he and Maryam might come out of this alive.

They drew up on the Corso Unità d'Italia with plenty of time to spare. Yosef had wanted to be sure that he had a clear line of fire and that his own position would be protected. To help in this, Doctor Momigliano had given them a metal filing cabinet from the sanitarium office. A small Fiat van pulled up behind them and two men got out. They had set the cabinet on its side at the entrance to the bridge. Yosef crouched down behind it and experimented with various firing positions. Satisfied, he nodded. The men had already brought several boxes of old bricks from the van, and these they now loaded hurriedly into the drawers of the cabinet.

"Thank you," said Yosef. "You'd better leave now. We don't Weiss getting suspicious."

The men drove off, leaving the car parked on the corso. Yosef remained crouched behind his barricade.

Weiss and his people arrived ten minutes after that in a long black car with windows that shimmered in the mid-morning sunshine and cast muted reflections across the river. The bridge was empty. No passersby had crossed it since Yosef had been there. From time to time, someone would walk past through the park behind, then silence would fall again and the tension of waiting would continue unabated.

A rear door opened in the black car and a man carrying a rifle got out. He made his way directly to the steps leading to the bridge and crouched down behind the top one. When he was in position, he raised one hand in a gesture of readiness.

A second man got out of the car and Yosef noticed that he held his hand discreetly inside his jacket. He was followed by Weiss. Yosef could have shot him where he stood, but what would have been the point in that?

Yosef raised his hand, and Leone Mortara came from where he had been waiting by the car on the corso. Mortara walked out onto the bridge and along it until he had reached the approximate center.

"Weiss!" he shouted. "We have to talk."

His voice shook in spite of his efforts to control it. The mantle that had been thrust on his shoulders was proving heavy, but he had accepted it in spite of the pain he knew it would bring. This was not a role he had ever sought for himself, but he knew he had no choice. He called Weiss's name once more.

The German came forward until they were face-to-face.

"Are you ready?" asked Mortara.

Weiss nodded.

"You have the woman with you?"

"She's in the car. And you?"

"He's ready."

"Good. We'll start them on their way without further delay."

"Not yet. There's one thing we insist on. You must remain in full view throughout the handover. We have a man with a rifle stationed at the head of the bridge. He will not be aiming at Krämer—that would be pointless. He will be aiming at you. Once Miss Shumayyil is safely in her car, you will be free to go."

"This was not part of our arrangement."

"You are in no danger if your people behave themselves. You have my guarantee."

"A Jew's word?"

Mortara shrugged. "It's all you've got."

Weiss opened his mouth as though to say something else derogatory, then seemed to think better of it. He was impatient now. And, on balance, he still had the edge.

"Very well. Let's not waste any more time."

They both turned and headed back to their respective positions at either end of the little bridge. An old woman came along the path on Mortara's side as though making to cross to the other side. She glanced at the group of people gathered there and changed her mind. Leone watched her walk off, muttering to herself. Once she was out of sight, he raised his hand.

Yosef watched her come. He held the rifle steady on Weiss, but he could not keep his eye on the sight. She was limping badly in her left leg and rough bandages had been wrapped round wounds on her head. They had not allowed her to change her clothes, wash her hair, or take a bath, and he knew she must be frightened out of her mind. She kept on walking, and he knew she was looking for him, but he could not risk drawing attention to himself.

He glanced down the sight again, then took his eye away to watch the old man pass. His head was held high and his step was as firm as he could manage without help. A stiff breeze came off the river, ruffling his white hair like strands of tinsel. He did not stop or look back, but went on walking. In his hands he held a small cardboard box as though it contained all his wordly possessions. The papers in it were heavy, but he bore them without seeming effort.

Around the middle, Maryam and the old man passed. She hesitated for a moment, looking into his eyes, then he took her hand briefly. He seemed to be saying something. Yosef could sense the impatience on the other side. He returned his eye to the sight. When he looked up again, they had parted, and Maryam was almost with him. She did not quicken or slow her pace, but continued to walk steadily forward, knowing all the time that a rifle was aimed at her back and that her life hung on a thread more slender than hope.

Suddenly, it was all over. Weiss's bodyguards converged on the old man, took him roughly by the arms, and bundled him into the car. The sniper stood, holding his rifle high. Yosef got to his feet and returned the gesture. Moments later, Weiss had disappeared into the car as well. The man with the rifle joined him and they drove off.

She was standing before him, shaking, all courage suddenly spent. He made to take her in his arms, laying his rifle down on the dusty ground, but she only stared at him as he approached, then turned and walked away. He watched her go, his heart aching for her. Listlessly, he picked up the rifle and headed for the car.

52

The car drew up outside a tall wooden lodge situated at the foot of a steep, wooded hill. A few miles to the north and west, snow-covered mountains rose in profusion to a silver sky. Storm clouds circled the tallest peak, a bent and arcane creation of frost, and from time to time a quick raiment of lightning would lie across its shoulders.

The old man eyed the mountains wistfully. They reminded him of his boyhood, a time so long ago and so cut away from the present by those dark years of war and slaughter. It was at least a consolation to see them again, to be able to hold them in his memory for the little time that remained.

The long journey had taken place in a tense silence. Occasionally, Weiss had barked out directions to his driver. Once he had spoken briefly on the telephone. Otherwise, he had been content to sit back and await his moment. He had Krämer and he had a box containing Krämer's notorious archive.

After a short drive round Turin, just to ensure they were not being followed, they had headed east for about two hours. They bypassed Milan to the north, then sped past Bergamo and Brescia before turning north onto the E45 west of Verona, and from there on past Trento and Bolzano, almost to the Austrian border. Here, high in the hills, they had at last come to this place, cold and remote, enclosed by a wire fence and inaccessible save by a narrow road that was closely guarded at all times.

Weiss got down from the car and headed into the lodge without a backward glance. The driver followed, carrying the cardboard box containing the precious papers. After a few moments, the two guards could be seen pulling their prisoner from the car and propelling him toward the lodge.

Weiss was already waiting for him in a long room at the north end of the building, a wood-paneled chamber with a high ceiling and a picture window that stretched almost the length of one wall. Beyond the window lay a broad terrace, covered now against the winter snow and rains, but in summer a place to sit and be awed or frightened by row upon row of high white mountains, so near that, had they been giants, it would have been but a short step for them to crush the villa and all its gardens to tinder.

"It isn't Berchtesgaden," murmured Weiss, "but it serves as a reminder." He spoke in German, in the lower Saxon accent he had acquired in his youth and never lost, though it had been many years since he last lived in Brunswick. "I was never privileged to be invited there, but you …You must have memories."

"You would not believe my memories," said the old man. He spoke with a different accent, but years of residence abroad had not impaired his German.

Weiss raised an eyebrow. "No? Perhaps we shall have an opportunity to see. What I do find hard to believe is that I am here in this room with a legend, a man I have idolized most of my adult life, and that all I can think of is how I mean to kill you. What I find even harder to accept is that you, out of all of us, should have betrayed our cause and brought shame on all our heads."

The old man did not answer this time. His legs were steady, and though his heart was beating rapidly, he felt quite calm and in control of himself. He tried to keep his eyes on Weiss, but again and again they turned, as if by their own volition, to the mountains outside.

"You were not just part of an elite," continued Weiss, "not a mere foot soldier in the service of the Reich, but a living link with the Führer in person. Men like you were the essence of Aryanism. That is why I do not understand. Where so many others remained faithful to the end and gave their lives for Germany, you betrayed us like a common criminal selling information to a police spy. How could you have sold yourself to the Jews just so they could parade you in front of their television cameras and use you as fodder for their propaganda?"

Weiss paused, glaring at his victim as though he was about to strike him. The anger in his face was visible, the stunted, resentment-fed anger of a child who has learned how to hurt and barely discovered the secret of self-control.

"Would it have achieved anything had you succeeded?" he asked. "Would it have given you a single night of better sleep? You were trained to be hard, trained to control your natural emotions and the prickings of your bourgeois conscience. And yet now, in your old age, when you might have expected to see the results of all those years of waiting and planning, instead you choose to run off blubbering like a little boy, a little boy who thinks he's done wrong when, really, nobody has even noticed a thing.

"Perhaps this would never have happened if we had met before this, long ago, before the doubts started. We could have talked it over, I could have brought you back to your senses. Do you think that could have happened, Otto? Could I have helped you?"

Still the prisoner persevered in his silence.

His eyes scarcely left the mountains now. He watched snow being blown down from a shattered peak, a long white flag against that perfect, silver sky. His silence only served to intensify Weiss's anger.

"No," Weiss concluded. "I see I could not. In any case, you're beyond help now. Your trial will take place here tonight. I shall be the court president, the other judges will all be men familiar to you. Some of them you will know by name only, others in person. They will start arriving in about six hours from now. In the meantime, you and I have much to talk about. Why don't you take a seat?"

The guards, who had been waiting behind the prisoner, stepped forward suddenly and forced him to sit on a hard, high-backed chair several paces to his right. Near the chair was a small table on which sat a black leather box. Weiss came forward and lifted the lid of the box. The guards held the old man firmly on the chair.

"Your trial is little more than a formality. I'm sure you have expected nothing more than that. The entire proceedings will be filmed, as will your execution, and copies will be sent to our groups round the world. You are to be made a lesson for the younger generation.

"But your death is only incidental at this stage. It eliminates the danger you posed, of becoming a public spectacle, but it does not remove the more long-term threat of your betrayal. We have to know just what you have told your Jewish friends about our organization."

Weiss paused and lifted two objects from the box: a hypodermic syringe and a small glass vial.

"Since you are clearly not to be trusted, you

will have to be questioned with a little pharmaceutical help. This is not a truth serum: You know as well as I do that there is no such thing. But it will allow you to relax to the point where you will no longer care what you tell me. And I insist that you tell me everything."

He nodded at the guard on the left. The guard reached down and, without ceremony, removed the old man's jacket and dropped it on the floor. Then, with the quiet and nimble movements of a trained nurse, he unbuttoned the prisoner's sleeve and rolled it above his elbow.

Weiss plunged the needle of the hypodermic into the rubber seal of the glass vial and filled it to a line about halfway along the cylinder. He withdrew the needle carefully, returned the vial to its box, and turned to the man in the chair. Two old men, joined by memories, separated by conscience. Weiss lifted the emaciated arm and searched for a suitable vein.

As he did so, his eyes caught sight of the numbers: 174 398, six simple digits tattooed on the left forearm, six digits that ought not to have been there. As though to wipe them away, his fingers brushed the offending numerals, but they had not been put there with a pen, and they had not been tattooed recently.

"Who are you?" asked Weiss. His anger had vanished, to be replaced by something like fear. Not complete fear, not yet: The reality had only begun to dawn.

"A *Häftling*," said the old man. He found it hard to keep a trace of mockery out of his voice. "An *Untermensch*, a Jew. I have no name, just the number you gave me. Don't you remember me?"

Weiss shivered. "Remember you? We've never met before. You tricked me into believing you were Otto Krämer."

"You tricked yourself into that, Herr Sturmbannführer. It was impossible for you to imagine that anyone would willingly take Krämer's place, so you never even bothered to check. You were not so careless when you wore a uniform and called yourself Emil Luders."

Some sort of enlightenment entered Weiss's troubled mind. He looked again at the old man in the chair. No, he did not recognize him, not even remotely.

"Are you trying to suggest that we met during the war? Is that what you mean? But it's impossible. I never served in any of the camps."

"We did not meet in a camp. It was at the beginning of 1944, in Turin. I had a name then. I was called Jacob Friedenson, a German just like you—until a gang of criminals decided I was not a German after all, but a Jew. In 1938 I came to Italy with my wife and children. We had relatives in Turin, and we thought the Italians would treat us better than our own people. And so they did, until the Germans took over in 1943.

"You and I met during one of your last roundups. You had a quota of Jews to send to the internment camp at Fossoli, and then to Auschwitz. My family was discovered in hiding and brought to the embarkation site along with several others. Everything was ready for the first stage of our journey, and then you arrived. You'd had instructions that only healthy and useful specimens were to be sent on. The transport would start for Auschwitz in a few days. They were looking for slave labor. My wife was ill, my children were too small to fend for themselves. So you shot them in front of me. You shot them, you shot several others, and you returned your pistol to its holster and fastened it, and you turned to me and smiled."

He had never forgotten that smile, never in all the years that had passed. In the camp, he had sworn, as so many others had sworn, that he would survive in order to bear witness, to bring Emil Luders and any other of his tormentors who might come out of the war alive to justice. It did not matter how. Tomorrow, in a courtroom in Milan, more of the record would be set straight, and for a generation at least the lie would be nailed down to the bloody floor from which it had attempted to rise. His own voice would be silent, but that scarcely mattered. By taking Otto Krämer's place, he had ensured his own victory and the defeat of his enemies. It was more than fate had granted to most of his fellow inmates.

He smiled at Weiss, remembering his wife and children more vividly than at any time in the years intervening, and as he did so his right hand slipped into his pants pocket and found the little transmitter that he carried there. The explosives strapped round his chest felt light, as though they were nothing more than air.

"All over now," he said. He stood up slowly and took a step toward Gerhard Weiss. With one hand he drew his wife's killer to him in a last embrace, and with the other he pressed the button on the transmitter. He smiled as he did so.

Part 9
THE SETTLER

53

"What is your name?"

"My name is Otto Krämer."

"Your nationality?"

"German, but I have held Argentinian citizenship since 1957."

The court listened in profound silence while the preliminary questions and answers were rehearsed. On their bench, the magistrates eyed the old man impassively, but not one of them was inwardly unaware of the significance of the testimony they were about to hear. Steadily, the state prosecutor worked his way through Krämer's background and education, then the details of his work under the Reich.

"Mr. Krämer," the prosecutor said. Out of the corner of his eye, he caught sight of Pier Maria Pacchia's tense face. In a matter of minutes, his self-importance had evaporated. He, too, understood the significance of what the court was about to hear, and after it, the entire world.

"Mr. Krämer, I wish to bring you to the topic under issue in this court with a simple question. The gentleman you see standing a few yards from you is Pier Maria Pacchia. He stands accused of writing pamphlets in which he denies that the event known as the Holocaust—that is to say, the extermination of European Jewry in the death camps and killing fields and ghettoes of the Third Reich—that this most notorious event did not take place. You are, by your own

423

admission, in a position to evaluate that assertion. I wish, therefore, to put this single question to you: Is Mr. Pacchia, in your opinion, telling the truth or not?"

Krämer looked at the prosecutor, then at Pacchia. Their eyes met briefly, then Pacchia looked away, half contemptuous, half frightened. Krämer returned his eyes to the prosecutor.

"I swear by everything that I hold sacred, that he is not only lying, but he is using his lies to build the fires that will ignite a second Holocaust on this continent. I deny him absolutely, and everyone who feeds that same lie to his children. What happened, happened. He was not there. I was. I made it what it became."

On a hard bench at the rear of the courtroom, Inspector Antonio Nieddu sat, unobserved by anyone, watching and listening. In a matter of days, his whole life had changed. He knew he could never return to Sardinia, never remain in the police force. Perhaps he would have to leave Italy entirely, take a new name, find a new profession. The thought of so much change frightened him, and yet the longer he had to reflect on what had happened, the more he grew certain he was doing the right thing.

In the past, he'd put up with the petty injustices and minor corruptions that were an everyday part of police work or of life in general. Now he was beginning to see how they fit into a much larger pattern, how men and women like himself were just cogs in a machine of corruption that permeated the whole of society. The bribes and the kickbacks were just minor symptoms of a much more serious malaise, a disease that turned men into killers and politicians into tyrants.

He had not been idle since coming to the mainland. A few more days, and he'd have all the evidence he needed. It would show who was really responsible for the killings of Butti and Gentileschi, and mark trails leading to the highest levels of the police force, the carabinieri, and the ministry of justice. And perhaps from there other trails would lead elsewhere.

Leaning forward, he listened to Otto Krämer speak. And he wondered whether he might not have been there to give his own testimony, had he lived in Krämer's time.

Qiryat Arba, Israel

A new moon grew, slanted and alone, against the head of a tall cypress at the corner of what had been an Arab field. The voices of worshipers could be heard as they made their way through the cool spring night from the synagogue to the community center. It was a special day. Prizes had been given earlier to children in the settlement school for poems celebrating the life and death of Baruch Goldstein, the fanatical settler who in 1994 had slaughtered thirty-three Muslims while they prayed at the Tomb of the Patriarchs in Hebron. Prayers had just been said for him, attended by almost the entire town. And tonight there would be a memorial concert and a short play in Goldstein's honor, performed by young men and women to whom he was a hero, almost a saint.

Yosef had not joined in the prayers, and he did not plan to attend the play. Instead, he had come out here alone to the edge of the settlement to watch, listen, and think. At first, he had thought it a simple thing to come home, to resume his work and life. But with every day that passed, it had grown harder.

He thought of Goldstein and the brutality of his attack on unarmed and innocent men at prayer. And he thought of his friends in the settlement and the words they used to describe the Arabs whose land they had stolen. He remembered using those same words himself, and he recalled acts of his own barbarity. He wanted to be sick.

Slowly, breathing the perfumed night air as though to hold it in his lungs forever, he made his way back to his own house. He opened the door and went inside as though he were the only living person left in the whole *yishuv*. The perfume from the trees outside followed him into the house. He would always remember it as the perfume of loneliness.

He pushed thoughts of Goldstein from him and allowed himself instead to think about Jacob Friedenson. Friedenson had been waiting for his chance all the time, housed in Momigliano's sanitarium until the moment might come. He had almost given up hope, and then everything had changed at once. Yosef had spent over two hours with him, trying to talk him out of his plan, but the old man had smiled gently and insisted that to die like that would make sense of his life, and slowly Yosef had understood. How many Jacob Friedensons, he wondered, and how many Baruch Goldsteins?

He looked round the room. Everywhere, boxes were piled, ready to be shipped out in the morning. He had spent the day packing, making his silent farewells. His old friends would only know he was leaving when they saw the moving van come for his things. He would be gone by then. For now, he would go back to Jerusalem. Home? Perhaps. And perhaps not.

There was the sound of a car pulling up outside, and, moments later, a knock at the door. When he opened it, Maryam was there. He remembered the first time he had seen her, in a doorway in Nuoro, framed by yellow light. It seemed as if years had passed since then. She was framed by darkness now, and the perfume of the night clung to her as though it began and ended in her.

She stepped inside. It was the first time she had ever been here, and it would be the last. Just coming through the road checks had distressed her. If Yosef had not made a prior arrangement, she would not have been allowed through.

"Are you ready?" she asked. She looked round the little room. It told her nothing about him. Whatever it had been, it was now just an empty room piled high with boxes.

He nodded.

She was dressed in a T-shirt and jeans, without makeup or jewelry. Her hair was untidy, and she still showed signs of the strain she had been under. He thought she was the most beautiful woman he had ever seen.

They had left Italy on a small boat provided by Leone Mortara. Beyond Mortara, a host of invisible friends and helpers had appeared. From

Italy, they had been slipped into Greece using false passports, and from Greece they had taken a ferry to Haifa. That had been a week ago.

He switched off the light, and they went out together. Yosef closed the door behind him for the last time. He touched the mezuza gently, then turned and walked to where Maryam was waiting for him.

The settlement was deserted. They could hear the sound of singing from the school building. The new moon hung at the bottom of the street.

He took her hand. It felt small and fragile, and he held it softly, as if afraid he might break it. He could barely see her in the darkness.

"When are we getting married?" he asked.

"I don't know," she said. "Maybe we are, maybe we aren't. I can't even think about it."

He had asked her to marry him for the first time onboard the boat bound for Greece, and she had refused him. She had offered to live with him, but said marriage was out of the question.

"I still don't see what difference it makes," he said. "You're willing to live with me, but you won't marry me."

"You're an observant Jew," she said, "and you'll want children to follow your tradition. That means you'll want me to convert, because you can't have Jewish children without a Jewish mother."

"Well, what's so terrible about that?"

"I'm a Christian," she had answered. "I may not be a believer, but it is part of what I am, like being an Arab or a Palestinian. If I were to marry you, I'd just be throwing my heritage aside as though it had no importance. I can't do that. Please don't expect me to."

The moon lifted above the low roofs of the little town, and all around it stars shone as though struggling to burst through the darkness.

"I love you very much," whispered Yosef.

"I know," she said. She turned and brought his face to hers and kissed him. They held one another for a long time, until the sound of loud applause from the school brought them back to the present.

"It's time we left," he said.

"I will live with you," she said. She could taste his lips on hers. "But I can't marry you."

"My family won't permit it," he said. "With them, it's marriage or nothing."

"I don't want to live with them, just with you."

"This isn't America," he said. "People don't just live together."

There was a brief pause.

"It's time they started," she said.

They climbed into the car. Out of the darkness, shadowy figures were coming from the direction of the school. Their voices were high and excited as they talked animatedly about the play. They were Yosef's friends and neighbors. He had shared their lives and hopes and fears, he had considered himself one of them, and now they were nothing more than shadows with loud voices passing him in the night. He looked at Maryam.

"Maybe you're right," he said.

As they drove away, he looked behind once. The moon lay on Qiryat Arba, a perfect silver crescent. He turned back again. The road ahead was empty for as far as he could see.

If you have enjoyed reading this large print book and you would like more information on how to order a Wheeler Large Print book, please write to:

 Wheeler Publishing, Inc.
P.O. Box 531
Accord, MA 02018-0531